Entwined

Fate, Tragedy, and Love
on the High Seas and Beyond

Entwined

Fate, Tragedy, and Love
on the High Seas and Beyond

A Novel

Laurel J. Schoenbohm

Entwined: Fate, Tragedy, and Love
on the High Seas and Beyond: A Novel
By Laurel J. Schoenbohm

Copyright © 2024 Laurel J. Schoenbohm

ISBN: 978-1-959239-17-8 (paperback)
ISBN: 978-1-959239-19-2 (hardback)
ISBN: 978-1-959239-18-5 (e-book)

Library of Congress Control Number: 2024903704

Interior layout and formatting by Scott Burr
Cover design and photographs © Laurel J. Schoenbohm
Edited by Leah Schoenbohm

Published by Inspirit Alliance
Buffalo, WY

Published in 2024

Dedication

To all those who have walked through my life, taught me something, and inspired part of these stories, and to all those who have lost their lives at sea or survived such a tragedy, especially to the crew and captains of the F/V Destination and F/V Scandies Rose.

If you assisted me in this process of writing and publishing this novel, or if you recognize some of yourself in any of these characters and stories, please take it as an honor and compliment. I dedicate this book to you.

Lastly, dedicated to my husband, Q, and mother, Leah, for supporting me in this endeavor.

Contents

Author's Note

Author's Note

THIS IS NOT a true story, although parts of it are inspired by true events, nor is it an autobiography, although some parts of it shadow my own life. Instead, this book is a blend of amazing and colorful people who have been transformed to create a rich story of its own, like a vibrant oil painting. Names have been changed to protect any identities of those who may be a part of a character, but all characters here are portrayed in a loving light with the utmost respect, as that is how I feel toward all who have come into my life. I view everyone I encounter as a teacher or potential teacher. I feel honored to be able to capture some of the wildness, pain, love, and joys of life that I have known and witnessed through the medium of this fiction story.

Chapter 1

The Black Seal

Late March 2013

HE TOOK A long drag off his cigarette. He only smoked when at sea; it took the edge off. The dark of the night accentuated the red glow, and the brisk wind grabbed the swirls of smoke, mixing it with the particles of spray under bright sodium deck lights. Todd finished the rest of his cigarette in a few inhalations. Just before he turned to enter the main cabin and join the rest of the crew already stripping off soggy sweatshirts on day five of a longline trip off the Aleutian Chain, a stony glimmer in a wave crest off the port side of the *Sea Ranger* caught Todd's eye. Taking a second look, he spotted it again. It was a seal, but its coloring was different from normal. This one was jet black. He paused a moment more to assure himself he wasn't seeing things, but it failed to resurface.

To Todd, a black seal was an ominous sign. He didn't usually believe in signs, but about three years ago, the last time he saw such an oddity, a day later a crew member, Warren, who had jumped on the boat last minute and whom Todd really didn't know, caught his leg in the bight of a line and was pulled overboard before anyone could react. Warren's face was blue with the kiss of death, his eyes glazed over by the time they'd recovered his body from the frigid water. Those eyes staring blankly at the cold night sky burned into Todd's mind an image that would always haunt him.

Todd felt a chill. Trying to shake it off and pull his salt-encrusted hoodie closer to his neck, he turned his back to the sea and put his shoulder into opening the heavy steel door into the galley, where he was immediately engulfed by blaring fluorescent lights and warmth.

"What took you so long?" asked Sam as he stood by the gear locker and turned his gloves inside out to dry.

"Oh, just finishing up my smoke."

"Those things'll kill ya, you know."

"Come on, Sam, you know I only have one after we finish a long day."

After a doubtful look, Sam switched topics. "Grub's on. Hope you're excited for more of Joel's 'cooking'. Probably spaghetti again."

"Oh boy," said Todd, his voice thick with sarcasm.

Todd ducked into the head before returning to the galley. As he warmed his swollen hands in hot water, he glanced into the mirror, shocked at the fatigue that painted his face. Bags lined his normally youthful brown eyes, stubble peppered his chin, his sandy brown and wavy hair needed a trim as it was starting to fall into his eyes. As usual, thanks to grueling boatyard work in February and early March and now fishing, he'd lost every trace of fat on his six-foot frame.

At the table the boys were hunched over heaping plates of steaming pasta, shoveling down mouthfuls of food, intent on ingesting as many calories as possible, no need or time for talk. Todd slid in next to Manni, and Sam took his usual place next to Joel.

"Skippy eat yet?" asked Todd as he grabbed the serving spoon.

"Yeah," grunted Joel.

After seconds and thirds were wolfed down, the skipper, Phil, sauntered down the stairs with his now empty plate and coffee cup in hand. He dumped his plate on the counter and made a beeline to the pot that was on twenty-four hours a day.

After filling his cup and taking one sip, his upper lip bunched up as he grumbled in a hoarse voice, "Who made this shit? Way too weak." With dramatic flair he dumped the remainder of the cup into the sink and headed back up to the wheel. Glaring at Manni (the last one to make the coffee), Sam got up from the table to make a new pot of joe. Manni simply shrugged his shoulders in apology.

"Hey, uh, whose turn is it for the first wheel watch?" asked Manni.

"Todd's," said Sam.

"Man, I get the middle watch again?" grumbled Joel to himself.

After cleanup, Todd made his way up top with a fresh cup of coffee for Phil. Ascending the steep stairs, he caught part of the NOAA radio weather forecast as he entered the wheelhouse. The familiar and somewhat nostalgic computerized male voice of the weather radio droned on . . . "Thursday night, east winds twenty-five knots, building to thirty-five, seas eleven feet. Friday, northeast wind forty knots, seas fifteen feet. Friday night—" Phil, who had already listened to all the forecast he needed, reached up and switched the radio to channel sixteen before Todd could figure out what area that forecast was for, then took off his wire-rimmed glasses and rubbed his bloodshot eyes. Phil was pushing sixty and hailed from Petersburg, the elite Norwegian fishing village in Southeast Alaska. His blonde hair was fading to white, wrinkles deepening, shoulders drooping, and belly expanding bit by bit, year by year.

Trying to bait his captain for more information without being annoying, Todd announced his presence with, "More of the same weather, huh?"

"Oh yeah, sounds like it's going to be a bit nautical the next few days," another way of saying it was going to be rough, choppy weather.

"Brought you some fresh coffee," said Todd.

"Oh thanks. Hey, you want to drive?"

"Sure thing," Todd replied as Phil slid out of the worn helm chair. Todd rubbed his eyes before checking over the chart plotter, radar, and engine gauges. The sodium lights illuminated flocks of gulls and painted the horizontal rain drops orange as they blew by in the stiff wind. With the soft thunk of the door, Todd turned to see Phil disappearing into his stateroom, coffee untouched on the dash.

Two hours. Two long hours of a watch, burning well into the wee hours of the night. Todd could remember the days when he had jumped at the chance to drive. But after days of minimal sleep and naps of only a few hours at a time, Todd had lost that greenhorn eagerness years ago. Now it was all a routine to get through. The days blurred into each other like runny watercolors. At least with taking the first watch he wouldn't be woken up right in the middle of a sleep. As Todd settled into the chair, the image of that black seal flashed in his mind again, setting off a nagging apprehension in the pit of his stomach.

But that feeling of impending doom waned for those few hours at least, minus the time he allowed his mind to wander and had failed to hit the Reset button on the helm alert (a device that would alarm every ten minutes unless you hit it—used to keep helmsmen awake on watch). It had screeched in a heart-stopping, high-pitched alarm. He jumped out of the chair seconds later to silence it, listening with fear for Phil to cuss him out from his stateroom in the corner of the wheelhouse. But his skipper must've been in a deep sleep already because his room remained quiet.

Filling the time with one daydream after another, Todd's mind wandered yet again to the events of that one unforgettable night last spring in Sitka, that night that, no matter what he tried, would not leave him. The memory of her clung to him the way a child on the first day of kindergarten grabs on to his mom's legs. The thoughts were *not* helping him get through the brutal longlining season. Instead, they were tormenting him. Todd looked up again at the helm alert. Only three minutes had passed since he'd last hit the button. Just fifty-seven minutes more until he could hit the rack for a few hours.

Okay, instead of thinking of her, I've got to think of something constructive. Hmmm, let's see . . . he thought. So instead, he focused on what he was going to do when he got off this goddamn boat. Images of the wide-open road filled his mind, windows rolled down, all the gear needed for a good adventure stowed in the back of his pickup truck. Then he pictured waking up to a sunrise in Hawaii and strolling down the beach in flip flops for an early morning swim in warm, clear water. *Can't believe this stone cold and angry ocean is the same tropical water of Hawaii,* he marveled. Then, *Can't believe it's the same water as back home.*

The thought of home, Port Townsend, WA, led to images of his family: a divorced mom and two sisters, both out of the house. He wondered, *What are they doing right now?* His mom Dianna, a doula and midwife, was probably spending the evening alone on her property of ten acres with ample space for gardening outside Port Townsend city limits. He could almost feel the walls of the now childless house closing in on her, the halls echoing with ghosts of the past. Both her daughters had gone to college out of state and were busy starting lives of their own, far away. And his dad, Rich McClelland, lived nearby on the Kitsap Peninsula close to the Olympic Mountains, in a small cabin on a property near Dabob Bay. He was a contractor and ran a small but successful construction business.

It was Uncle David, Rich's brother, who got Todd his first fishing job seining for salmon when he was in college. David had been the black sheep of the family, leaving Washington and taking off for Alaska with nothing but a duffel bag and worn pair of boots on his feet. After decades of hard work, guts, and grit, David had made a name for himself as a skilled fisherman. He called Kodiak home; his family now included a wife and two sons, two and five years old. Uncle David kept an eye out for Todd like a son but treated him just as hard if not harder than the other crew. After four summers fishing with Uncle David, Todd had mastered seining and was addicted to the fishing lifestyle of hard work, good money, and adventure.

Thoughts of his family and the dreaming of what he'd really like to be doing in his time off, having someone by his side as he walked that beach or started that long road trip, inevitably led him to thoughts, yet again, of . . . her.

Her name was Emily, Em for short. He'd first heard Em's name tossed around years before he first ran into her in Sand Point. The commercial fishing community was so small and tight-knit that certain characters in the industry were known up and down the Pacific Coast. Boats became like people, and crew became like family. He would see the same boats and crew members squidding off the coast of California, crabbing in the winter off of Oregon and Washington, seining and gill-netting summers in Alaska, then longlining springs all the way from Dutch Harbor to Sitka, then back down to Seattle for shipyard. Longlining, crabbing, seining, gillnetting . . . different gear, different season, same boats, same people. It would be no surprise to run into someone he knew from Cali hiding from the wind in a bar in Dutch Harbor, Alaska.

There were women who commercial fished in Alaska, but they were few and far between, and often they got their start by being born into it. Therefore, Em was somewhat of a "unicorn" and gaining status in the fishing world, especially as she did not grow up in a fishing family, or a fishing village, but instead hailed from the South, AND she'd participated in just about every fishery over the years. She'd started out on a whale watching boat for a summer gig after high school and had fallen in love with Alaska so much, she'd stayed and worked her way onto tugs, then commercial fishing boats. Todd's ears always perked up at the mention of her name, so in time, he'd gathered a good deal of secondhand in-

crew, asking so much of each of them. Todd and Phil had grown closer over the last few years. Once in a while Phil doled out a hint of more responsibility to Todd than the other crew and even went so far as to ask Todd his opinion on a matter, such as whether to reset in one spot or try new fishing grounds. Todd was careful not to broadcast these small treasures of trust to the other crew but took them to heart as small pats on the back.

Todd beat Manni to the shower, a rarity since Manni usually spent the most time grooming before going up to town. Thus, Todd was the first to head off the boat to decompress and up the winding gravel road toward the Tavern. Since it was late winter/early spring, the streets were deserted.

Sand Point, a remote Alaskan village of a thousand year-round residents, contains a small ramshackle group of houses nestled around a natural bight that serves as a harbor and accommodates the main cannery. It lies on the northwest side of Popof Island, about halfway between Dutch Harbor and Kodiak Island. Not a tree dots the landscape, except for a few stunted conifers planted by the Russian Orthodox Church back in the day. Besides that, grasslands, tundra, and willow compete against the near constant wind. On the east and southern sides of the island, sheer cliffs drop straight into the sea, cliffs populated with colonies of thousands of seabirds and gulls. It's an island that feels as if it's on the edge of the world, the last remaining outpost of the wild, wild West. Most of the souls on the island are employed in fishing, either for subsistence or commercial purposes, or work at the cannery, the tribal government, marine trades, or the school. In the summer salmon season, the population of the island swells with trouble-making, rowdy fishermen and cannery workers. At the end of August, there is a rush to get off the island, the planes are overbooked for weeks, and in September, the locals, mainly of native descent, have the island back to themselves, and the winter pot fishing for crab and cod season to get ready for.

So when Todd walked into Sand Point's dilapidated drinking establishment on that fierce March night, he knew without a doubt it was Em
when he saw her sitting across from the bartender, Derrick, engaged in
animated conversation with a tumbler of whiskey in her hand.

She truly was her own woman. Not flashy and prissy, all dolled up
with too much makeup and eyeliner. Instead she was natural, effortless,
and all the more beautiful for it. She wore her shoulder length black hair
in pigtails. Her Xtratufs tapped at the bar stool, her worn and abused
Carhartt overalls in need of a few patches, and her closely fitting shirt
hinting at her toned arms. Trying to see through the dim haze of smoke
floating around the bar lamps, Todd took a glance around the room.
Three small groups of locals huddled around the tables closest to the
bar, all taking a long glance at him, but none acknowledging him. Even
though it was late, Todd didn't expect many more to saunter in besides
his fellow crew who'd soon be on their way up after their showers, so he
calculated he might only have a few minutes to make his move with Em.

Trying not to look at her, Todd sidled into a bar stool just one to the
right from her, leaving three stools empty on his right for his boys. As
Derrick paused his conversation with Em by putting up an apologetic
finger, he asked Todd, "What do you want?" Even though Todd had
seen Derrick multiple times, the question was coated in gruffness, as
most locals were not overly friendly to the non-local fishermen. Em
took the pause in the conversation to look his way and judge his choice
in beverage.

"I'll have an, uh . . ." changing his mind last minute after looking over
the meager selection of beers on tap, "I'll have some Glenlivet on the
rocks." *Fuck it,* he said to himself, as they'd just gotten in from a scratch
of a fishing trip.

"Interesting choice," he heard her say with a hint of her Southern
accent. He turned his head in her direction and almost froze in place
when he made contact with those green eyes. He decided to play it nonchalant and gave her a casual nod.

She continued with, "So where are you from? I don't think I've seen you around before."

"Washington."

"What boat are you off?"

"Oh, the *Sea Ranger*. Just got in."

"Oh yeah, had a few buddies that used to work on there, but that was a while ago." She paused and took a sip. "I'm Emily Bancroft, but I go by Em, by the way," she said as she extended a hand.

"Todd, Todd McClelland," he answered as he took her hand in his for a quick shake that revealed her strong grip.

They had no time for more introduction as the door slid open, followed by a stiff breeze that hit the back of his neck. Just Joel and Manni stepped inside, their newly shaved cheeks raw from the wind. Manni was stout, standing about six foot three, built of nothing but muscle. He had Hawaiian blood running through him, giving him a dark and mysterious look, his arms and back covered in South Pacific inspired tattoos. His soft black hair, puppy dog eyes, and linebacker form melted ladies' hearts like chocolate in a sauna. There was often a mischievous look on his face, and he was constantly barely avoiding trouble. Manni was the baby of the boat, ringing in at twenty-four. He loved having fun, be it playing pranks on the guys, going out dancing, or cracking jokes. Since Manni was a fairly new husband and dad, Todd had come to notice a more serious shade of him, as all his spare attention was now devoted to his little one-and-a-half-year-old baby girl back home in Anchorage, and an exuberant and dedicated father he was shaping up to be.

Joel, forty-six, was the grandpa of the deck crew and also acted more maturely than the others. He stood a few inches shorter than Manni. His love of beer had contributed to a slight belly, barely noticeable, and the first gray whiskers had begun mixing in with his blond stubble when he didn't keep up on shaving. Part Norwegian, he had fitting baby blue eyes and an unstoppable determination. On deck, he was the anchor of the crew, seldom losing his temper, observing and assessing a situation before reacting, just as he often thought before he chose his words. He could quietly outwork just about any man, and then pick up their slack, too.

"Hey, what's up, buddy?" Manni shouted when he spotted Todd.

"Come over and grab a seat, man! What do ya want to drink?" asked Todd.

The boys sauntered over, draping their thick coats over the stools, Joel fishing out a cigarette. Derrick opened two beers.

"Where's Sam at?" asked Todd, surprised not to see him.

"Oh, he said he was going to stop by his buddy John's house. Guess he went crab fishing with him last year on the *Mary K.*"

Sam, a native of the Gig Harbor area, had gotten into fishing after a fellow construction buddy hooked him up with a seasonal job on a boat. For a while he did summer salmon seining in Southeast Alaska and winter construction work in Tacoma, just as his friend did, but in a few years switched to year-round fishing, getting hooked on the big money and chunks of free time to go skiing in between. Just a year younger and with about the same amount of fishing experience, Todd sometimes compared himself with Sam. They had a lot of similarities, especially when it came to their Pacific Northwest roots and getting in the mountains skiing and mountain biking in their time off, but Sam was born with something Todd never had. Every time Sam walked into a room, he had a magical way of wooing the ladies and even befriending the guys, even more so than Manni with his chocolatey looks melting women's hearts. With Sam, the saying was true, he often did have a "girlfriend" in every port, and sometimes even more than one. Joel, Manni, and Todd loved to scratch their heads at just how Sam did it. Even though his unbounded confidence kept him like a Leo, center of attention in every room, flashing a winning smile with hazel green eyes and sandy brown hair, Todd, who enjoyed trying to figure people out, guessed that deep down inside, the show was a sort of cover for some deep loneliness that Sam felt. Anyways, Todd was relieved Sam was absent tonight, as he didn't need Sam's Cool Hand Luke aura competing with his own while Em was around.

"So, are you gonna introduce me to your 'friend'?" whispered Manni into Todd's ear.

"Hey, back off," Todd hissed. "She's mine!"

"Who says?"

"I got here first."

"That doesn't give you no right," he mumbled into his glass.

Todd wasn't really worried about competition from Manni since he was faithful to his baby's momma, and Joel had just started dating a new woman with an exuberance that Todd had never seen in him before.

From there, round after round ensued until Derrick announced closing. Once the boys had joined Todd, his chance for intimate conversation with Em died like fire in a monsoon, but he'd had enough time sitting next to her, exchanging stories, cracking jokes, and making eye contact that he could feel the touch of warmth in his soul and not just from the alcohol. Derrick flicked the lights once more and everyone fumbled for their wallets and signed steep credit card bills with a drunken hand, not bothering or caring to look at the damage.

"Bye, my love!" Em shouted to Derrick, as she closed the door, following the three *Sea Ranger* boys into the frozen gravel streets of Sand Point. Joel and Manni started down the hill, just ahead of Em and Todd. Em zipped up her black down parka and threw the hood over her head so just her nose, eyes, and a few wisps of black hair stuck out.

"You, uh, need or want a walk home or anything?" Todd asked, swept with a sudden loss of confidence.

"Oh no, I'm just fine, thank you," she replied. "I'll walk with you to the streetlamp." As the streetlight neared, Todd tried to slow his steps, but all too soon they were under its orange glow.

"Alright kiddo, I'll see ya' around," said Em, her breath forming magical clouds in the cold air.

"Yeah, okay," stammered gun-shy Todd.

"Go load 'em up on your next trip." And with that she turned on her heel and headed up toward the AC, the village grocery store, to where exactly he did not know. Joel and Manni stopped just down the street, realizing they'd lost their companion.

"Hurry up, man!" Joel shouted. "I'm freezing my balls off."

"You get her number?" yelled Manni.

"Shut up!" he hushed them.

As Todd hustled after them, he turned his head once, hoping Em hadn't heard his gregarious friends' banter and caught a glimpse of her as she slipped out of the light near the AC store.

🪢 🪢 🪢

AFTER THAT NIGHT, Todd wasn't sure if they would ever cross paths again. It seemed there were too many uncontrollable variables involved. How long might it be until the rare random coincidence would lead them to the same place at the same time, if ever? He'd rather not live off unrealistic hopes anymore, his heart crushed too often in the past for that. The next day, he'd had way too much time to replay every moment of the night, as they stood for hours in the bait shed, jamming thousands of hooks with cold, chopped herring. When he had been able to get a word in to Em, he'd tried to play dumb to the fact that he'd heard about her for years. As he moved on to another skate of gear to bait (a coil of line with hundreds of hooks), he started kicking himself that he had not mentioned the *Adelyn Abby*. That would've been a sure way to connect and leave a lasting impression with Em. They could've reminisced over the quirks of old Skipper Stew: how he was missing half his teeth but still opened up beer bottles with the remaining few, how he talked to himself when he thought no one was near, or refused to wash his coffee cup, ever.

Chapter 3

Howl to the Morning

Late March 2013

WITH A START, Todd remembered the helm alert. Glancing up, he saw the seconds ticking down from fourteen, thirteen, twelve . . . *Close one!* he thought, as he hit the Reset button and focused back on watching the gauges, chart plotter, and endless sea of rolling waves. Daydreaming had whittled his watch down to only about fifteen more minutes.

Suddenly, "What the fuck are you doing?" came Joel's voice from behind Todd's shoulder. He didn't wait for an answer, but continued with, "Picking your nose or something?"

"Jesus H. Christ, Joel!" replied a startled Todd. "Can't believe I didn't have to wake you up this time."

"Yeah, fuckin' Sam woke me up with his snoring again."

"Tell me about it," Todd said, rolling his eyes in sympathy. "Well, nothing exciting to report to you from up here. Just a lot of seabirds and a few porpoises to keep you company."

"No mermaids?" Joel teased. "Hey, I'm going to make a fresh pot of coffee first, then I'll be right back up."

"Roger."

"DROP YOUR COCKS and grab your socks!" came the standard but crude and lewd wake-up call from Phil as he poked his head into the fo'c'sle and flicked the lights off and on, and then on for good. Todd groaned as he shielded his eyes from the harsh light and tried to re-member what they were doing and where they were as he glanced at his watch, which read 4:39 a.m. His stomach sank as he pieced together that they were still out at sea, still fishing, and now on day six of their trip. Eyes now adjusted, Todd fumbled for the pile of fishing clothes he'd been donning every day, crusty from salt and sweat. From his messy bunk he maneuvered into a polypro shirt, long underwear, fleece pants and a hoodie. Next he rolled out of his bunk, vying for space in the crowded fo'c'sle as three grown men all struggled to don clothes and Xtratufs, essential boots on a fishing vessel, while still half asleep. As usual, Joel was the first one out, then Todd, and pulling up the rear, Manni.

"Here you go, Sunshine," said Sam, who handed Joel a cup of coffee. Sam had woken early to get breakfast started and was no longer in the zombie stage of waking that the other three were still in. The smell of biscuits and gravy filled the air, making Todd's stomach rumble. Todd saw the head was open and took his opportunity to relieve himself be-fore someone held it up for their morning "routine." Inside, he glanced out the porthole to see what was in store for the day. The toilet paper, which hung on a string, swung from side to side with the roll of the boat. Still dark outside, he could make out the moon, about to disappear behind the rolling swells and smoking water. The smoking water meant it was clear, and because of that, bitterly cold.

Back in the galley, Sam dumped a pile of plates on the table and then began to dish up a heaping pile of food for the captain. With a steaming plate, Sam then headed up the stairs to deliver the dish to Phil, signaling for the rest of the crew to dig in and eat as fast as possible. No time for reading the daily paper they didn't have or slow sips of coffee. Instead, Joel reached up to the volume control of the house speakers and filled the room with Led Zeppelin, his morning psych-up, "Let's go fishing!" ritual that all had to succumb to, Zeppelin fan or not. Manni sat beside Todd, chewing his food in loud mouth-open smacks. It was not a way Todd would normally choose to spend his mornings, but this was fishing, and all you could do was learn to not let little annoyances push buttons. They were here to make money.

Plate now empty, Todd piled his utensils on top, and with one look at Manni, gave him the head nod to get up off the bench so that Todd could slide out. As he pushed up his sleeves to start in on the pile of greasy dishes, Manni came up from behind and said, "Yo, man, I'll do those, think you did 'em last night." Todd didn't complain and handed off the sponge, but suspected that Manni really just wanted to stay inside the longest. So instead, Todd headed off to begin the process of donning his rain gear.

Sam was the first one out, and he greeted the fierce wind and dark morning with an "Oh, fuck!" howl. *Great, here we go again.* Todd braced himself for the biting wind and followed Sam out the door with minimal enthusiasm in his step and even less as he glimpsed the green and white "Attitude is Everything" sticker, faded and cracked above the door.

Once on deck, the bright work lights blinded him for a few moments. Eyes adjusting, he saw the weather seemed the same as when they'd halted last night, if not worse, but the clouds were thinning. The air temperature with wind chill hovered around five degrees Fahrenheit, and the seas pitched the boat enough to keep everyone on edge. They were in for a long day of hauling gear.

Since the crew of the *Sea Ranger* had longlined together for a few seasons straight, the men worked without words, none needed as they prepared to pick their first string of gear (or long line of baited hooks). They'd left it to soak on the seafloor overnight, allowing the halibut time to smell the bait and come in for a deadly bite. Phil appeared in his rain gear just as the flag and buoy attached to an anchor on one end of their longline set bobbed into view on the starboard side. Phil slid into his place at the rail with the gaff hook. Todd and Joel, having worked for Phil the longest and therefore yielding the most seniority, manned the filet table, while Sam coiled the skates of line, and Manni headed to his station in the shed, baiting more hooks with odiferous herring, already blasting death metal music over the bait shed speakers. Phil maneuvered the boat up to the end of the line with the throttle and controls on deck, while Joel swung the grapple hook, catching the buoy line at the first throw, allowing them to pull the line aboard, which Todd then ran to the coiler. The whine of the hydraulics, a steady drone, combining with the loud reverberation of the diesel engine and gen-set, forced words to be spoken in raised voices. Phil hunched over the rail, squinting his eyes in anticipation for the first hook to appear out of the inky depths.

"Damn it," Phil cussed under his breath as it came up empty. The next one came up empty, and the one after that, bait gone. Todd couldn't help but roll his eyes. It was probably the sperm whales going after them again. But the fifth hook came up with a forty-pound halibut.

"Whew," Phil sighed under his breath. He gaffed it with expertise and slung it on the deck where it flopped in death throes, before Joel knocked it hard in the brain to end its thrashing and slung it up on the table for Todd to clean it of guts and gonads.

And so they repeated the same process over and over. Just as with most fishing, they became machines. Haul the gear in, set it back out. Haul the gear in, set it back out. Sometimes you got fish, sometimes you didn't. In reality, it was not the process of fishing that hooked a man or got under his skin, but the elements of the unknown, or the gamble of it all, or the hard work for sometimes huge payouts. When Todd felt he was about to lose his mind in the boredom of the routine, all he needed to reassure himself of why he loved fishing was to glance up and gaze at the ever-changing ocean, or think of pranks to play on crew members, or how he'd spend his settlement check.

As Todd and the guys started to settle into the day ahead of them and the sun peeked its first rays out over the horizon, Todd found his mind drifting back to . . . Emily. This time, though, he relived that second of the three times he'd crossed paths with Em thus far.

Chapter 4

Tote Sledding

March 2011

IN HIS DAYDREAM he could almost still hear the wind beating on the glass panes of the Tavern bar, smell the stale cigarette smoke, and feel the vibrations of the jukebox. It had only been ten days after he'd parted ways with her under that streetlamp in Sand Point. They'd gone out for one trip, but weather and poor fishing brought them back into port. He huddled with his boys, nursing some beers at a corner table. With no sign of Em, Todd felt glum.

"What's the matter with you?" Sam poked at Todd in an almost annoyed tone. Sam on the other hand was happy as a dog on the loose, already scoping out his next feline prey, which was one of about two choices.

"Oh nothing."

"I know what's his problem," piped in Manni. "He's sad 'cuz he don't see his girlfriend here."

"Yeah, whatever," said Todd, brushing their teasing off. "She probably doesn't even remember my name."

"Well, did you even tell her your name, dipshit?" said Joel.

"Uh, yeah, thank you very much, I did."

"Bet you didn't get her number, though," said Sam.

Todd just rolled his eyes and proceeded to excuse himself, feigning interest in the jukebox in the far corner of the one-room bar. After another beer, and little to no excitement, Todd pondered heading back to the boat. Only a few more people straggled in, and with each creak of the door, Todd felt a rush of excitement, followed by a bitter letdown.

"Hey, I'm heading back, anyone wanna come?" Todd asked, the disappointment of the evening coating his question.

"Sure, I'm feeling wiped," admitted Joel. Manni nodded in agreement as well. They didn't bother asking Sam, as he'd just placed himself next to one of his prey and was immersed in putting his moves on.

The three trudged back in silence, only the howl of wind and crunch of their boots on the frozen gravel breaking the quiet. It was about a ten-minute walk down to the harbor. To cut a few minutes out of their walk, they veered to the left and opted for the shortcut down the side road. There were two rows of small houses before the road dead-ended and the trail continued past the church and its small graveyard filled with white Russian crosses, and down across the main road to the walking bridge over the slough, and finally, to the harbor.

Most of the houses they passed lay dark and in shadow, yet one emitted a warm glow. Nearing the bright house, its door to the Arctic entry opened (an Alaskan version of a mudroom), spilling out a pile of four bodies bundled up against the cold, making it hard to recognize faces. At first Todd only heard male voices, but then one or two female voices joined in the mix. A few steps later, he picked out a slight Southern twang.

Joel nudged him in the ribs and whispered, "Looky, looky!"

"Well, good evening, gentlemen!" came her voice.

"Hey, what up, yo," replied Manni, trying to sound tough and nonchalant.

"Wanna come join us? We were about to go have an adventure," asked the girl with a thick Filipino accent.

"Oh hey, it's the *Sea Ranger* boys!" exclaimed Em. "Long time, no see."

With that, the two groups converged on the dark street and joined as one. Turns out it was Em and her friend Brena along with a few other local fishermen. Brena was originally from the Philippines, but had married Lex, the town's welder, whom she met when she first came over to work at the cannery. Also in the crowd were two guys, Stephen and Ivan from the *Calysto,* who Todd recognized but didn't know well. Names and brief introductions were tossed around, but that didn't matter so much. It was Em who counted.

Ivan pulled out a flask from his pocket as they walked and passed it around. Em and Brena led the pack, arm in arm. The rise in numbers and cheer pushed away any thoughts of hitting the rack for Todd, Manni and Joel. Soon everyone was in good spirits and creating a ruckus. The cold didn't matter with all the whiskey flowing through their veins.

They had just arrived at the harbor when Em broke away from Brena toward a big blue fish tote that was perched at the top of the dock. It was a bomb-proof plastic cube, with an open top and sides that stood three feet high. The cannery used them to transport fish once they came off the boat. It was rare to find one so far away from its home.

"Hey! Look what I found," yelled Em, as she neared the tote. Before anyone could react, she threw her leg over the side and climbed in.

Brena followed, and the two of them started trying to rock it back and forth, but they couldn't budge it. It didn't take long for the boys to join in and push it toward the ramp. Sand Point's ramps were made of worn and smooth wood that, when wet, invited many a youth to get a running start and slide handsfree all the way down like a skateboarder. That night it was low tide, and the wooden ramp slick with frost had a vertical drop of close to twelve feet.

"Push us down the ramp!" cried Brena.

"Come on, get in," urged Em.

Todd boldly climbed in and wrapped his legs around Em as if they were riding a toboggan. One of the *Calysto* boys, Stephen, also climbed in, sliding in next to Brena. That left Joel, Manni, and Ivan to push them over the lip and down the dock.

With Brena counting down, "Three, two, . . . one!" they were launched into a steep and swift flight downwards. The girls screamed and Todd grabbed on to Em, pulling her in tight. As they neared the bottom, Todd closed his eyes, bracing for impact. He felt a powerful blow that jolted Em even closer to him, and then, as if in slow motion, the tote tipped ninety degrees, spilling its cargo out onto the dock in a pile of legs and arms.

"Everyone, okay?" yelled Ivan from the top of the ramp, apprehension thick in his voice.

Em, Brena, Stephen, and Todd all glanced at each other, then broke out in uncontrolled laughter.

"Sounds like they're fine," said Manni. "My turn next!"

And so the crew spent their night, passing around the flask, dragging the tote up and down the dock, until their voices were hoarse with gleeful screaming and fingers numb from the cold. Nothing extra special happened that night between Todd and Em, but every time he made eye contact, his heart went wild.

The party ended once Joel looked at his watch to see what time it was and declared, "Fuck, man, it's two a.m. Phil said we're all starting at eight. We gotta get back to the boat." Standing at the top of the dock, the *Calysto* boys muttered in agreement.

"See ya round sometime," said Em, looking in Todd's direction.

"Yeah, sure," said Todd, not sure that such an encounter as this could be so lucky as to happen again.

"Later," said Manni as he put his arm around Todd's shoulders to start leading him back, sensing that Todd was reluctant to say goodbye to Em.

As they walked with Joel toward the *Sea Ranger* at the very end of the float, Manni warned Todd, "Don't look back, dude. Don't look back."

It took all of Todd's strength not to turn around and watch Em walk off into the darkness with Brena.

Back on the boat, the three crept into the galley like guilty teenagers sneaking back into the house, afraid of waking Captain Phil. Todd, the first one in the galley, gasped in surprise at Sam sprawled out on the galley bench, feet sticking off the end of the bench, boots still on. Bloody paper towels lay crumpled on the table and a few on the bench near Sam's head. His hood was pulled over his head and face nestled in his arm as he slept.

"What the fu— " said Manni as he came upon the scene next.

"Uh oh," said Joel. After a pause to assess the scene, Joel strode forward and poked Sam in the ribs.

Sam emitted a long groan and swatted at Joel's hand. "Leave me alone," he muttered, still half asleep.

"Dude, wake up," hissed Joel in urgency. "You can't let Phil see this!" motioning at the mess of bloody paper towels and trail of blood spots on the table that led to the sink where an ice pack lay thawing and a box of Band-Aids sat half opened. Meanwhile Todd and Manni had both begun cleaning up the outer periphery of mess.

"Let me see your face," said Joel.

"No, leave me alone," Sam grumbled, his eyes still closed as he lay on his side.

With an exasperated sigh, Joel grabbed Sam and rolled him over, Sam half protesting and covering his face in his arm. Finally Joel wrestled Sam's arm free, the fluorescent lights blinding Sam, but revealing a swollen nose, dried blood still caked on, and a very swollen and black shadow over Sam's normally gorgeous hazel right eye.

"Who'd you get in a fight with this time?!" asked an excited Manni, the gossip of the bunch.

"I don't fuckin' know his name! You think he wanted to shake my hand before he punched me?"

"Well, what happened then? Last time we saw you, you was kissing that cute girl up at the bar."

As they were talking, Joel eased Sam up into a sitting position. "Easy man, I got a few hits to the ribs, too!" Sam snarled in pain as Joel bumped a tender spot.

Most of the evidence now cleaned up, Todd poured a glass of water for Sam, and sat down at the table on Sam's other side.

"Here, try to drink some of this," he urged. "Got any other injuries?"

"Naw, just some bruised ribs, nose, and eye. No big deal," replied Sam, trying to brush it off.

"Come on, tell us!" pleaded a relentless and gossip-hungry Manni.

"Okay, okay," Sam caved after a long slow sip of cold water. "So after you guys left, I was really hitting it off with that chick, uh . . . think it was Sandra. Had another drink or two with her and then was just giving her a friendly little kiss when all of a sudden someone grabs my shoulder and yanks me off the stool."

Manni across the table was leaning in closer, engrossed in the details.

"It didn't mean nothing, I was just flirting . . ." Sam said in self-defense, although all three knew there were other intentions and rolled their eyes at Sam. "So this dude I've never seen before yanks me back. I don't even have a chance to get to my feet. He's got his two buddies with him. That bartender Derrick is yelling at him to take it out of the bar, and Sandra's yelling at her so-called boyfriend to stop, but he grabs me by the armpits and drags me out."

"No shit!" interjected Manni.

"Well, outside he let me get to my feet, then all he says is 'Yo dude, that's my woman,' and takes a huge swing at me. It was three to one, so I didn't have a chance. I got a few hits in, but was outnumbered. Can't remember if Derrick eighty-sixed me or not," Sam continued, wincing as he took a deep breath.

"You know any of 'em?"

"I don't think so, it was pretty dark. Definitely locals."

"You better be careful next time we come to town," warned Joel, alluding to the story of another outsider a few of the locals took a dislike to for similar reasons and ran out of Sand Point.

"I know, I know. She wasn't even worth it," Sam muttered, taking another sip of water before the guys helped him slide out of the bench and into his bunk.

Chapter 5

Deadhead

Late March 2013

"WAKE UP, MAN!"

Todd lifted his head to see Manni standing across from him at the cleaning table and then looked down to see the knife in his hand, about to make a sloppy cut on the thirty-five-pound halibut in front of him. His daydream had only lasted a few moments, as the sun was still working its way over the horizon of the ocean. *Focus, Todd. Focus,* he reminded himself.

The men of the *Sea Ranger* continued stacking the fish on deck. Once gutted, they were thrown into a weigh box. When the box was almost full, a quick reading was taken and recorded before the fish were dumped into the hold, where later they would be carefully packed and layered with ice. More often than not, the hooks came up empty, bait stolen. Or hook after hook came up with a squirming rockfish or green-eye shark that Phil flipped back into the sea.

The sun climbed higher over the southern horizon, warming the air by a mere five degrees. Sometime in the late afternoon, as the sun was just about to dip below the horizon and Phil had gone up to the wheelhouse to drive them to where they'd place a new set of gear, Todd hustled back to the bait shed with a skate of gear in his arms. Suddenly the boat shuddered, momentarily stopping dead in her tracks, so much so that it knocked Todd off his feet and sent him sliding across the deck and slamming his back into one of the steel shelves that lined the walls. As he slid in slow motion, the image of the black seal he'd seen the night before popped back into his head.

"What the heck was that?" Todd cried out in pain and shock as the impact was hard enough to leave a softball-sized bruise on his lower back.

As he pushed the now tangled skate off of himself and stumbled up and out of the shed, rubbing his back, he saw the rest of the guys picking themselves up and looking around in bewilderment. The seas were ten to thirteen-footers, but no rogue wave felt like that. This was different. This felt like they'd hit something. Todd ran back to the stern to watch the wake and see if anything popped up.

"Well, I'll be damned," Todd exclaimed a few moments later, loud enough to bring the guys running. About thirty yards behind them bobbed a four-foot-diameter log. *That seal sure was a sign of bad luck.*

"Fucking deadheads!" cursed Joel. Instead of the behemoth lying horizontally in the water, it was floating straight up and down, hard to spot and hard to avoid, hence the nickname of deadhead, because a collision with one often left a boat floating dead in the water, or worse.

"Goddamn it!" cried Phil in disgust from the loudhailer, and then asked them, "What'd we hit?" He then brought the throttle slowly back up to speed and the *Sea Ranger* started limping along like a car with a flat.

"Oh no," groaned Manni.

Phil dropped it back down, then tried it in reverse. Same effect. Then he put it back in forward, testing the vibration at different RPMs. Since Sam was the engineer, Phil called down on the loudhailer, "Go check the engine room, Sam. And Todd, you check the laz. Take a real good look at that rudder post."

Flashlight in hand, Todd crawled around on his belly in the dank lazarette storage area in the stern belowdecks, searching for flooding or leaking. Everything looked normal, so Todd headed to the cabin to report what he'd seen. There he saw Sam emerge from the engine room. Waiting for him to take off his earmuffs, Todd asked, "Find anything?"

"Everything looked okay down there and in the fo'c'sle. How about in the laz?"

"All good."

Todd headed up the wheelhouse stairs, grimy rain gear still on (a taboo act unless there was an emergency), to report to Phil and see if he needed help with anything. Like any good skipper worth his salt should, Phil was already on the radio, making calls and arrangements. Phil had been on fishing boats since he'd been in diapers, his mom a native of Petersburg and his dad of pure Norwegian descent. Phil's mom and dad had met in that town, and after a few years of struggling marriage, they divorced, leaving Phil's dad no choice but to take his toddler with him during the summer salmon seining. Back in the day Phil's father had a reputation for catching more fish than any other, going out in the worst weather and returning with a full hold, and for burning through crew like a construction worker burns through work clothes. Now, it was clear that Phil had inherited his father's knack for finding fish, but he had *not* inherited his father's "screamer" tendencies. Instead, during times of crisis, Phil remained stoic and silent.

Phil interrupted his conversation on the satphone to quickly explain, "Looks like we're going to have to limp back into . . . well, back to Sand Point, the closest village. With the bad vibration we got, I don't think we can go much over five hundred RPMs, so it'll take us a good long while to get back in."

He then turned back to the satphone with, "Hey, so I'm going to need the boat pulled out. When's the soonest we can lift her?"

Todd nodded and then headed back down to fill in the others. At the mention of Sand Point, Todd's heart had taken a momentary leap. *Em!* he thought, but checked himself by following with, *I doubt she's around, or that I'd run into her.* As he shouldered open the door to the deck, Manni and Joel looked at him with an inquisitive look. Todd informed them, "We're going to haul the gear back, then head into Sand Point to get the boat pulled out."

A distraught look passed over Sam's face. "Goddammit, I hate that blow hole!" After a pause, he asked, "You think they still remember me there?" referring to the fight he'd gotten in two years ago.

"Wouldn't doubt it, my friend," replied Joel. "Wouldn't doubt it."

Chapter 6

Unplanned Return

Early April 2013

TWENTY-SIX HOURS later, the *Sea Ranger* limped into Sand Point, too late in the day to catch the shiplift, so they'd have to wait until the eight a.m. opening time the next day to get hauled out, inspect the damage, and replace the prop if needed. But before they could tackle that, they first had to offload their fish, the hold only half full due to their abbreviated trip. Only one other boat was tied up at the dock, the usual buzz of forklifts and cannery workers quieted for the winter. The orange florescent lights of the cannery reflected off the still water and their dock lines were stiff with cold and frozen sea spray, slowly creaking against the tar-stained pilings.

On their long and slow crawl back to Sand Point, the crew had plenty of time to do the standard deep clean of the boat (always extra thorough before pulling into port), and then catch up on sleep. Now they stood in the cold, waiting for a few year-round cannery workers to stumble out and begin their offload. The boys smoked cigs and taunted the harbor's few resident sea lions with bits of bait, noting the precious time that the cannery was wasting in their disorganized offload. This time it took thirty-five minutes for the workers to appear, even though the cannery had known well in advance of their arrival. Phil had disappeared into the main building to talk shop with the office and make use of the skipper's lounge, a small room kept under padlock combo that skippers and lucky deckhands that knew the code could use to make phone calls and hit up the one, neolithic computer. Sand Point still didn't have Todd's cell service carrier, so he couldn't check his messages. From the back deck he watched two figures, one small and petite like Em, climb up the stairs to the upper warehouse where the town's general store was located, and his heart flipped for a beat, but it was not her.

Todd was stuck with late dinner duty while the cannery offloaded their catch tote by tote. That's when he allowed himself to reminisce on his third and last, but most precious memories about Em.

Chapter 7

"Let Her Go!"

April 2012

TODD WAS HANDS deep in a project, this time on a different boat, different crew, different fishery, and different place, as that spring he'd decided to take a little break from longlining. Phil said he'd save his spot for him the next year, and Todd trusted him. It was early April in 2012, over a year since he'd seen Em those two times in Sand Point, but his mind still wandered back to her. Her memory didn't haunt him quite as much, but she was still there, like the rain of Southeast Alaska, slow, steady, and frequent. Just as the rain was coming down now, in Sitka.

Todd had been there for two weeks getting the *Lori Lou* ready for the brief but lucrative herring seine fishery. The *Lori Lou* was a classic wooden seiner built in the 1950s. He'd met the skipper, Ray, at Sitka's Pioneer Bar, locally known as the P Bar, during a spring longline trip, and Todd must've impressed him because Ray kept his number over all those months and then called him out of the blue and offered him a job that next spring.

The Sitka Sound sac roe herring fishery was like no other. It was fast and furious. Some years the forty-eight permit holders only had a few openings to catch the quota. It was a hurry-up-and-wait fishery, as the openings depended on catching the fish when the roe were mature, but before the fish had spawned. In recent years the guideline harvest was capped at about twenty-nine thousand tons, but sometimes the fishermen were only allowed to seine for half of that. Last year the fleet could only take ten thousand tons. Sometimes they would catch so many fish that the processors could not keep up, also causing closures. So when there was an opening, it was a full-on greedy slaughter of fish, a wild West, get-your-guns-out, hold-on-for-the-ride, and cork-the-guy-next-to-you atmosphere. Hopefully you got your net *and* your boat back in one piece. Big money was involved. From the air (many fishermen hired spotter planes to lead them to the largest schools of herring), the scene looked like mad chaos: almost fifty boats seining in a small area, the water frothy with nets, boats, and skiffs, in most cases just a few yards away from each other.

After two weeks of dirty, wet, and cold boat projects on the *Lori Lou*, Todd was ready for the first opener. The harbor was alive with eager fishermen all waiting for the standard two-hour notice for an opener as the department of "Fin and Feather" (Fish and Game) waited until the mature roe were above eleven percent. Now with the main projects completed, Todd and the two other crew—Zach, a lean, young native boy from Craig, and Jake, a tall and curly-haired twenty-five-year-old from a longlining family in Cordova—were tinkering with a few small details. Todd's hands were deep into a gob of Splash Zone, working the two-part epoxy to cover over a sharp spot on the back deck where the net could catch and tear, when Ray hollered down from above, "Put all that shit away, it's time to go fishing!!!"

In a matter of moments the word spread throughout the harbor.

Diesel engines sputtered to life, and black smoke choked the air. Skippers cried out, "Cut her loose," or "Let her go!" Deckhands waved to each other as they sped out of the breakwater, friendly now, but soon to be stiff competitors when they reached the fishing grounds.

Once out on the grounds of the shoreline of Kruzof Island, a short ten nautical miles northwest of Sitka, the crew had just enough time to stash the tools from projects they'd been working on in town, get their gear on, and double and triple check that the net was ready to set and all the lines were hooked up correctly, buoys stowed, and maybe grab a cup of coffee to amp up the already ecstatic energy of the fishery just one notch higher. Boats circled, hungry as ravens, crews stood at the ready, each skipper vying for the best spot. Beads of sweat painted many a skipper's brow, as a few bad decisions could cost the boat thousands and thousands of dollars, and maybe even the season. Ray ordered the crew to help him keep an eye out for boats approaching too close. Just about every year at least one boat got rammed, never clear if the incidents were intentional or "accidental." Ray kept a close eye on the clock. Setting too early could result in a hefty fine from Fish and Game of several tens of thousands of dollars or even seizure of the boat.

"Everyone ready down there?" asked Ray on the loudhailer.

Zach, standing closest to the intercom yelled up, "Yes, Rog-o!"

"Stand by, it's almost time."

Todd stood in the middle of the deck, one hand on the pancake, or rather, the pull cord attached to the spring-loaded skiff release. Once he heard the order from Ray, he'd give it a yank and the line holding the skiff to the stern of the boat would be free, allowing the skiff to detach from the "big boat" and pull the net away and out in a circle. As Todd glanced off the port side, he witnessed the white froth of water and cloud of black smoke from the nearby *Copacetic*'s skiff pulling away with their net in tow, then, the *Intangible*, just seconds behind, then all around, boats began setting their gear, skiffs revving their engines, deck crew watching the nets peel off the back deck. Yet Todd heard nothing from Ray. He looked at Zach, and he shrugged his shoulders in bewilderment. A minute went by, then two.

It seemed that the *Lori Lou* was trapped between seiners in every direction. Then, just as Todd started to wonder if Ray had lost his marbles, the loudhailer rumbled, "Okay, let her go." Somehow Ray, and Jake in the skiff, found enough space to squeeze the net in and come back full circle. Zach and Todd had seined before, so there was minimal rust to work out of the routine. Todd took the leads and Zach took the corks, and since they were shorthanded, both handled the web when they could as they began the process of piling the net back on the boat. Ray ran down from the wheelhouse to run the hydraulics and purseline, which would close up the bottom of the net.

Superstitious of saying anything too early, Todd held his tongue as they retrieved the net, but he was burning with the questions, *What'd we set on? Are we going to get anything out of this?* Ray ran the block at full speed, making Todd break a sweat, as was usual the first few days of seining. Soon the bunt, or end of the net where the fish were forced into, came up to the port side of the boat. Todd tried to glimpse in as he stacked the leads, and saw a frothy mass of herring, flip-flopping away.

"Woohoo!" he shouted, loud enough for Zach to hear and give him a big grin. Most of the boats around them had already stuck their pumps in the frothy water and were shooting the herring into their holds. Some were even done and looking to make another set, which was a bad sign because it meant they hadn't caught much. There were still a good number of rings to the purseline left when Ray stopped the block and Zach and Todd came forward to set up the pump. The size of the bunt was bulging with weight, some of the corks sinking.

It took over an hour to pump their catch into the hold. They'd done better than anyone around them. Ray's initial delay in setting had planted doubt in Todd's mind, but in the end, as usual, Ray proved himself a wise and fishy skipper. The clock was ticking, as the opener was only open from two thirty to five p.m. But thanks to their good first set, their sixty-ton hold was almost full, the fish packed in so tight the plunger pole would only go a few feet down before hitting resistance in the mass of refrigerated water and herring. They'd just started setting up for another set and were hosing off the deck of herring escapees, when Ray came over the hailer again.

"Hey guys, we're going to go help the *Jean C.* The *Williwaw Bay* rammed them good, and now they're taking on water. Get out that dewatering pump, you know where it is, in that box on the top of the house, by the chest freezer."

Zach hurried up to the top house to grab the pump. Todd helped him wrestle it down over the ladder to the deck with the help of a spare line to ease the heavy load. Some boats carried a dewatering pump made for emergency flooding situations, others did not. Ever since the *Lori Lou* had a close call a few years back, Ray never went anywhere without one, although it hadn't been test-run in over a year. Zach, Todd, and Jake were tossing down the pump hoses, which had been stashed behind the chest freezer, when they pulled up next to the *Jean C.*

"I got this, if you and Jake want to go toss them our lines," suggested Zach. They had crash bags and lines out and ready just in time as they pulled near to the starboard side of the *Jean C.* She was a tough-looking steel boat, covered in a fresh paint job of green with white trim, but not tough enough to withstand the full speed ramming from the *Williwaw Bay.* About ten feet back of the bow the upper railing was caved in, along with the steel plating of the hull. It looked like the bulbous bow on the *Williwaw Bay* had made the most impact, denting in the plating like a crumpled can.

The *Jean C* crew looked flustered. Only one guy in a yellow and blue Grundens coat could break away from the madness to catch their lines. Another boat, the *Clipper Star,* was already on the port side, their pump up and running, spewing forth a steady flow of water. As Todd stood at the bow and coiled the line, then split it in half, one coil for each hand to make for a better throw, he made eye contact with the guy on the *Jean C* to make sure he was ready before flinging it across the twenty-foot gap. That's when he gasped—her dark hair spilled out from under her baseball cap, and green eyes widened when she recognized him. It was Em.

"Hey, stranger, fancy running into you like this," Em called over to him before he could react. "It was Todd . . . right?"

"Yeah, good memory," he blurted out, wishing he'd thought of something more smooth.

"Well?" she called back, and when he failed to get it, clapped her hands and made a catching motion.

Oh, right, I'm supposed to be throwing her the lines.

"Ready?" he asked.

"Born ready," she said, and with that he hurled the line across the now only fifteen-foot gap. She caught it with ease and slipped the eye over the cleat while he tied off his end and then rushed down to toss her the midship line.

"Secure!" he yelled to Ray, who was leaning his head out the window watching them tie up, hand on the throttle. Once alongside, everyone burst into action and grabbed a side of the pump to walk it over to the *Jean C,* which was listing to the starboard at an ominous fifteen-degree angle.

"Where's the water coming in at?" he asked Em as she hustled by.

"Below the water line up in the fo'c'sle," she answered as she disappeared back into the cabin. A hole below the water line was always bad news, as even a quarter-sized hole could do considerable damage if it went unchecked.

With a quick look around to see what needed to be done, Todd grabbed a five-gallon bucket of water and poured it down the suction hose to prime the pump, while Zach manned the pull cord. Meanwhile, Ray conferred with the skipper of the *Jean C,* who was up in the wheelhouse on the radios.

Just before the rumble of the pump started, Todd overheard Ray yell over, "So you've got the Coast Guard coming with one more pump?"

After only a few pulls, the pump came sputtering to life, and Jake grabbed the suction hose and ran it in through the galley and down through the engine room to the fo'c'sle. Soon water started shooting out the discharge end. As Jake emerged onto the deck, Todd quizzed him for information.

"Well, the water's up over the floorboards in the engine room. You can see the side's all dented up in the fo'c'sle and there's this gash on one of the weld seams that the water's gushing through. They're trying to stop it with wedges and pieces of neoprene cut off an old survival suit," Jake relayed.

With both pumps running, there wasn't much to do until the Coast Guard chopper arrived on scene. Todd recognized a few of the guys on the *Jean C* and *Clipper Star*, but didn't know any names. There were boats making sets all around, but the *Williwaw Bay* was nowhere in sight.

The captain of the *Jean C* ran back and forth between the wheelhouse, where he was communicating with the Coast Guard, and his crew trying to stop the leaks.

"Looks like the pumps are keeping up!" he shouted on one of his passes by the deck.

And another time, he reported, "Coast Guard should be here in about fifteen. Make sure we're ready for 'em!"

Throughout the emergency, Em spent most of the time with the rest of her crew in the engine room trying to dam the gash, so Todd had no chance to ogle or even slip in a word to her, although he wasn't sure of what he'd say, anyway.

"I see the chopper! Straight off the stern," yelled Zach, picking out the tiny speck over the horizon long before Todd could spot or hear it. But soon, the red and white chopper hovered above them, sending out circles of spray, wind, and a deafening roar.

The "Coasties" (a common nickname for US Coast Guard personnel) lowered a red line to the water, called the tagline, that was attached to a dewatering pump, still in the helicopter. Todd looked around to find a boat hook and ran it back to the deckhand standing at the stern so they could pull the line out of the water. Once they had control of the tagline, the Coast Guard lowered the pump from the helicopter on another, sturdier line. This method of delivery allowed the helicopter to stay a safe distance from the rigging of the boats, while the tagline helped the crew pull the pump toward the boat as it was being lowered. Adrenaline coursing through everyone's veins made pulling the pump on board an easy task. Once out of its waterproof box, the well-maintained pump started after one pull.

After fifteen minutes of pumping with three machines running, Ray reported that the flooding was almost under control, only a few inches of water in the fo'c'sle.

"We're gonna untie. Since the *Clipper Star* has more horsepower than us, they're gonna tow 'em back in," instructed Ray to his crew.

At last Em emerged from the engine room, face flushed, looking exhausted, just in time to see Todd working the stern line, and ran over to help him.

"Hey, thanks for your help," she said as she slid the eye off the *Jean C*'s cleat.

"Uh, yeah, of course, no problem." They moved up to the spring line, as Jake already had the bow free. "I know you guys'd do the same for us if we ever needed it," Todd added after more thought.

Jake interrupted them with, "You're queer!" shouting the smirky and very un-PC way of letting the captain know he was "all clear" right into Ray's ear.

"See ya 'round," Em called as the distance between the two boats widened.

"Roger," he said as she was already turning her back to him.

There was no time to daydream about Em anymore, as they had missed the closing of the opener but still had to get back to town as fast as possible to line up for offloading. It was first come, first served, and no one enjoyed an offload at three a.m.

The *Lori Lou* pulled back into Eliason Harbor, one of the largest of Sitka's four boat harbors, with a full hold loading her down. As feared, it was a long wait to offload, since there were only so many processors and many more full boats. They didn't finish pumping out until after two the next afternoon. Just as they'd tied up back in their permanent slip and Todd was in the galley washing his hands, Ray sauntered down from the wheelhouse.

"I need you guys to . . ." and spouted off a long list of projects and fine tune adjustments he wanted the boys to fix. The boat itself was still a little "rusty" after not working for months.

"Okay, sure thing," answered Todd, as Ray disappeared back up the stairs.

Jake flipped through a *Pacific Fishing* magazine at the galley table across from Zach, who was eating a bowl of Cheerios, looked up, and asked, "And why didn't he tell us this when we were sitting around waiting to offload all morning?"

Todd rolled his eyes and shrugged his shoulders. Zach whispered, "Because he was sleeping off his usual hangover, that's why."

Forgetting any thoughts of freedom and running around town, the guys instead pulled out the tools and coveralls. As Todd stood on the net switching out a hydraulic fitting running to the power block, disappointed that he couldn't spy on Em, he thought, *Why couldn't we be at a slip near the ship lift?* During the wait to offload, gossip about the *Jean C* had spread the way kudzu vine takes root in the South, and each mention of Em's boat sent a jolt to Todd's heart.

"Heard the *Jean C* is pressing charges against the *Williwaw Bay*," reported one friend as he walked by.

Then, "Looks like they're probably gonna miss the whole herring season," commented another friend as he stepped in the galley to grab a cup of coffee.

And also, "*Williwaw Bay* claims it wasn't their fault, that the *Jean C* got in their way as they were setting," from a friend of Jake's.

Todd never got a chance that day, or the next, to get off the boat or look around town for Em, as the next day another opener was suspected to take place and Ray made them take off from town that evening. He wanted to be on the grounds early to ensure his whole crew was actually on the boat and not in jail or showing up with black eyes, trouble that sometimes ensues when in town. As they motored out of the dark harbor that night, Todd glimpsed the forlorn looking *Jean C* on blocks, a welding truck parked by her side, lights on in the galley and on deck, but no one in sight.

The second opener was as chaotic as the first, minus any boats getting rammed. Ray kept up a furious pace, working Todd's already sore muscles. The problem with herring fishing was that just as your body got back into seining shape, the season closed, and it was another two months until salmon seining would start.

The next closure lasted two days, giving Ray time to dole out more maintenance orders, one of which was, "Oh hey, I need two of you to go over and get our dewatering pump off the *Jean C*."

"I'll go!" offered Todd, a little too eagerly, causing Ray to pause and raise his eyebrows in a slight arch.

"Okay, you and Jake go use the work truck and pick it up. They're over at the dry dock. You'll see 'em right away by the entrance." Then he added, "Hard to miss a crumpled-up boat like that."

Jake was ready to go get it over with so they could be free to prowl town sooner.

"Just one minute," said Todd as he ran into the head to give his appearance a quick once-over in the mirror, not wanting to show up with grease or something embarrassing on his face. Neither Jake nor Zach knew of Todd's long-standing crush on Em.

As they pulled up next to the *Jean C*, Todd noted the three other trucks parked in a haphazard fashion around her, then moved his gaze up to the damage on the boat. The welder stood on scaffolding near the starboard bow, visor down and sparks flying, as he made a cut around the caved-in plate.

"Wow, that's bad," said Jake.

"I'd say so," agreed Todd. It did indeed look like one of the rumors was true, that the *Jean C* wouldn't be fishing any time soon, at least not if the season closed in a few days. But Todd was only half looking at the damage. He was also half scoping out the scene for signs of Em.

"Yo, anyone up there?" yelled Jake before climbing the ladder tied to the deck, ten feet above. "We're here to get our pump."

A head in a gray cap peeked over, answered, "Come on up," then disappeared.

The deck was littered with tools, scrap metal, welding equipment, and various water-damaged articles from the fo'c'sle and engine room, laid out to dry on the rare sunny day that it was. Todd's hope dropped like the ball on New Year's Eve when there was no sign of Em. Over in the corner of the deck lay the *Lori Lou's* pump. Todd and Jake introduced themselves to the crew members who were around, Ryan and Shay. After taking a minute to have a smoke and talk about how they were coming along with repairs, Ryan and Shay lowered the pump with a line down to Todd and Jake into the back of Ray's T100 work truck. Just before they took off, and Todd was tasting disappointment like acid in his mouth, audacious Jake leaned out of the driver's side window and bellowed up, "Hey, where's that chick?"

"Oh, you mean Em?" asked Ryan.

"Dude, she's hands-off, just like my sister would be," warned Shay.

"Okay, okay, just wondering. She seemed like a hard worker," said Jake, trying to save his dignity.

"She just ran out to get some more parts from the chandlery, if you must know," Todd heard Ryan give in as they were pulling away.

Instead of dealing with talking to Jake, Todd turned up the volume to the one decent radio station in Sitka, KIFW. Bon Jovi poured out of the battered speakers, muting out the sound of gravel crunching under the tires. Just as Jake made a hotrod turn out of the shipyard, spinning the tires to make a dust cloud, a battered old red F-250 pickup with a white camper top signaled to turn into the yard. As a custom of habit, Todd peered through the window in hopes that it might be Em. This time, for once, it was.

Jake, concentrating too hard on his hot rod moves, didn't notice her, but she also failed to notice them. Todd turned his head to follow the truck with his eyes out the back window, as it sputtered over to the *Jean C* but soon disappeared out of sight as Jake sped away.

"What are you looking at?" Jake asked, noticing Todd's craned neck.

"Oh, nothing," he replied with frustration at their timing, as he turned back his head to face the road ahead.

ʄ ʄ ʄ

AS THEY WENT through the routine the next few days, including two more successful openers for the *Lori Lou*, the fact that Todd knew Em was near drove him mad. Every time he entered a local shop, whether it was a hardware store or during grocery shopping runs, he looked down every aisle in anticipation of running into her; every red F-250 that drove by piqued his attention. Yet there was no sign of her. The town of Sitka, population of only nine thousand, began to feel like a metropolis. Toward the end of those few days, Todd started to give up hope of ever seeing Em again.

So, feeling defeated on the night after the last opener, Todd didn't even bother to put on his nicest "town" clothes or go through with the effort to shave his three-day stubble when he and the *Lori Lou* crew joined the rest of the fishing fleet in hitting the bars in celebration of a good season. They started with dinner in the small Fly-In Fish Inn, squeezing into a table by the windows looking out over the channel with a clear view of the sun setting behind Japonski Island.

But the men were not gazing off into the sunset. Instead they were busy devouring sloppy burgers and greasy fries, and slamming pints of beer.

From there, they rolled downtown for a few at Victoria's Poorhouse where they graduated from beer to mixed drinks. It was a long and narrow bar, every stool already filled with the male species since it was a Friday *and* the last night after the season closed, so Ray led his crew to the rear with, "Come on guys, follow me." The three shuffled behind Ray, drinks in hand, where he held open the beaded curtain to the back room. Inside was a cozy lounge filled with pillows and comfortable couches, a flat screen TV with the remote lying out on the low coffee table.

"Sweet!" declared Zach as he grabbed the remote and flopped down into the enveloping sofa.

"I never knew this was here," admitted Jake, a regular at the Poorhouse.

"What do you guys want to watch?" asked Zach. Not waiting for an answer, he continued with, "ESPN or . . . ESPN?"

Todd found a corner spot on the sofa and took a sip of his drink. After living on the boat for so long on a flimsy foam mattress and thin cushions at the galley bench, it felt good to melt into the pillows and couch. After a handful of empty glasses lined the table, the jukebox, located just outside their "lounge," kicked in, making their laidback conversation difficult.

Todd, already feeling antsy, pulled himself out of the couch, and announced, "I'm going to the P Bar. Anyone want to come?"

"I'll be down later, I still want to say hi to a few folks here," said Ray.

"Yeah, me too," muttered Zach, still engrossed in ESPN.

"I'll go with ya," said Jake, struggling to a stand.

As they pushed their way out of the crowd, cold spring air followed them as they walked the few blocks back toward the infamous Pioneer

Bar, central nightlife nerve of Sitka. They could hear the pounding of music and loud voices from half a block away. Todd didn't pause before he pushed himself through the door and headed straight for the bar, where they had to elbow their way in to place an order.

Soon after, Jake got pulled off into a conversation with a buddy from Cordova, so Todd took the opportunity to take a look around. The sobering photographs of wrecked or grounded ships that lined every inch of the walls were a little more yellowed from cigarette smoke than the last time he'd been there. The pool table was mobbed with fishermen either waiting their turn or playing, most of them with ladies at their sides. A group of young and hip looking local kids huddled around the jukebox between the pool tables and bathrooms. Then, there were the old familiars slumped over the long wooden bar, who pretty much owned their bar stools. Todd glanced over at the horseshoe-shaped booths, all full of fishermen, a few of whom he knew and recognized. The tables were cluttered with ashtrays, glasses, and empties. He took a sip of his drink, and then performed a second once-over of the booths.

And that's when he saw her, unmistakable in her pigtails. When he'd first walked in, he'd walked right by her, as she was at the crowded table nearest the door. She was surrounded by about five young guys, two of whom were Ryan and Shay from the *Jean C.* Anxious now, with this turn of luck, Todd took another drink and swirled the ice around, giving him time to ponder how to proceed. She hadn't seen him yet. There was no way he could break into that group right now. He'd have to wait for her.

But, he decided, he had all the time in the world. He was prepared to wait it out like a hunter in a deer stand. The night was still young, as it was only half past ten, so he passed the time striking up conversations with the old-timers next to him while keeping an eye on her table.

"What boat were you on, kiddo?" asked the fifty-year-old man in the patched green flannel to his right.

"Oh, the *Lori Lou*," he replied absently.

"Oh, I know Ray! He and I were neighbors back in the day. How'd he do?"

Never giving out the truth is the fisherman's trademark, so Todd replied with modesty and ambiguity, "Oh, we did okay."

He listened to the men complain about the usual three "f's": fish prices, fuel prices, and federal taxation. As he nodded from time to time to agree with their ranting, Todd glanced over at Em's table where she was still wedged in the middle, a warm glow on her face as she laughed at some joke one of the guys had made. Good news was it didn't appear that any of the guys with her was a significant other.

After drink number two, he glanced over and she wasn't there.

Oh fuck, please don't tell me she left!, his heart beat faster.

"Excuse me, gotta hit the head," he interrupted his neighbor in the middle of a fish tale, finished his last gulp of whisky and headed toward the bathroom, searching for any sign of pigtails. Nowhere to be seen. He poked his head outside. Nope. So he made his way to the men's room, giving him more time to think. It was crowded and smelled of piss, so he got in and out as fast as possible, but still had no good ideas. Lost in his mind, he didn't notice when he neared the women's restroom and the door flew open, spilling forth a group of giggling girls. The door made direct contact with his face, his nose taking the brunt of the impact.

"What the fuck?!" he cried out in shock. As the door slid back, holding his nose in pain, he stood face to face and eye to eye with the now shocked, silent girls.

"Oh my god, you're bleeding!" cried one.

"I'm *so* sorry!" said the other.

And, "Oh, Todd!!" said Em, standing right there in front of him.

His face flushed as he noticed the unmistakable feeling of blood run out his nose and pool into his upraised hand still covering his nose. Glancing down, drops of blood fell onto the floor, spattering his shoes.

Before he could turn away in embarrassment and before he could protest, Em grabbed his arm and said, "Oh jeez, let's get you cleaned up," and steered him into the women's bathroom. "I got this!" Em told the other two girls still standing in disbelief in the hallway, as she pulled Todd toward the sink.

Compared to the men's room, the women's bathroom smelled of chemical deodorizer, and its walls were decorated with a few tacky paintings of flowers in vases. Todd avoided looking into the mirror at the damage and didn't have time to, as Em turned on the faucet, ran her hand under it to test the temperature, then eased his head forward. "Let me clean you up a little," she said.

"Oh my god, I feel like such an idiot!" Todd lamented into the porcelain basin.

"You feel like an idiot? I'm the one who flung the door open like that!" she tried to soothe him.

"I haven't had a bloody nose in years," he said. Then, "So, I'm afraid to ask, but does it look broken?"

Now that most of the blood was washed away, turning the tap water rose pink, she gently turned his head to the side to take a look. There was a long, dreadful pause.

"Oh no," he groaned in fear and anticipation.

She pursed her lips a little, then answered in a serious voice, "Yeah, it looks pretty bad," but then burst out laughing as she guided his head up to the mirror for him to look, showing him an intact, but swollen nose. "You better pinch the bridge of your nose," she ordered.

It took over ten minutes for the bleeding to completely stop. The door opened two or three times and Todd sheepishly explained to incoming bewildered ladies why he was hanging out with Em near the sink with a fist full of paper towels shoved in his face.

Alone again, she said, "Let me take a look at that," as he let her slide up so close to him he could smell her scent.

"I think it's stopping," he said. "I'll be fine."

"Well, Todd," she said. Hearing her use his name made him feel surprisingly content. "I really owe you a drink now . . . what with helping us when we were sinking and now this!"

"What are you talking about? No, you don't," he answered, playing dumb.

But she grabbed the remaining paper towels out of his right hand and threw them in the trash, then grabbed his left hand to lead him back out to the bar. Not believing the turn of events, Todd followed like a sheep led home by its shepherd.

"I want to get this guy . . ." she paused looking for a clue as he mouthed his answer, then, "a rum and Coke . . . make that two!" she informed Eliza, the redheaded bartender who'd worked at the P Bar for as long as Todd could remember. There was only one bar stool open, and Todd insisted Em take it, but she insisted they share. Taking the chance to get closer to her, he caved in with no resistance.

Looking back on that night, unfortunately, due to his buzz, Todd still couldn't recall much of what they'd talked about. He did remember at one point swearing he'd beat up the *Williwaw Bay* guys for ruining her herring season, until she hushed him with a finger to his mouth, trying to avoid a bar fight in case one of those boys overheard Todd. He also remembered finally mentioning the *Adelyn Abby* and laughing with Em over Skipper Stew stories. And at last, he remembered gathering all of his remaining courage and whispering in her ear, "Hey, you wanna get out of here?"

The second it took her to reply seemed to last eons. "Sure thang," she answered in her hint of a Southern twang.

Once outside, Todd linked his arm under Em's and she didn't protest. Without consultation, they both started walking toward the harbor, giggling, and laughing the whole way, making the fifteen-minute walk seem like three. Standing under the streetlamp at the top of the dock with her fleece zipped up to her neck to fight the cold, Em looked up to Todd. "So, what now?"

"My boat's that way," he said, nodding down J dock. She returned his suggestion with a contemplative stare. "I'm sure Ray's still out drinking, Zach has a place to crash in town, and I saw Jake leave with a local girl," Todd tried again.

"Well, you can at least give me a tour," she consented.

What does that mean? Todd wondered, confused. *Does that mean she only wants to stop by for a minute?* But he soon got his answer.

🪢 🪢 🪢

AS THEY NEARED the boat, it was clear she was deserted, as the *Lori Lou* lay dark and quiet, her dock lines creaking in the wind. On his "tour" of the boat he showed her the galley, she feigned interest, then the engine room, she feigned interest again, and finally the fo'c'sle.

"And this is Zach's bunk, and here's Jake's. And here's mine . . ." he said, trailing off. She looked up at him and blinked her green eyes. Heart thudding, Todd leaned closer to her. He took a big gulp, then moved in to kiss her.

She didn't protest, but instead leaned her head in closer. Her lips were soft, tasting of the Pomegranate Burt's Bee's she'd put on during their walk back to the boat. She closed her eyes as he continued to kiss her, putting one hand behind her head and the other to her slender waist as she grabbed on to his strong arms. She didn't protest, either, when he unzipped her fleece, or when his hands moved to the button of her jeans. Instead, she helped him when he fumbled, letting the clothes fall to the floor, as when the velvet curtains concealing a masterpiece are dropped for the unveiling. Both still half dressed, he eased her into his bunk, climbing in on top of her with care, as they continued to fumble with their remaining clothes in between bouts of kissing. She moved her hands over his bare chest, feeling his small patch of chest hair, then fingered his navel, toying with the idea of dropping her hand lower. Her resistance all the more excited him. Then she brought her hand up to finger his tattoo of a manta ray on his shoulder. She was naked, so small and strong, her small breasts perfect to cup his hands over. Her skin was smooth as butter, but he could feel the calluses of her palms, as she pulled him in closer, running them over his back. He kissed her neck as she decided to stop playing around and moved to slide his briefs down. Breathing into her ear he made her giggle with delight. Then she guided him into her. They made love in silence and muffled sounds, she touched him in all the right places, they moved together, everything fluid and without thought, as if each could read what the other wanted. Passionate and urgent. He had never experienced sex to be quite so effortless before. She was more aggressive than most girls he'd been with, and he liked it. He could feel her almost on the verge, and just when she climaxed, he could hold himself back no longer, and the two collapsed, sweaty and smelling of sex, together into a pile of tangled sheets.

"Wow," was all she said, as he spooned her and traced the grapefruit-sized circular tattoo, a native-style depiction of a raven in red and black ink, in between her shoulder blades.

"Wow is right," is how he replied, still catching his breath. With his thick arm he pulled her in closer to him and nestled his nose into her hair. He fell asleep to the rhythm of her twitching and breath deepening, melding with his own.

Sleeping two in a bunk is an art. Every time one moves, the other must move, too. But Todd didn't mind. Sometime in the early morning, heavy footfalls, banging pots and pans, the smell of coffee and bacon filtered down from the galley. Todd woke first, in disbelief that he had his arms around her. He took a deep breath to take in her scent, moved his hand to her head to run his fingers gently through her silky hair. His mind replayed the magic from the night, all of it playing out like a movie, but all of it real, the proof in his arms. Em moved, slowly waking, turned her head to smile at him, blinking the sleep out of her eyes.

"Hey there," she whispered.

"Good morning," he replied, bliss emanating through his body.

Footsteps banged across the floor above them, the head door slammed shut, muffled voices floated down through the wire chase.

A shadow crossed Em's face. "Oh my god, what time is it?" she said, afraid to know the answer.

"Let me check." Todd pulled his arm out from under her to see his watch. "It's 8:19."

"Shit!" she cried as she jerked herself up, almost hitting her head on the low ceiling. "I'm late! We were supposed to start work at eight!"

The magic of the moment over, Em started fumbling for her clothes strewn across the fo'c'sle.

"I hope my skipper is late like usual. Maybe I can get the boys to cover for me." She'd already gotten her bra and T-shirt on, but was still looking for the bottom half. "Where are my underpants?" her voice edging on frustration, as they were nowhere to be found.

"I don't know," Todd replied as he sensed her urgency and got up to search the neighboring bunk and cluttered floor, moving the pile of miscellaneous stuff that always gathered there.

"Fuck it, I'll go without," she said as she shimmied into her jeans and slid into her shoes.

"Hey, I know a better way out, if you want!" Todd said as she put her hand on the door to go through the engine room and up to the galley. She paused, and Todd pointed to the Freeman escape hatch above his bed.

"Oh perfect! I didn't really feel like making small talk and answering any questions with your crew this morning," she said, stepping back towards him and jabbing him in the ribs in a teasing way, topping it off with a heartwarming wink. She then climbed back up to his top bunk, where he twisted the heavy handle and popped it open, poking his head up with caution to make sure the coast was clear.

"Okay, it's all clear!" he whispered to her, as he slid back down to let her escape.

Before she climbed all the way out, she paused, "Thanks, Todd, I had a really fun night." She gave him one last kiss. It was soft, ephemeral, and urgent all at the same time. And then, she was gone, slinking off the boat like a panther in the jungle, leaving Todd with an empty bunk, a pair of underwear he'd find later, and no chance to slip her his number. A memory, that dang memory, that still haunted him, aching and heavy.

Chapter 8

Boys will be Boys

Early April 2013

DISHES DONE, THE water drained out of the galley sink, leaving nothing but suds, just as the memories of Em remained with Todd. A gust of wind rocked the boat and snapped Todd back to reality: Sand Point, broken boat, slow offload, dead of cold Alaskan spring, wind, and dark. Pulling on his jacket, Todd stepped out onto the deck, the bite of cold air further awakening him. Joel and Sam stood next to the fishhold supervising the offload, while Manni stood on the dock, clipboard in hand, recording the weights, making sure the cannery didn't short them any hard-earned, precious cargo.

Sidling up to the edge of the hold, Todd took a peek, finding it about two-thirds unloaded, or about two more hours of work, including clean up. Joel, standing next to him, offered a cigarette without even looking at Todd, which he accepted gratefully.

"Alright, alright!" came a shout from the cannery worker in the hold, a full brailer of halibut ready to be hauled up to the dock.

Sam relayed a whistle to get the crane operator's attention along with the hand signal to hoist the brailer upwards. Todd dodged the pink, icy gurry oozing from the mesh bag as their catch took flight. Just then Todd caught a glimpse of Phil returning from the cannery, paperwork in hand, inspecting the dock operation before he climbed the cold, steel ladder back to the boat.

"Hey, boys," he called to rein in the crew. "So with our appointment at the haul out tomorrow morning at eight, get this cleaned up, get some sleep, and be ready for the haul. You know what to do."

"Roger," Joel replied.

No one even brought up the idea of going up to the bar, it wasn't in their realm of thought after the average of about three or four hours of sleep a night. Todd tried to push images of Emily out of his mind, all the fresher for being back in the town where they'd first met.

Yet as hard as he tried, there was one reminder he could just not escape, all due to an unfortunate work of gravity. Shortly after the fateful night in Sitka, when Em had to rush to leave without finding her underwear, well, Todd found them, at the foot of his bunk, crumpled up in the sheets as he was doing laundry. There is one sacred space for each person on a boat that no one else is allowed into, unless invited, and that is the bunk. Knowing this, Todd grabbed them quickly—they were purple with just a touch of lace around the edges—not wanting the guys to see and tempt them into breaking his hallowed space. Guys will be guys, their minds often on sex, and it sure doesn't get any better being on an isolated fishing boat. The site of some sexy underwear might just be a tad too much for them. The underwear felt soft and silky under his rough hands. Of course he brought them up to his nose for a good smell, and by god, her arousing scent was definitely still there.

Todd had quickly tucked them under his pillow, knowing he'd want that smell again later. And he did, plenty of times. He kept them as almost a good luck charm, all until that fateful day when he'd been tossing and turning in bed, and had then gotten up in a rush to begin a long day of fishing. They must've been stuck to his shirt, but anyways, they somehow found their way onto the dirty sole, or rather floor, of the fo'c'sle.

There they sat for hours until, tired and worn, the men came back in after a late dinner and galley cleanup, and Manni spotted the splotch of purple first. He stooped to pick them up, muttering, "Looky what we have here!" and turned around, proudly spinning them on his finger.

Joel was next behind him and his face lit up like a downtown street lamp on a winter night, "Hey, where the heck did those come from?"

"It's too early to be Christmas!" piped in Sam, who was third into the tiny, smelly space.

Todd was last and felt his cheeks burn with a mix of embarrassment and then anger when he realized he'd now forever lost them. Those guys were not giving up such a treasure.

"So where'd these come from?" asked Manni, turning around to look over the faces, then resting on Todd's.

There was no hiding it, so he gave up and said, "They're mine, now give them back." Hey, he at least had to try. Manni was close enough to get to and Todd stepped forward, standing tall, holding his ground. They stared eye to eye for a long moment. Joel, sensing the tension and possibility of blows to follow, sidled in sideways, prepared to play referee.

"They're common property now, man. They were on the floor," Manni retorted.

That was it. Todd took a swing, blood and anger and frustration rushing in before he could stop himself. But Manni was big, and fast, and he blocked Todd's blow.

Sam, seeing the situation turn, and taking the moment of distraction, used it to swipe in and nab the panties from Manni's hand, slip between their bodies, and out into the galley. That brought everyone back out to more open space.

Sam, seizing the moment, said, "Well, see now, we have a little situation here. They're no longer in the bunk, and they weren't ever *actually* Todd's to begin with. So, they will remain out here, for all to enjoy." He grabbed a bag clip, clamped an edge of the purple cloth, and attached it to the bottom of the American flag that was hanging over the galley porthole.

Over time, as men working sometimes very mundane jobs come up with strange rituals, the purple panties turned into a reward. Whoever did the most rounds of dishes in one day would be able to sleep with the panties that night. Todd knew he'd lost Em's panties the moment they had been discovered, but at least he could get a turn with them. And as ridiculous as it was, it did assist in the piles of dishes getting washed with more enthusiasm. But sometimes, glancing up and seeing them there staring him in the face, a reminder of that magical night but with Em nowhere to be found, they tormented him, and he was tempted more than once to tear them down and throw them out the window.

Chapter 9

Skunked

Early April 2013

BANG, BANG, BANG, the hammer reverberated against the brass prop.

"More heat!" Phil ordered. The hiss of the torch made everyone raise their voices. Joel gave it a few more seconds of heat from the torch. Phil followed with another few whacks, and Todd got one more turn on the prop puller. They'd been at the process for the last half hour, with a mix of patience, brute strength, hope, and determination. Todd gave the puller one more yank, all the forces fighting against them, like the energy built into a fault line, and then at last the seismic release, and the broken prop popped.

"Hell, yeah!" exclaimed Sam.

"Phew!" said Joel as he high-fived Todd. Phil just stood, hammer in hand, with a grin of satisfaction.

After pulling the boat up on land, or "on the hard," in the morning, it was obvious why the old girl didn't want to run. The deadhead had bobbed alongside the boat, but failed to miss the prop, bending two of the three blades at unnatural angles. But Phil, being as connected as he was, had started making the right phone calls immediately. Luck was on his side, as he found a spare prop that actually worked with their boat at a friend's web locker. Without that incredible luck, the crew would've been stuck in Sand Point for weeks, waiting for a new prop to come in on a barge from Seattle, *if* the weather allowed.

Todd was relieved to not be stuck, eager to get the season over with and get back home to Port Townsend, but couldn't help but feel a little disappointed to know they'd be back in the water in a few hours and steaming northeast toward Kodiak, with no chance of looking for Em. This would be their only stop in Sand Point this season, with no chance to sneak away, no chance to chase down this ghost.

"Okay boys, get her on," Phil said as he kicked his toe at the spare prop, lying on a pallet on the gravel. "I want to be out of here by three."

Phil turned back to his buddy's truck and with a spin of tires headed up "town" to do "skipperly" business, whatever that was. With his departure, the boys burst into a flurry of activity, feeling the clock ticking and all that had to be done. Everyone had partaken in a prop change before, so the crew worked with efficiency, no head scratching or tire kicking. As usual, putting the prop back on was easier than taking it off. Soon the boys were putting tools away, and the *Sea Ranger* was back in the slings and into the water on short notice. As Todd trudged through the galley to put away a bucket of wrenches in the engine room, he nearly collided with a cupboard door Joel swung open.

"Hey, watch it, buddy!" chided Todd, half kidding.

"Oh sorry, man." And then, as an afterthought he said, "Hey, you need anything from the store? Phil wanted me to run up to the AC to grab some fresh produce before we leave."

"If they have any, you mean," joked Todd. He forced a smile, but inside, his heart dropped, knowing he had no excuse to run up to town now.

"I thought you were about out of hemorrhoid cream," said Joel.

"Naw, I've been using yours."

Joel had been gone for about forty-five minutes when Todd, Sam, and Manni finished putting gear away and getting the deck back together to go longlining. Manni, always anxious to get off the boat first, took a peek at the clock in the galley. "Whoopee!" he exclaimed. It's only two! I think we got time to go get a beer at the Big Bar," Big Bar being code for the larger, Tavern bar in Sand Point, as opposed to the only other drinking establishment, which was the slightly smaller, not often open, Anchor Inn, otherwise known as the Little Bar.

"Yeah, I don't know," said Sam, "What if Phi—"

"Who cares, he said three o'clock," said Manni.

Todd just shrugged his shoulders, feigning nonchalance, but inside, he was siding with Manni.

"Fine, you go for it, I'm going to make myself a fuckin' sandwich." And with that Sam stormed off, already feeling a short fuse after the unforeseen mechanical delay and pissed at himself that he'd gotten into a fight and was now not so welcome at the Big Bar.

Manni turned back to Todd, "Well brotha', let's get going before it's too late."

The two grabbed their wallets from their bunks, then climbed off the boat and made the shortcut past the Russian Orthodox Church and its few lone trees. They were almost up to the top of the row of houses where Todd had run into Em that one glorious night he got to wrap his arms around her as they sledded down the ramp in a fish tote, when they spotted Joel heading down toward them. His head was barely discernible, floating like a cork or piece of flotsam atop a sea of paper grocery bags.

"Nice try, guys," he shouted when he recognized Todd and Manni. "Hate to break it to you, but I just saw Phil heading toward the boat."

"Fuck," said Manni, shoulders drooping.

"Fuck is right," Todd added, and meant it.

"Well, you might as well give me a fuckin' hand, then, goddamn it," replied Joel, reiterating the fishermen's salty choice of words and handed off some of the groceries for them to help carry back.

Joel filled their ears with stories about how much the peppers cost, or how bad the lettuce looked. "You wouldn't even believe what they want for milk," he continued, chatting their ears off the whole return trip, leaving Todd to brood in his thoughts, his maybe, possibly only, shot to maybe, possibly ever see Em again, gone.

Chapter 10

Pasagshak Road

Sunday-Monday, April 7-8, 2013

SAND POINT WAS a distant speck behind them now, and they'd been motoring slowly to the continental shelf south of Kodiak Island. With a chance to rest up and catch up on sleep, it still felt like a rude awakening once they'd reached the fishing grounds and Phil was back in the fo'c'sle flicking on the lights shouting, "Get up, you lazy sons of bitches! Time to go to work."

And with that he left them to rub sleep out of their eyes, reorient, find sweatpants and hoodies, socks and boots, and crawl out one by one, like a family of ducklings emerging from their nest in a tree.

It was five or so days of a grind ahead of them now. Five days of slate gray skies, five days of being tossed around, ripping out gonads with aching hands, and five days of sore muscles and little sleep. Days and time blurred in a way only possible when fishing hard.

⚓ ⚓ ⚓

THE *SEA RANGER* finally pulled into Kodiak with a loaded hold and a crew with red eyes and slime caked on their rain gear. Unloading at the cannery in Kodiak took most of the morning. Joel had coffee going and the second pot was almost empty, dishes piled in the sink coated in oil from an egg, bacon, and potato breakfast. Sam and Manni were on the dock, overseeing the unloading process, and Joel was standing on deck, watching the work being done in the hold. As Todd was about to tackle the mess in the sink and counter, a shadow filled the galley door.

"Hey, Shrimp!" Without having to turn around, Todd knew it was none other than Uncle David, who never let Todd forget his childhood nickname.

A smile spread across his face and Todd turned to give his uncle a manly hug (stiff, with a pat on the back), only hinting at how much he loved his uncle. "Hey, good to see you! How'd you know we were here?"

"Really?" he laughed, "Us old birds got nothin' better to do than drive around and see what boats are in. You should know that by now!"

"Oh, of course," he said, taking a step back. Todd could see his uncle had aged just a little since he'd last seen him two years ago when he was stopping over on another halibut and black cod trip. The crow's feet around his eyes and the ratio of gray to brown hairs had changed slightly in favor of gray, but besides that, David was a chiseled man, with a body shaped by a life of hard work. His hands were the most telling sign —big paws, weathered, scarred, and ever highlighted by black grime around the fingernails.

After a few minutes of catchup about the latest misadventures that little Gunnar and Oscar had gotten themselves into and what latest social activities his wife, Tammy, had signed him up for, David said, "Alright, Shrimp, better get going, hope to see you stop by if you get a chance. We've always got something on the stove."

"Right on, Uncle. You know if I get "freed" I will be there!"

This time, instead of a hug, they departed on a handshake. The happiness Todd felt from seeing his uncle floated him throughout the day. There was nothing so comforting as seeing someone who knew you from a little tyke, who watched you grow, then taught you, and fostered you, in a place where you were mainly a stranger.

Shortly after David left, Phil sauntered into the galley, deep in a conversation on the phone, grabbed a piece of leftover bacon, and continued out on deck.

Dishes done and sink dried (one of Phil's weird pet peeves), Todd dried his hands and went to check out the offload. Joel sat on the rail, sharpening his knife, so Todd decided to join him.

"Hey, how's it going?"

"Oh good, almost done," he said over the whine of the hydros, as a brailer bag stuffed with stiff white carcasses emerged from the hold.

Since Phil was nowhere in sight now, he asked, "So, any word from Phil?"

"He went up town to do some errands, but I think he said we were going to leave as soon as this is done."

"Oh, okay," Todd replied, trying to hide a hint of disappointment, as an hour off the boat would have been nice, at least.

Joel, watching Todd's face fall, waited a few seconds, then burst out laughing, "Naw, man, he said we're staying the night!"

Sam, who had been half paying attention while he wrote down the numbers, let out a sly smile. "Yeah, you know what that means . . . PARTY!"

🐟 🐟 🐟

THREE HOURS LATER, it was midafternoon. Frozen slush from the city streets coated Todd's boots and his worn Carhartts as he headed up the hill for Uncle David's. The sun was just peeking out of the low stratus clouds, and the wind whipped down his hoodie as Todd approached the small downtown of Kodiak. Pulling his hood just a little tighter to ward off the biting wind, Todd glanced across the street at Tony's Bar, sure that Sam, the true partier of the crew, was already comfortable there with one or two beers downed. The reflections off the window-panes made it hard to see into the dark interior, but just as he was turn-ing his eyes back to the sidewalk, Todd did a double take. He rubbed his eyes, blinked, and looked again. *Wait, was that—???? No, it couldn't be! Must be a look alike.* But goddamn it, that girl walking by the window sure looked like Em. The sight halted him in his tracks and he felt a kick of adrenaline speed up his heart rate. *Shit, the last time I saw her was, oh my god, on that oh so good of a night in Sitka.* Memories of her breasts, the scent of her, her urgency, taste of her sweat, flooded back. *Oh goddamn! I can't keep walking by now. I could never live with myself if I didn't find out.*

He took a deep breath and paused. His nerves were jittering as he approached the heavy, oak bar door. One more step and his hand was on the stainless steel handle. One more second, and he was enveloped by the dark of the bar, eyes adjusting, and he could feel all the locals' eyes on him. First, he spotted Sam at the bar, already chatting it up with a cute redhead. Then, a group of old-timers in the booth and a few middle-of-the-day, sad solo drinkers. No sign of the ghost he'd seen in the window. His heart dropped like porcelain on a marble floor. Feeling sheepish, and Sam too engrossed with his next victim to notice him, Todd took an embarrassed step back towards the door. But then he saw shiny black hair and a big, cute grin pop up from behind the bar. Of course. *Oh my god, it is actually Emily!*

"Oh, hey cowboy, how you been?" she asked him as they made eye contact, and after a quick pause, confirming to him that she remem-bered him, "It's been a while, huh? Looks like your nose healed up okay," she said with a playful smirk.

"Uh, yeah, I guess it has," he mumbled. "So, uh, how *are* you?"

"Oh, just passing time working here until I get another fishing gig." Then she pretended to whisper, "Don't tell the boss!" as she winked toward the man who must have been the owner, hidden in the back counter going over the books. "Well, are you going to stay for one?" she asked after another awkward pause.

"Oh yeah, I guess I could have one, was headed to my unc—"

"Hey you!" Sam finally noticed him and motioned to an empty seat next to him at the counter. On his other side was the pretty redhead. "There's plenty of room."

Todd shuffled toward the bar, feeling heat burn across his face. He'd felt as nervous and flustered as a teenager on a first date.

"What can I make you?" she asked. Then, "I think last time you'd been downing the rum and Cokes. Would that work?"

"Oh sure." No matter how he sat on the black bar stool, Todd felt he was oozing awkwardness. As she handed him the drink, they made eye contact again, not just casual, how are you, but deep, soul penetrating contact. Her green eyes to his brown. It only lasted a second, but it felt like minutes. A warm smile brushed one corner of her mouth and she whispered so her boss wouldn't hear, "It's on me."

After he took a swig of the sweet brown liquid, she asked, "So what have you been up to?"

Words started spilling out, words pent up like a house cat. They talked and talked as if no time had passed. Every now and then she filled a glass or cracked open a beer for one of the locals, but always returned directly to where they left off. Engrossed. Captivated. The hour hand on the clock on the wall had wound round, Todd's glass barely touched.

Since they'd last parted from that sweaty bunk in Sitka, Em had spent the summer seining in Sand Point. The skipper okay, the crew worse, she dealt with a grumbly old skiff, keen on not running more often than not, and with low prices, she'd only made a modest check that season. The pinks never showed up. Sockeye and chum runs were mediocre, the prices not great. Dreading another winter in Sand Point and having to go pot fishing again, Em hightailed it to Kodiak, where she'd gotten an apartment with a friend she'd made and gotten a job at the bar until she lined up another fishing gig.

Noticing Todd's glass was finally empty, Em took the opportunity to lean closer over the bar, and as Todd leaned his head in, too, she whispered, "I got the day shift, so I can be out of here by seven when the next bartender comes in." After a pause, she added, "Want a little tour of the town? Last time it was *you* giving me the tour," she said with a devilish wink.

Todd chuckled, "Well, a tour of a boat goes a little quicker than a tour of an island, but sure, I'd take you up on that."

With that, she grabbed his glass and turned on her heel to refill the rum and Coke. He couldn't help but watch her from behind. A scene with her in his bunk flashed across his mind and he could feel himself getting aroused, remembering how perfect she looked beneath those clothes. As she turned sideways, he quickly looked away toward Sam. He and Redhead were engrossed in a flirtatious conversation, and Todd turned his gaze right back to Em. When she returned with the drink, ice clinking on the cold glass, he said, "Hey, how about this—I'll let you finish up here, and I'll go grab some food for us."

"Perfect!" she replied. "Then we can have a picnic in the truck as I show you around the town."

"What's your favorite place here?"

With her to-go order and restaurant recommendation in his mind and excitement in his heart, Todd finished his drink a little faster this time, and decided to give her some space as there was a steady trickle of newcomers to the bar as it approached beer thirty.

"Okay, see ya soon," he called to her as she was ringing up a weather-hardened man.

"Roger," she called as she gave him a heart melting wink.

SEVEN COULDN'T COME soon enough. Nervous and excited energy mixed with rum made for a caustic concoction in his gut. But seven came and went, and no sign of Em. The Old Powerhouse where they'd decided to meet was dead, as it was a Sunday night in a hibernating fishing village. Todd couldn't stop from tapping his foot, and not a word of the newspaper he'd found in the empty waiting area stuck in his head. His to-go order was getting cold. Every time the door opened, wafting in a bitter wind, he glanced up in hope, only to have spirits plummet like a waterfall. Just as he was about to check his watch again and feel guilty for skipping out on dinner at Uncle David's, the bells on the door jingled, and in waltzed Em.

A burgundy scarf poked out of her navy peacoat, and tips of her black hair from her gray woolen cap. The tip of her nose was dusted in pink from the bite of the cold. "Hey you, sorry I'm late!"

"Dang, I was about to give up and eat it all myself," he kidded, as he grabbed the plastic to-go bag and held it up for her to see it remained untouched.

"Sweet, I'm starving! Ready for your tour?"

"More than you know," he said, clenching his teeth at how cheesy that must have sounded and wishing he were more witty.

He followed her out to an old Toyota pickup, black, beat up, a two-seater with stick shift. "It ain't much, but the old girl gets me around," Em said as an explanation.

Todd didn't need explanation, he loved it. It fit her like a pair of beloved and worn blue jeans. It turned over with a healthy grumble. Todd didn't pay much attention to the quick "tour" as he already knew Kodiak like the back of his hand from his early days of summer seining with Uncle David and exploring the island during time off from the boat. Not a thought of the *Sea Ranger* and Phil and his agenda had even entered his mind since Em had taken its place. They wound up heading south on the Pasagshak Road. As they neared the beach, the sliver of moon peeking out from the blanket of clouds was sending glitters across the expansive ocean. The small gravel parking lot was empty, and as Em rolled down her window the muffled roar of breakers meeting their final destination drifted in over the light drone of the radio.

Em moved to grab the takeout order and get out to show him the beach, but without thinking, going on pure impulse, Todd reached over and took her hand reaching for the door handle, then turned her toward him, and leaned in to kiss her, heart in chest, groin pulsating, on fire, every nerve ending alive with desire. One hand on the small of her back, he pulled her closer, up against him, he could smell her intoxicating scent filling his nostrils like a drug. Heck, it was a drug. Fumbling around the stick shift, she squirmed in as close as possible. As her lips brushed his ear and then his mouth, she tasted of peppermint, her lips as soft as tulip petals. His hand on the back of her neck spilled off her cap to let her tresses run free, and he ran his hand through her silky hair. God, it had been soooo long. He had forgotten how indescribable it was. Time stood still, there was nothing but her, and him, in that truck with the ocean and moon and the sound of pebbles rolling in the surf.

SOMEHOW THEY PARTED long enough to drive back to her place, clamber through the dark, tripping over a desk, boots, and bicycle in the hallway, until they found her bedroom, surely waking up Em's house-mate and best friend, Jess, in the process. Then it was a tangle of sticky sheets, pulling off a sock here, shirt there, then the pants, and oh my god, there she was, naked underneath him, and waiting, wanting, her hands on his chest, grabbing his back with abandon, trailing down to his belly button, then grabbing him, hard, yearning, and leading him in. Ohhh, he felt his body shudder, he was inside of her, she felt so tight and wet and wanting. They made love slowly, then hard, a year's time apart speaking, then slowly again, and finally, until he thought he could stand it no more, a release proportional to the time apart.

He lay on top of her, both catching their breath, heads spinning with what had just happened. "Holy shit," was all she could manage.

All he could return in agreement was an "Oh my god."

He glanced at the clock, reading 12:53. He was spent, physically and emotionally, and felt sleep taking over as he turned toward Em, folding her into him, arm around her chest, hand on her firm breast.

THIS TIME, IT was Todd who woke up with a start. It took him a minute to recollect where he was, move his arm and feel her warm, smooth body wrapped up next to him; then it all came flooding back, the magical, epic evening. His movement sent her groaning. Next to her on the bedstand, the clock read 9:10.

"Oh fuck!!" Todd cried out. That woke Em fully.

"What, what??" she mumbled, sleep and alarm in her voice.

"This time, *I* am so late for the boat," replied Todd, already fumbling for his clothes strewn across the floor. As he wriggled into his pants, T-shirt already half on and jacket in his hand, he said, "Hey Em, I'm so sorry, but I gotta run. Phil is going to give me so much shit for being late. He has zero tolerance for that."

Em, half sitting up, covers pulled up over her chest, watched Todd dressing, enjoying the show, admiring his sculpted chest and big ripped arms. "Alright, cowboy, don't you be getting in trouble now," she replied, laying on her Southern accent as a tease.

Haphazardly dressed now, Todd crawled back on the bed long enough to give her a gentle, slow kiss, the smell of sex still lingering between them.

THE BRISK WALK through town and down to the harbor seemed to take forever. Todd could see the rigging of the *Sea Ranger* from afar, tied up at the cannery, a thin plume of exhaust rising from the stack. Climbing down the slimy ladder, he could feel Phil's eyes on him from the wheelhouse. Joel was on deck splicing some lines and gave Todd a little wink for his disappearing act that night.

Before he could get into the galley, he heard Phil's voice from up top. "Todd, need you up here, now!" he said, strict and stern.

Thinking he was going to get a good shaming, Todd entered the wheelhouse with apprehension, head hanging. But instead, Phil had a grave look on his face as he said, "So, I just got a call from Old Joe, you know, one of your uncle's buddies." Todd couldn't even guess what was coming next. "Joe said that last night as your uncle was driving down to the harbor to check on his boat, someone, probably some drunk, hit him head-on around a blind curve." Seeing Todd's face turn white, he added, "He's going to be okay. He's at the hospital, was unconscious for a few hours, but came to. Both legs are messed up. He broke multiple bones, including his femur, some ribs, maybe some internal bleeding . . ."

When Phil trailed off, Todd realized he'd been holding his breath. "Oh no—oh my god, I gotta get up there!"

"Yeah, that's fine, I expected that," replied Phil as Todd was already turning on his heel, a blur of color rushing down the wheelhouse steps. Phil called after him, "I'll get a replacement for one trip . . . and one trip only!"

Todd grabbed a few essentials from his bunk, shoved them in a big garbage bag, and ran off the boat without any explanation to the guys except, "I'll be back as soon as I can!"

"What the hell?!" asked Manni as the galley door slammed shut.

Phil had overheard from up top and yelled down the stairs, "His uncle's in the hospital. Guess I better go round up a deckhand."

Chapter 11

Desperate Measures

Monday, April 8, 2013

AFTER DOZING BACK to sleep for an hour or so, Em slowly stirred awake. She felt like the normal gray world was tinted in rose colors as she moved about her morning routine, making coffee, taking a long hot shower, although she was reluctant to wash off his scent. Out in the kitchen, Em was careful not to wake Jess in the room next door, since she'd probably heard them last night. In picking up her clothes from their hurried disrobing, Em came across Todd's forgotten sweatshirt. She couldn't help but hold it up to her chest and take in a deep breath of it. *God, he smells good!* she thought to herself, as she felt an electric jolt in her gut accompanied by a flash of a memory of him last night, his sweat dripping onto her, her tasting him. *Jeez! I gotta get my head on straight!* she scolded herself, trying to shake the erotic scene out of her mind.

A lazy wind blew down the alley behind Tony's Bar, but it was strong enough to scatter a few pieces of trash from the dumpster, chased by scavenging ravens and crows. The back screen door opened with a creak as Em took a deep breath to prepare for the long day ahead of her, sleep deprived. She liked the early shift because she usually had the first hour or two mainly to herself, giving her time for a coffee and making sure everything was in order for the day. She'd already been at it awhile and was in the process of emptying the dishwasher when the first customer of the day sauntered in. He was an older man with white hair and wrinkles radiating from his eyes, wearing a jacket that was more worn than not, collar pulled up to his ears to keep out the wind. He headed straight for the bar, so Em put a glass in her hand, ready to pour, but instead he didn't sit down at a stool and order as she'd expected.

"Hey," he said, as he fumbled with a stack of coasters to keep his hands busy. "So one of my crew on my boat just had a family emergency and is going to be out for a few days. Do you know *any* of the local guys who might be looking for a quick longlining job? I'd go shorthanded, but we already are."

Em hesitated in her answer as the wheels in her head started to spin.

He continued, "I'm just hitting up every place I can think of since it's so last minute, and I cannot afford to sit around and wait," still occupying his hands with the stack of coasters.

Before the wheels in her mind could complete their circuit, her mouth blurted out, "Yes!" That got the man's attention, as he nearly knocked over the ashtray sitting next to the coasters. "I do know someone," she continued.

He just looked at her, waiting for a name. "Well?"

"It's me."

"Ha!" he laughed to himself and started to turn away.

"Wait, skipper," she retorted, "I'm not just some barmaid."

At that he paused in his step. "Well?"

"I've been fishing about seven years now and am just working here until salmon season starts."

"Well, have you ever gone longlining? That ain't the same thing as no salmon seining."

"Yes sir," she said, a hint of her Southern accent coming out again. "I've worked on the *Cape Fearful*, *Aleutian Warrior* and the *Adelyn Abby* longlining and the *Vicki V* for pot cod, and a few different Sand Point and Kodiak boats for seining."

"Oh," he answered, as he knew and respected a few of the skippers of those boats.

"I can totally fill in for at least a trip, my roommate works here too, wants the extra hours, and could cover for me no problem."

"Well, I don't hire girls," he replied. Em stared back at him, firm and defiant, not breaking eye contact. Then his eyes softened and he said, "I suppose you'll have to do . . . for just one trip."

"Thank you, yes sir!"

"We're leaving at two this afternoon."

"Okay, I'll be there,"

His hand was already on the door, as Em called out, "Wait, what boat?"

"The *Sea Ranger*."

Chapter 12

Turn and Burn

Monday-Tuesday, April 8-9, 2013

RUSHING HOME, EM didn't have time to process the fact that the gig was on the *Sea Ranger,* Todd's boat. She'd deal with that when she got there and saw him onboard, but for now she had to focus on packing, and packing quickly, as she only had an hour or two. Em fumbled with her keys at the door and almost knocked a cup of water off the kitchen counter as she dashed to her room. Grabbing her duffel from the back of her small closet, Em threw it on the bed and started haphazardly throwing armfuls of warm clothes towards it.

Let me think, she told herself, trying to quell the excitement in her stomach. *One week, longlining, what do I really need . . . ?* Sifting through the selection of clothes on the bed, she grabbed a few sweatshirts, including one gray one, which she didn't realize wasn't hers, some long underwear tops and bottoms, two heavy fleece pants, a load of warm socks, undies, sports bra, two ratty T-shirts, then in a second duffel she crammed in her fish gloves, Stormy Seas hat, rain gear, boots, and Xtratufs. Soon the bags were bursting at the seams, barely enough room for her toothbrush and hairbrush. Em had already called Jess to fill her in and check if she could cover for her, so no need to write her a note. Taking one last look around her now messy room, Em sighed, turned on her heel and closed the door.

As she started heading down the hill, she gritted her teeth into the cold air off the ocean and noticed the butterflies building in her stomach as each step brought her closer to the *Sea Ranger*. Thoughts of *What will Todd think of this, and how will he react?* and *Oh my god, I sure hope I can keep up with these guys,* crowded her head, as the *Sea Ranger* was known as a highliner, turn-and-burn boat. To counter her building anxieties, Em called on memories of going out pot cod fishing in the dead of dark winter in Sand Point during one of the biggest storms of the year. If she could handle that, she could handle a week on the *Sea Ranger*, she thought to herself.

As she rounded the corner, the harbor came into view, and there by the cannery dock was the black *Sea Ranger* trimmed in white and yellow. A few more minutes of huffing her duffel bags along allowed Em time to collect her thoughts before she found herself dockside of it.

"Hey!" she yelled down, as nobody was in sight. The tide was out, so the boat's back deck was a good ten feet below the dock.

After a few seconds she gave a louder, "Hey!! Anyone home?" Thirty more long seconds passed with no answer. As she leaned over to rap her knuckles on the cold hard steel of the *Sea Ranger*, she saw a shadow pass by the galley window, and a hoodie and sweatpants-clad figure emerged on deck, hunched over to light a smoke.

"Hello!" she tried for the last and final time.

The man looked up. Just enough light from the dock above cast on his face to let her know it was Todd's crewmate, Joel.

"Can I help you?" he asked, somewhat surprised, unable to make out who the silhouette was under the backlighting.

"Hey, Joel!" After a pause where she realized he wasn't recognizing her, she added, "It's me, Em. You remember me from Sand Point?"

After a second, the warmth of recognition came out in his voice, "Oh, hey! The tote girl! How the heck are you? What are you doing down here?"

"Well, uh," Em stammered, suddenly losing some of her confidence. "Your captain wanted me to fill in for a trip. Guess someone had some family emergency up town, right?"

She could see from that glow of inhalation on his cigarette stop when she mentioned she'd be crewing for a week. He tried to hide the surprise in his voice, but failed.

"Oh, uh, well, that's cool." He took a step forward, realizing she'd need help getting her bags down. "Hope you can fill Todd's shoes okay."

Em's stomach did a flip in disbelief. It was Todd who had the family emergency? She didn't even know he had family on the island. "What happened?!" she couldn't help but ask.

"His Uncle David with the *Tammy Sue* got hit by a drunk, he's in pretty bad shape now, but I hear they think he'll be okay. He's in the hospital, probably for a while now."

"Oh shit," was all she could manage, as she did know David and his wife Tammy. She had actually tried to get a job on the *Tammy Sue,* but his deckhands usually did so well they rarely gave up their spots, and if they did, there was usually a wait list.

Trying to cover her shock, she remembered her duffel bags and told Joel, "I've got nothing fragile in these," as she tossed them the ten feet to the deck below and proceeded to turn and climb down the ladder on the dock.

"Okay, well, welcome aboard. Let me show you around," replied Joel cordially now.

He reached down to grab her bag, but she firmly stated, "I got it," and he backed down.

Opening the steel, salt-stained door to the galley, warmth poured out. As she stepped over the threshold, she saw the guys had all their hooks for rain gear and boots to the right and a stacked washer and dryer to the left. Just past that was a door that was half ajar, with a steep ladder leading to the bowels of the boat, where the hum of a generator roared up to blend with the rap music blaring over the galley speakers. Taking a quick glance down into the engine room, she noted it looked clean and orderly with lots of yellow. *Must be a kitty cat* (meaning a Caterpillar main engine), she thought to herself as she dropped her rain gear bag by the door and continued to follow Joel forward.

Inside the galley, she saw Manni with the freezer door open, reaching for a gallon of ice cream, while Sam sat at the table, flipping aimlessly through a hotrod magazine. The flatscreen TV, lashed down for rough weather in a corner above the galley table, flashed a movie that no one was paying attention to.

"Yo, guys," Joel said, to gain Sam and Manni's attention. Both looked up, eyes flickering in recognition with a touch of confusion, "You remember Em, from Sand Point, right?"

"Oh, hey," said Sam nonchalantly.

"Hey, weren't you the one we went tote sledding with?" asked Manni.

"Yup, that was me. Pretty fun night, huh?" she said with a hint of a sigh in her voice.

"You looking for Todd or something?" Sam asked.

"Oh no, I wa—"

Before she could finish, Joel jumped in and replied, "Yo, dude, she's actually filling in for Todd on this trip."

"No shit!" Manni inadvertently exclaimed with surprise in his voice.

"Yes, shit," Em said with firm gumption in her voice. Changing the subject, she asked, "So where's my bunk?" motioning to the heavy packs she'd dropped by the engine room door.

"Oh, right, let me show you," Manni replied quickly, trying to cover himself.

Through the galley, past the head, and down a short hall, lay the fo'c'sle. Even though it was a decent sized fishing vessel, there was only one private stateroom up top in the wheelhouse and one below, which was now used for storage of miscellaneous boat parts, fuel and oil filters, O-rings, wrenches, boxes of potatoes, paper towels, etc.

Manni led Em into a black cavern at the bow of the boat filled with the scent of bait, dirty socks, and sweaty laundry. He paused in his steps for a moment, realizing there were only enough bunks for four crew, two on each side.

"Guess you're going to have to take Todd's," he said as he pointed to the upper port bunk. A towel placed over a string served as a half curtain. Manni reached up to turn the reading lamp on, while Em pushed the "curtain" aside and peered into his bunk. His sleeping bag was still in a crumpled mess, which she realized was a godsend because in her haste, she had forgotten hers. The rest of the bunk was a rat's nest, with clothing mixed into his bedding and pillow, books, spare change, even a sheathed Vicki knife all in the mix.

Oh boy, she thought to herself, as she shoved some of the mess to one side to allow room for her sea bag.

"I'll give you a few to get settled and go tell Phil you're here," said Manni as he was already turning to leave.

"Okay, dear, I'll pop up there in a sec."

Em then seized the opportunity to fish out her knife and flashlight, two things that out of habit she carried with her at all times on a boat, and put them in her pocket. A strong flash of déjà vu of sharing a bunk with him once before hit her. As she moved a dirty sock to the long shelf between the bunk and the wall, she noticed a few pictures taped up by his reading lamp. One was a photo taken quite a while ago that must have been his family, as Todd was a youngster in it, surrounded by two other young girls, a man who looked strikingly similar to Todd in a red and black flannel, and a woman with frizzy hair cozied up next to him, both their arms sheltering the children. It looked wet and cold out, the background full of small conifers, and the man had a handsaw. *Hmm, must have been Christmastime.*

Finding a shirt flattened between the mattress and pillow, Em couldn't help but take a quick smell of it. As the overwhelming scent of Todd hit her, memories of the night before flooded in. While unpacking part of her clothes, she realized one of the sweatshirts she'd brought was *huge!* She took a quick smell of it, definitely not hers . . . and definitely smelled like the one she'd just sniffed. It dawned on her that somehow she'd grabbed Todd's from when he'd forgotten it in her room . . . and she wasn't sure she'd ever give it back.

While a warm flood of reverie ran through her body from the memory, a loud clanging and clunking of the main engines starting up jolted her out of her day dreaming. *Oh shit! We must be leaving already!* In a hurry, Em grabbed her Stormy Seas float coat and fish gloves, rushing out of the stateroom to go help untie. The galley was empty and Em beat herself up for not being ready. Out on deck she saw Joel at the spring line, Manni at the stern line, and Sam on the bow. *Ugh! Great way to make a first impression,* as there was no line for her to grab and no way for her to be helpful. She stood there awkwardly as the boys coiled the lines.

"Where you put the lines at?" she asked Joel as he walked by her with a soggy tar-stained line on his shoulder.

"Throw 'em up top," he grunted as he handed it off to her and turned to finish setting up the deck for another round of longlining. Climbing her way up the dark and slippery ladder, Em glanced around, seeing no obvious spot where the lines were stowed. She did get a glimpse of Phil at the wheel, but decided this was not the time to check in with him. He obviously knew she was on board. Thankfully, Sam rounded the corner with the bow line, saw her in her state of indecision, and pointed to a nook near the chest freezer and wheelhouse wall.

"Over there," was all he muttered, as he dropped his and headed down to the main deck.

Arghhh, Em groaned to herself. The first few days on a new boat were always hell, as she was constantly torn between wanting to help as much as possible to try and prove her worth versus observing and not getting in the way because she didn't know the routine of the boat yet. It was the rock and the hard place of being the greenhorn, wanting to look good but not yet knowing how. Taking a deep breath to find her composure, Em turned back to go down the ladder, and set her mind on finding a way to be helpful in the next task of setting up the longlining gear that had been stowed away for their last delivery.

They had just rounded out of the harbor, the red flashing nun bobbing in the swell off the port side. Just as she was turning to ask Joel what she could do, the loudhailer crackled and the deck lights flickered on.

Through the weathered white speaker above the door, Phil's voice sounded, "Sam, I want you up here driving, and you other two show the new greenhorn how to set up and what we want her to do when we start setting gear tonight."

"Roger, Roger," yelled Joel back toward the intercom.

As Sam stood up from what he was doing, tightening down the bolts on the fishhold hatch which had been previously opened for the offload, he walked past Em and handed her the wrench without a word. Out of the corner of her eye, she saw Joel nudge Sam with an elbow and whisper so Phil couldn't hear it over the loudhailer, "What'd you do to get on his good side?"

"Oh, wouldn't you like to know," teased Sam back, who was happy to escape the cold deck work.

Em looked at the wrench in her hands. She bent down to the wet deck, thankful of the water resistant patches on her fleece pants and cotton liners in her fish gloves, to finish the task Sam had started.

It took about a half hour to refasten the hatch, deck boards, and the scale. All the while, the swell and roll of the ocean rocked the boat from side to side. Em noticed that in spite of being in the trough, the *Sea Ranger* rode the waves with a smooth finesse. Once the deck was ready to go, the real work began.

There was still the never-ending baiting to catch up on. At the stern of the boat was a covered shed that housed the chute where they would set the gear from, and behind that, a table to bait hooks on. Lining the sides of the shed were shelves that held rows of all the skates of line. Each skate was a stacked coil of six hundred feet of line with hundreds of hooks attached and spaced out at three foot intervals. As they set the line out, about ten skates would be connected to create a full string over two miles long from end to end, with an anchor and buoy line on each end. Joel, Manni and Em began the weary task of baiting the hooks by hand with frozen chunks of herring on the sheltered table. Each skate could take up to twenty minutes to bait. Hours upon hours of longlining were spent baiting hooks. This boat was still old-school and did not have the fancy new auto-baiting equipment like a few of the most cushy long-line boats had. Thus, the significance of the *Sea Ranger* not being short of a deckhand.

Hours later, tired and sore, Em stripped down to her long underwear and climbed into Todd's bunk for a quick nap of an hour or so before they began setting gear. She glanced at her watch before closing her eyes and saw the numbers blaring 3:24 a.m. *And why did I want to do this?* Em asked herself as she tried to relax and not think of Todd, but as she turned her nose into the pillow all she could smell was him, just as he smelled as they made love the night before, and their legs, arms, hands, hair, heart, sweat all intertwined as one.

IT WASN'T UNTIL that next morning, when they woke up around five and had time to get some breakfast and coffee together in the galley, when she stopped to take in the details of the space around her. The galley was fairly organized with food stuffed in every available space and cubby, like a well stocked ship should be. There was the typical light-house poster framed behind the galley table, screwed into the wall to prevent it from falling down, and then the small American flag on the starboard side porthole. Her eyes did a double take, for there was also a splotch of purple by the flag. Since she was at the end seat of the bench, she took the opportunity to get up, refill her coffee, and inspect what the purple was. As she got closer she gasped, choking on her coffee, re-alizing her worst suspicions were true: it was her very own underwear! No doubt about it. The guys looked up from the table.

"You okay?" Joel asked.

"Uh, yeah, coffee just went down the wrong pipe," she coughed, try-ing to cover her shock. Those were definitely her old underwear that she'd bought back in Virginia, complete with the lace edging. *What on earth . . . why are they up on the wall for all to see??* The blood rushed to her face and roiled through her veins. Her memory flitted back to the last time she was with Todd, and quickly recalled her haste to leave and maybe, well, not finding all of her clothes. Her next thought was, *That bastard!!*

But there was no time to ask about it, as the guys dumped their plates in the sink and were already heading out to gear up for the day. Em made it through that first set, barely. Not only was she new and not fit-ting into their routine, or rather, Todd's shoes, her mind kept jumping back to anger and confusion at him. *Why the fuck is my underwear on the wall?* She could not even begin to fathom the why's except that he was some sort of sick bastard and she'd been completely fooled by him, which set her into anger at herself for being messed around with. More than once, one of the guys had to call her attention back to the deck, to pay attention or hurry up what she was doing. She felt like one of the fish flopping around in their last gasping breaths. Only later that evening when they finally had a chance to sit down, the guys intent on shoving massive amounts of lasagna down their throats to make up the calorie deficit they'd just burned through, did she have a chance to ask.

"So . . ." she said, clearing her throat and pausing.

The boys continued to eat, but all looked up at her, waiting for something, having no clue what was coming next.

Em gulped, and looked back at her undies on the wall, then in a barely controlled voice, asked, "Why do you have women's underwear on the wall over there?"

Sensing this was a trap, that she was some feminist about to scream at them about their chauvinistic ways, Sam jumped in.

"Oh, Em, that's really just a silly thing we do to help us motivate and clean the dishes."

"What??" she asked, more confused now than ever.

"Yeah," Joel helped, "we just found those in the fo'c'sle on the floor one day and thought, well, what can we do with these?"

Now Manni said, "So yeah, we uh, thought, since we'd been having a problem with getting dishes done, that whoever did the most dishes in a day would get to sleep with the underwear that night."

"And then they get hung back up each morning," finished Sam.

Em looked at them all in disbelief; disbelief if it was true, and if it was, how pathetic men could be.

"Hey, don't blame us . . . we haven't been trying it for that long, but it's been working real good!"

Once this settled in, Em felt her blood begin to boil again, largely out of self-embarrassment. "And you don't know where they came from?"

Secrets on boats are near impossible to keep, so the guys all knew back when they first found them, but never had to ask Todd whose they were. So to protect everyone involved, Joel made up an explanation, "Of course not, they just showed up on the floor. We all thought they got mixed in when we got our laundry back from the cannery."

Before she knew what she was doing, Em jolted up from the bench, marched over and tore down the purple and now worn undies, then walked past all the guys, and turned into the fo'c'sle. She shoved the undies into her duffel, took a minute to recollect herself, and walked back out to take her place at the bench again.

Sam said, "So, I guess we know who those belonged to now?"

"Yes, you sick perverts. Sorry to ruin your little game, but it's over. And underwear is not cheap, so I'm taking them back. Go buy your own," she said, voice near a shout, the boys looking like puppies caught in the act of doing something wrong.

Feeling an air of awkwardness from the situation settle in like fog, the guys looked down at their plates and started eating again in silence.

Manni muttered to himself, "It's not the same when they've not been worn before," only audible to Joel across from him, and he received a stern kick in the shin.

After that outburst, her boiled blood was still simmering and she couldn't get to sleep that night, and wasn't nearly as comforted by Todd's smell in the bunk as she had been the night prior.

Chapter 13

Family Matters

Monday, April 8, 2013

BEFORE PUSHING THE door open, Todd took a deep breath, but instead of calming him, it only accentuated the sterile and stale antiseptic smell of hospital. He didn't know what to expect, he didn't know how he would react, but *Here I go* he thought, bracing himself for it. As he cracked open the door, the faint sound of a heart monitor beeped and a newscaster on the flatscreen TV flickered on the wall. On the bed, covered in thin hospital sheets and blankets, lay Uncle David, sleeping. Todd tiptoed over, sliding into the armchair next to the bed, and gently pushed away a bedside table littered with get well cards, flowers, and balloons. As the table accidentally screeched across the linoleum, Todd held his breath, hoping not to wake David. But it did wake him. He turned his head, which was covered in scratches and deep purple bruises, and slowly opened his eyes.

"Oh, hey Shrimp!" he said in recognition, his voice dry and raspy.

"Hi, Uncle David." Todd paused because he couldn't think of what to say next.

Thankfully, David took charge, sensing Todd's unsureness. "Man, that nurse out there is a sweetheart. Maybe we should ring for her . . . think I need some more water," and gave him a big joking wink. Todd cracked a smile, relieved the tension was lifted.

"Jeez, if you look this bad, I can't imagine how the truck turned out," said Todd, glancing down at the bed. David's leg was in a body cast, slightly elevated, the other leg in a smaller cast. He had bandaging around his torso and was hooked up to an IV and monitors. Parts of his head were shaved where the doctors had given him stitches. He looked like, well, like he'd just survived a head-on car crash.

"Oh, the old Chevy is probably already in the junkyard. I'm just glad I didn't follow directly behind it." Todd was glad to see David's ever-present sense of humor still pervaded the pain and seriousness of the situation.

"They'd have to drag you to the junkyard kicking and screaming," Todd said.

David started to laugh, but was soon thwarted from the pain of broken ribs.

"So, uh, where are Tammy and the kiddos?" asked Todd, glancing at a chair near the TV draped with their jackets.

"Oh, she took the little terrors down to the cafeteria to get some grub," he explained. "Hey—weren't you guys leaving today?"

Todd was impressed he remembered that after all he'd just been through, including over three hours of unconsciousness.

"Oh, well, Phil told me it was okay if I stayed back this trip. He probably picked up a guy in town to sub for me. They'll be back in a week or so, and I can jump back on then. Oh, and uh, Phil sends his best wishes," Todd added at the end.

"Oh, I'm sure he does," David muttered, rolling his eyes, as they both knew that wasn't in Phil's character to show empathy, even though he did genuinely care. Uncle David tried to squirm around in the narrow hospital bed, but with little success as pain severely inhibited him.

"Easy there, Uncle," urged Todd.

Just as Todd was going to ask how the hospital food was, he heard the door handle twist, and a flurry of little voices flooded into the room. In burst his cousins and his always cheery Aunt Tammy.

"Daddy!" cried Gunnar, the five-year-old. "Guess what we did!"

"I have no idea," replied David, putting on a smile for his enthusiastic son.

Gunnar ran right past Todd, not even noticing him yet, and went straight to David's bedside and held up a half eaten soft serve ice cream cone and proceeded to explain to David his first experience with a soft serve machine and the wild array of sprinkles and sauces the cafeteria provided.

In the meantime, Todd stood up and sidled over toward Aunt Tammy, who was holding their two-year-old, Oscar, in her arms. Her face lit up when she saw Todd.

"Hey, you!" she cried, as Todd moved closer and gave the two a half hug. "I heard you were in town." As he stepped back, he could see the worry and stress hiding behind her green eyes. Oscar played with her long red hair that stuck down from under her blue hand-knit cap.

"Can I see the munchkin?" Todd asked, and Tammy disentangled little fingers from her hair and necklaces and passed him over to Todd. It was the first meeting of Oscar and Todd. He stared in disbelief at the little miracle squirming in his arms. The following hour flew by. Todd held Oscar until he got too antsy, and Tammy caught Todd up with the events of the town and their lives while David listened and kept Gunnar busy with a coloring book.

Todd liked Aunt Tammy, she was a good strong woman, of Midwestern descent, and her kind manners and loving hospitality shone through. She and David had met one summer when Tammy was vacationing with her family on summer break from college. Her dad, an avid outdoorsman, had dreamed of Kodiak Island's burly brown bears and monster king salmon plying its streams for years. While her dad went out on one of his fishing forays and her mom, engrossed in a new book, lounged at the motel, Tammy had been sipping tea at the local coffee shop. A distracted David had walked in and almost spilled his coffee all over her, but luckily most of it landed on the nearby table. As he helped clean up the mess something sparked, and they ended up sitting and talking for over an hour, or so the story goes. He managed to get her phone number, and they kept in touch every other month or so until she made another trip that following summer, this time without Dad and Mom, and this time, the main goal was not to hunt for bear. Todd looked at their love and saw just how much they adored each other. Tammy was quite a bit younger than David . . . by fifteen years. *And* they had waited until just now to have kids, she at thirty-five and David at fifty, but the love of those two was so deep, the age difference didn't seem to matter. They emanated what Todd could only hope to someday find, himself.

"So, since I have this whole week off, I want to help out as much as I can," urged Todd to Tammy while Gunnar distracted Uncle David. Tammy was already shouldering a huge load in taking care of her two little ones and managing the successful knitting shop, The Net Shed, that she'd started ten years ago.

"Oh, honey, you don't need to do a thing, we'll manage just fine." Todd knew this was her Midwestern roots kicking in, and he knew he would have to play the game and offer to help two or three more times until she would cave in. So he was persistent, and in the end she agreed to let him help with babysitting and some cooking and cleaning while she did errands or stayed at the hospital to assist David. Since they lived in a small single family home they didn't have a guest room, Tammy offered Todd to stay on the boat, the *Tammy Sue*, named after . . . you guessed it, the one and only Tammy. Todd gladly accepted the offer as he usually felt much more at home on a boat than on land these days.

"David was working on a small boat project, so he's had the diesel stove going in that old girl, so it should be nice and toasty for you," Tammy said.

"Yeah, Shrimp, take the stateroom up by the wheelhouse. I think it's even got fresh sheets on the bunk," piped in David.

"Well, if you guys insist. I'll take good care of her. You know I know that boat like the back of my hand, Uncle David," said Todd, reminding him of all the countless hours of so many summers fishing on that boat back in the day. "I'll take good care of her."

"Well, you might not recognize some of the instruments. I just got a new VHF and chart plotter installed this fall." David liked to brag about how well he kept up his boat, as it was his pride and joy.

"Okay, well, I'll go check her out. Key still on that float hanging above the galley door?"

"You betcha," replied David.

The sugar rush had long since crashed in Gunnar, and Todd could tell the kiddos were getting grumpy and hungry, so he offered to run down to the Peking to pick up some Chinese takeout. This time Tammy only protested two times and slyly slipped a wad of cash into his pocket as Todd turned to embark on his new mission.

"Okay, see you guys in a few."

"Don't forget the fortune cookies!!!" reminded an excited Gunnar.

"I won't, buddy, but you gotta promise me we'll save 'em for last!"

"Okay, okay," he said, looking up from the picture he was now coloring with crayons just long enough for Todd to give him a big old wink. Gunnar tried to wink back, but failed, instead giving Todd a cute double eye blink.

Chapter 14

Proving Grounds

Tuesday, April 9, 2013

IN THE FLUORESCENT lit bowels of the boat, Em donned oil-smeared headphones and was feeling the sweat start to drip down her brow as Sam communicated in hand gestures for her to pass him the new fuel filter, since speech over the roar of engines was impossible. On a quick run between strings, Em had overheard Phil ordering Sam to check on the Racors (fuel filters) of the new 60KW generator since it had just died two-thirds through the last set.

Being both ambitious and curious, Em had followed Sam down the ladder to the immaculately clean engine room to see if she could at least be a wrench monkey. Sam moved around the crowded space with ease, making it obvious he knew where every tool, spare nut, bolt, or O-ring lived. She enjoyed watching Sam work, trying not to get in his way, and he didn't seem to mind having her down there with him. He, too, was starting to sweat in the heat of the overworked engine, with it beading up on his forehead and running down his neck in trickles.

Several times Sam pointed to a tool over at the workbench, and Em was able to hand it to him, saving Sam from having to get up for it. Luckily, this malfunction seemed to be an easy fix, as it was indeed a clogged fuel filter. Like every good boat should have, this one had multiple spares of every filter for every piece of machinery, including many other miscellaneous spare parts. It made Em feel safer to be on such a prepared vessel. In her brief poking and prodding of the *Sea Ranger*, which she did with every boat she stepped on in an attempt to memorize where all the important tools were in case of an emergency, she even found a flooding and damage control kit, which most skippers usually scoffed at or overlooked the importance of.

With the filter back in place, Em grabbed some oil absorbs to sop up the few small puddles of red-dyed diesel. Sam caught her eye and gave her a dashing wink as he moved to turn over the ignition key. She held her breath and after a second the generator lurched back into life, making the deafening roar of the room even louder. Sam held up his hand for a high five, but as Em reached up to return it, the boat pitched, just as it had been doing progressively more and more violently throughout the day, and she missed her target. So instead, she shrugged her shoulders and Sam returned it with an understanding smile. Mess cleaned up and generator back online, Em followed Sam up and out, both hanging their headphones on the hooks mounted above the stairs.

In the hallway between the gear locker and galley, Sam paused to wipe the sweat off his face with his dirty T-shirt. "Hey, thanks for the hand," he told her.

"Oh, no problem," said Em, trying to be nonchalant about it.

"You know Todd's the only other one who ever offered me any help down there on his own."

"Oh really?"

"Yeah, he's always one step ahead of everyone else." Hearing that filled Em with a glow, as working on a boat inevitably brought out the best or worst in a person.

As Sam politely squeezed by Em, he said, "Gotta go tell Phil we're back up and running," and Em followed him to the galley where she attempted to wash the fuel off her hands with Lava soap.

Nobody had brought up the topic of where Todd had disappeared to that last night in Kodiak, so she didn't know if the guys knew they had hooked up then, although they obviously had figured out those were her underwear he'd had from a ways back. Now, at every mention of Todd, Em's ears perked up in a mix of adoration from her original feelings toward him and present dismay at how he'd turned her undies into a game. Yet, from having to fill his shoes, and such big shoes they were, she was getting an inside glimpse at his world and who he was, and her anger was softening a touch.

That evening while they had taken twenty minutes to shovel down dinner, Manni had reached over Em to grab seconds of the meatball spaghetti still steaming on the non-slip pad of the table.

Realizing in most situations that would have been considered rude, he grunted, "Oh, oops," and then followed with, "Hey, how's that bunk treating ya?"

In between a bite, Joel managed, "You find enough space to squeeze between the messy pile of socks and underwear?"

Not waiting for or needing an answer, Sam piped in, "Tell me about it! Half the time he tosses and turns so much I wind up with half his smelly shit in my bunk!"

With that comment Manni's face lit up, "Oh my god!" he said. "You gotta tell Em about that one time!"

"Oh fuck yeah, that was a good one," asserted Joel, a smile at the memory, already spreading across his face.

"Okay, okay!" said Sam, as he turned to face Em directly and relived the tale for her. "So one night, I think this was a season or two ago, after we'd been out for what seemed like forever, Phil let us catch a little nap. We were all dead tired and pretty much zombies by that point."

Manni interrupted, "And Todd had been coiling the line all day long, which he doesn't normally do."

"Oh yeah, right," said Sam continuing. "So out of all of us, Todd usually talks the most in his sleep. I had finally dozed off and woke up suddenly to Todd screaming and yelling, 'Stop the coiler! Stop the coiler!!!'"

Em gave Sam a puzzled look, and he continued with, "Well, he'd apparently been having a nightmare about falling behind on coiling the hooks and line, and they kept coming in on top of him faster and faster, and I guess, uh, burying him, and he was trying to yell at Phil to shut it off."

This time Joel interrupted, "But it didn't end there . . ." urging the story on.

"Right, so we are all awake now, wondering what the fuck is going on and where the hell we are . . . I was completely disoriented, and as Todd continued to scream to shut off the coiler, he was tossing and turning and suddenly . . ." Sam had to stop to laugh out loud in remembrance for a second, "so, suddenly, he rolled right off the bunk and into mine, still asleep and screaming!"

Sam was laughing so much Manni picked it up and continued for him, "So I'm up in my bunk trying to figure out what the hell is going on and finally get my light on and look over to see Sam holding Todd in his arms, pretty much spooning him, trying to wake him up and calm him down. Yeah, all I remember is hearing Sam say, 'It's okay Todd, I got you, I got you. It was just a dream.'" With that final image, all four of them burst out with uncontrollable laughter, Sam even wiping tears away from his eyes.

When they regained enough composure, Sam finished with, "Next time we made it to town, I made sure to get him a teddy bear to spoon with instead of me. It must've worked because he hasn't wound up in my bunk since."

A crackle on the intercom interrupted the regaling of their story as Phil warned, "Okay, we got ten minutes 'til we're there."

With that they all took a few last bites of warm and comforting pasta, then piled the dishes in the sink, making sure nothing would slip and fly away as there was no time to do dishes, and the seas had kept building.

Em struggled into her stiff Guy Cotten pants and a wet and cold Grundens rain jacket, trying not to elbow or bump into the other guys in the crowded gear locker room. The whole process took a good five minutes, as winter fishing required so many more layers, especially for her, as she had always been prone to get cold easily. Joel led the charge on deck and Em brought up the rear, a blast of wind and rain greeting them to another long night of hauling gear. As Em stepped over the threshold, she glanced up and saw an old and faded "Attitude Is Everything" sticker above the door. She caught herself pausing and calling on her inner strength to greet this evening's challenges with a touch of grace and bravery.

Chapter 15

Fortune Cookies

Monday, April 8, 2013

THE STREETS OF Kodiak were dead. It was around four o'clock, the sky a dull gray. Mounds of frozen gray slush lined the streets, forcing Todd closer to oncoming traffic than he'd normally like. Cars were few and far enough between to momentarily blind him with their headlights. It was a good thirty-minute walk from the hospital to the small downtown area. As each step brought him closer to Tony's bar, Todd's apprehension ticked up with an equal pace. The Peking restaurant was just two blocks past Tony's, on the same side of the street, and there was no way he could bypass Tony's for his main errand at the Peking without taking a quick look for Em.

The sound of music and flash of neon signs greeted Todd before he actually saw the bar's store front. Todd paused in a nearby stairwell to fumble in his pockets for a small tin of mints, and then popped one in his dry mouth. The mounting jitters in his stomach surprised him, and thus he attempted to take a few deep breaths to quell the roiling nervousness. Todd tried to pump himself up with *Well, it's now or never,* as he stepped out of the stairwell and headed to Tony's door.

Smokey haze greeted Todd. The bar was as dark and dim as the day outside, hiding the stains on the floor. Only a few small groups of patrons were hunkered down inside. Todd's eyes scanned the bar, searching for Em. *I swear she said she was working tonight,* and with no sign of her he took his first steps to the bar counter. *Maybe she just ran to the back,* he told himself as he now waited awkwardly at the bar. He heard a tinkle of bells from around the corner, and Todd's heart leapt, but it was not Em. It was not Em at all. Instead, a tall and slender girl with long shiny brown hair, freckles, and a green V-neck T-shirt strode forward with a rack of still steaming glasses from the washer.

As she glided by and made eye contact with Todd, she said "Hey, I'll be right with you," giving him a small, half smile.

That gave Todd's mind time to start spinning. *Where is Em? She was supposed to be here! Did I miss her shift? What time is it?* Glasses now stowed on the counter, the woman turned her attention back to Todd.

"What can I get you?" she asked, wiping her hands on a short server's apron.

"Oh, uh," he hadn't planned for this, so he stuttered. "I, uh, was just looking for my friend. I thought she was supposed to be working tonight."

"Oh," she said, her voice lighting up with a hint of curiosity. Todd was too confused to answer, so she prodded, "Were you looking for Emily?"

"Uh, yeah . . . do you know where she's at?"

"Well, who should I say is asking?" she inquired, trying to affirm her suspicions.

"Oh, yeah, my name's Todd, uh . . ." Not knowing what to continue with he paused and the woman's eyes lit up in affirmation.

"I see. I'm Em's roommate, Jess. I don't think I've met you yet, but I think I've, uh, heard you."

At that Todd's face turned beet red. "Oh shoot, I'm so sorry," was all he could manage.

Jess, sensing his embarrassment, let out a little giggle and wink. "No worries, I have ear plugs." She started putting glasses away and allowed Todd's face to regain some of its normal color, then continued, "I hate to break it to you, but Em got a spur-of-the-moment fishing job and took off this afternoon. I'm covering for her."

Todd couldn't help but let his heart sink to the floor in a puddle at his feet. "What was that you said?" he asked, still digesting the news.

"She got offered some spot on a longlining boat, threw her stuff in a duffel bag, and rushed off."

"What boat was it on??"

Seeing his shock and disappointment, Jess struggled to give him answers. "I didn't catch the name of it, she left in such a hurry. Oh, but she said she'd be back in a week or so, just doing one trip."

"What?" was all he could manage again, his brow furrowed in confusion.

"I guess one of the crew had a family emergency so she's just covering temporarily," explained Jess further, hoping the knowledge that she would be coming back soon would ease the disappointment on Todd's face.

That's when it all started to click, the gears turning in his brain, the puzzle coming together. Could it actually be possible that Em was on the *Sea Ranger*? Could it be possible that she was with his boys right now, probably sleeping in *his* very own bunk? Why didn't she tell him? And *Oh my god, my bunk was such a disaster!* he thought in horror. Gleaning enough information from Jess, Todd thanked her, apologized if he'd woken her up the night before again, and turned for the door, lost in his thoughts.

Distracted, he almost walked past the Peking, barely even smelling the distinct odor of sesame oil and soy sauce emanating from its doors. Inside, Mimi, the five-foot tall Chinese lady who, with her husband Lei, had been running the Peking for as long as Todd could remember, was on the phone taking an order. As soon as she saw Todd enter, her face lit up in a cheek to cheek smile. Hanging up quickly, she came out from around the checkout stand and gave Todd a big hug.

"Long time no see! You stay out of trouble?" she asked in a thick Chinese accent. Mimi was like a second mom to many of the transient fishermen in town who popped through year after year. She greeted each and every one with a big hug and smile, watching the boys grow into men over the years. Her husband Lei poked his head around the kitchen over a steaming vat of white rice to see who Mimi was flirting with this time. After a quick hello, Todd told Mimi what had happened to Uncle David, and a shadow cast over her face.

"I hope that son of a bitch who hit him rot in jail!" she exclaimed with a touch of vengeance in her voice. With a little more poking and prodding, Todd got the full story out of the all-knowing Mimi. If there was a rumor floating around town, she was known as the one who could confirm or deny it with startling accuracy.

Pots and pans clanged in the kitchen as Mimi moved in close enough for Todd to see the lone black hair sticking out of the mole on her chin. She spoke in almost a whisper, explaining that according to her un-named sources there had been a party at a guy named Skylar's house, just south of town before the Coast Guard station. The party spiraled out of control pretty early in the night, so the cops were called in. That sent all the kids spreading away, some via car, some on foot (most of them be-ing underage). The thing was, Mimi swore, they weren't even just drink-ing and smoking pot, since in the last year or so popping pills had be-come a thing on the small island.

"So," she finished with great dramatic flair, "it was young Taylor who wrecked into poor dear Uncle." She further explained to him that the paramedics got Taylor out with the Jaws of Life and took him to the hospital, but he had suffered even more serious internal injuries and a crushed pelvis that required immediate surgery, so he was airlifted down to Harborview in Seattle. You never want to be told you or a loved one have to go to Harborview because that's where the most serious of serious accident victims get sent. "They say they do drug test, but have no result yet," Mimi concluded.

"How long does that usually take?" inquired Todd.

"Oh, who know, but your uncle, he so lucky he not down there, too." With that, Lei crept around the corner of the kitchen holding out a big plastic bag brimming with Todd's order and then some. He gave Todd a big hello and handshake, but quickly returned to the kitchen.

"I so sorry," she said in an even thicker accent. "I make extra order spring roll, egg roll, and crab Rangoon for your family."

"Oh, you didn't have to do that!" Todd replied in genuine gratitude.

"I know, but I want to."

"Well, thank you, thank you. I will tell David you two send get well wishes." Todd almost forgot to get Tammy's change as he was so distracted with this new information, but Mimi remembered and pressed it warmly into his hand and took the opportunity to reach up and give Todd a peck on the cheek.

"Oh Mimi, you better be careful," Todd teased, "you'll make Lei jealous."

"I know, that why I do it," she replied, giving him a sly wink.

Stepping back out into the cold air, Todd took a peek in the bag, seeing it filled to the brim with extra fortune cookies. It put a smile on his lips knowing how happy Gunnar would be, as he tucked the warm bundle into his chest and headed up the hill to the hospital, thoughts beginning to swirl back in, like the pelting snowflakes that were starting to drift in on the wind.

For an unusual moment, Em receded to the recesses of his mind and Taylor came to the forefront. *Taylor* . . . the name turned over and over in his thoughts, but no face was associated with it. *Do I tell Uncle David?*

How would he react to all that information? In anger, sadness, or worry? I mean first of all, David needs to focus on recovery. Does David know Taylor? It was a small enough island that chances were he knew the kid or at least the family. He had the whole walk back to ponder the dilemma. In the end, he decided since David was bound to find out sooner or later, if he didn't already know, he should slip it in at the first chance he got when the kids weren't around.

A black Toyota pickup came whipping around a corner, waking Todd from his thoughts, splashing his feet with a spray of slush. Instead of a typical reaction of annoyance, Todd only noticed the truck looked exactly like Em's and a new type of longing flowed into his core.

Chapter 16

Galley Table

Monday, April 8, 2013

A FEW HOURS later, after all the Chinese food had been devoured, including every fortune cookie, Tammy gave Todd a ride back down to the harbor. Oscar was asleep in the back seat of the Suburban, and Gunnar, also tired, hummed a song to himself, only managing a weak and weary, "Buh bye, Unckie Todd," when he cracked the door, ready to step out.

"Hey, thanks for the ride, Tammy," Todd said as he reached down to grab his bag of the few items he'd thrown together in his frantic leaving of the *Sea Ranger*.

"It's the least I can do . . . so you know where the key is, right? The diesel stove's on for heat. I think you know the rest of the routine."

"Don't worry, Aunt Tammy, I'll take good care of the *Tammy*," he replied, unable to resist the jab at her namesake boat.

"Oh, I know I don't have to worry, just make yourself at home. There's even some leftover grub like crackers and cookies in the cupboards if you get hungry for a midnight snack."

"Thank you, but I think Lei's cooking will hold me over," he said, patting his stomach. "I'll be up at your place . . . eight?" She nodded an approval. "Okay, see you in the morning." And catching the worry lines on her forehead, he added, "You get some good rest now, it will be a new day tomorrow and I'm here to help out however you need."

With that, Tammy took a deep sigh and replied with a crack in her voice, "I don't know what I'd do without you right now. I'd be a mess, so thank you." And more emphatically this time, "Thank you." Todd leaned over to give her a hug and one last reassuring look before he climbed out of the Suburban and embraced the winter air.

A thin layer of snow had fallen on the docks, revealing the tracks of just a few pairs of feet heading down the floats. All had been clad in Xtratufs, the Alaskan sneaker. Several lights along the float were flickering off and on, and Todd watched his footing carefully on patches of black ice over even blacker water lapping at the dock. About two-thirds down the float, just past the *Danny Anderson*, Todd saw the bow of the *Tammy Sue* peeking out. It felt like spotting an old friend in the midst of a crowd. *There she is and looking good!* She sat regally, with not a spot of rust, dock lines neatly coiled, and paint looking fresh and new.

Todd threw his bag up over the rail, then straddled it himself. His hands grew cold and numb as he fumbled with the Hide-a-Key attached to the float. Managing just the right twist and force, the lock clicked and the stout stainless steel door opened outward, allowing a wave of heat to escape and the familiar smell of the boat to wash over him. Just as every home has its own distinct but subtle smell, so do boats. He took a deep breath and the scent soothed him. Moving into the galley, Todd dumped his bag on the floor and ran his hand over the worn galley table, taking a moment to allow some of the memories of times past to filter in and flicker by, like light playing through the tree canopy on a sunny, windy day. Different faces, some still here, some now gone forever, countless meals, thousands of cups of coffee, sea stories, getting through long and grueling fishing days, drinking around the table late into the night, it all had happened over the worn wood of that table. After a sigh, Todd grabbed his bag and headed to a bunk to collapse.

Chapter 17

The Sea and Satellites

Wednesday, April 10, 2013

IT HAD BEEN a long day. In a typical Kodiak late winter, it was just barely turning into spring (albeit only marked by the return of more daylight), so skies were lead gray and laced with a stiff wind. However, when it did get dark in Alaska, the light from the snow on the mountains helped to light up the night, unlike the dark and suffocating winter nights in Port Townsend. Everything there was just black and wet, light getting sucked into a black hole, if it could penetrate at all.

Todd had spent the day between visiting Uncle David at the hospital and helping Tammy with the kids. He did drop-off and pick-up duty for Gunnar at preschool, made his after school snacks, and rough-housed with him a bit to help burn up some of his overflowing five-year-old energy. For Oscar he did diaper and chasing-around duty. The silver lining of this situation was that he was getting more time to spend with the kids than he'd ever had before. But even after years of the hard work of fishing, this was a new kind of tired that was seeping into his bones after just a few bouts of chasing tots around. Todd felt a growing new admiration for the fact that Tammy and David did this every single day, without a break.

So now, back on the boat, Todd glanced at the clock. It was past ten o'clock. He could hear the creaking of the dock lines in the wind and the steady clang of a nearby sailboat's halyard slapping against the mast in the steady wind . . . he'd have to go tighten that up one of these days. The tea kettle started to whistle, which brought Todd up from the galley bench where he had strewn about a few magazines and a book he'd been reading in spare moments. He grabbed his favorite mug hanging from its hook under the cupboard and opened an herbal tea bag. Steam warmed his face as he tightly gripped his fingers around the worn mug and used his other hand to haul himself up the steep ship's ladder to the wheelhouse, where the only proper type of seat on the boat existed. Todd had found it comforting to have a cup of tea up there to unwind and process the day, and watch, from the cushy captain's seat, the harbor's orange glow from the dock lights. It was almost as good as a La-Z-Boy.

Settling into the chair, kicking his slippers off and putting his feet up on the dash, his thoughts moved from Uncle David and family to his other family, his fishing family. *What are they doing right now? Hauling another set? Steaming to a new fishing ground? Having a very late dinner? Is Em in my bunk, catching a short rest? Are the guys being nice to her?* His eyes wandered up to the top of the dock; the ramp was steep, as the tide was out. Then his eyes wandered to the radios. Several of them were mounted within arm's reach of the captain's chair. Two were normal VHF radios with a fairly short hailing distance. But one was the satellite phone, commonly referred to as the track phone on commercial fishing vessels. He looked at it again, and then one more thought of Em urged his hand up to flip the On switch. It took a moment for the orange light to come on, indicating power. Todd punched in the four-digit number for the *Sea Ranger,* grabbed the mic, and settled back in the chair, thinking of what to say.

Nothing good came to mind, but his thumb pressed the mic's button, and he heard the delayed beep letting him know when to talk. With track phones, there is always a slight delay that takes some getting used to, marked by a beep to let you know when you can start to talk. His heart started to accelerate a touch with the question of who would answer?

"Hello, anyone there?" he asked.

Pause, pause . . . he took a sip of his tea, noticed the tension gathering in his stomach.

"Hello? This is Todd, anyone there?"

Pause. *Dang, they must all be out on deck,* which, while disappointing that he might not get to talk to anyone, also made him appreciate being warm and comfortable on the *Tammy Sue.* Then came a reply, and it was *not* a deep male's voice.

"Hey, Todd." He couldn't believe his luck that it was Em. "I couldn't figure out how to turn the volume up."

Delay, pause . . . At least the track phone delay allowed him some time to think about his next sentence, then came the beep.

"Em, how're ya doing? I'm so sorry my bunk was such a mess!" is what came out. He felt dumb even with the extra time to think of something witty to say.

"I've seen worse," was her reply.

There was a weird coldness in her tone, which confused Todd.

"You okay?"

"Uh, I've been better." She hadn't expected to run into Todd until she was back on land, but with him now on the line, she couldn't contain her anger about the panties. Hearing his voice brought up the whole goddamn embarrassment again.

"Oh no, what's up?"

"What's up? How dare you! What's up is my panties were hanging on the fucking American flag, *in* the galley, for *all* to see!" She paused to take a breath. "HOW COULD YOU! YOU MOTHER FUCKER!" she said in as loud a whisper as she dared. Iciness coated every word, and anger dripped from them at the same time. She wanted to yell, but was afraid to wake up Phil whose stateroom was in a corner of the wheel-house.

Todd's jaw dropped, shock set in, and he felt nauseated. He keyed the mic, "Oh my god, Em, I can explain!"

"You better be able to, I don't see how any story could make that right again."

"Em, please! I didn't want them up there!"

"Right," she said, rolling her eyes even though he couldn't see her. "All you guys are the same—dirty, perverted, immature bastards!"

"You're right, you're right." He was feeling desperate. How would he dig himself out of this one? "Em, come on . . . I found them in my bunk after that last night in Sitka. I kept them a secret from the guys. I missed you, and they were really special to me. For sure I didn't want them to know." Then he explained what had happened, how he attempted to fight Manni over them. He talked himself in a circle, and she remained quiet.

"Em, come on! Please don't be upset at me. It broke my heart when they took them from me. They were the only tangible reminder I had of you!"

After a moment that seemed to last to eternity, she came back on. "Hmmm, well, you're marked!"

"What?" Todd asked.

"You heard me, you're a marked man. I *will* get you back someday in an equally or more embarrassing way. And they are no longer hanging up in the galley. I took them back."

"Oh my god, yes, please do, or give me a slap across the face. I totally deserve it." He was starting to feel he was almost back in the safe zone.

Then she asked, voice calmer, "Where are you calling from? Did you switch boats?"

"Oh no, definitely not. I'm just staying on my uncle's boat, the *Tammy Sue*. Their house is a bit cramped. I was having a cup of tea, and thought I'd try to see how you guys were doing out there."

The conversation relaxed further and turned back to the basics more so with each transaction. "We're just running up the hill to our other set. Everyone's taking a nap." She was still talking quietly, so he reached up and turned up the volume some. It was a far cry from what he'd rather do, which was be in the same space as her, lean in closer to hear her, and to get lost in her eyes. He could imagine her on the other end of the mic, maybe cozied up in a hoodie, with a cup of coffee on the dash . . . God, he wished he could be there with her!

FOR EM, IT had also been a long day, but a very different kind of long. She tried not to let it show when Todd caught her off guard and his voice came filtering into the wheelhouse. Even though she was confused and angry at him about the underwear, her heart had betrayed her upset mind and released a flutter of elation when she had first heard his voice.

They'd been up since four a.m. or so, but fishing hadn't been that great. As they'd run through the gear several times now, she was starting to get in the groove and figure out her role and where she fit in (or rather, where Todd had fit into it). She'd also undertaken a study of the guys, analyzing them, trying to figure out who they were, what other quirky rituals they had (like always starting out the mornings with Led Zeppelin), who usually got out of their bunk first when the wakeup call came, how to interact with them, how they were receiving her . . . was she cutting it or not? Being the rookie on the boat, she had to pick up some of the duties no one else wanted, because if she didn't, she'd definitely not gain any respect. So when Phil announced they'd have a two-hour drive to the next spot, his eyes gazing at the crew as they hastily cleaned up dinner in the galley, Em had volunteered to drive.

The weather throughout the day had stayed consistent: miserable. A biting wind, sleet, and steep, choppy waves. The first few days back on a boat after extended time on shore had led to some queasiness in her stomach, but after another night she'd have her sea legs under her and be good to go. Currently, the steep erratic waves and riding in the trough was getting to her, as she could barely hold down her dinner. The last thing she wanted to do was puke in front of everyone . . . that would be seen as a sign of weakness. Just before Todd had called, she'd turned on the weather radio, and it didn't sound good. Wind speeds and wave heights would only be increasing for the foreseeable future.

Her body also took a few days to adjust to the hard physical labor. Currently she was all aches and pains. The worst was the biting cold from the wind and constant struggle to keep her hands warm. After their last set, she'd again had to take the least favored duty and hop in the fishhold with Manni. It was still so packed with the ice they'd just loaded up on in Kodiak to keep the fish frozen, they had to constantly shovel it around and sometimes even lie on it as they stacked the first fish in one of the sectioned off corners of the hold. As Manni splayed open the body cavities of the fish that needed packing, even with insulated fish gloves, Em's hands grew more numb with each handful of ice flakes she had to shove into the fish. Manni seemed impervious to the cold as he'd been whistling a tune to himself and seemed quite comfortable. It took all Em could muster to hide her discomfort. Ten more minutes of the task, and she wasn't sure if her fingers could've lasted.

When she was finally back at the gear locker area, trying to get off her raingear, she waited until Manni disrobed and slid into the warm galley before she struggled with the buttons and clips on her gear, numb hands making it awkward, not wanting anyone to see just how numb they were. Once she was in the head with hot water running over them, she wanted to scream with the burning sensation of rewarming them. But she couldn't really capture all that in a track phone call. Nor could she capture just how sleep deprived she was . . . only a few hours at most, each night, for the last three. But Todd knew. He'd been there many times. She was literally filling his shoes, or rather his sweatshirt that he'd left at her place and she'd accidentally brought. She'd thrown it on that morning, as hers was already dirty and crusted in salt.

So instead of dwelling on all that, she turned back to what most fishermen turn to, what they'd do when they were back in town. "So, Todd, when we get back in, how about we continue that date we started? I never finished showing you around Kodiak."

"So, Em," he said, his voice so deep and sexy, even from a track phone, "How about you continue showing me around your body."

She just about spit out the gulp of coffee she'd just taken. "Goddammit, Todd!! Keep it down. I'm not sure how soundproof that stateroom door is." And after a pause she finished with, "If you're lucky, maybe, if you keep it up, maybe—"

"I'm sure I can keep it up."

"Oh my god, stop, Todd. You're too much," she demanded, but there was a smile and playfulness in her voice, even transmitted over the magical airwaves that were allowing him to talk to her, way out in the middle of the Gulf of Alaska.

"Are the guys treating you alright?"

"Oh yes, they're being gentlemen, when not sniffing underwear," she just had to add. To be more serious she continued, "They're definitely giving me a chance and letting me get my hands dirty." *And cold*, she thought to herself.

"Well, when ya get back, I've got a private bunk here on the *Tammy Sue*. It's a wide one, and nice and quiet down here." His mind continued with the image of undressing her real slowly and gently, then pulling her into the bunk with him, the feel of her skin, warmth of her body . . .

"You know I have an actual bedroom, right?"

"Well, yes, I do recall that, but I also recall meeting your roommate at the bar, and she said something about earplugs."

Em laughed. Before hitting the mic button again, she reached up to reset the helm alert, (no need for it now as she felt alive with electricity talking to Todd and was not about to fall asleep at the wheel), but she didn't know where the Off button was yet. Then she took a quick sip of coffee, just as the boat rolled violently, making the coffee slosh out and onto his hoodie. A little surprised at the unusual jolt, she thought it must've just been a wave that hit them just the wrong way. She took a scan out over the bow. The halogens lit up the gulls and a few shearwaters, flapping with effort, trying to keep up with the boat, then they'd suddenly veer off to the side and glide away. The spray came flying up over the bow with every wave, rolling off the Rain-Xed windows. *Good luck spotting any logs,* she thought to herself as she pushed the mic button again.

"Well, I could use ear plugs here . . . for Sam's snoring. My god, how do you put up with that?"

"Luckily I'm a hard sleeper," was Todd's reply. Not so for Em. Her light sleeping was one of the curses she faced in this lifestyle where sleep was so precious yet sometimes so hard to attain. The anxiety of knowing she desperately needed it, yet only having a few hours for it, usually left her barely just drifting off when it was already time to get up. Just then, Em jolted as she heard someone come up the stairs unexpectedly. Glancing over her shoulder, she saw the wavy top of hair of Sam's head, then the rest of him, slight bags under his eyes, but he had a cup of coffee in his hand.

Em flushed, hoping to god Sam hadn't heard any of that ridiculously flirtatious conversation she'd just been having. If he did, he didn't provide any sign of it.

"Hey, Em."

"Hey."

"Go get some rest, I can take over."

"What?" She asked in disbelief. It was rare for anyone on a longlining boat to give up sleep if they didn't have to.

"You heard me, I woke up to pee, and thought I'd spell ya."

Well, she wasn't going to fight him over it (even if she doubted she'd have time to get any sleep in), but he was staring at her over the rim of his steaming coffee cup, making his intent clear, like she was an idiot not to see that with coffee already imbibed, he was committed.

"Okay, if you insist."

"So, where we headed?"

Sam stepped closer to get a better look as Em pointed to the marked spot on the chart plotter.

"Hey Em! You still there?" came in Todd's voice from the radio.

Sam's eyes widened, then a smile broke out on his face, and he reached toward the mic in Em's hand. She sheepishly handed it over.

"Yo, yo, Todd!"

"Sam!! How's it going man, what are you doing up?"

"Better question is, what are you doing? Where you calling from?"

Todd explained to Sam and they started to catch up, so Em slipped soundlessly down the stairs, her head still spinning from the surprise conversation with Todd. As she pulled herself into Todd's bunk, she could only hear the distant beeping of the track phone and mumbled tones, a relief, as she doubted anyone could have heard their conversation . . . except maybe Phil. Even if she couldn't sleep, she'd at least get some rest, which she knew she'd need to get through the next few days.

Chapter 18

Big News

Thursday, April 11, 2013

"SO, UNCLE," TODD could feel a lump of anxiety in his throat, not sure how David would react to what he was about to tell him.

"What is it?" David rolled his head over so he could look Todd in the eyes, sensing this wouldn't be the usual bullshit they talked about. It was Thursday night, and the TV was on with the evening news, a broadcast from Anchorage in the background. Todd had brought some Chinese takeout again, as the hospital food sucked, but hadn't yet started unwrapping it.

Todd cleared his throat. "Well, you know the guy that hit you in your truck?"

"Yes, I knew Taylor."

Phew. Todd was partly relieved to confirm that at least someone, probably Tammy, had already told him who it was. But now that part of it seemed easy compared to what was to come next.

"Well, when I stopped by to pick up our dinner, I was talking to Mimi." Todd paused to take a breath. "She told me that she'd just heard that Taylor didn't make it. He passed away this morning."

Todd stopped again, to gauge David's reaction. There was none besides a slow inhale and exhale of breath. Unsure how to proceed, Todd added, "They couldn't stop the bleeding in his brain. They tried everything they could." Again silence. "I'm not sure if I should have told you or not."

Todd's mind was racing. How would he feel if he were in Uncle David's position? He was severely injured, recovery a very long way off, work and normal life ground to a halt for probably months, if not more. And then to hear that the person that had been driving recklessly and crashed into him was now dead, *and* it was a person he knew and had watched grow up on the island? He was a young man that David had probably witnessed start off as a sweet and innocent kid, then once teen years hit, had been sucked into the dangerous party scene of a sleepy fishing town with ready access to drugs. Would he feel sadness, or guilt, or something more complicated?

His uncle took a deep breath and said, "Todd, thank you for telling me."

There was another long pause. Up on the TV the annoying ad from Mattress Ranch in Anchorage filled the void.

"Please let me know if you find out when the service will be. I will try to be there, if I at all can. I'll reach out to his parents, too." In reflection, it was the type of answer that made sense coming from Uncle David. As a fishing skipper, he was skilled at hiding his true feelings, keeping his cards close.

"Okay, sure thing," Todd replied. Sensing that was all Uncle David wanted to say about it at the moment, he gave him some time to process it, and started untying the tight knot of the plastic bag the takeout food was wrapped in.

The TV again filled the void. Now the meteorologist was back on.

Todd glanced up and saw him standing in front of the weather map, arm stretched out to the center of a big low pressure system.

"We can expect gale force winds and freezing spray. It will be moving in, starting on Saturday and strengthening on Sunday night, so batten down your hatches and secure your garbage cans. Temperatures will also start out above freezing, highs at thirty-five, and then drop below freezing by Sunday morning."

In Todd's profession, one had to learn the weather, as it affected everything. And he knew that low pressure system looked serious. His thoughts flitted to the *Sea Ranger*, a small ship, just a speck of metal on the vast dynamic ocean.

Chapter 19

Reaching Out

Sunday, April 14, 2013

NOW THAT IT had been a few days and he was in the routine of kid care, hospital visits, and helping Tammy out, time started to slow down for Todd after the initial first few days since the accident. As it was a Sunday, the streets were deserted and the docks a ghost town. Down in the harbor the rigging of the sailboats began to scream, and halyards clanked against many a mast as the wind increased throughout the day. A tried and true mariner could tell the wind speed just based on the sound in the rigging in the sailboats alone. The rain hadn't started yet, but usually that came after the initial bursts of wind. As Todd jumped off the *Tammy Sue*, he inspected the dock lines, all holding steady and in good shape, but visibly stretching and then easing under the strain. He headed up to the hospital to check on David before heading over to make dinner for the kids (and let Tammy get some time with David alone).

The nurses knew him now, so just gave a quick nod as he trudged in, throwing back his hoodie and stuffing his wool cap into his back pocket.

"Hey, Uncle," he said as he entered.

But David didn't answer, he was asleep. The recovery was definitely taking it out of him, more than he tried to let show. The TV was on again, and as he stood for a moment, deciding what to do, Todd caught the tail end of the five o'clock weather report: "So folks, this storm is building. Be prepared for power outages and winds topping sixty miles an hour, gusts possibly over one hundred."

Oh shit. A bad feeling started to seep in, and Todd's stomach took its time rising back up from its initial drop. With Uncle David in a deep sleep and still needing what rest he could get, Todd didn't see any point in waking him. Since Todd still had some time to make it over to Tammy's before six, he quietly padded out past the busy nurses, put his cap back on, pulling it over his ears, and headed back out into the wind, down to the noisy harbor again. Waves were now kicking up over the docks, freezing on the walkway, making things slippery.

Once back onboard, Todd leapt up the stairs to the wheelhouse and grabbed the track phone, flicked it on, dialed their number, and keyed the mic, "*Sea Ranger, Sea Ranger,* anyone there?"

Silence. The boat rocked in the waves, wanting to be free of her lines.

"*Sea Ranger, Sea Ranger,* do you copy?"

Silence again. Todd reached up and turned on the VHF radios to channel sixteen, used for emergencies only. With the USCG base nearby, he'd hear any chatter that might be going on, at least one side of it. Then he turned on the other radio and tuned it to the weather broadcast. The automated male voice was in the middle of a report, Todd was not sure which area it was for, but it wasn't good: "Gale force winds northwest. Winds at sixty knots, gusts to eighty, seas twenty to thirty feet." The unsettled feeling in his stomach grew.

"Hey, anyone there?" he tried again, more desperation in his voice. His mind was racing, coming up with all sorts of imaginary scenarios as to why they weren't answering. Maybe they were busy on deck (although unlikely as they'd never fish in that kind of weather), or busy talking to someone else?

The increasing feeling of something being not quite right linked his mind to an image of that black seal he'd ominously seen in the waves near Sand Point. He'd disregarded that omen, as hitting the deadhead had started to seem like a blessing in disguise after he'd run into Em in Kodiak. But now the thought ripped through his mind like a siren, *Oh god, please no, don't let the black seal mean it was a sign for something yet to come . . .*

Chapter 20

Building Seas

Sunday-Monday, April 14-15, 2013

THEY'D STOPPED FISHING late Saturday night as finishing the most recent set of gear had proved a struggle, and there were hardly any fish on it, anyway. The boat pitched and rolled, throwing Emily off her feet twice. Once she was thrown as she was carrying a skate of baited lines. The coil went flying, she slammed against the bait shack, and landed with a hook from the now jumbled skate just inches from her left eye. However, they still had a set or two out that had been soaking since the previous day that they'd have to come back for later.

Presently it was the wee hours of Sunday morning and they were all in the galley having eggs and toast when Phil came down the stairs and refilled his coffee mug, some of it sloshing out with the onset of a forceful wave that rocked the boat. He had a hand on the galley counter, maintaining the adage to always keep a hand for the self and a hand for the boat in weather like this.

"So guys . . ." he stopped when he glanced around and saw Em, "er, and gals," he added, pathetically. Em just shrugged and rolled her eyes. "The weather is supposed to come up. We're about an eight-hour steam to the Sitkinak Strait. We're going to have to make a run past Sitkinak Island for Akhiok, the closest shelter around."

The guys all exchanged glances. They'd set their gear toward the edge of the continental shelf, about seventy nautical miles from the island. They were all internally calculating that they were now going to have to add an extra few days to their trip to make the run back out and retrieve the gear.

Phil continued, "I'll start with a longer watch, then one of you, I don't care who, can start with two-hour shifts. Also, make sure the deck's secure." He didn't need to say that. The crew already knew the drill. "After that, make sure you get some rest, looks like we might get some freezing spray on top of it all."

Manni let out an audible groan by accident. Freezing spray when fishing in Alaska in early spring as they were doing was the norm, but it was exhausting to deal with. They knew with the rough seas and being far away from any protection of land, they couldn't stop to safely beat off ice while underway. So, once they got into shelter they would be in for grueling work with sledge hammers and shovels, heaving around heavy ice. Hopefully it wouldn't add up to too much until they got toward Akhiok. Icing could add tons upon tons of weight to the topside of a boat, changing the stability and making it much more likely to roll, and not be able to right itself. It was an even bigger danger to the crabbers when their crab pots were on, as the netting and pots themselves were havens for ice buildup, the pots commonly referred to as "ice cube trays."

Em had just started to doze when Joel came down and tapped her, "Hey, it's your turn," and she groaned and rolled over. But after a moment she gathered her willpower and sat up, feeling all her muscles ache as she did. Em threw on sweats and Todd's hoodie over her long underwear and climbed up to the wheelhouse.

"It's getting real nautical out here," Joel muttered, scanning the seas. The sky was dim, the sun somewhere behind the blowing spray and miles of thick gray clouds. Not even the usual crowd of birds seemed to be present. The halogens lit up the whitecaps and froth of an agitated ocean. Em could see ice starting to build on the railings of the bow. It didn't look too thick, but it could add up fast.

The radio was quiet and her shift went by swiftly, but she did note they'd lost some speed, going from ten knots down to eight, pushing their estimated time of arrival even further behind. As they steamed northwest, the wind was coming at them on their port side. Thus, the ice was building up more heavily there. Five minutes to the end of her shift, approaching nine a.m., still a ways off from the Akhiok Bay, she calculated that they might not make it there until late that night. Em went down to tap Sam awake.

Ten minutes later Sam appeared, hair disheveled and sleep still in his eyes. After looking over their location on the chart plotter, sizing up the scene out the windows, and giving a big yawn, he said, "Looks like another day in paradise."

"Oh, yeah, livin' the dream," she agreed, with sarcasm.

After handing over the helm to Sam and making sure he was briefed on the route and plan, Em turned to go down the stairs, but as Sam eased into the chair, he asked, "How much has this ice built since you started?"

"It was barely just sticking when I began." They both looked out the windows again. In two hours it had grown to about half an inch. Still nothing of note or worry, except, if they had hours to go. Em could see the gears spinning in Sam's head as he calculated ice accumulation rates.

He sighed and said, "I think after my shift is done, I'll go transfer some fuel to the starboard side, as we're taking all the ice on the port," more to himself than to her. It was standard practice for a seasoned engineer to know when it was needed to transfer fuel and to not need to bother the captain about it.

"Sounds good," said Em as she turned to do an engine room check before crawling back into her . . . well, Todd's bunk.

🪢 🪢 🪢

IN A SLEEP-INDUCED fog, she heard Sam and Manni switch out, marking the passage of time. Next was Phil's turn, and again he took a longer shift. As she drifted off to sleep, she heard Manni rummaging about in the galley, trying to make a sandwich, but not very successfully based on the sounds of it, dishes crashing, forks flying. Nothing was easy to do in twenty to thirty-foot choppy seas.

Next time she woke, it was Sam who was up, heading down to the engine room. She guessed he was checking on the fuel transfer again. But there was a funny feeling in her gut that something wasn't right. Working on boats, one becomes attuned to subtle differences, as paying attention to small changes like a new sound in the engine room or different way the boat rolled could be a sign of a potentially imminent danger. Em couldn't get back to sleep, and she had to pee anyway, so she decided to get up. Out in the galley, she glanced at the clock on the microwave, reading 17:11. Gripping the wooden rail along the counter (all boats had them around the counters and galley tables to keep kitchen items from rolling off), Em grabbed a cup already in the sink (versus the risk of opening a cupboard in these seas), and filled it up for a drink of water. With the boat pitching so violently, it was hard to tell, but it almost felt like they had gained a slight list to the port side. Outside, through the galley window, she could glimpse the back deck. *Oh my.* There were now inches of ice coating everything, and more of it on the windward, port side. *This is not looking good. At all.*

Thirst satiated, Em made her way carefully up the stairs to the wheelhouse with a hand on the rail. The list was more evident. Phil was at the helm, his white wispy hair illuminated by the glow of the radar and other electronics. He was sitting forward, hunched over the jog steering stick, one hand on the satphone mic. After the track phone beeped and then a voice on the other line came on, Em's heart dropped just a tad, realizing it wasn't Todd but probably a captain from another boat.

Phil turned his head, seeing Em, and nodded to her, but then went back to his conversation. As she drew up to the dash, she glanced at the chart plotter. At least now they were nearing Sitkinak Island and about to turn into the Strait, but it was still a good twenty-three nautical miles or so through the Strait and then into the protected waters of the Akhiok area and Alitak Bay. Sometimes around islands or points of land, the ocean currents become confused, as waves bounce off of land, leading to notoriously choppy and turbulent seas. She hoped getting closer to the point off Sitkinak Island wouldn't have this effect on them. The ice on the bow railings was thick now.

It sounded like Phil and the other guy were talking about the normal stuff—boats and fishing and the weather. The other skipper mentioned they were just pulling into Seward and glad of it, to be out of the weather. It sounded like they'd be shooting the shit for a while, so Em carefully went back down to the galley. Her stomach rumbled, so she headed to the fridge. Her hand was on the fridge's latch, waiting to time it with the waves for a quick chance to grab something before items spilled out like a cracked gumball machine. Still waiting for just the right moment, the door to the engine room opened and the roar of the machinery filled the room until Sam closed it behind him.

"Hey, how's it going?" he said, seeing her preparing to battle the waves for a peek in the fridge.

"Oh, good, was just hoping there was something I'd be able to grab quick and easy."

"Good luck."

"You transferring fuel?" she asked. "Need a hand with anything?"

"Oh, yeah, I started a little bit ago."

"Hopefully that helps."

"Yeah, it should. Usually does." Then after a pause he added, "Just a pain if the wind changes," implying he'd have to go back down to change the fuel over.

"Well, let me know if I can help with anything."

"Naw, you're good."

Sam turned and went up to the wheelhouse. As she cracked open the fridge, grabbed a Tupperware with some leftovers and latched it shut again, she could hear his and Phil's voices float down, discussing the boat's port list.

Leftovers and fork successfully in hand, Em turned and saw that Joel had sauntered in and was sitting at the galley bench without her realizing it.

"Couldn't sleep," he said with a shrug.

"Me, neither."

"Hey, you feel that list?"

"Yeah, I do. Sam's transferring some fuel to help out with it."

He nodded without saying anything. There was a touch of melancholy to him at that moment that she hadn't picked up on before. He looked a little defeated, tired of being beat up, at the whim of the wind and sea and skippers.

A moment later Em could hear the thud of Sam's feet as he came back down from the wheelhouse. "Dang it, I jinxed it, Em. We're starting to make a turn down into Sitkinak Strait. I'm going to have to switch the fuel back already."

"What?" asked Joel.

"Yeah, the ice is on the port side, but now we're going to be beating head on and a little starboard to it, so I've gotta even it out again or we won't be balanced anymore."

"Right on. Man, I hate having a list," he said with a discernible shudder. "Maybe the wind will help even the ice out." Em wondered if he'd known anyone who'd been on a boat that capsized that way. Most people who have worked on a boat instinctively know a list is bad, as boats depend on stability to not sink, but Joel's edginess around it seemed extra palpable.

"I sure hope so," said Sam. What they didn't know was that the wind had been doing them a favor when it was coming from the port side. Even though the ice was building there, the wind was also acting as a righting agent to keep the boat pushed up and over toward the starboard. Now, the wind was not assisting in pushing the superstructure of the boat up against the weight of the ice. Rather, with their new change in course it was pushing the port side down, along with the currently uneven fuel tank levels and tons upon tons of ice. Sam yanked open the engine room door again, put on earmuffs and disappeared down the ladder.

Joel started talking, not looking at Em, staring out straight ahead. It didn't seem like he was talking to her, but she was the only person in the room, so she moved a little closer on the bench and listened in. "My aunt once got a plane ticket to visit family in Nevada. But she was always one with her 'senses,' having crazy premonition-type dreams. Well, the morning before the flight, she had a nightmare that she was on a plane that was starting to crash, starting to free fall, and then she woke up. So the whole drive down to the airport, she just couldn't shake the feeling. To the disappointment of everyone, she decided at the last minute not to board. I mean she'd even gone through security and everything." Em, listening intently, raised her eyebrows in surprise. Joel nodded and continued, "Well, she headed back home, and when she saw on the flight tracker that the others made it just fine, she felt like a royal idiot. But then, as a few other folks from the family were all arriving at the same time, the car that had picked them up got in a head-on with a semi, and half of them didn't make it."

"Oh, wow," Em said.

"Yeah, well I got this bad feeling building about this. I hope I didn't inherit any of her premonition skills."

"Well, if it makes you feel any better, I didn't have any bad dreams," she said, trying to console him. He gave her a doubtful look with one raised eyebrow. "And it sounds like we're making the turn into the Strait, so hopefully it'll get better soon, being protected from the wind and getting closer to Alitak Bay."

"Oh yeah, I know, I've been through worse seas on this boat. I'm sure we'll be fine—still I just can't shake this feeling."

Not sure what else to do, Em looked at Joel and offered him some of the leftovers, Tater Tot casserole. Even being a few days old and re-heated, it was surprisingly satisfying.

Joel accepted and stood up to snatch a bowl out of the cupboard. They sat in silence, but a comfortable silence. The side of the wrap-around galley bench they were on was against the bulkhead to the fo'c'sle, so it ran along the width of the boat. Em noticed she had to put more pressure on the port-leaning side of her body to keep from sliding down toward Joel.

Em only had a few more bites left. Glancing over, she saw Joel was about half done with his serving, when WHAM, the boat jolted violently to port. It shuddered, the steel groaning in protest. Em waited for the boat to lift back up, her heartbeat quickening. Three seconds passed, then finally, *finally* it came up, but not *all* the way up as it should have. Normally when a wave knocks the boat over, there's a pause, but then it quickly rights itself all the way back to center. It shouldn't have taken more than a second, but this pause was uncomfortably long. Her eyes grew wide and she looked at Joel, his eyes looking just as anxious.

Without needing to say anything, both slid out of the bench like patrons smelling smoke in a movie theater. Em grabbed their dishes and threw them in the sink. Joel leaped up the stairs to the wheelhouse, Em right behind. Phil wasn't casually seated anymore. All the cords from the radios were hanging at an odd angle. His hands gripped tightly not on the jog stick, but now on the wheel where he had more control. Near the compass, centered in the dash of the wheelhouse, there was a small clinometer mounted to the cabinets, a common feature of most boats, to show the degree of a list. Em's eyes went straight for it, and saw the little needle oscillating between fifteen and twenty-five degrees to the port side, depending on the size of the wave they were in. Her throat went dry, and her hands began to sweat.

"Phil! What's going on?" asked Joel with urgency.

"I'm not sure." Now that they'd changed course around the island, they were at the wrong angle to the waves. "I think it's the ice, and we're in a bad trough here, too."

The boat still hadn't come up above fifteen degrees of tilt. It was enough to make it hard to walk normally and stand up now.

"Are we almost around the corner?"

"Yes, we just made the turn, but now the wind's on the wrong side of us."

"Yeah, Roger," said Joel with a gulp.

Another big wave hit them. Em saw the clinometer hit thirty-five degrees, almost knocking her over.

"This ain't right," Joel said to nobody in particular.

The waves kept coming, confused and angry, bouncing off the island as they neared the rugged shores of Sitkinak Island. Em felt her nerves switch on to high alert. The maritime safety course she'd taken two years earlier down in Seattle came rushing back: how to don a survival suit in less than a minute, how and when to release a life raft, how to make a Mayday call, how to use the EPIRB, the device that could send out their location via satellite if it was either manually activated or submersed in water. *God damn it*, she cursed, realizing she'd never received the *Sea Ranger's* full safety rundown. As soon as they'd left Kodiak they'd either been working, eating, or trying to get precious sleep. At least she had located a few items on her own like the damage control kit, but she knew that would do zero good in this situation. *So, where are the survival suits stored? Is there one small enough for me?* she wondered, trying to quell panic.

She took a wild look around the room. She guessed they were stowed under the big bench against the back wall and rear windows, or maybe out behind the wheelhouse. Yet she didn't want to ask just at that moment, not wanting to imply impending doom. She did remember seeing the EPIRB in the standard spot outside the wheelhouse door starboard side, and the life raft was obvious, perched out on the upper deck by the chest freezer. But when was the last time it was serviced? A knot was growing in her stomach, and her mouth went dry. Her eyes went back out to the sea in front of them.

By this time Manni had woken, probably from the odd list, and had climbed up to the wheelhouse. Sam was still down in the engine room.

Manni entered the space with a, "What the fuck is happening?" question, one to which Phil didn't have a good answer or one that anyone wanted to hear.

The waves kept coming. Now that they were around the island and turning in to the Strait, turning in to what was supposed to be nearing safety, the wind was blowing from the bow and starboard side. And what that meant was the wind was pushing the boat over, the ice helping to drag it down on the port side.

With urgency in his voice, Phil ordered, "Someone go get Sam, NOW!"

Manni, nearest the stairs, nodded and turned around, getting pushed into the side of the wall. The tilt was so severe, it was closer to thirty-five to forty-five degrees now.

Phil took a gulp, then turned to Joel and Em. "I think we're in a bad spot here, guys. She's not coming back up like she should be," fear and acceptance, both, in his voice. "I'm going to have to make a Mayday call. We're still too far away to make it."

Holy shit, this is really happening, thought Em. Her fight/flight responses switched on. What was she going to do, fight or flee? There was nowhere to run to, so it was more like fight or freeze. The thought again screamed through her mind, *This can't be real! Please tell me it's just a bad dream . . . I'm not really on a sinking ship. Is this really how I'm going to die?*

Phil had his arm around the captain's chair, holding tight to stay upright. With the other hand he reached for the VHF mic.

It took him a second to gather himself, but Em watched the surreal scene unfold as he held down the button and said, with regal stoicism, in a calm yet tense voice, "Mayday, Mayday, Mayday. This is the *Sea Ranger*. We're at 56° 36' North and 153° 54' West. Five persons on board. We are rolling over, and the boat is not coming back up. Repeat, we are going to sink."

There was no immediate reply. In the distance, Em heard the engine room door open. Manni must've made it at least to the engine room stairwell.

"Get the survival suits out—now," Phil directed.

Joel, who had been frozen, now spurred into action. They were indeed where she'd guessed. Joel tore off the seat cushions, and ripped the seat boards up, which now went flying down to the port side of the boat, revealing the big orange and green bags containing the only hope of an Alaskan mariner for lasting more than a few minutes in the frigid waters.

Another big wave rocked the boat, Phil began a second Mayday call. On top of that, though, the track phone beeped. It was Todd's unmistakable voice that came through the speaker: "*Sea Ranger, Sea Ranger,* anyone there?"

Phil glanced at the track phone unit, but couldn't get to it with his hand gripping the chair, and then a stranger's voice came on over the VHF radio. "Roger, understand the vessel's name is *Sea Ranger* at position 56° 36' N, 153° 54' W. Break—Break. *Sea Ranger, Sea Ranger,* this is the United States Coast Guard, Comm Station Kodiak Alaska on channel one six, over."

"Yes, this is the *Sea Ranger*, go ahead."

"Vessel *Sea Ranger*, we understand you have five persons on boar—" And then the radio crackled and cut out.

"Yes, we have five persons on board," Phil yelled back. "We are rolling over and she's not coming back up!!"

"*Sea Ranger, Sea Ranger,* do you copy?" Todd's voice broke into the chaotic wheelhouse again. He didn't sound too worried, but there was a hint of urgency in his voice. *If he only knew what's really going on!* Em despaired.

Em could hear the engine room door open again, and Sam and Manni began clawing their way up, fighting the awkward angles as they scrambled through the galley and up the tilted stairwell to the wheelhouse.

As all that was happening, Joel was pulling out the Gumby suits (a nickname for the awkward, full-body suits that have mittens, booties and hoods attached, and once donned, do indeed look like the green Gumby character, but dressed in orange). Most of the bags had XXL or XL labels on them, but Em did glimpse an orange bag with an L and one with an M. Knowing the size could make a big difference, she kept a sharp eye on the Medium bag. Em was trying to hold on and help out at the same time, but with the list and violent waves, the bulky bags kept dropping and rolling down the floor to the port side.

Since Em was facing the stern of the boat, she could see the portside deck rail was now completely under green water. A steep wave rocked the boat, sending her tumbling down to the port side. Her fall was cushioned by the multiple Gumby suit bags that had rolled down with the gravity as well, so taking advantage of the situation she fished out the bag labeled L for Large and ripped open the snaps, unfurling the rolled-up suit like a sail. All her training from the maritime safety class came back, but this time it was on a rocking, tilting ship with panic coursing through her veins and her hands shaking. She remembered the plastic bags shoved in the hood were to slide over her shoes to make sure she could get in fast. She could've laughed at how unrealistic the maritime training course had been on a flat, stable, concrete floor, compared to the chaos and terror she was now immersed in.

Joel was simultaneously getting started on his suit. Her instructor's advice pounded through her head: *Get yourself safe first, so you can then help others.* The suits had no separate hand pieces, so as soon as she slid the arms on, she lost almost all dexterity in her fingers due to the suits' huge, awkward mittens. Joel had his suit about halfway on. Em got her hood up and could feel just how large the suit was on her, but it was going to have to do. Then she tried to grip the zipper with the mittens and yank, but it got stuck halfway.

The Coast Guard hadn't come back on, but Phil tried again, in hopes someone would hear, "Mayday, Mayday, Mayday. This is the *Sea Ranger.* We are at 56° 36' N, 153° 54' W. Five persons on board. We are listing and on our side, taking on water, and have taken on too much freezing spray. We are about to go down." Em knew that must've been the hardest thing for Phil to say in his life.

THE NEXT FEW moments became a blur. As Em was struggling with getting the suit zipped up the rest of the way to her chin, out of the corner of her eye she spotted a foaming wave crest, higher than most. It came from the starboard side and was on them before she could shout out a warning. The boat leaned over with it, and after the wash flowed away, the boat didn't come back up, not at all. Instead it hung at a solid fifty to sixty degrees of list. Em, already on the port side, was flung to the wall again, which was now pretty much the floor, but luckily it was only a few feet away. Joel, who'd been more in the aft middle of the wheelhouse, was flung down, but had grabbed onto the benches as he was thrown. Phil, standing in the middle of the space, had managed to get a hand on the ship's wheel, but the violent motion was too much, and he lost his grip after a few fraught seconds. Flying down he went, arms flailing, landing on the port windows with a sickening thud and crash, jumbled up a few feet away from Em.

Phil's head had hit hard, and blood smeared the window and his face, yet he was still able to look Joel and Em in the eyes, check if his crew were okay, then yelled at the top of his lungs, "Sam, Manni, get up here! Everyone get your suits on now! You've gotta do it before she lays too far over and you can't get out," he ordered.

"Hey, anyone there?" It was Todd's voice breaking in again. This time she could hear a little more worry in his question, as there was almost always someone on the helm. She wanted with all her being to scream out to him for help, but couldn't, the mic too far away. Instead, she stared at it helplessly. They never heard his last call.

Sam's head finally appeared at the doorway. "What the fuck is happening?" he shouted. As he and Manni had been in the narrow stairwell when the last big wave hit, they hadn't fallen far, but then slid and fell the rest of the way into the wheelhouse. Em got one last look at the back deck before the lights flickered four times, then cut out completely. Now they were without power, fully at the whim of the sea, and the dark gray sky outside their only light.

THE DECK WAS half underwater, any open vent or crack into the ship filling with green, foamy seawater, the normal hum of the engine and generator silenced. Forever. The portside windows that normally stood tall above the waterline were now submerged below it. The lights flickering out allowed sheer terror to replace any shred of order that had remained.

A pile of suits, charts, cushions, boards, coffee cups, you name it, anything that wasn't bolted down was now on the port side crashed against the window and wall. The wall was now the floor, and the only door on the starboard side was now a good fifteen feet straight up and a tough climb to get to. Everyone was in a pile and reacting differently.

Manni lost his shit, "My girl, my little girl, I'm never gonna see her again! We're gonna die!" he kept shouting.

"Get your suits on," Phil ordered in a severe, stern voice, trying to restore calm, but he failed to move himself. Maybe he'd broken some bones in his long fall to the port side.

Joel was manically fumbling with the bags, his own suit on, but not fully zipped. Joel managed to snag another bag out of the chaos and toss it to the dark shape where Manni was, but he was in shock and just held it, not ripping it open to get at the only thing that had a chance of keeping him alive.

"If you've got your suit on, get out before it's too late!" ordered Phil, yet his shadow still showed no sign of moving. Em was silent, but inside was screaming with disbelief. Everything had been fine not more than fifteen minutes ago, eating Tater Tot casserole in the galley with Joel. How could it turn into this nightmare, so unbelievably fast?!

Stay calm, stay calm, stay calm! she thought, but not feeling calm at all. At her feet she started to feel something cold.

"OH, FUCK!!!!" Manni yelled, also noticing the water that was now infiltrating into the wheelhouse and coming in fast.

Em finally got her suit zipped all the way up. She looked up at the door. It was so far away, and way too steep to climb out, especially now that she had only oversized mittens for hands.

Something bumped her shins, and reaching down she realized it was a still unopened survival suit bag. "Who still needs one?" she asked.

"I do!" said Sam. "We need one more, for Phil!"

"I don't want to die, not here, not right now!" Manni kept repeating, near hyperventilation state, not making any progress in donning his suit.

Em couldn't believe how fast the water was coming in, already at her waist. More fumbling and sheer naked terror. Visions from movies of flooding ships blinked through her mind, but this was real.

Joel, now fully geared up and noticing the fading opportunity to make it out of the wheelhouse, had started to climb, grabbing onto whatever he could, breaking cupboards and cabinetry as he tried to ascend the steep angles. After a moment, his voice called down from up above. "You gotta get out! Now!"

That gave Em the real jolt she needed. She followed his path, adrenaline coursing through her veins and giving her the strength she wouldn't normally have had to climb and pull herself up. As she neared the top, the water was already almost to head height. She could see Joel's silhouette in the frame of the door, his hand reaching down for her.

"Take my hand!" he yelled.

She made a lunge, missed, but still held tight with her other arm, then gathered all her energy up again and made another lunge. This time . . . contact.

"I got you!" Joel shouted with assurance. His strong arms pulled her and her bulky survival suited body up and out. Even though it was a few hours before sunset, the stormy sky was ominously dim, the steel boat creaking, swaying back and forth, screaming in its own way against what was happening. Sound everywhere, but none of it mechanical anymore. Joel turned back to the cavernous hole though the wheelhouse door.

"You guys gotta get out of there. Climb up to me!" Joel shouted. His suit was still half open, so Em took a moment to help him, and they almost got washed overboard in the process, but finally with an adrenaline-induced yank, she got the zipper up to his chin. Now she realized why her instructors in the class had recommended waxing the zippers once a year.

There were muffled shouts and yells from below. Em scanned for where the life raft was, her heart dropping when she realized it was already underwater and hadn't deployed. Another wave washed over the boat, and it listed further, almost straight on its side now. Em knew the life raft had a mechanism with a hydrostatic release to cut the line when it reached a certain depth under the water and it should float up to the surface and automatically open and inflate . . . *if* it didn't get caught in any rigging, and *if* everything else went right. Her maritime instructor's words, *Never leave the boat until you absolutely have to,* rang in her head. And the EPIRB? That should also release on its own, but she couldn't see it in the chaos of the storm.

Em knew they'd only have maybe a few more moments for the other guys to get in their survival suits, and the longer they waited it'd be near impossible to climb out against the force of water rushing in, so she tried to find a secure spot near the door to shout down to them.

"Come on guys, you got this! Get your suits on, then you can swim out."

She couldn't see well enough to verify, but she imagined how cold they must be without their suits on yet. The water was near freezing and they were probably now completely immersed in it.

From below, Phil's muffled voice remained stern, but restrained from panic. She could hear him trying to calm Manni down and help Sam with his suit. Not all their words were audible, but she did make out Sam saying, "I'm not going to leave you, Skipper."

Joel and Em continued to shout to the three trapped inside who continued to struggle, without any progress. Once the water started flooding in from the stairs, the boat not only was all the way on its side, but also sinking deeper in the water. The *Sea Ranger* was showing signs of going all the way under. With the boat's change in position, Joel and Em had to reluctantly abandon the wheelhouse door and Sam, Manni, and Phil inside, and start climbing on the bulwarks and superstructure, trying to find a flat place still above the water. She knew a boat could seem like it was going to sink, but then end up floating with an air pocket, so she was determined not to leave it until it left her. Looking around, she tried to grab some lines, as that might help tie her and Joel together, so they wouldn't get separated, but all the lines were frozen, caked with inches of ice.

Em realized she had her hand through a scupper from the starboard side of the deck, now a safe distance from any dangerous rigging that might entangle her.

"Joel, we've got to stay together!" she screamed, knowing that would increase their survival odds. The boat started to shift in an odd way, as if the stern were going down.

Then a huge wave smashed on top of them and ripped Em's tenuous grip free from the scupper, and she was set adrift from the boat, a miniscule speck in an incomprehensibly huge ocean. Now fully dependent on her survival suit, she was relieved at how well it kept her floating, but she had to fight to keep her head up, as she hadn't inflated the extra buoyancy chambers by her upper back and couldn't find the air valve to inflate them in all the pandemonium. Her strobe light was working though, flashing at the ghastly scene with an eerie flash every second or so. Joel was still clinging to the side, but then suddenly the vessel jerked straight upright, bow pointing to the sky. The *Sea Ranger* was in its last fight for air.

"Joel!" she cried. "Joel!" "JOEL!!!!"

Nothing could be heard over the wind and the steel groaning of the boat. Em was a good fifty feet or so away now, when the boat suddenly lurched even more violently, bow now fully perpendicular to the horizon, shaking Joel off at the same time. It was a final salute, but no trumpets were playing. There the *Sea Ranger* paused for a good thirty seconds and then began her descent straight down, deeper, and deeper, until she was completely gone, air bubbles and debris the only sign a boat had ever been there. It was a scene she knew that would be burned into her memory for the rest of her life, and something that would be indescribable to others. One minute your boat, your lifeline to life is there, the next minute it is swallowed whole, and all that is left is you, a tiny unimportant speck on a raging sea amid freezing spray and angry ocean, miles from land. The finality of the disappearance of the groaning ship partnered with an odd sense of acceptance that this was it. This was going to be how she was going to die.

With the ship gone, Em had lost sight of Joel. Last she'd seen him, he was trying to get away from the sinking ship, but it was hard to stay oriented riding in the constant up and down swells of the sea. The terror that had filled her before, shifted into acceptance of death, mixed with a yearning: such a strong yearning to get one more chance, a chance to do . . . anything.

A buoy, then an ice shovel appeared. They made her wonder what else was around. The smell of diesel started to permeate the wind. Water had seeped into her neoprene suit, taking energy out of her already exhausted body to heat it. As she was squirming to get the tube attached to her chest pocket to inflate the air pouches which would help keep her upright, she glimpsed a light out of the corner of her eye. Hope pulsed through her heart. *What was that? Please let it be Joel! Or the life raft.* But at this point she was still afraid to hope.

"JOEL!!!!" she yelled at the top of her lungs. There was no way in hell she'd have the dexterity to try to fish out the tiny whistle from her suit's chest pocket, although it was a much more efficient way to communicate. So she resorted to yelling again, "JOELLL!" No answer, but she started swimming toward the light with everything she had left in her.

As she got closer, she finally confirmed it was the raft, not Joel. The wind was helping push her toward it, but at times it felt like she wasn't making any forward progress at all. The raft bobbed up and down between every swell, and the suit still wasn't properly inflated, making it incredibly difficult to swim.

"JOEL!" she kept trying to yell periodically when she could catch a breath. He had to be nearby; she knew he must be close.

As she was drawing near the life raft, the wave she was on rose. Em got a glimpse behind it and saw another strobe flash, about two hundred fifty feet away.

"JOEL!!!!!"

It had to be him. That was a game changer. Her voice probably only carried about twenty-five feet, but Em didn't care. She kept yelling between short bouts of swimming, throat hoarse. Her energy and stamina were dangerously depleted, but as she got closer her willpower grew, and she noted Joel's strobe was moving . . . toward the raft.

Finally she was within reach of the bright orange and towering raft. The canopy was flapping wildly in the wind, but the raft's light had stayed on, helping her fumble with the line along the side to find the entrance. She pulled herself around until she spotted the door in the canopy. She pulled on some lines, and a small ladder plopped out. The extra weight in her suit zapped every last ounce of her energy, but one last surge of adrenaline helped her up and in, into a puddle of water.

She took a second to breathe, to collect herself, to look. Now she had something besides despair to focus on: survival. She remembered from the class that there should be some pockets along the sides with emergency supplies, such as a first aid kit, food, water, and flares. Now that she was inside, she couldn't keep an eye on where Joel's strobe was, so she would call out periodically. As Em was fumbling with the first of the survival pockets, she heard a faint voice—it was Joel! She called back, and they kept in communication the next five or ten minutes as he drew closer. At the door of the canopy, she leaned out and finally caught sight of him. Tears rolled down her cheeks, indiscernible from the salt of the ocean, and emotion gripped her—to see another live human being—for a while she'd thought she would never be so lucky again. Joel looked as exhausted as she felt. This time it was her reaching out and giving him a hand in. They collapsed in a pile in the foot or so of water inside the raft, wet, but safe for now.

"Em, I can't believe it," he managed.

"Joel, are you alright?"

"Yes, just cold. You?" They had to speak up, as the flapping of the canvas was deafening in the wind.

"Same here." After a moment, Em asked, "Hey, Joel, did you see if anyone made it out of the wheelhouse after I did?"

Joel shook his head, no.

Conversational silence fell on them, as they lay, still gripping one another, trying to digest what had just happened, but not fully able to grasp it.

Then the light at the top of the canopy dimmed and went out.

"What the fuck?" Joel swore in disgust. "The goddamn light just went out??"

That got them back into motion again and digging through the survival packs. It was hard to keep things from spilling out and floating around in the bottom of the raft. The waterproof case where the flares and flare guns were was key, as well as one working flashlight. She didn't think they'd survive long enough to worry about the food and water or first aid kit.

"Joel, you think anyone heard the Mayday call?"

"Yeah, for sure. Plus there were a few boats nearby that I remember seeing on the plotter with their AIS on." AIS is a satellite tracking system that all large boats have, to show their locations on other chart plotter, tracking, and emergency response systems.

"So if they heard our call, and we're not that far from the air station at Kodiak, how long do you think it'd take them to respond?"

"Hmmmph," he said, thinking. "Maybe an hour or less?" It had felt like hours since the ship first went down, but Em knew things had been going in slow motion, so it was probably more accurate to guess only forty-five minutes or so.

"Okay, well we have the flares ready, and I suppose we can use the flashlight and shine it on the canopy walls to help illuminate our position if we see them," suggested Em.

So it turned into a waiting game. The cold crept into their bones and waves splashed relentlessly through the door. Em curled up next to Joel in a fetal position to conserve warmth. He did the same. It was not a time to talk much, it took too much effort over the wind, nor did they really want to. But every twenty minutes or so, Joel tried to crack a few jokes to keep their spirits up.

After a time, Joel stirred, "Hey Em."

"Yeah?"

"It feels like it's been well over another hour. I was thinking . . ."

"What?"

"Well, on my last watch, I for sure remember seeing one or two other boats nearby on AIS. They'll have heard the Mayday from us or heard it relayed by the Coast Guard. I mean the Coast Guard should've been here by now. Maybe we should shoot at least one of our flares off. They may be searching, but maybe our EPIRB didn't go off and they can't find us."

Em mulled it over. It was a risky proposition. They only had six flares total. If they shot them off now, and a rescue chopper came later, they might risk not getting seen.

But . . . he had a point. The boats were near enough that they would probably be in sight of a flare by now.

She consented to shooting one flare off and said, "How about this: let's shoot one off now. Then if we don't see anyone, in another hour or so maybe shoot off one more, then save the rest for if we hear a chopper or see a boat."

Joel paused in thought, then agreed, "Okay, sounds good."

They both sat up, waist deep in water in the raft now. The waves were unyielding, so she tried to push out the worry about the raft sinking, and instead focused on finding the flare kit in the dark and sloshing water. Finding the waterproof box, Em cursed and fumbled with the latches and her giant survival suit mitts until she finally got it open, and Joel clumsily grabbed the gun and one flare, similar in size to a shotgun shell.

"This survival gear is absolute crap!" he screamed in frustration, as everything was impossible to handle when wearing the Gumby suit. Em struggled to snap the case back, terrified of losing anything, but most of the survival kit was rolling around in the foot or two of water, anyways. They don't tell you how fucking hard it is to do anything useful in a survival suit in the safety class. Jumping into a flat calm heated pool for thirty minutes to practice seemed a joke to her now.

Joel leaned out the door and shot off one of the flares. It left an eerie trail and glow on the sea, an arc of light that fizzled into nothing. And nothing happened. Just more waves and wind and water. They worked to put the flare gun back in the case and returned to their huddled positions.

After another hour or so came and went, they shot off one more flare. They both knew there was only a small window when rescue was likely, and it was closing in on them. The more time that passed, the farther they drifted away from their ship's last known coordinates. The wind was pushing them away from the islands, but who knew what the currents were doing. And who knew how long they could last in their survival suits. Mariners often joked and called them "body bags." And it was true. Way more often than not, they were found with the occupant long since deceased. It was getting difficult to think straight now, which Em knew was a sign of hypothermia. They spoke here and there, but again, the wind made them keep it to a minimum.

Em spent those long desperate hours deep in almost dreamlike thought. She went from fighting off panic, to getting her breath back into control, to acceptance of the situation, not wanting it to be true, to thinking of regrets and things she still wanted to do. She felt anger build in her chest that they'd made it this far, and now hope seemed to be dimming with each passing minute.

She was again wondering, *Has it been another hour already or two?* From her curled up position, she could glimpse a section of sky out the door and all she could see was inky blackness. With the coming of night, the waves and sea became even more terrifying, if that was even possible.

Then, during one of her skyward glances, she suddenly glimpsed a light near the horizon. She stumbled up to her knees and leaned out of the door to make sure she wasn't hallucinating. Joel sat up too, reacting to her sudden movement. If she was getting truly hypothermic, she knew she'd likely be hallucinating soon, but no, this was not imagined. The light suddenly shot up, in the way only a helicopter can do, and then came a distant but brief sound of the throb of helicopter rotors on a blast of wind.

It was the best goddamn sound she had ever heard in her life.

Em and Joel looked at each other, words not needed, as relief and joy flooded their faces. Rescue was so close, it looked like they were going to make it! They were going to be able to return to the land of the living, and Em would fall down on the earth and kiss it and never want to let go.

That spurred them into action. Em grabbed the flashlight, flicked it on and started shining it on the flapping tent canvas. Joel fumbled with the flares, but in his now hypothermic state he was having trouble. So Em just kept shining the light at the raft's canopy roof, praying someone on that chopper would see their tiny speck of light on the big, hungry sea. If the EPIRB had never turned on, or if it did cut free from the boat, it could be drifting in a completely different direction, confusing the search. Nor had their survival suits been fitted with a personal locator beacon, so the USCG might not yet spot them. Survival was close, but still not guaranteed.

After the light she had seen had shot back up in the sky, she heard the sound of the rotors grow closer, and closer, and then, goddamn, she looked out and the Coast Guard had their strong searchlight trained right on them. Em choked up, tears blending with the spray, and eyes blinded momentarily by the light and ears deafened by the roar of the rotors.

The red and white rescue helicopter lowered, a door slid open, and a rescue swimmer jumped out, making his way to them in less than five minutes. As he drew up to the raft, all she could see in the dark night and blowing spray was light blue eyes under some tight fitting goggles and a snorkel mask. As his wetsuit-clad frame filled the raft's small door opening, Em wanted to kiss and hug him, but could only manage a yes nod of her head when he asked if she was okay.

Soon a basket lowered, and the swimmer helped Em in. She was swinging in the air, wind whipping everywhere, then multiple hands pulled her into the helo, attended to her, wrapped her in blankets, checked her vitals. She completely succumbed to them, nodded to yes and no questions, and tried to breathe. Joel was next, then once the rescue swimmer made it back and the door closed, they rose and took off to Kodiak. The chopper rocked in the gusts of winds, but after forty minutes, they landed on the very ground Em had wondered if she'd ever set foot on again.

She didn't get a chance to lie down and kiss that sweet earth though, as hypothermia was now fully setting in. Upon landing, the rotor blades still whipping, two guys from the helicopter jumped out and helped Em and Joel to an EMS chopper waiting on the landing pad, to take them to the Providence Hospital in Anchorage, where a better facility could take care of them and treat them for hypothermia and shock.

"Don't separate me from Joel!" Em remembered shouting as they were whisked into the busy ER when the chopper landed in Anchorage. Like an anchor line disappearing beneath the surface, he was her only connection to what had just happened, and the thought of being separated from him, alone in a giant hospital, seemed terrifying. She'd just gone through losing him at sea one time and couldn't stomach it happening again. To her luck, they kept them in the same alcove, separated only by a dividing hospital curtain. She could call over to him whenever she needed as the nurses and doctor rushed to warm them back up. And he, the same to her.

By now it was well into the early hours of the morning. The initial prodding and poking had come and gone, replaced with the steady beeping of heart rate monitors and hospital machinery, when Em finally collapsed into sleep.

Chapter 21

Spaghetti on the Stove

Sunday, April 14, 2013

"*SEA RANGER,* ANYONE there? Please pick up!" Todd waited, hoping an answer would come forth, but it never did. *Well, maybe they're just out securing the deck, or whoever was on watch ran down to do an engine room check,* he tried to assure himself, but it didn't sit well. Deep down in his bones, something felt wrong. But Todd knew he had a tendency to worry about things that never came to fruition, so he hung up the mic from the track phone and tried to shake off the feeling. With a glance at the clock, he knew he should be heading up to Aunt Tammy's to help with dinner.

By the time he arrived, he was soaked and frozen, the prayer flags on David and Tammy's porch fluttering like the Tibetan prayer flags on top of Everest. It was a good ten to fifteen-minute walk from the harbor up to their house. His uncle had scored a home in town with a view of the water and the Woody Island Channel. The warmth and coziness of the well-loved house enveloped him like a big hug as he pulled off his Xtratufs. Wood stove heat was like no other. Gunnar immediately came running up to him and hugged his legs.

"Hey, Mamma! Unckie Todd is here!" he shouted with glee.

Tammy came around the corner and gave Todd a big hug. "Good to see you!"

"You, too. I just stopped by the hospital a little bit ago and David was deep asleep, so I didn't wake him."

"Ah, okay, thanks. I think I'll still go up, though. He hasn't been napping for more than an hour or so at a time. I started the spaghetti, and everything for dinner should be ready and laid out for you." She turned to lead him toward the kitchen, but sensing something was wrong, paused. "Hey, everything okay?"

"Oh yeah, I'm fine." Not wanting to reveal his true worry he said, "Just was hoping to check in with the *Sea Ranger,* before I headed up here, but no one answered."

"I'm sure they're fine. They're probably just busy." Tammy tried to assuage his apparent underlying worries with her soothing voice and a kind look as well. They headed to the kitchen with its big windows overlooking the inlet, but no view tonight—just pounding rain on the windows and gusts of wind that were visibly shuddering the glass panes. After Tammy got Todd lined up for dinner, she bundled up, kissed Gunnar goodbye, and headed out the door. Oscar was down for a nap, and Gunnar retreated to playing with toys in the living room. As Todd chopped an onion, he caught a distant sound over the low thrum of the Black Keys playing in the background. It came from the south, getting a little louder. Todd put the knife down and walked over to the corner of the kitchen where the stereo was and turned it down. Yup, the sound was definitely there, reminiscent of a plane or helicopter. *Coming from the south,* he pondered. His brow furrowed. *No way in hell a civilian flight would be going out in this storm.* Queasiness replaced the hunger in his stomach. To the south lay the US Coast Guard Station.

Pretty much every skipper on the island kept a VHF radio in their household. It was handy to talk to those already out on the sea, or get reports on fishing or the weather, or listen to what the heck was going on out there. Todd knew David had to have one somewhere . . . *Where would David keep it?* It'd help if the antenna had a direct line of sight to the water, but the unit inside could be anywhere. Todd knew David had an office in the back corner of the living room and he figured that would be a good place to start his search. He turned off the stove momentarily and strode out to the living room, dodging Lego blocks and toy dinosaurs as he went, the plush Oriental rug hugging his feet.

One glance around at the desk with its computer, stacks of papers, receipts, and fish log books, and Todd spotted the VHF unit. He flicked it on and turned it from channel sixty-eight, where most of the guys chatted about nonessential stuff, to channel sixteen, used only for emergency or important notifications and comms with the USCG.

It was silent for a few, but then the radio crackled, "Pan-Pan, Pan-Pan, Pan-Pan. Attention all mariners near 56° 36' N, 153° 54' W. We have received a Mayday call from this location. If you are in this vicinity, contact USCG on channel sixteen." A Pan-Pan was a notice to all mariners about something to watch out for, like a deadhead or drifting vessel, or Mayday call relay.

Oh my god, which boat is it? He yanked the chair out and woke the computer, opening Google maps. He typed in the coordinates and saw it was near Sitkinak Strait, an entrance toward safer waters.

He heard the USCG call out the Pan-Pan notice again.

Todd wondered if the USCG had switched with anyone to their working channel, usually twenty-one, so he flipped up a few and caught the tail end of a discussion, "Roger that, we're heading there now."

"Copy that. What is your estimated time of arrival?"

A discernible pause, they were probably calculating the timing, then

"We estimate to arrive on scene at 20:30." Todd saw the clock on the computer read 17:53. That was a dang long ways away, especially when people were potentially in the water.

WHAT BOAT IS IT?!?! He needed to know! Even if it wasn't the *Sea Ranger,* it was one he probably knew.

"Received, *St. Andrew.* Please contact USCG once you approach from two nautical miles away." Yup, Todd definitely knew that boat and crew.

"Yes sir," came the reply. "*St. Andrew,* en route and standing by on channel sixteen and twenty-one."

In the break after that communication, another call came in. "USCG Station Kodiak, this is the *Viking.*" Todd knew them, too, another large crabbing vessel. "We are approximately seven nautical miles from the *Sea Ranger's* last known position."

Todd's world stopped and dropped when he heard the *Sea Ranger's* name over the radio, loud and clear, no denying it. There was a buzzing in his ears, all other noise fading away. He stared at the radio. Nothing else the *Viking* said registered with him. *Oh my god, what the fuck? What happened? This can't be real!* He didn't know how long he sat there stunned. Slowly the sounds of Gunnar playing, the rain on the windows, and crackle of the wood stove came back.

His pulse was beating through his ears. With shaky hands, he fumbled for his cell phone. Thank god Tammy was on speed dial, as he didn't know if he'd be able to manual dial in the state of shock he was in.

It rang twice. He hadn't planned out what he'd say, so he just blurted it out as soon as she picked up.

"Tammy! The *Sea Ranger* put out a Mayday call! I don't know what to do!"

Chapter 22

Hospital Gowns

Monday, April 15, 2013

IT WAS THE smell that drifted into her senses first, of sterility, commercially laundered sheets, and the overall distinct odor of hospital, a smell that made Em cringe. *Where am I? And why, oh god, does it smell like a hospital?* She cracked her eyes open, and, to her disappointment, confirmed it was indeed a very hospital-like environment she was in. *Well, this isn't good.* The beeping and humming of monitors in the alcove she was sharing with Joel confirmed it. As the nurse messing with her IV bag noticed Em stir, the events of the last twenty-four hours came flooding back to her like bombshell bursts from a battlefield.

"Hello, how are you feeling?" asked the nurse, as he moved toward her bed to converse more directly with her.

"Uhnnnn," was all she could manage, as the reality of the situation kept hitting her like the waves that had been bashing her just hours ago.

The boat sank. Manni. Sam. Phil. They didn't make it out. It's gone, they're gone.
No undoing, no way to change it, the only thing to do was to accept it
like a brick falling from the sky. It was going to fall where it was going to
fall. And it was going to hurt.

With her awake, the nurse took her vitals again, poked and prodded a
bit, then said, "Your vitals all look good. The doctor should be here
soon." He then turned and hurried off into the corridor. It looked like
she was in the emergency room still, as lots of hustle and bustle filtered
in, and the space didn't have any actual doors. She was also in a pile of
blankets and some sort of warming device.

Left to her own devices now, Em continued to process and relive the
previous day, and started to feel a frenzied panic build from her stomach
and work its way upward.

"Joel?" she called, urgently. No answer. "JOEL?" with more trepidation. There was still a curtain dividing the small space, but she couldn't
tell if anyone was on the other side of the curtain.

Just as she was debating crawling out of bed to check, the doctor
came in.

"Good afternoon." She flipped through the charts and said, "Good
news! Your vitals have stabilized, and your core is now at a normal temperature. You're no longer hypothermic."

Em was feeling more with it and more panicky, enough to manage
talk now and demand some answers, "What is going on? Where is Joel?"

This doctor must've been fresh on shift. She looked confused. Usually patients didn't know each other. She didn't even seem to know much
more than that Em had come in and had been treated for hypothermia.

"He was over there last night. Can you please check. I was on a goddamn boat with him that sank! I NEED TO KNOW WHERE HE IS!"

The rise in Em's emotions was enough for the doctor to walk over
and slide the curtain, allowing Em a glimpse of Joel, deep asleep, monitors beeping.

Feeling a little calmer, but not all the way, she pleaded next, "Hey, I need a phone, I just lost everything. My clothes were cut to shreds and I just survived a boat sinking. I need to call my family."

"We can get you a phone. You have stabilized, but we do want to keep you at least another twelve hours or more to monitor and get you rehydrated."

"Okay, I don't care, I just need a phone . . . NOW."

⚓ ⚓ ⚓

NEVER HAD SHE been more grateful for having at least a few phone numbers memorized in this day of cell phones where it's rarely needed anymore. The nurse came back a half hour or so later with what looked like a loaner cell phone the hospital kept for such situations.

It rang four times before her mom picked up. "Hello?" she asked tentatively, confused by the strange caller ID.

"Mom!!!" It's me, Em!" She didn't expect it, but tears started pouring out from her eyes like she was pouring out some of the sea she'd just swallowed in her ordeal. Then big sobs followed.

"Sweetie, what on earth is the matter?"

Em was sobbing so much, she couldn't get anything out, but her mom kept trying to reassure and calm her. Finally, she managed, "The boat . . ." then some more bawling, and then, "it sank."

After she finally got the story out, her mom, Kathy, a registered nurse practitioner, tried to reassure Em she'd be alright, and that she was getting on a plane as soon as she hung up.

"But mom, I don't have anything here, I got lifted in with nothing but the sweats I'd been wearing and I don't even know where those are now! I need to know some phone numbers. Can you call Tony's Bar and get Jess' number? I've gotta let her know what's going on, and that way she can let everyone else know what's happened."

Next she called her dad, Bruce. He'd always been the yang to her mom's yin, maybe so much so it was part of why they divorced when she was four, just too different to reconcile it all. After the divorce, he moved to Montana and never looked back. He was logical and rational, but with a hidden sensitive side, while her mom was the nurturing, emotion-driven type.

Her next call was a little easier as she'd calmed down a bit by then. Her dad also said he'd be there on the next plane he could get on. She didn't have any other siblings, and she knew her parents would fill in the rest of the extended family.

As she was hanging up with her dad, she heard a rustling of sheets and blankets from behind the thin curtain. Em pondered whether she could get up. After a quick assessment she saw that there was only an IV in her arm, probably just rehydrating her, and a few vital sign monitors hooked up to the same stand. So she slowly sat up fully, swung her legs over, grabbed the IV stand, which was on wheels, and padded over to Joel's bed in nothing but a hospital gown.

His eyes fluttered open and she could see him going through a process similar to what she had just been through, of confusion followed by realization—realization of all the terror that had just happened and that it was real.

"Joel, I'm here," she said as she pulled up the bedside chair, trying to calm his widening and terror-stricken eyes.

He sat up a bit in the startle of his realization. Em reached a hand out and took his, looking him in the eyes. She felt tears, yet again, spill down her cheeks.

"Em . . ." he said. The few lines on his face prior to yesterday now looked deepened and hardened. There was a weariness in his face like she'd never seen before, as if his life had just fast-forwarded ten years.

Chapter 23

Mess Hall Matters

Sunday-Monday, April 14-15, 2013

TODD HUNG UP the phone with Tammy. The VHF Coast Guard talk was still going on in the background, and as she had suggested he do, he began searching the Internet for the USCG Public Information Line number for the Kodiak Station. Tammy filled in David on what had happened and rushed back to the house. After five minutes of frustrating and frantic searching on a typically frustrating government-created webpage, he finally found a possible phone number for the Kodiak Station.

After multiple tries, he broke through to a real human, who answered in a monotone, "US Coast Guard Seventeenth District, Station Kodiak, how many I help you?"

Todd tried not to let his voice crack with emotion.

"Hello, I heard the Mayday call from the fishing vessel *Sea Ranger*. That's the boat I work on. I've gotta know what's happening! My skipper and best friends are on that boat!!! *I* was supposed to be on that boat!"

After further discussion, the Coastie explained that if Todd wanted, he could come down to the base and explain who he was at the guard station, and they'd have someone meet him to usher him in. If he really wanted to, only because he was a crew member from the vessel, they'd have a place where he could hang out and wait for news and get the most current updates.

When Tammy burst into the house with a blast of cold and damp shrouding her, Gunnar ran over, a bit scared, and started crying, as even though he'd stayed quietly playing with his Legos the last fifteen minutes, he had perceived that something was very, terribly wrong. Tammy called a babysitter who lived a few houses down, and in thirty minutes she was driving Todd the ten minutes to the base in her beat-up GMC Suburban.

Though he'd never been on the base, he knew it was one of the biggest and most famous US Coast Guard bases, largely due to its location and response area covering some of the deadliest waters in North America. They rolled up to the guard shack and the attendant slipped open the booth's window a crack to hear what they had to say.

After their explanation of the situation, the guard, clad in the classic blue Coastie uniform, said, "Just a second," slid the plexiglass closed, and picked up a phone, glancing at Tammy and Todd in the rumbling GMC. When he hung up, the guard cracked the window again and said, "Pull over just behind the guard station, and someone will come out to walk you in."

The car rocked in the wind. The base was more exposed than in town, the shadow of Barometer Mountain looming behind them. Eventually someone came out and led them to a parking lot at a large building nearby, just to the north of the guard shack and entrance. They followed him inside. In the fluorescent lighting Todd could tell he was young, probably a few years younger than Todd, in his early twenties. It was just after dinner, and all the offices had doors closed and lights were out.

As they walked down the hall the Coastie explained, "We don't know anything besides the original Mayday call, and then they went silent. We have an MH60 Jayhawk rescue helicopter on the way." He paused and then continued to explain more, "And we have diverted the Coast Guard Cutter *Mellon* from its route near Sand Point. However, it will take up to fifteen hours for it to reach the site of the last known position. In addition, a C-130 has been dispatched from Elmendorf-Richardson base in Anchorage."

"How the fuck will an airplane be of any use in a storm like this?" asked Todd before he knew what he was saying.

"We often dispatch one for a search like this to act as a communications base and aid in any search grids," the Coastie explained.

They walked down a long hall and came to a large mess hall, with a serving area attached to a galley on the right side and then some rows of cafeteria style benches. Being just almost seven o'clock on a Sunday night, it was empty. The Coastie (Todd noticed his name tag read "Blakely") stopped by the serving area. There was a large coffee machine with a hot water tab, some tea bags and paper cups, cream, and sugar available twenty-four seven.

"Feel free to make yourself some tea or coffee. There's a TV you can turn on over there," he said, pointing to a corner with a big flat screen circled by a few comfortable chairs, and then pointing to where the remote was kept. "Bathrooms are just down that hall. We don't have any new information for you now, but I'm working the night shift, so I'll make sure you get notice of any developments. You'll be the first to know."

"Thank you," Todd said at first fast, and then repeated it again, slower, to emphasize his true gratitude for at least feeling he was closer to knowing what was going on.

With that Lieutenant Blakely turned, and the click of his black lace up boots faded away down the linoleum hallway. Now alone except for a security camera on the wall, Aunt Tammy and Todd looked at each other, and as the reality of it set in, Todd's face dropped. Tammy leaned in and gave him a hug. Her motherly instincts were just what he needed right now and he let out wrenching sobs. Once he'd quieted, she thought a distraction would be good for him, so put a warm cup of tea in his hand and walked him over to the TV where they flicked through the channels until she found the evening news to serve as distracting background noise, she hoped. Word of the unfolding tragedy hadn't yet spread out past those with VHF radios, so there was no mention of the *Sea Ranger* and unfolding rescue attempts on the news.

"Todd," Tammy asked after a few moments. "Do you know the numbers of any of the guys' families?"

Todd thought for a few, then said, "Hmmm, no I don't. I only had their own personal cell numbers."

The crew came from all different towns. Phil was from Petersburg, Manni from Anchorage, Sam from Gig Harbor near Tacoma, Joel from Kenai, and Em from . . . Kodiak? At least for now she was, as he realized he didn't actually know what exact town she was from in Virginia.

Todd mentioned that Em's roommate Jess worked at Tony's Bar, though. *This is so not cool, being the messenger of uncertain and bad news,* he thought with dread. But it'd have to wait since when Tammy gave the bar a ring, no one picked up.

Time dragged on, minute by minute, slow and sluggish, and still no word or updates. The anxiety building in his body, from nausea, sweaty palms, to tight and heavy chest, grew to a debilitating level. He remembered it had been about five forty-five when he first heard the chopper take off and he had turned on the VHF. There was an old school clock on the wall to the left of the big screen TV. Now the clock read eight forty p.m.

"Hey Shrimp," Tammy said, calling him Uncle David's nickname, "I'm going to have to take off here, the babysitter can only stay until nine. She has school tomorrow."

After they hugged again and talked about next plans (she'd come back as soon as she could in the morning, and he was to call her as soon as he learned anything, no matter what time it was), he couldn't stand to sit anymore, and started pacing. One or two Coasties came in and out, filling coffee cups and giving him sad nods, as they knew what it meant when there was a civilian in their mess hall.

Then around nine forty-five, he heard boots in the hallway again, and Lieutenant Blakely returned with another Coastie, Chief Petty Officer Christianson. As they walked past the coffee area and up to him, he knew it wasn't just a caffeine break they were on, and he felt nausea build in his stomach.

"So, Todd, we have some news," said the elder officer. He must've been around for a while, as he had a few gray hairs mixed into his short cropped hair, and he wore wire-rimmed glasses.

"Okay," he said, mentally and physically bracing himself.

"The Jayhawk arrived at the *Sea Ranger's* last known position and started a search grid. They have not found any sign of the vessel, but they did find a survival raft."

Todd let out a deep breath, bracing himself.

"There was a light shining from it, so they dropped a rescue swimmer and retrieved two survivors."

"Oh, my god." He was waiting for names . . . *Which two? What about the others? Are they still out there?*

"They're en route to the base right now. Both are in a hypothermic state, so we'll be transferring them directly to Anchorage."

"WHO?!?" he finally blurted. "Who is it?! Where are the others??? Tell me!"

"We don't know which two at this point. The C130 is going back to continue the search pattern. There were two fishing vessels nearby, but they had to desist in search efforts until the weather gets better. It was getting too risky for them to continue searching in those seas."

"Okay, thank you," Todd said, digesting this news.

As they were turning to leave, Todd called out, "Wait! Can I see them when they come in? Can I go with them to Anchorage?"

Lieutenant Blakely replied, "Unfortunately that is not possible. We should have their ID's, though, from the air crewmen when they return."

After they left, Todd felt a crescendo of nervous energy wash over his body. He felt like he needed to run, and run as hard and fast and as long as he could until he'd collapse into exhaustion, to get it all out. But he couldn't. All he could do was pace and wait, pace and wait, look at the clock, glance at the TV, check his phone. About twenty long minutes later he heard a chopper. Not able to help himself, he rushed out of the mess hall to the front doors of the building just in time to see it land, but of course he couldn't see it once it went behind the hangar.

He figured Blakely would be back any minute to update or scold him for leaving the waiting area, but then it turned into over a half hour since the chopper landed. Todd felt like his nerves were starting to come out of his skin, when *finally*, he heard footsteps again, and it was Blakely and Christenson.

"Who was it?!" he cried, rushing to meet them at the hall entrance.

"Now, we haven't made any contact with their families yet—" started Officer Christenson.

"Just fucking tell me!" Todd pleaded with desperation in his voice.

"It's Joel Arneson and Emily Bancroft that were rescued," broke in Blakely, getting a scolding look from Officer Christenson for jumping in.

He was filled with joy and fear at the exact same time.

"The plane is still out searching, they think they may have found an oil slick and some debris, but still no sign of the EPIRB or boat or other survivors."

Blakely added, "You can stay here all night if you want, but if you decide to leave, just make sure to check out with the guard. You can also call that Public Information Line and ask for one of us, and we can update you that way. We've got your name and contact information, and we may contact you later with questions."

Todd sensed how erratic his breathing had become. *'Em and Joel are alive!'* And there was still some small hope for the other three. One could last a few hours at least in a survival suit in Alaskan waters.

Todd decided to stay, so he turned back to his phone to update Tammy.

Eventually, around three a.m., he passed out in one of the TV chairs. When he woke, it was to Aunt Tammy gently tapping him. "Todd," she whispered.

Even with the gentle wakeup, he was still startled, and it took him a few seconds to place where he was and why. Then his heart fell when he realized he was back in the Coast Guard station mess hall and that this was all really happening and not just some horrendous nightmare that he could wake up from.

"What time is it?"

"It's six. I figured we should get you home for some rest. Plus, I'm guessing breakfast here may start up soon, and you might prefer to be elsewhere." He could indeed hear pots and pans clanging around in the galley.

"Okay."

"I just called the information line and nothing new, still the only sign of anything is an oil slick and some random debris."

Hearing that, his head and shoulders dropped in despair and tears filled his eyes. That was probably it then, for Phil, Sam, and Manni. Hope for their survival was thinner than a sliver of the moon against the vast night sky. Tammy rushed in to hug and comfort him and let him cry on her shoulder for a good while, long enough to dampen a patch of her sweater's shoulder where he'd laid his head.

"Come on, Shrimp, let's get you home. I've got some warm oatmeal made on the stove for you."

He tried to hold back his tears all the way home and walked into their house like a zombie. Gunnar had donated his bed, happy to sleep in a makeshift "fort" Tammy had allowed him to make in the living room. Todd crashed into Gunnar's tiny bed and its dinosaur sheets, clothes still on, mind numb from the pain and wishing that this wasn't what was really happening. But it was. So he sobbed himself to sleep and didn't stir for five hours.

Chapter 24

Sink and Settle

Monday-Tuesday, April 15-16, 2013

TWELVE OR SO hours since the transfer to the ER, Joel and Em were cleared, but sent to private rooms on the same floor for further monitoring until they got their full strength back. Both Em's parents arrived by late Monday night, while Joel's girlfriend and family drove up from Kenai, only a three-hour drive away.

Her parents smothered her with love and care, helping to distract her from realizing that even though the USCG was still searching, chances of survival for the other three after twenty-four hours were basically nonexistent. At moments Em felt okay, grateful to be alive and smiling at her mom, her dad making a goofy joke. Then she'd have a flashback to the nightmare of the memories, feel the grief and guilt rise in her chest, and tears would be at her eyes before she could hide it. It all washed over her as big as the waves had during that dark night—small crests, then huge deep drops.

Another helpful thing about having her parents there was that while they were divorced and could tolerate each other, they generally tried to avoid each other, so they took turns individually lavishing her with distraction and support while the other would go out and do errands. As she'd showed up at the hospital in nothing but some wet and cut-up sweats and polypro, Kathy helped with getting her a few changes of new clothes, and Bruce helped her get a new phone, worked with the phone company to keep her original number and contacts, and figured out where to start in getting her IDs and credit cards replaced as her wallet and phone had gone down with the boat.

When she first powered up the new cell phone and got logged in, it started lighting up. The dings and beeps of messages and texts seemed to go on for more than a few minutes. Her mom had been standing at the window, bathed in the dim midday light of April in Alaska, staring out over the woods and up into the foothills of Anchorage, wind-whipped and white.

The first few texts and messages were all from Todd. *Oh my god,* she thought to herself, *Todd's sitting there in Kodiak, no idea what's going on, and he was supposed to be on that boat.* By just a twist of fate, he wasn't. One could go through the whole "butterfly effect" and discover that fate started at the very first action at the beginning of time, maybe all the way back to the Big Bang or further. But, she wondered, how was it that Todd's uncle had been in the exact spot at the exact same time as another car? She let it sink in and settle. If he would have left a few seconds later, then David would've made it to wherever he was going with no incident, and Todd never would've stayed back from that trip. Then it might have been Todd who had drowned, and she wouldn't be in the hospital in Anchorage right now. *What might it feel like to be Todd, the one who was supposed to have been on the boat, but somehow wasn't?* She could almost glimpse the repercussions of the small twists of fate leading up to where she was now, and then spreading out into the future, like a crack on a windshield can spread and grow over time in unpredictable patterns. Goosebumps prickled her skin with the thought.

Kathy glanced at Em and sensed through maternal instinct that Em wanted privacy. "I'll go grab some snacks down at the cafe," she said. "Do you want anything in particular?"

"Naw, I don't care, just something with calories in it," was her reply. After being so cold for so long, she had felt ravenous the last few hours. Maybe her body was trying to make up for a calorie deficit of all the energy it had burned during that long trying time in the frigid seas.

With her mom gone, she pulled up Todd's name in her phone's address book and hit the call button.

It rang once, then half of another ring and he was there, "Em, my god, oh my god! I can't believe it. I don't even know what to say. Are you okay?" Worry and concern and sorrow filled his voice all at once.

"I'm okay, feeling better, just really hungry and feeling a little weak."

"And how's Joel?"

"Same, he's in a room nearby. His family is here with him."

"Any word on when they'll release you? I looked at getting a flight to Anchorage, but the storm messed all the flights up and the USCG wouldn't let me ride with you guys. I was on the base when they brought you in. Are you coming back?"

"Yes, I am . . . I think they'll let me go for sure by tomorrow morning. Any updates on the search?" It struck her hard that he had been on the base when they'd touched down at Kodiak, so close and so worried, and she hadn't even known it.

There was a pause from his end of the line. "No." He sounded defeated. "I think they'll be calling it off by tomorrow."

Since Monday at dawn when the wind had gradually eased, several vessels, including a few USCG boats and planes, had begun to make search and grid patterns over a vast portion of the sea, based on the last known position and estimates of drift with the currents and wind. All that searching had turned up nothing but a few pieces of debris.

"Em, please let me know when you'll be getting back to Kodiak. I'll be at the airport for you, I must see you."

"Of course, I'll let you know. Probably it'll be in a day at least. My parents aren't staying for long as they both have full time jobs and dropped everything to get up here from the Lower 48 so quickly, so they won't have time to come out to Kodiak, too."

"Okay, thank you." He paused, and then said, "Em, I love you."

Wow, I wasn't expecting that. But, oh my god, after their last day together in Kodiak and then her near death experience and realizing, at that point, that she might not get a chance to do anything ever again, she was more than grateful for his confession of love.

"Todd, for a while there, I didn't think I'd ever have a chance to see you again." After a pause, she added, "You know, we heard you trying to call us. It was right as everything was going to hell."

"You did?"

"Yes, I remember wishing I could grab the mic and cry to you for help, but no one could reach it. And it was right when the USCG was trying to contact us."

It brought her to tears to relive that fraught moment, and Todd was floored in the realization of what they had been going through at the exact moment when he'd tried to call. They talked a little bit longer, but she had a call come in while she was on the line with him, so excused herself earlier than she would have liked to. As she hung up, an image blasted into her head of Phil after he'd landed on the window, blood on the pane and his face, trying his best to stay stoic. Then an image of Manni as Joel handed him a suit and he just stood there holding it and his eyes wide with fear, then came the sounds of the boat groaning as the engines shut down, then the silence after it slipped away. The terror filled her chest, making it hard to breathe.

Chapter 25

Solid Ground

Wednesday, April 17, 2013

THE COAST GUARD called off the search on Wednesday, April 17th, at 11:39 a.m. The weather had calmed, and by Wednesday some blue skies were even poking through the cloud cover. The last day of searching had been in good conditions and allowed for intensive coverage. Nothing of import turned up, except about a quarter mile-long oil slick, all signs of the *Sea Ranger* and the life it held, gone into the depths of the sea.

That same day, around the same time, Em had a quiet and lovely goodbye with her parents and Joel and his family in Anchorage, and they all went their separate ways like leaves blown from a tree in the fall. Her parents drove her to the airport as they had arranged flights home shortly after hers, and before she knew it her plane was descending onto the rocky island of Kodiak.

Em was in no way prepared for what awaited her when she walked out of the Arrivals gate. The exit was crowded with friends and the fishing community, people with flowers and "Welcome Home, Em!" signs. Right in front center was Todd, his dark brown eyes something she could melt into within the sea of color and people. She strode right for him in his green wool sweater and solid frame, and he welcomed her with open arms. He smelled so good, like being home. She felt his strong arms wrap tightly around her, the muscles in his back flex as he held her, and she let tears seep onto his sweater. The chaos of the airport faded while they embraced.

But it didn't last as long as she'd like. She was jostled and prodded by friends vying for their hugs. Of course Jess was there, too, with a big, freckled smile, her hazel eyes moist. A reporter from the local paper tried to enter the mob but was quickly shooed out by the protective community. Thanks to Em's job at Tony's, she'd gotten to know quite a bit of the town, the who's who and who's doing what. And of course, fishermen being the tight-knit clan they were, especially in times of tragedy, always came out to support other fishermen. She saw Tammy and her kids, but of course no David, and her boss from the bar, and a bunch of the guys she knew from fishing, and many more of the folks she'd met during her time living in Kodiak.

After many teary hugs and kisses with the crowd, Todd took her hand and whispered in her ear, "You want to get out of here, just squeeze my hand," as he took hers in his. She immediately squeezed it.

It took another ten minutes to say goodbyes and make their way to the exit. Sun fell on her cheeks, and she had to squint to adjust to the rare bright day.

"Where do you want to go? I'll take you anywhere."

"First, take me to the park. I just want to do something there, then please take me home."

She climbed into Uncle David's spare work truck, a gray and blue 1980s vintage Ford F-250. The engine rumbled to life and Todd eased it into first gear, heading toward the park. The truck was messy, full of random fishing gear, receipts from the ship supply store, and empty coffee cups, but Em couldn't have cared less.

When Todd found a spot to park, Em got out and walked toward a big cottonwood tree, Todd following her lead, unsure of what Em needed. Even though there was still snow and ice on the ground, Em went up and gently hugged the tree, then lay down beneath it on her back, gazing through the branches. Todd was confused about what he should do, but she motioned him to lie down next to her. She was silent for a good long while, her eyes moist but staring up through the bare branches gently rocking in the breeze to the sky beyond. A lone bald eagle soared on the thermals high above them.

They were silent for a while, then Em took a deep breath and began, "Todd, you know when I was out there, waiting for what seemed like forever for an uncertain rescue, I had time for lots of thoughts besides survival." He nodded to show he was listening. "One of the biggest things I wanted to do if I ever got a chance again, more than anything else, was to just lie on the earth and be."

He didn't say anything, how could he? So he let her take her time.

"I can't believe I'm here. I mean, how did I make it, Todd? I'm so grateful for this, I really didn't think I'd ever set foot on land again." He moved closer and put his arm under her neck and around her far shoulder. "Todd, nothing will ever be the same, though," sadness crossing over her face. "Why did I make it out?"

"Em, that doesn't matter. We can never know why, and we can't undo it. But you did make it out, and I'm here for you now."

She turned over toward him, looking him in the eyes, just inches from him now. He reached out to caress her cheek.

"How do I live with this . . . with what happened? The fact that I survived and the others did not?"

"I don't know," he said, "How do I? I mean if it hadn't been for me, you'd have never been on that boat. I feel so bad about that, Emily. Words can't really describe it."

She looked up into him, her lip quivered, and they both started crying. He hadn't known he could hold so many tears inside of him.

"Todd, it was so horrible. I can't keep the images away. It's like they're chasing me. I can't make it right again, ever, and I don't know how to escape it!"

He held her tight and let a wave of anguish wash over her. Slowly she calmed. The ground, being frozen, was starting to zap the warmth out of him.

"Come on, Em, let's go get you warmed up."

TODD KEPT HIS arm around her thin frame as he helped her up the apartment stairs. He had watched her gazing out the truck's windows as they drove through town, her mind in another world, seeing everything differently now. There was no going back to the same Em as she had been before.

Jess had beat them back, and when she heard them on the stairs, came to open the door. The smell of fresh baked muffins wafted out, and the apartment was decorated with balloons and a Welcome Home sign. Jess helped Em down onto the couch, getting her a cup of tea, warm muffin, and blanket, along with the same for Todd, too.

After a day or two since the shock of the situation had settled in, Todd had sprung into action in communicating with the families of Phil, Manni and Sam. He also ended up talking with Jess a lot, as she had naturally become the de facto point person for the Kodiak community to pass information along as they heard search reports back from the US Coast Guard. Jess was one of the few who had come down to the station once she first heard the news. Phil's wife, Carmen, had also been there at the station after she'd taken the first flight she could out of Petersburg. So over the last three days, Todd had gotten to know Jess in a unique way, due to a circumstance he wished had never happened.

They all sat in the small living room area, not really knowing what to say. There was no guidebook or training course written for situations like this. After the initial rush of coming back through the airport, and then their quiet time under the tree in the deserted park, Em was starting to feel a sense of numbness settle in.

"Say, Em, how are you feeling . . . really?" Jess asked, point blank. She and Em had a tight relationship and had become friends instantly when they'd first met at the local laundromat. They'd had a mutual *We could be friends* feeling.

"Jess, it sort of feels numb right now, like a weird, surreal dream. To be back in the apartment and sitting with you, I didn't think that'd ever happen again. And then I feel so grateful to be here and be alive and get this chance to live life all over again that I thought the door had closed upon. But now I'm getting these strong flashbacks to the boat, and what happened, and why was it me that made it out? What if I'd stayed below and helped them with their survival suits more, or, or . . . all the what-ifs?" Her voice cracked with emotion.

"Em, I know you, and I know you did everything you could." Jess hadn't heard the full story, nor was she sure if Em would ever want to relive it and tell her, but what else are you supposed to say?

They talked a little more, and they could see Em was looking exhausted. "What do you need right now?" Jess asked.

"I don't know, besides changing what happened. Maybe a hot bath, and then to crawl into bed," she said, glancing at Todd, indicating she wanted him there for that part of it.

"Alright, sweetie, I'll go draw you a bath," said Jess, grateful to feel helpful again. "You want the lavender bath salts?" Em managed a thankful nod, to indicate yes.

Enveloped by *warm* water this time and the silence and privacy of the bathroom, Em slipped into some of the memories again, flashes of terror hitting her like cards in a deck being shuffled in front of her. She wanted to cry and scream, but oddly no tears would flow. It was a suffocating feeling, wanting to cry and release but not being able to. It felt like too much for her to process, what had happened, and why she was still here, so after the water cooled a bit, she hit the plug and stayed in until it emptied, wishing she could release the feelings away as easily as the water had disappeared down the drain.

DRYING OFF, SHE looked at herself in the mirror. She had already been slender, her muscles well defined from the hard physical labor she usually made her living by, but now she looked gaunt, and there were deep lines on her face. Turning away from the mirror, Em wrapped herself in her light gray, fuzzy bathrobe and padded silently down the hall to her bedroom. Todd, hearing the bathroom door open, made his way to Em's bedroom door and stood silhouetted in the frame.

"Em, you want to lie down together?"

"Yes, please, Todd."

And with that, he stripped down to his briefs and she slid out of her bathrobe, and they crawled in under her covers. He spooned her, let her curl into the folds of his body. She smelled fresh, of lavender and soap from the bath, and he kissed her neck. This was not a time to make love, but a time to love.

Todd whispered, "I can't believe I'm holding you again, Em. For a while there, I thought I'd lost you forever."

"Please don't let go of me, Todd."

"I won't, I promise."

Chapter 26

Reminders

Saturday-Sunday, April 20-21, 2013

IN THE FOLLOWING days, with it being clear that the *Sea Ranger* and its remaining three souls were now lost forever at sea, their names to join the fishing memorials in permanent engravings, celebration of life service events started to unfold.

The first gathering was held in Kodiak. Even though the boat didn't hail from there (its home port was Seattle), it was a well-known vessel of Kodiak. Phil had many skipper friends from the island, and Em from Kodiak was a survivor. So a gathering was planned at Tony's Bar the Saturday evening of April 20th, almost a week since the fateful night, planned mostly by Phil's wife Carmen and Jess.

In the dim lighting, the bar was packed. Even a few off-duty Coasties in civilian clothes had stopped by, ones who had been involved in some way in the search and rescue. You could identify them by the way they carried themselves. The rescue crew members usually oozed confidence, a requirement of the job of plunging oneself into deadly seas in the grip of Alaskan winters on a regular basis. Along the wall a table was set up with photos of the three—Phil, Sam and Manni—and cards laid out to write remembrances of them.

About a half hour after the event officially began, Em and Todd entered arm in arm, but were subsequently separated by the crowd. Different people wanted to talk to them, trying to offer condolences and none really knowing the right words to say. Em appreciated that they were trying, but unfortunately there were no magic words to make it better. Beer and drinks were flying around the room like birds at a migration stop, and within minutes upon arriving, Em had a drink in hand.

She had always been a sensitive child, prone to strong feelings and emotions, coupled with bouts of depression, but as she grew she had found remedies and had been doing fairly well, handling her strong emotions and the ups and downs of life with a learned grace. The two key tools she'd discovered to help fight her predilection to slip into depression had been hard work and adventure, as they forced her out into the world, and the hard work was a good release for her intense emotions. Thus, the fishing profession was a perfect match for her. Yet now, ever since the horrific night, the emotions had come up from depths where she'd checked them years ago, oozing out like waste from a clogged sewer drain, making it hard for her to focus, find her purpose. It was the very beginning of the old vicious cycle, reaching out its claws to grab and pull her in.

So, she gladly took the first drink, hoping it might help her get through the night or ease social awkwardness. By the time Jess gave a toast to the Coast Guard, the room was starting to spin a bit, and Em knew she should stop, but fuck, just over there across the room, were the pictures of Phil, Sam, and Manni staring back at her. It was as if every time she looked over, she could hear Manni's screams, "We're gonna die!" And she could feel Phil's stoicism and Sam's concern for the others like she was right there with them again.

As she was turning her back to the table, she saw Todd out of the corner of her eye talking to three fishermen from the *St. Andrew*. She glanced back to the pictures of the guys, then to Todd, standing there living and breathing, then back at the pictures. The narrow line between life and death jarred her. She turned so she couldn't see him or the pictures, it was just too much at that moment, too much of a reminder that it could've been either one of them this memorial was for, and maybe it could have been Sam standing there talking to the *St. Andrew* guys instead.

In between conversations, she saw one of the presumed Coasties make eye contact with her, and he stepped a little closer. Em looked at him for a second, having to gaze up, as he stood a good foot and a half taller than her. And then in a flash, she saw those same light blue eyes that had stared at her behind goggles and a snorkel mask. It felt like the whole room disappeared and all she could see was those eyes.

"Were, wer—" she stammered, unable to get the words out of her mouth.

"Yes, Ma'am," he said with a slight Southern drawl similar to hers. "That was me."

She took a breath and felt a flood of wooziness wash over her already tipsy state of mind. His face coming up out of the waves, the thud of the chopper blades, the biting wind and ice slicing into her face felt real again. She remembered his presence and his taking command, grabbing her and getting her into the basket with ease, ordering them to hoist her up and away from the absolute nightmare.

She felt faint but steadied herself by leaning in to give him a long hug, as her breath had become increased and irregular with the anxiety of the flashback. She didn't even know his name, but he hugged her, patting her on the back, not knowing what else to do. Finally pulling away, she asked, "What's your name?"

"It's Chris," giving her just his first name, intentionally leaving out his formal titles, as this was an intimate moment. There are some rescues you just never forget, that stay with you your whole life, and he knew this would be one of them.

"Everything I want to say sounds cliché," she finally managed.

"It's okay, you really don't need to say anything. I know. I was there."

Then his buddies called him, asking him what he wanted to drink. Chris said, "Excuse me," and turned toward the bar after a pause to look deep into her eyes in an understanding and sorrowful way, one last time.

Jess moved in then, pushing a Rainier into Em's momentarily empty hand, then Phil's wife, Carmen, rang the bell (normally reserved for a round on whoever rang it). With her black curly hair, she looked like a just-barely-managing trainwreck. Em hadn't talked to her yet, didn't know if she could find the strength to look her in the eyes, knowing that she'd witnessed her husband's last living moments. The room quieted, and with that quiet, words of love, sorrow and loss poured forth from Carmen. She spent time remembering Sam and Manni, as over the years she had known all the crew and had heard countless stories of them from Phil. Then she ended with some more detailed and moving stories of her husband.

"And this round is on me," she ended. "Phil wouldn't have wanted it any other way,"

By now Em knew she should have stopped drinking a few drinks ago. She tried to shoulder her way to the bathroom, but there was a long line so she pushed out the back exit into the cold and full moon night. If it wasn't raining and windy, it would be cold and clear in a Kodiak winter. Tonight was a cold and clear one. The channel lay in the distance, inky dark water laced with slivers of silver and the orange glow of the harbor, boats safe and sound and floating.

Em was a good ten-minute walk from her apartment. She felt bile rising in her throat, knowing very well what was soon to come. She rested her back against the building, wondering what to do—the dumpster looked like a convenient place to puke into—when the back door opened and slammed, a wave of voices escaping out into the night air with it.

"Em!" It was Todd's voice. "I've been looking all over for you."

"I'm right here, Todd."

"Are you okay?"

"No, I'm not. Are you?"

"No, not at all."

"Todd, I need to get home, as soon as possible."

He was slurring his words a bit, too, "Hey, I saw Frankie's son, Max. He's sixteen, so he's sober, or at least he should be. He can drive us to your place. Let me go get him."

It took a few minutes, but Max arrived just in time to get her into the car, windows open just in case, and then into the apartment, where she collapsed by the toilet. Todd was too drunk to hold her hair back, as he also needed to find something to throw up into.

She woke, stiff, contorted, achy, with cold linoleum on her cheek. She felt like hell. What the fuck had she just done to herself . . . ? Then she remembered the service, the staring faces of those three men she'd watched die, now only looking on from photographs, and then she realized why she'd done that to herself and sunk herself into oblivion: because she wanted to forget, to make it go away, to wake up and find everything better. She'd go back out on deck and finish that set with Joel, Manni, Sam, and Phil. Then they'd come back ashore, and Todd would get back on the boat, and everyone would be happy like it was all supposed to happen. She felt nausea rise again and let more out. After she released all she had, basically water and stomach acid now, she crawled up onto her knees and dragged herself to her bedroom, making sure a garbage can was near her bed. Todd was already there, passed out. Being a deep sleeper, he didn't even twitch when she got in, the smell of alcohol heavy in the air.

🪢 🪢 🪢

THEY HAD SLEPT well past ten o'clock. When she slowly drifted back awake, she looked up at the ceiling and saw the faint outline of the glow-in-the-dark star stickers some kid had put up a long time ago. She looked out the window and could tell by the angle of the light that it was midmorning. Besides a strong headache, she at first felt okay, like she could handle the day. Then she looked at Todd, his living, beautiful body lying there next to hers, a stark reminder of the *Sea Ranger* and the three bodies that didn't survive, that were somewhere trapped under the sea, and she was not okay. The devil of memories took another whack at her, and flashbacks again began flooding her mind. She noticed the flashbacks had been increasing over the last day or two, maybe because the trauma had had more time to soak in and set its hooks in to torment her.

Finally coming back to the world, Todd woke to hear Em sobbing.

"What is it? Are you okay?" he asked as he rolled over to face her. He reached for her shoulder, and she flinched, shuddered away.

It took her a minute, but he waited.

"Todd, it's not you, it's just," she wiped away tears, "I just looked at you when I woke up, and all the bad memories came back. You reminded me of all of them and what happened."

That hurt him. He wanted to be a source of joy and steadiness to her, not pain. He didn't respond, but she didn't say anything more.

"Em, what do you need?"

Eventually an answer came out, and it was what he had been afraid to hear.

"I think I just need some space, at least for a little bit."

Taking a big swallow, he said, "Okay, I understand," but inside, his world was ripping apart. After the tragedy, he'd felt the need for her more than anything before. He attributed it to feeling like he'd lost everything with the boat and his friends going down, yet here Em was a survivor, someone to cling to and cherish, a link to the past *and* someone he'd already been in love with for years now. But apparently, she was feeling the opposite. *How messed up is this whole situation?* he thought.

It didn't help that his head was pounding and he felt like absolute shit. Her request for him to leave felt like salt rubbed in a wound. Em lay on her side in the fetal position, curled away from him, quietly sniffling.

After he found all his clothes, as he threw on his hoodie he said, "Em, I'll be down at the *Tammy Sue* or at their house."

She nodded to show she heard him.

"I love you, Em. Let me know if you need anything."

She nodded her head to show she understood. As he quietly closed the door, he reflected, *She hasn't returned my "I love you yet."*

Chapter 27

Mud or Stars?

Tuesday, April 23, 2013

IT WAS ONLY Tuesday, but just a day away, on Wednesday the 24th, there was also to be a memorial service in Petersburg, where Phil had grown up and raised a family of three now-adult daughters, and finally, a bigger memorial the following Saturday, April 27th, down in Seattle at the Fisherman's Terminal in Ballard, home to one of the biggest maritime memorials on the North Pacific Coast.

Sam was from the Gig Harbor area, so most of his family would be at the Fisherman's Terminal Service. All of Phil's immediate family were going to fly down for it, too. Even though Manni had lived in Anchorage for the last seven years, he originated from Seattle, so most of his family was also going to be at the Seattle service. Joel could only attend the Petersburg service.

Todd planned on being at both.

In between booking plane tickets and trying to acquire some of the things he'd lost on the boat, like a laptop and some clothes, Todd tried to be with Emily as much as she would allow him. Yet ever since that memorial night at Tony's, things had been strained. It was as if something had changed in her. It was hard to get her to smile or want to get up out of bed. Tony's Bar had told Em to take a few weeks off to recover and allow her time to go to the services, as Jess and a few of the other bartenders could cover her shifts and wanted to, especially if they knew it'd help Em out. Todd was also conscious of giving Em some space over the last day or two, not smothering her too much, but wanting so badly to be close to her. Yet it seemed to him that the emotions had fallen heavily upon her like a weighted blanket.

So in his time apart from her, he started assisting in some of the service plans and visiting Uncle David, who was still in the hospital but very close to being released to come home, and helping Aunt Tammy with the never-ending duties of toddler rearing. He was keeping steadily busy, which he knew he was using as a crutch to keep all the thoughts of worry, grief, and guilt at bay rather than deal with them.

Uncle David, skipper that he was, was usually a man of action, so being stuck in a hospital bed while all this was going on had driven him up the wall. But as usual he was a master at checking his emotions, noticing and then either shoving them into a box to deal with later or noticing them and letting them go. The thing keeping him going was realizing he was very close to being released and starting physical therapy, and he'd been making plans with Tammy so he could get around the house. They'd have to make a few modifications to the house to cope with the full-length cast that still needed another month or two and the partial one on his other leg, but they were resourceful, and David was confident they could figure it out. This was nothing compared to running a fishing boat.

When Todd came to visit that Tuesday mid-morning, just under a week after Em had returned, David could smell a hint of the sweetness of alcohol on Todd's breath. Todd pulled out a flask and offered it to David with a wink. Fishing and social life in a small town in Alaska often went hand in hand with drinking, but David was surprised, as he'd never seen Todd with a flask before, nor had he seen him drinking this early in the day. David, being a "tough" fisherman, took a quick sip before the nurses caught on, but he didn't want any more than that.

Todd's words slurred just slightly, "Hey Uncle David, how do you deal with it?"

"Deal with what?"

"Deal with what happened, when something happens you can't undo . . . like your accident, and Taylor dying from it. I mean it wasn't your fault, he hit *you*, but then *he* . . . died, and you know his parents and watched him grow up. He's never coming back."

David understood now what might be getting to Todd to drive him to the flask that morning. He thought for a moment. "Well, Shrimp," he swallowed and thought about what to say. "I don't spend a lot of time on it, honestly. I see that it happened and there's not a goddamn thing I can do about it, so I've been spending a lot of time in this here goddamn hospital bed thinking about what I *can* do when I get out of this goddamn hospital bed."

"Okay, but you see, well, I'm just, well . . ." he trailed off.

"You know the Serenity Prayer, right?"

"I think so . . ."

"You know, the one that goes, 'God grant me the serenity to accept the things I cannot change, the courage to change the things I can, and the wisdom to know the difference,' or something like that?"

"Oh yeah, I've heard it."

"Well, for whatever reason, you were not on that boat. You stayed back to help a family that needed it. Even if you would've been on the damn boat, you couldn't have saved it from sinking. You probably couldn't have saved any of them. You might have not been able to save yourself. Now for whatever reason, you are here, you are alive, and what can you do with that? What can you change and what can you not change?"

He paused. Todd was staring off at a point of space on the bed somewhere.

"You have two choices now, you can stare up and look at the stars and make something of the life you've been gifted, or you can look down at the mud and get lost in the what-ifs. It's up to you."

Todd took another sip and offered some to David, but he declined. He saw a tear on Todd's cheek which he quickly brushed away, trying to hide it.

"Now you've got people out there to take care of, to support all the family of Phil, Manni, and Sam at these services. We'll be fine up here. I'll be out of here very soon and can start to help out again. And I'm sure that sweet gal Em could use someone. That gives you purpose. Be strong for them."

"Yes, but I should've been there . . ."

"Stop it! You weren't, you weren't meant to be there. Maybe you've been given this chance to do something good with it. Put those other thoughts out of your head—*now.*"

Todd nodded, but didn't seem convinced. He seemed a bit despondent, and his eyes had a slight glaze from the whiskey.

"Hey, thanks, Uncle," he said, sitting up, getting ready to leave. "I've gotta go, I'm flying out for Petersburg tomorrow morning, then I will be down in Seattle and then back to Port Townsend. Don't know when I'll make it back up here."

"We'll see ya when we see ya. Love you, Todd. Take good care of yourself," said David, with concern in his voice.

Chapter 28

Whales and Wolf Tracks

Tuesday-Wednesday, April 23-24, 2013

IT WAS TUESDAY evening now, nine days after the Mayday call and the next morning Todd was going to hop on a plane for the Petersburg service. After his usual routine of helping Tammy with dinner and the kids, he stopped at the Chinese restaurant to pick up some takeout. He wasn't hungry, but thought it would be nice to bring something to Em. Now that some of the hubbub around the tragedy was starting to fade away, she seemed depressed and more despondent each day.

The Peking was dead on Tuesday nights, so Mimi had every opportunity to slather all her attention on Todd. Looking up from the cash register, she rushed over to the counter where his takeout was ready and headed toward him with it.

"Hello, my Todd! We have order ready for you! I see it's only for two.

You not need for whole family?" she asked with prying curiosity in her voice.

He was sure she'd heard Em and him were an item, and a curious one at that, considering the tragedy surrounding the *Sea Ranger*. Unfortunately, as this was his last night in town, he was in a rush to see Em, so he tried to keep it short, which was a tricky task with her.

"Oh yes, Mimi, it's just for two. And I'm a bit late already!" He didn't need to divulge. He knew she knew, even though she pretended she didn't.

"Ah, I see," she said and gave him a big wink, confirming his suspicions. He paid and thanked her, and as he turned for the door she rushed over to hold it open for him and still managed to get a peck on his cheek.

Bag of warm food in hand, he walked up the steps, not sure what sort of state Em would be in. She was on the couch, wrapped in a blanket. It looked like she'd been trying to read, but he noted some crumpled-up tissues nearby.

"Hey, babe," he said, trying to sound cheery, "How about we finish that tour, but this time I'll drive. I know a good spot to share some Chinese takeout and look out over the water."

The thought of looking at cold, black water made her shudder. But at that point, she felt too weak to argue, she just wanted to be near someone living. They grabbed some blankets to be cozy in the truck with and headed out. Some classic Rolling Stones played on the radio. The overlook that Todd drove them to was deserted, moon just coming up.

"So I'm flying out tomorrow," he said, putting the truck in Park.

"Yeah, I know."

"I'm really going to miss you."

"And I'll miss you, too," she said. Todd couldn't discern just how much, though, from her rather flat tone, a flatness which painted a lot of her words these last few days.

Looking out at the shimmering water, he remembered the night he saw the black seal. He wasn't sure if it'd help or make things worse to tell her about it, but it seemed important enough to him, so he decided to.

"I don't think I ever told you, but right when we started fishing this season, when we were off of Sand Point, I was on the back deck smoking a cigarette." He braced for her reaction to that . . . she gave him a questioning eye, "Hey, I only smoke when fishing. It helps get me through some of it. I seem to be able to have just one and be okay," he added. "Well, anyways, before I headed back in, I saw something strange in the crest of one of the waves. It was a black seal. It was definitely not their normal gray or mottled color." Maybe she didn't know the superstition, so he went on, "They say seeing a black seal is a sign of something bad to come. Shortly after that we hit a deadhead and had to limp into Sand Point, so I thought that's what the seal symbolized. But now, I think that maybe it was an omen of the boat sinking."

She thought it over for a minute, then said, "You know, I think a lot of those superstitions are crap, like obviously there's the one about women on boats being bad luck, and I hope to god that's not what people are thinking about my winding up on the boat."

"Oh my god, no! That's not it at all." He hadn't thought of that. Why on earth did he bring it up? He prayed that thought wasn't going to set her into a tailspin. But to his surprise, Em kept talking, more than she had in the last few days combined.

"I know, I've worked on plenty that didn't sink. But some of the old-timers may think so, especially now. Anyways, there are certain things I will never do, like talk about the weather while on a boat in fear of jinxing it. So, maybe the black seal did mean something. The world is pretty strange sometimes."

Recalling an old story of hers, she continued, "One time, I was tormented in making a decision between two very different jobs. One was land based, and the other was working out on the water on whale watching boats—how I got my foot in the door in the maritime world," she added. "Well, I was taking a walk along the beach pondering what decision to make, and said, 'Show me a sign!' to whatever higher powers there may be, not really expecting anything, when lo and behold, when I looked up a humpback whale surfaced once, and disappeared. It's incredibly rare to see a whale that far up in the bay, and I, for sure, took that as a sign. So of course I took the whale watching job instead of the land based one, which is eventually what led me to fishing and why I'm here in this truck with you now."

"Wow, that's crazy . . ."

"And it happened one other time. As a young girl I absolutely loved wolves and wanted to be a wolf biologist. I was up in Denali National Park, right near the entrance, but in the dead of winter. I had a short snowy path to walk between parking lots and the Visitor Center. I had just thought to myself, *I would really love to see a wolf in the wild someday,* and as soon as I had that thought, I looked up and there was a wolf about thirty feet in front of me, coming along the path. It looked at me eye to eye, like it was staring into my soul for what seemed like a half a minute or so, and then it took off, vanishing into the woods. It was so surreal I actually had to double check that there really were wolf tracks there in the snow."

It seemed like there was a narrow door open to getting her talking, so Todd prodded her with more questions. Discussing signs and life and twists of fate ensued. Were things fate, or just chance? He pulled the flask he'd had on him all day out of the glove compartment, offered her a sip, but she shook her head. He took a pull of whiskey, hoping to shake his nerves off. Feeling the evening slipping by, Todd braced himself for what he didn't feel ready for, but had to do.

In the next natural break in the conversation he turned to her and started with, "Emily, I know I live in Port Townsend, and you way up here, but I want to see you again. I am so in love with you, the thought of not being near you is driving me mad already."

"Todd, but how . . . ?" How could they make their lives work, he knew she was asking.

"Look, I don't know. We could figure out a way. Maybe we could just spend a few months together at least and see how it goes."

"I don't know . . . I can't just up and leave here, I worked hard to get to where I am."

"Well, I'm sure Tony's would always take you back if you wanted, and Port Townsend is a boat town. There are tons of marine-related trades down there, and fishing boats . . ." he added, but was unsure if she'd ever want to fish again. They hadn't talked about it yet.

She seemed to flinch at the thought of fishing. "Todd, I don't know if I ever could do that again after what happened. I just don't know yet."

"Well, that's okay. Anyways, my mom has a big property down there, like ten acres. And on one corner there's a cute little cabin. She's always said it's mine if I want it. You could come down and we could stay there. It's small but it's quiet, in the woods. Plus, we're used to small spaces, right?" He grinned, hinting at their time in bunks meant for one person. "My mom's only stipulation is that any guests must help in her garden and do some chores around the property . . . like feeding the goats," he added in hopes that sounded enticing to her.

"Todd, it's a lot to think about. I'm just trying to get through a day at a time right now."

"You know it's easier to find counselors and stuff down there, too, if that might help you."

"I don't know, Todd." She sounded a bit stressed.

"It's okay, there's no rush. I just wanted to throw it out there." He took a bigger, longer sip of whiskey, feeling a bit crushed. "Take your time and think about it." He gave her a few seconds, and she still didn't answer, so he tried instead, "Well, are you coming down to the Seattle memorial service?"

"Oh, I didn't get a ticket yet. I'm on the fence about it."

"Okay, no worries. I'll be at the Petersburg one and stay there for a few days. Then I should be in Seattle by Saturday morning, and the service is that night." He paused, then added, "It'd be really great to see you there."

In the following silence in the conversation, Todd could hear the classic rock station on the radio that'd been turned down play "Into the Mystic" by Van Morrison, a fitting song as they watched the moon reflecting up off the water. He turned it up a bit, and Em nestled her head onto his shoulder. But as soon as she closed her eyes she had a flashback to that last fishing day where they had music going on the deck speakers, connected to Sam's iPod. He had really good taste in music, and she clearly remembered a Van Morrison song playing, the guys all working, covered in fish blood and guts, each doing their tasks seamlessly, happy, and alive and thrumming—and then in just over twenty-four hours, three would be gone. She took in a sharp breath, feeling the nausea and ache come back.

"Todd, can you please take me home?" she said, her voice wavering, hinting at emotional pain she was trying to control.

"Yes, Em, I can, no problem. You okay? Did I say something? I wasn't trying to overwhelm you."

"No, it's not your fault, it's, well, I just had another strong flashback. I just need some time to myself."

He hung his head and let out an exhale, feeling defeated. He'd been dreaming of crawling back into bed with her. Instead it sounded like he might have to spend his last night alone in the bunk of an empty fishing boat. How lonely and depressing did that sound? He really needed to be with Em. He worried that without her near, the ghosts of his lost friends would creep in and take her place.

The drive back to her apartment was too short. As he pulled up to the curb and put the truck in Park he gave her a long kiss before she pulled back, gathered up her blankets, and opened the door. It was a moment he didn't want to end and knew he'd spend way more time remembering it than the actual time it had taken to elapse.

"Bye, Todd, thank you for everything, and thanks for the takeout, too."

"Hey, Em, come on, maybe I'll see you in Seattle in a few days."

"Okay, I'll try. Good night," then added, "Love you."

Wow! That was the first time he'd heard her say the "L" word to him.

"Love you, too," he quickly returned. She blew him a kiss dusted with sadness and turned to go up the stairs with her pile of blankets.

"HEY!" he called through the cracked window, "Please Em, let me come up, I just want to sleep near you."

It seemed she didn't have much resolve left, as she just said, "Sure," and shrugged. Maybe she was just too mentally tired.

Again, Todd curled into her bed, just holding her, feeling her struggle with some emotions, not saying anything but just being there with her. He still felt like he hadn't had time to process it all, either, as if he was on a whirlwind with all the services and people reaching out, but he was starting to get the feeling he, too, should brace himself for some strong emotions to hit once all the hubbub faded away.

He had an early flight, so in the morning after a restless night of sleep, tossing and turning but not wanting to wake Em, he kissed her neck gently and whispered, "I have to go now, I love you," but she did not stir.

Picking up his clothes, he saw a pair of her underwear on the floor. This time they were blue with lace trim, and for old time's sake, before he knew what he was doing, he reached down and swiped them. He knew he'd want something to remember her by in the tough days ahead without her.

Chapter 29

Needed

Wednesday, April 24, 2013

THE PETERSBURG MEMORIAL service had gone okay. It was again a blur as he'd taken a few too many drinks that had been offered to him. It was overwhelming how many people of Petersburg had come out, it being an even smaller town and tighter-knit fishing community than Kodiak. He remembered taking a break from the gathering and stepping out to try Em on his phone.

She picked up on the fourth ring, and he begged her one last time to come to Seattle. He was drunk and emotional.

"Em, I can't do this alone. I need you by my side," he'd pleaded unabashedly this time, and started crying. So far, he'd been pretty solid, but something was different now, he sounded like he was in despair. She finally consented, thinking how selfish she must be, being the one having such a hard time with it. Heck, those were *his* boys that he'd fished with for *years*. They were like his brothers, and she'd only known them a few days.

"Okay, Todd, I'll come down to Seattle for the memorial. I'll work on getting a ticket tomorrow."

Stifling a sniff, he said, "You promise?"

Wow, he must be feeling really vulnerable. "Yes, I do. I'm not sure how long I'll stay, though," she added, sensing he wouldn't want her to leave.

"I don't care, any length of time you can stay for is fine with me. I just really need you, Em. This is so goddamn fucking hard."

"I know, Todd, I know. I'll be there."

"Okay, just let me know when you get in. I'll come pick you up. Ethan said we could stay on his boat. It's right there at the Terminal."

Todd's head was spinning, both from this hopeful turn of events and the alcohol. Just then, some guys burst out of the doors at the Sons of Norway Hall where the memorial was being held, right across from Petersburg's Fishermen's Memorial Park, where three newly-etched names had been added that morning.

She heard some guys calling his name in the distance, and he said, "I should go Em, they're calling me back in."

"Okay, good luck. I'll let you know when I get my plane ticket."

Chapter 30

Bronze Names

Saturday-Sunday, April 27-28, 2013

SEATTLE WAS DRIZZLY and blustery when Em landed, but as it was April and a cold spring, the cherry blossoms were just at the end of their bloom. This time as Em exited the Arrivals gate, it was only Todd waiting for her, but she rushed into his arms just the same as she had a week and a half ago. They embraced for a good while, people stepping around them, then he ushered her out to the Temporary Parking lot.

Todd navigated his dark green Toyota Tacoma pickup through the hellish Seattle I-5 traffic all the way north until they pulled off into the Ballard district where they were finally close enough to live cherry trees, after the miles of concrete, to see the delicate blossoms dancing on the branches. Em had been to Fisherman's Terminal a few times, prepping for various fishing seasons, so she knew the basic lay of the land.

Her flight had been delayed due to bad weather in Kodiak, so it was only an hour or so before the memorial was set to begin. The parking lot in front of the big concrete building guarding the entrance to the Terminal was already full. The complex of buildings held a fancy restaurant, Chinook's, on the west wing, then a covered open-air walkthrough to the Terminal and the Seattle Fishermen's Memorial, which was front and center on the promenade. On the east side was a small sundries store, the Bay Cafe, a barber shop, the Highliner Pub, laundry, showers, and bathrooms. The celebration of life gathering was going to be held in Chinook's, which had expansive windows overlooking the harbor, and then it would move outside to where the tall marble pillar of the Memorial overlooked the marina and fishing fleet.

They parked near the pub, and Todd, wanting to be a gentleman, carried Em's pack as they walked down toward Ethan's boat, a wooden green and black-painted seiner called the *Patricia Ann*. It was one of the many seiners home for the winter from the summer salmon season, nestled in along one of four docks, all devoted to fishing vessels of various sizes, shapes, and sorts, most of which spent time up in Alaska. In another month or two the harbor would be buzzing with pre-season boat and net work. As soon as Em saw the rigging and bright colors of the vessels from the parking lot, she felt her anxiety tick up, and it increased with each step.

Will I be able to do this? Will it bring back too many of the memories?

Sensing her internal resistance, Todd stopped.

"Hey, you okay?"

"It's just, uh, thinking of stepping on a fishing boat again, it's, uh, something I'm not sure if I'm prepared for," she stammered. "Or if I can do it."

"Oh," he said, then beat himself up internally. Why hadn't he thought of that himself when he'd made the plan? He'd gotten the day bunk up in the wheelhouse ready for them, even bringing some bedding from home, and my god, what an idiot he was. Last time she'd been in a wheelhouse was when Manni, Sam, and Phil were trapped inside and

Em had been struggling for her life. While he was dealing with incredible guilt and grief, he had none of the terror of the actual memories of what had happened in his mind, only imaginings of what had happened, nothing as real as Em must feel, nor had he even gotten the play-by-play, minute-by-minute explanation of what had happened from her. How could he ever ask her that without her offering it herself first?

"Well, how 'bout I walk your stuff down, we can go up to the restaurant and grab a drink, and then if you still feel not good about it after the service, we can always go get a hotel room nearby."

Seeing no other viable options and not wanting to make a big deal about it, Em conceded. She waited up at the Terminal while he ran down to the boat with her pack. Em entered the hallway by the bathrooms where the walls were lined with old black and white photos from the 1900s of fishermen and their boats. She scanned the bulletin board, perusing old and faded signs for "Crew wanted," or "Engine for sale," or "Need net repairs?" notes pinned up to the corkboard. There were a few beat up books for borrowing as well. She wondered if any of them had been taken out for a fishing season, where they'd traveled to, and how they'd wound up back here.

Soon Todd was back, his arm naturally going to her side, and he led her over to Chinook's, ever the gentleman and holding the door for her, something which she wasn't used to after years of trying to make it on her own and work in a male dominated industry. But as usual, lately, she didn't fight it. As they walked in, Todd marveled at how beautiful she looked, even with sadness painted on her face.

One whole side of the restaurant was reserved for the memorial, only a few folks mingling there, so they went over to the bar first, and ordered two gin and tonics.

Feeling nervous, Em asked, "So, are you ready for this?"

"No, that's why I'm going to have a few of these," Todd said, raising his glass slightly, ice clinking. He toasted to her glass, and they both took a sip. "Also, I want to warn you, my parents will be here."

"Oh?" she asked, surprise in her voice. *That would've been nice to have some warning about.*

Sensing her reaction, he said, "It's no big deal, they just live nearby and want to show their support. In case you meet them, my mom's name is Dianna and my dad's is Rich. They're divorced, so you probably won't see them together."

As this was the biggest and most organized memorial event, it started to fill up early. Fishermen, cleaned up and in semi formal clothes, which was about as fancy as they got, milled about. Em could pick out some who she guessed were family members. There was a more solemn air to the room than at the quainter, small-town events in Kodiak or Petersburg. As people filtered in they fingered appetizers, or wandered over to the memorial table, where yet again the gazes of Phil, Manni, and Sam were placed with wreaths and memorials decorating their photos.

Faces blurred together, but this time Todd did a better job of staying hitched next to Em. He needed to keep tabs on how she was doing with it all, which preoccupied him enough that it didn't leave much room for any other of his emotions to storm in.

Em's emotions had turned again to numbness, for the moment. She'd felt so much, cried so much, been so terrified, and now even if she wanted to cry, she felt like nothing would come out, except when a flashback sprang upon her. The event was too busy to allow for those to creep in, so she stood hollowly, saying hello, accepting sympathies for going through what she did. Todd's mom Dianna appeared, definitely resembling Todd, but with gray and slightly frizzy hair. Todd must've given his parents a heads up about who Em was, as she didn't seem surprised to see her son holding Em's hand, or that Em was one of the two sole survivors.

She welcomed Em warmly, gave her a hug and said, "Can't wait to see you in Port Townsend!"

When they pulled back, Todd, to his dismay, received a very stern and questioning look from Em. He restrained himself from kicking his mom in the shin, and said to Em, "I'll explain later."

Dianna, realizing she must've caused a snafu, excused herself and someone else filled her spot. A few people later, Todd's dad rotated in and gave his son a manly hug. He was chiseled, with salt and pepper hair, weathered skin from a life of working outdoors, wearing a stately blue and black flannel jacket. Rich shook Em's hand awkwardly, then moved along.

Carmen, Phil's wife, looked a bit more put together than at the Kodiak event. Em guessed she was running on autopilot and would collapse later, once all this part of it was over. After about an hour or so, Carmen dinged her glass with a spoon and led the group in some reflections, shared a few more stories about the men, and then let the mic pass around the group, allowing anyone to speak who wanted to share a memory. That went on for a very long time. Dry eyes in the house were rare. Todd grabbed Em's hand, holding it tight for that whole time. Neither of them felt strong enough to share anything. Todd knew he would have only been able to get a word or two out before breaking down and having to pass the mic along.

With so many stationary bodies, it had begun to grow hot and sticky, so there was an unsaid sigh of relief by all when Carmen announced it was time to go out to the memorial and have everyone come up, one at a time, to lay the flowers and wreaths and memorial items at the foot of the monument. The sun was setting in the pink and orange sky, just a slight ripple of wind on the water. Emily could hear the traffic buzzing by on the Fifteenth Avenue Bridge. She couldn't even hear the words anymore, she felt lost like a bird blown into a strange land by a storm. Todd was currently her only pillar of strength. After two hours of going from one drink to another, she felt, yet again, woozy. *This is not a good habit to get into,* she scolded herself, but then thought, *Fuck it, who gives a shit?* in a defeated manner.

When it came their turn to place flowers at the foot of the pillar, it was already overflowing. There was a granite pillar in the center of the memorial, with fish and sea creatures cast in bronze at the base, and another bronze statue at the top of the twenty-foot pillar, of a longliner fisherman with a halibut on a hook. On the west side of the memorial stood a long marble block that held all the names from 1988 onwards that had been lost at sea and hailed from Seattle, and on the east side there was another long marble block with the names of those lost at sea continued, up until the present. Much of the space on the east block was still blank, eerily waiting to memorialize the names of those still yet to be lost at sea. As Em ran her fingers over the names of her crewmates, realizing her name had been unfathomably close to being listed there as well, the thought made her sob out loud. In reaction, Todd hugged her closer while she looked down in embarrassment. But this was not a crowd to judge. In the past Em had been around many similar mariner memorials since just about every harbor has one, but what those names on the lists meant had never fully sunk in before. Now she knew, on a whole new level. Those names felt like kin and she was connected to them in a way that no one else could ever fully grasp.

Soon it was growing dark. People were starting to wander back into Chinook's or take off. Todd received many hugs from the crew's families, as many of them knew him, or of him. Few besides direct family members of Phil, Manni and Sam had figured out exactly who Emily was, as she'd only been on the boat so briefly, and her name had not gotten out into the news yet.

Todd looked over at Em. Her face seemed set in stone, grim and blank, like she wasn't fully there with him. She probably wasn't, he thought.

"Hey, sugar," he called to her, trying to brighten her up a little. "You ready to go?"

She squeezed his hand back.

"Okay, let's just make an Irish goodbye and try to sneak out without too many more hugs."

He spotted a path out, as people had drifted back into the restaurant after the wreath laying to get out of the chill, drink more, remember more. He had a feeling many of them would be at it up to closing, then take it down the street or uptown to Ballard and close out those bars. It's how fishermen seemed to deal. Drink until it doesn't hurt anymore, just as he had done. Getting him and Em out of there and down to the boat was going to take real concentration in his current drunken state.

In this condition he did a poor job of checking how Em was doing, and instead he just sort of guided her down, like he had been doing all night. She didn't resist, but gosh, how many drinks had she also had? Then he picked her up and lifted her over the rail of the *Patricia Ann's* back deck and into the galley.

As he flicked on the light switch, he observed her eyes look around wildly and could sense the terror build, her reliving those last moments on the night of the sinking. Every fishing boat of that size is built in a similar manner, and he guessed it was easy to see herself in the *Sea Ranger's* once cozy galley again. He could see her eyes darting about, calculating, flicking here and there, probably remembering the whole scene all over again. She started to breathe rapidly and grip the galley counter with white knuckles.

"Em, Em, it's okay. Here, let's go back up to the truck."

She nodded with wild eyes, her breath starting to morph into a panic attack. He pushed open the door and she bolted out like a released hound, over the rail and onto the dock.

Catching up to her, he said, "Breathe, Em, breathe. It's okay. I've got you." She couldn't control it. "Breathe, please. Nice and slow for me."

He led her back up the dock and into his truck as she gasped for air. Thinking fast, he realized he'd left his homemade camping bed set up in the back of his truck, so in the worst case scenario they could crash there, at least until he was sober enough to drive somewhere.

She got in the truck and slammed the door, still breathing in panic attack mode. He tried to talk soothingly to her, assuage her fears, have her sip some water, and eventually after what seemed like forever, she calmed down. He had her lean across the seat and put her head on his shoulder while he stroked her hair, knowing gentle touch and contact might help sooth her.

"Hey Em, we're in luck. I've got the back of my truck made up into a bed. We can crash back there."

Finally calmed down enough to manage communication, she managed a, "Hmmph," as an okay.

After kicking off their shoes, crawling into the back, and shutting the camper top door, they wrestled into the sleeping bags, passing out into fitful sleep shortly after.

🪢 🪢 🪢

TODD WOKE WITH a raging headache, the condensation from their breath dripping down on them, coating every surface like they were in a terrarium. He rolled over and looked at Em: she was lying on her back, her green eyes open and staring up at the ceiling.

Turning her head slightly toward him and making eye contact, she said "Hey Todd, I'm so sorry about last night . . . you know, my panic attack on the boat." He moved his hand to brush the hair out of her eyes. "I'm just . . . I'm just really struggling right now."

"Em, no worries. It's going to take time," he said, trying to comfort her. "I'm so glad you were there with me, though. I don't know how I could have gone through all that without you."

"Yeah, same here . . ." but she didn't sound convinced. "Todd, I don't feel so good."

Todd fumbled in the bed he'd made of plywood and foam mattress, and fished out a Nalgene bottle, unscrewed the lid, and handed it to her.

"Here, drink some water."

After a few big gulps she handed it back to him, and he followed suit.

"Hey, Todd. What'd it mean when your mom said she was excited to see me in Port Townsend? I never said how long I was going to stay, or that I would even go to Port Townsend at all."

"Oh, yeah, well . . ." he felt at a loss. What should he tell her? In a romantic and grief-stricken, irrational moment, he'd talked to his mom about Em, and how she was coming to visit. Hearing that, his mom offered up the cabin to them on the longstanding agreement that they could stay there, but just help out with some chores. In her over-excitement, she'd decided to get the cabin ready for them. That got the romantic and hopeful side of Todd going, a side which he himself had never experienced before, and he'd sheepishly asked his mom if she could buy some fresh flowers and candles, you know, to make it romantic. His mom, who had a little too much enthusiasm at times, had sent him about fifteen pictures of how she'd "spruced" it up. He was planning on keeping it all a surprise for Emily in hopes that she'd be interested in going up there to see Port Townsend with him. Now it all seemed like whimsy, a foolish fallacy . . . how could he yet again be so stupid?! Well actually, he knew, it was because he'd never felt this way about anyone before. It was because he, for the first time in his life, was in love, and more in love with her than ever, in spite of everything she was going through, maybe even more so because of it.

He had a foreboding feeling in his gut that he was about to be hurt, and it was going to hurt bad. He licked his lips before answering, "Em, I, well," he was still a bit tongue tied. She just looked deeper into his eyes. *Just rip the Band-Aid off,* he decided.

"Well, I know you didn't say how long you'd stay, but I was hoping to offer to take you up to Port Townsend, see my hometown, maybe spend a little more time with you."

Her face was blank, and he couldn't read her reaction. Instead she closed her eyes for a moment. When she opened them again, he could see that far off look, like she'd gone somewhere else. Then her eyes came back to his.

"Fuck, Todd, I can't do this."

"You can't do what?"

Her heartbeat was elevating again. "I can't . . . I can't. I just have to go back. I know this is going to hurt to hear, but sometimes seeing you triggers me as you remind me too much of what happened."

"You want to leave, like, today?" he asked, his throat starting to choke.

"Yes, Todd, I'm so sorry. I'm in no state to be around you. I am only going to hurt you worse if I stay."

"Really? Please, please don't . . . I need you!" It was as if there were an earthquake breaking up the very ground he was standing on. First he'd lost some of his best friends, and now it appeared he was losing the love of his life. The image he'd had of them cozying up in the little cabin in Port Townsend, sipping coffee together, sleeping in, talking, loving each other, started to sting like salt in the wound—just a stupid, delusional fantasy. He couldn't tell her what a fool he'd been to imagine that could ever happen. He felt his own pulse increase.

"Em, please. Please stay, just a little bit longer . . ." He started to feel panic, the thought of her leaving him now, alone, no one to relate to who had just been through this and having to navigate it on his own seemed impossible, suffocating. My god, he didn't think he could bear a second of it. He tried to sit up, but hit his head on the camper ceiling.

"Todd, I'm just going to hurt you. Trust me." Trying to explain again, she said, "I can't do that to you. And there are too many memories . . . sometimes when I look at you, it's all okay, and then other times I look at you and think of . . . well, I think of all of them. And I just can't bear to hurt anyone else more than I'm hurting myself right now."

She started to sit up. Her voice had been rising with emotion, too.

Things felt like they went into slow motion then. Em found her jacket, rolled out of the sleeping bag, and slid down to the tailgate door, pushed it open, and clambered out, fumbled for her shoes, slipped them on . . . all while Todd sat back on his elbows dumbfounded at how the rug had just been pulled out from under him.

"Todd, I just need some air," she said, almost on the verge of a panic attack again, and she turned quickly, walked a few steps, then he saw her pick up her pace and jog away from him. Todd felt big hot tears forming, disbelief and horror flooding in. He felt so goddamn alone, like he didn't even know how to tie his own shoes anymore, or breathe, for that matter. He didn't know how long he sat stunned and shaken as he pondered how disillusioned and naive he'd been to dream up this future life with her. Several people walked by, as it was now early morning, keeping their eyes averted to the strange man lying in the back of his truck in the parking lot, sobbing.

It was maybe twenty minutes until reality filtered back in through his still splintering hangover headache and heartbreak, realizing he had no idea where she had gone. And now she was alone in a big city, no ride, or even her own pack, which was still down on the boat. Where would she have gone? He had to find her! And in growing panic he scolded himself, *How could I be so fucking stupid?!* Why had he been such a dumbass and not run after her?

He doubted she'd be down by the boats, but maybe by the memorial? Did she have her phone or wallet on her? He tried her cell. It rang and rang, with no answer. Shoes finally on, he closed up the back of the truck and started jogging to the memorial. She was not there, but the mountain of flowers remained. He knew she'd been at the Terminal before, so guessed that she at least knew her way around the direct vicinity. He continued past Chinook's, across the street to Cafe Appassionato, a popular coffee spot. He poked his head in, but she wasn't there. Then he headed up the street past businesses and parked RVs to Seattle Marine Supply. She was nowhere in sight. Beyond that, there wasn't much of interest or any logical place a desperate soul would want to go to besides the climbing gym down the street, and he was sure she was in no mood for climbing. He decided to turn around and try the other side of the harbor, toward the bridge. Maybe she was back behind the net lockers. He was running at a good clip, jacket open and flapping. He must've looked insane, but he didn't care. As he was nearing Chinook's again, he saw someone sitting with their back against one of the memorial blocks. As he got closer, it was clear it was Em.

"My god, Em! Where did you go and what are you doing?! I was looking all over for you!"

She jumped at his surprise appearance, her eyes red and cheeks traced with tear tracks.

"Todd, I'm so sorry . . . I just have to go home."

He sank his back into the marble with her, putting an arm around her shoulders.

"Em, I was so scared. I didn't know if you were okay," his breath was finally catching up.

"I'm sorry, there's just nothing else I can say or do right now. I never should have come down. I've only hurt you."

Her phone rang as it was lying in her lap. He could see the caller ID said "Jess." She looked at him with an apologetic face and picked it up.

So she'd had her phone on her, he realized, feeling stung. He could hear Jess on the other line, giving Em some directions. It sounded like, well, flight information.

"Okay, thanks, I'll check," she said as she hung up. He already knew what it was about. In defeat, he nodded, yes, he could take her back to the airport—that day.

They eventually got up from the cold stone and walked back over to the cafe, got a cup of coffee, walked down to the Ballard Locks, and then back to his truck. They pretty much walked in silence, sipping the coffee, observing the world rushing by about them. Both souls in totally different forms of heartache.

Their last few hours together were fraught with tension. He felt like there was no way he could do or say anything that would be right or could make it all better. Compared to the hours of waiting for word from the US Coast Guard, these were the next hardest hours of his life . . . knowing he had precious little time with her, but not able to do what he wanted to with it. He knew this might be the end, this goodbye would set her free back into her world in Kodiak and set him adrift down here, and would their lives ever entwine again?

Then it was time to fight the traffic, get her over to SeaTac, let the radio fill the silence. It was hard to find an open spot to drop her off, no place for an extended goodbye, but the morning had already painfully done that. He hopped out, truck still running, door half open, got her bag out of the back, met her at the passenger's side on the curb, and gave her one big giant hug that he never wanted to let end, but of course it did, way too soon, and then she was walking away, out of his life. She'd snagged a thread to his soul and was now unraveling him further and further with every step she took. He waited to get back in the truck, hoping to see if she'd look back. She did, and he saw tears glisten on her cheeks. With a final wave, she and her black pigtails were gone.

Todd drove straight back to the Fisherman's Terminal, called up his friend Jason who was always up for grabbing a drink, and proceeded to deal with his anguish in an exceedingly rash and unhealthy fisherman fashion, by getting as drunk as he could, as quickly as he could.

Chapter 31

Same Same, but Different

Late April to May 2013

EM'S RETURN HOME did not go well. Jess picked her up from the airport and could barely arouse a smile. Jess understood what had happened in Seattle with Em and Todd, and also knew that the hardest part of grief and trauma comes well after all the services, memorials, flowers and dropped-off casseroles and sympathy cards taper away. So Jess was bracing herself for a tough few weeks or months for Em, but it started out worse than she expected. The rough days immediately after the tragedy seemed like a false summit now. With the quiet after the storm, Em's horrific memories and PTSD of the sinking would not relent, compounding into a downward spiral of depression and restless sleep.

It'd been about a week after Em's return, and Jess had been picking up extra shifts at Tony's for her so was gone for large chunks of time, not able to monitor how Em was doing. Jess would leave numerous leftovers in the fridge, hoping Em would eat them while she was away, but upon return, rarely saw a dent in any of them. In that week, Em had also not left the house, barely gotten out of bed, or spoken to anyone, including Jess. She was rapidly slipping away, more so each day. Jess had never seen anyone in such a deep depression before and was feeling overwhelmed about what to do.

Jess had just worked a double shift, so it was about three a.m. when she returned to their apartment. Hoping not to wake Em, she tiptoed to the bathroom, flicked on the light, and instinctively grabbed for her toothbrush, when her foot touched something hard and cold on the floor. Looking down, she saw a pair of black scissors on the linoleum, splayed open. Jess' stomach lurched, as it was odd to see them misplaced like that. Her mind rushed to Em and the depressed, catatonic state she'd been in ever since her return from Seattle. Scissors dropped on the bathroom floor and depression don't usually mix well.

Before she knew what she was doing, Jess bolted toward Em's room and barged in. In the darkness she could make out a crumple of blankets and hoped somewhere inside was Em. Jess reached the bed and turned on the lamp by the nightstand, sitting down at the side of the bed. Em groaned and stirred. The dread Jess had felt started to ease in seeing Em was alive and breathing. Em opened an eye slightly, against the blare of the light.

"What are you doing, Jess?" she asked.

"I need to make sure you're okay. Let me see your wrists."

With that, both of Em's eyes opened wide.

"What the fuck, Jess?"

"You heard me, I'm really concerned," and she started to reach toward Em's arms, hidden under the covers.

Sensing Jess' reach, Em jerked her arms away in anger. But Jess was fast, caught her right arm, and brought it toward the light. Em struggled and broke free, but it was enough for Jess to see. There were red angry lines, fresh cuts, all along Em's wrists.

"Get out!" Em ordered.

"Em, I'm really worried for you. We need to get you help."

"Fuck you, leave me alone. You can't understand."

"Em, I know I can't understand, but this is too much. I don't know what to do."

"Don't do anything."

The conversation continued to hit a wall, Em angry and combative at being found out for trying to hurt herself, and Jess feeling at a loss for what to do. In the end, Em just stopped talking, rolled over and turned her back to Jess, which left Jess feeling heartbroken and scared. This was more than she knew how to handle. Realizing there was nothing else she could do at the moment, she finally stood up and turned out the light, gently closed the door, and whispered, "Em, I'm here for you, and I love you," as she exited.

By then it was about four a.m., but eight on the East Coast, so as soon as Jess was in her own room, she searched her contacts on her phone and called Em's mom, Kathy, who answered on the third ring.

"Hello, Jess." Instead of words, muffled sobs came out, Jess not wanting Em to hear her.

"Whoa, whoa, whoa, what's wrong, dear?"

Eventually, Jess got to words. "I'm so worried about Em, I don't know what to do!" She started sharing about how things for Em had slid deeper into depression each day, no sign of relenting, and how she'd just caught Em harming herself. Kathy, knowing Em since her early, very hypersensitive days with bouts of depression, also grew concerned, as in spite of her painful past, she'd never known Em to go so far as to hurt herself . . . How much more would it take before she went further with it?

"Jess, don't take it all on yourself. Ultimately it's up to Em to get herself out of it. All we can do is provide support and maybe therapy, but this is way too much for you to handle on your own. I will be there as soon as I can."

"But what should I do now? I'm afraid to leave her alone, and I have to work extra to help cover some of her shifts. Luckily Tony's is being understanding and giving her a few weeks off . . . but I'm going be terrified to leave her out of my sight now."

"Don't worry, I'll be there on the next flight I can get on. In the meantime, I think you should quietly gather up any sharp or dangerous objects, so they're out of easy reach."

After more thorough discussion and assurances from Kathy, Jess hung up and hugged her knees to her chest and cried, relieved Kathy was going to be there soon. Exhausted from worry and overwork, Jess then rounded up every sharp object she could find as Kathy had suggested and hid them away in her bedroom. She then collapsed into her bed with only a few hours left before she'd have to get up and start work again.

🪢 🪢 🪢

WHEN KATHY ARRIVED two days later, Jess felt like it was her own mom coming home to the rescue, taking off some of the intense pressure she'd felt in the impossible task of trying to take care of someone who didn't seem to want to live.

As Kathy, bundled up to the extreme against the April Alaska temperatures, slid into Jess' gray Honda Civic, she asked, "So, how is she? Any changes?"

"Well, ever since I called you she hasn't talked to me, but I had to work both days. The anxiety of not knowing if she's okay is more than I can handle. I've just been opening her door to check if she's breathing, but every time I do, she's just lying in bed."

"Oh my," said Kathy, bracing herself for what she was guessing might be the toughest task of her life, to get her daughter out of an immensely deep depression and PTSD.

"So she still doesn't know I'm coming, right?"

"No, I haven't told her. I was afraid of how she might react."

"Okay."

Anxiety mounted for both Jess and Kathy as they climbed the stairs to the apartment, unsure how Em would feel about her mom's unexpected arrival. Kathy opened the door to Em's room and said to the figure on the bed, "Hey, honey, it's Mom!"

Em groaned from under the blankets. "Did Jess call you up?"

"Yes, sweetie, she did. She was too worried about you not to."

"Mom, I'm fine. Sorry I wasted your time. You should go back."

Kathy took a deep breath, "Em, you are *not* fine. I am here, and we are going to work together to get through this. I know you can do this."

Em rolled away from her, and said in a dull tone, "Mom, get out. Leave me alone."

Kathy sucked in her breath. She'd been bracing for this. The hurt that came from depression was often directed most toward those who cared or were trying to help, but still there was no dulling it.

"Okay, Em. I'll leave for now, but I am staying up here, and we are going to work through this, whether you like it or not."

"Mom, leave." Em said more forcefully.

Not wanting to push too hard on this first interaction, Kathy did rise and leave, but before closing the door said, "Em, you can't run from what happened. You're going to have to face it, just like you've done in the past. I'll be out here and checking on you frequently. We are going to start small. First step is you are going to have to sit up and eat some dinner with me. I'll be back in an hour or so. Let me know if you need anything."

Kathy moved in and onto the living room couch, then in the next few days flew into full mom mode and offered any remedy she could think of to get Em out of her pit of despair and to find treatment options. Jess continued to work, so didn't see a lot of either of them.

Kathy tried all manner of tactics, drawing on some she'd learned from the past when Em was still a child—pampering Em and being gentle, then trying to give her a little kick, motivation to get out of bed, trying to get her out to get some fresh air. She at least managed to start getting her daughter to eat again. In her spare time Kathy searched for counselors and therapy options. Kodiak was dismal in that department and offered next to nothing for mental health assistance. Even if there had been options, Em wasn't interested in giving anyone or anything a fair try.

About three days into her stay, though, after a late night of Internet searching for how to deal with trauma, Kathy randomly stumbled across something called Dialectical Behavior Therapy, or DBT, for short. It had some glowing results, and after more searching, Kathy found a therapy group that met online. "Hmm," she thought. "Maybe if I try it out, then sit in with Em and do it with her, that might make a difference."

$$\mathit{\widehat{\mathcal{S}}}\ \mathit{\widehat{\mathcal{S}}}\ \mathit{\widehat{\mathcal{S}}}$$

TODD'S RETURN TO Port Townsend didn't go well, either. After a wicked bender in Seattle with Jason and some fishing friends, he crawled back to Port Townsend to crash at his mom's cabin, which was an ordeal in itself, going back to the spot where he had hoped to spend time with Em. His mom had wisely removed all traces of the decorations and flowers she'd set up for Em, but still, it was painful to walk into the now cold, lonely, and empty space, with Em nowhere in sight. The first night he spent there alone, he was too tired from his bender in Seattle to think, and passed out, sleeping the whole night through and well into the morning.

It was the second day being back where everything hit him, like luggage from the back of a car hitting him in the head after a hard stop. He woke up alone. Utterly alone and no purpose to the day—no job, no point in doing anything. In his state, there seemed nothing to live for anymore. His friends were dead, and Em now seemed dead to his love, as well. He probably should have been dead too, but somehow he wasn't. He felt nauseated, but not from drink this time. It was an unsettling feeling, making his skin want to crawl, but no remedy to any of it seemed possible besides somehow turning his mind off. The feeling of aloneness closing in on him, Todd picked up his phone and started scrolling through names, searching for buddies from Port Townsend who might be around. It took three calls until finally someone picked up. It was Caleb who did.

"Hey man, what are you doing today?"

"Oh, hey, buddy! I didn't know you were back . . ." there was an awkward pause. Caleb must've heard about the *Sea Ranger* sinking, but had no clue what to say about it, so instead avoided it and continued, "I'm down at the harbor, just working on the *Roatoa.*" Caleb was a local Port Townsend boy who spent summers seining in Southeast Alaska and winters picking up jobs in the shipyard. On the side, he was working on fixing up an old sailboat he'd acquired called the *Roatoa.*

"Oh, right on."

"Why don't you come by. I can show you how far I've gotten with her, and then we could grab a drink."

"Sounds good, I'll stop by later," said Todd as he hung up.

It wasn't until late afternoon that he made it down to the harbor. Instead, once he'd hung up, Todd decided to take a shower to try to wash some of the pain away, which didn't help. He then just sat and stared at his bag, stuffed with clothes and still unpacked, in a stupor of sadness, unable to move or get dressed. That's when Dianna knocked and came in, seeing Todd in a towel, just staring off at space.

"You okay, Todd?" she asked, concern lacing her question.

It took a second to snap out of it, but he managed a weak, "Oh hey, yeah, I'm okay."

Seeing his state and understanding her son was probably heartbroken in more ways than one, she demanded, "Todd, get dressed, and then come over to my place. I'm going to make you lunch."

"Okay, Mom," he said with a sigh, knowing there was no way to get out of it.

She purposefully distracted him from some of the sadness for a few hours, serving him an elaborate lunch, then tasking him with chores, showing him the new garden bed and her latest addition to the goat herd, Alby. But around four o'clock she got a call from a patient showing signs of labor, so she had to grab her midwife kit and head out, apprehensive at leaving her son in a state she'd never seen him in before.

As soon as Dianna was gone, the suffocating feelings came rushing back with full force. It took all he had to get in his truck, turn the keys, and head into town. But once he pulled up in the shipyard to the double-masted *Roatoa*, seeing Caleb's truck full of tools and hearing the sound of a grinder coming from the depths of the boat, Todd felt a small amount of relief at this new distraction.

As he climbed up the ladder, Caleb came out, covered in a dust mask and coating of wood dust. His face lit up upon seeing Todd, and he gave him a big hug once they both stood in the cockpit of the forty-foot vessel. Todd could sense it was a longer, tighter hug than normal . . . again, Caleb's way of saying he knew and was sorry about what had happened.

When he made eye contact, Todd decided to get it over with, "I'm sure you know about what happened, but I don't really want to talk about it right now."

"Oh yeah, man, no problem," Caleb replied, not sure what to add after that, so he tried, "I'm so glad to see you. Let me show you my latest project and then buy you a drink!"

"Sounds good to me," Todd said, relieved he'd soon be meeting his new friend, alcohol, again.

Caleb had been hard at work, his boat repairs moving along. In another year he'd probably be able to resell it for three times what he'd bought it for. The yard was busy year-round as it was one of the largest centers of skilled maritime craftsmen around.

Todd jumped into Caleb's messy pickup for the two-minute drive over to the Pourhouse, a local favorite pub, close to the harbor and right on the water. The large open indoor space was mostly empty as it wasn't yet the dinner rush, but after Caleb and Todd grabbed a beer and picked a table in the corner, a steady stream of patrons trickled in. As it was a decent day, most gravitated to the picnic benches outside. Avoiding the elephant in the room of the *Sea Ranger* tragedy, Caleb carried the conversation, chatting away about his projects, plans for the summer, town gossip. Two beers downed, then some buddies from another fishing boat sauntered in, dirty from shipyard work but thirsty for beer. They joined Todd and Caleb, and drinks continued to flow. Todd welcomed the distractions and free beers. It seemed to be everyone's way of paying him back for what he'd gone through without having to talk about it.

The night began to ebb and flow like so many drunken nights do. People came and went, then new ones filtered in. Soon he found himself downtown at Siren's. It was a pub up two flights of stairs on the backside of a historic brick building that faced the water, with a Victorian sort of ambiance. Dark wood interior and burgundy paint on the ceiling, stained glass lamps, and oil paintings lined the walls, making it feel as if time outside had stopped. He skipped eating, opting for a liquid dinner instead. Siren's that night was intimate and crowded and filled with mixed drinks. The background music was loud, blurring out his thoughts. Caleb and the original guys he'd started the evening with were long gone, but now it didn't matter, he had new people and drinks to distract him from his black hole of loneliness. Time slipped by, as it magically does in such states of altered consciousness. Before he knew it, it was midnight and closing time. Todd found himself alone and out on the street, zipping up his jacket against the cold, his truck a twenty-minute walk back at the harbor.

The world seemed to close in on him. He could barely walk or think, which is what he'd wanted. Next to the towering brick building that housed Siren's and a few other shops, was the Adams Street Park by the water. Todd instinctively made his way down toward the gravelly beach, knowing there was no way he'd make it back to his truck, and collapsed near the high tide line. This time the nausea was real, and he let his emotional pain and stomach contents spew out, until he collapsed in a blackout, drunk and cold, by the sea.

Dawn came too early, and Todd cracked open his eyes, confused as to why he was shivering and could hear the sound of waves. *Oh my god,* he despaired as he flicked his eyes open, realizing where he was. He was that drunk guy on a beach, while other, normal people were starting their days, going to the office, walking their dogs. He quickly sat up in a pool of shame as large as the ocean, then he remembered the *Sea Ranger* and Em, and all his heartache, and he threw up again. He was a mess, vomit on his flannel jacket. And he had a long walk back to his truck. In a panic he realized he didn't know where his keys, wallet, or phone were. He patted his pockets, relieved to find all three still on his person, but cursing himself at how careless he'd been.

He glanced at his phone, knowing it would only make him depressed not seeing any calls from Em. There were only two messages, both from his mom, demanding to know where he was and if he was okay. The walk back down Main Street exemplified a true walk of shame. He had to find another garbage can to puke into along the way. And the nail in the coffin was that Caleb was already working, busy inside the bowels of his boat when Todd finally got back to his truck. He sheepishly slid into the driver's seat and started the truck without saying hello. Then he crawled back to his mom's cabin, pulled the covers over his head, and tried to escape the world and his mind again, this time in sleep.

More long, lonely nights and no work in the days led to a worst case scenario mix, which led to turning to the bottle more and more, and hanging out with friends who also drank to excess and spent all their nights at the bars. Todd rarely came back to the cabin in the evenings, wising up and crashing in his truck instead of trying to drive home drunk.

Before the tragedy, Todd had only drunk socially. He did like a good party, but he had never carried a flask, or drunk solo, prior to April and the *Sea Ranger* sinking. Now his addiction to alcohol was growing impossible to hide. And his mom, even though she lived across the property and largely left him alone except to dole out some chores and tasks, was on to him, the way only a mother can be. Now when Todd woke in the morning, he started the day with a bloody Mary, then a stiff mixed drink or three at lunch, and a free-for-all after dinner. He knew this was not a good sign, but the moment he let up, all the grief and heartbreak came rushing back. He didn't know what to do with it or how to deal.

$$\mathscr{S} \ \mathscr{S} \ \mathscr{S}$$

ONE EVENING, AS he was sitting down with a glass of wine this time, to watch an action movie (another way to numb the pain), he heard something outside, then a knock on the cabin's front door. Guessing it was his mom, he glanced at the recycling box overflowing with glass bottles as he strode to the door, curious, as his mom usually stayed well away from the cabin, giving him space.

"Hi dear," she said, sliding in before he could protest.

"What is it, Mom?"

"Well, as hard as this will be to say, it's my duty and really important to talk to you about this. See, I'm really concerned for you." Todd could sense what was coming over the horizon. She continued, "If you keep this up, drinking and not working, I'm really afraid of where you're going to end up. Todd, you need to face your emotions. You can't just keep stuffing them away. How many of your friends have wound up dead from drinking or drugs?" He had started to lose track, as it was a silent epidemic in both fishing and in small Alaskan villages. "Do you want to be one of them?"

Glancing around the room, Dianna sized up the recycling box, then spotted the very large glass of wine sitting by the small couch. She strode over to it, picked it up, and dumped it down the small kitchenette's sink. Then she opened the cupboards and started to rummage around. At first he was confused as to what she was doing, then it hit him . . . "Mom, NOO! Get out of my space!"

"Excuse me?" she replied, "Whose space is this??" She had found some of his stash—a bottle of whiskey, some wine bottles, one of vodka. What was he supposed to do? He couldn't go so low as to physically fight his mom, and she knew he wouldn't stoop to that level either, so she started to pull them down, uncork them, and pour them down the drain. Instead he raised his voice, "MOM, get out now! I'm fine, I can deal with this."

Dianna matched his voice, standing up tall to him. She knew this was going to be tough, but it was this or watch him die slowly.

"Todd, you are NOT okay. You need to get help. You've just gone through a lot. I've signed you up for a recovery center down in Bellevue."

His world started to spin in anger, shock, and disbelief that his mom would take such measures. In a rare, alcohol-enhanced rage, he grabbed the now empty wine glass and threw it at the wall, shattering it into a thousand shards, several wine drops painting the white wall like blood splatters. He stared at his hand, as if in disbelief he'd actually thrown it, then looked down in shame.

"Son, we are going. Now. Pack a few things."

He couldn't believe this was happening. He refused, so she did it for him, then forced him out the door and into the car she had waiting for him.

Chapter 32

Small Steps

May 2013

"MOM, I CAN'T believe you signed me up for this without asking," Em said, anger in her voice. "It's not going to help. It's a waste of money and time."

"Sweetie, I don't care, it's worth it to me. And I'm going to do it with you, as well. I'm sure it could help me figure a few things out, myself."

"And why is that a good idea?"

"Because, I'm going to put in the work, too. I want *you* to hold me accountable, as well. I know we are supposed to meet online once a week, and then we'll get some homework, and I am going to commit and will need someone to do this with me, too."

"Arghhhhh . . . Mom, go away. NOW." Em sighed in annoyance, but she knew there was no talking her mom out of this idea. She rolled over, hoping her mom would give up and leave soon, which she did.

After the bedroom door swished shut, Em closed her eyes and let her mind wander. It'd been weeks now since the tragic night, and she felt like she was in a hole she could not climb her way out of. She couldn't focus, she had no energy, her thoughts were in a ruminating spiral of negative guilt and self-hatred. Everything around her seemed flat, black and white, dull, while her heart felt heavy, hurting to even breathe. Thoughts incessantly bounced around her head. *What's wrong with me? I should be happy to be alive. I'm pathetic for being so weak. Why did I hurt Todd like that? Why couldn't I have done more to save them? I don't deserve to live, but THEY did.* All were thoughts that helped feed the monster of depression, feeding on itself like a black hole, none of them logical or true, but at this point she was too far gone to fight them.

Then on top of all that, would come the flashbacks. They'd come at her with no warning. She'd be trying to butter her toast, or read a book, or trying to take a shower, then BAM! She was right back on the *Sea Ranger*. She could feel the cold water seeping in, hear the panic, see the look of sheer terror in Manni's eyes the last time they made eye contact, feel the terror that rushed in as the lights went out and engine died. Then she'd be bobbing cold and alone on the immense Gulf of Alaska thinking she was going to die, watching the ship slip down, swallowed by the froth and waves. When the flashbacks came, adrenaline flooded her body. She'd tried to shudder and hide from the images, but they'd roll over her like a semi on a runaway truck ramp, not caring if she was in the way. All she could do was cower and let them leave her behind as wreckage on the roadway.

More than anything she wanted to let her mom and Jess know how much she loved them and needed them, but it felt like her mouth was taped shut and nothing but cold and mean words could exit. The meaner and colder they were, the more desperately she wanted love and comfort from them. About the only time the pain lessened was when she had found a way to transform the emotional pain to physical, like when she'd cut herself, or her mom and Jess with words.

SO, IN FIGHTING with all of that, the first DBT meeting did not go well. It was about a week since Kathy had first arrived, and she still couldn't get Em dressed or out of bed. So when it came time to log on to the online meeting, Kathy brought the laptop into Em's room, and joined on her own, hoping Em would at least overhear it. The counselor who was to lead the year-long venture with eight other women from various parts of Alaska spent the first two sessions laying out a foundation and expectations, and then they dove into practical applications and discussions.

Em must've indeed overheard some of the first meeting or two, and to Kathy's surprise, during the third meeting, Em sat up in bed, pretending to read, but obviously listening. Then the fourth meeting went a little better, and Em actually joined her mom on the couch, although she didn't say anything. After a month or so of constant care and work with Em, she was able to function, at least on a basic level, and Kathy felt it was okay to head back to Virginia again.

It was a year-long course, and as Kathy continued the DBT sessions after she had returned to home, Em also still logged on. Over time, a slow transformation ensued. At first Em was no help doing the weekly practices or exercises in between classes, but Kathy was persistent, and eventually Em did start to participate, and she even helped to hold Kathy and herself accountable throughout the week. The group was patient and supportive of Em. After about three months, Em started to share here and there during the sessions. Slowly her walls started to open, like a flower during a cold spring, hesitant but slowly and surely unfolding.

The premise of DBT is gleaned from the basics of Eastern thought and Buddhism, focusing on observing emotions, not attaching to them, letting them go, meditating and learning how to observe one's mind, so one can recognize how the emotions arise and fall away. Through observation, one can realize that emotions *can* be let go of, that they merely serve as signals, and one can choose to latch on to them or not. The goal is to use the "Wise Mind," a balanced middle ground between the emotional and logic-based sides of the mind, and a good way to deal with PTSD.

Jess, the one living directly with Em, noticed even more small changes. As soon as Em was able to finish more shifts at work, and then after a few months of very slow progress, she even started looking for a more permanent job. The reality that she might never mentally want or be able to go fishing again had sunk in, especially after the incident on the *Patricia Ann* in Seattle. Em had also started with just a five-minutes-a-day meditation practice, then upped it up to ten, then fifteen, and now was often practicing at least twenty minutes at least once or twice a day. As more and more positive change slowly started to unfurl, the results started to provide more and more positive feedback reinforcement.

Chapter 33

Standard Operating Procedure

May to June 2013

IT WAS FOUR long weeks at the rehab center in Bellevue that specialized in alcoholism. Four long weeks where Todd was being constantly monitored, all his personal effects taken away and locked up, then forced to sit in circles and "talk." In a way, the being stuck where he was, whether he liked it or not, felt like being on a fishing boat. Maybe some of those skills he'd acquired in having to deal with whatever was going on with no place to escape helped him adapt to life at the recovery center.

The first week or so was physical hell, though. Todd's cravings and withdrawal were overpowering, but even worse were the second and third week, although for mental reasons this time. Getting through the worst of the physical condition he could do, as it was a world he was familiar with in pushing his physical limits on the boats and in his skiing and climbing. But then, oh then, the fears, grief, and guilt he was trying so hard to keep at bay came roaring in like an ice dam bursting into all his being. The facilitators weren't quite prepared for that, so once they got a little more of the story about the boat's sinking from checking in with his parents, they called in a special grief and trauma counselor who worked with him one-on-one, daily, for the rest of his time at the center.

Growing up in the fishing world, Todd had always guarded his emotions as much as he could, shucking them away, not dealing with them, seeing it as a sign of weakness. But during one of the early one-on-one sessions that seemed to be going nowhere, as Todd refused to open up about the hurricane of grief roiling in him, he flashed back to that day when he'd gone to see Uncle David in the hospital. He remembered what his uncle had said about life being his choice whether to look up at the stars, or down at the mud. Something clicked. The thought hit at just the right moment, like a key inserted into a lock. Here he was in a goddamn recovery center, dealing with a mountain of grief and sadness, but also, here he was in a center, being supported, and he was alive. If Phil and Manni and Sam had another chance, what would they do with it? Certainly not drink it all away.

So after that point, Todd decided, *Fuck it, I'm here. Might as well talk.* As he did, his biggest fears, guilts, and memories started to percolate out, which served to loosen up other deeper things. To his surprise, the grief counselor shared decent tools in how to deal with these emotions, and by the end of the fourth week, he felt like he'd come to a new way of coping and accepting.

Yes, he was going to be sad, he was going to grieve for his friends and Em, and yes, he had a lot of heartache, and he couldn't undo anything about what had happened, but that was okay. It was okay to feel grief and sadness. They trained him on how to observe it, feel it, be okay with it, and let it go. He started to see this pain as a legit "challenge" hurled at him. Todd could operate on that level, as that had been his standard operating procedure, or rather, code to life: throw a challenge at him and he'd face it head on. With this reframing of the situation, he felt like he indeed was learning how to look up and see the stars.

Chapter 34

Window Views

October 2013

"MOM!" EM EXCLAIMED excitedly as her mom picked up the phone.

"What is it, dear?" Kathy responded, surprised, as she hadn't heard any excitement in Em's voice since before the accident a half a year ago.

"Mom, you know how I started applying to whatever jobs in Kodiak that I could recently?"

"Yeah, I remember you telling me that you'd gone down to the job center and updated your resume and they helped you find some places that were hiring."

"Well, a lot of them led nowhere, but the Department of Fish and Game posted a temporary job opening at the Kodiak Fisheries Research Center. So *not* their enforcement part, but doing fish research." As a former fisherman, she didn't really want to get tangled in enforcement and regulations, but research sounded interesting to her. "It's just a temporary job in the winter, I think mainly crunching numbers and helping with data entry, but they offered me an interview!"

"Wow, honey, that's great!" Kathy was deeply relieved as she had been worried about what Em would do to support herself now. With a resume for the last seven years filled with working on boats and at a bar, that might be hard to match with many land-based jobs. This seemed like a golden ticket for Em to get her foot in the door into a new field. Even if it wasn't glorious or interesting work now, it was a place to start over.

Em had reported in their DBT class that her PTSD was still present and would sometimes come on unexpectedly, but overall was much more manageable. Through the DBT class and support group, she now had multiple tools to deal with the trauma when it did hit her. Kathy was confident Em was healed enough to at least hold down a temporary job for a bit. And if it didn't work out, it didn't work out. Em's whole life, she'd thrown herself at whatever job she had been given, learned it well, excelled in it, and then tended to move on to a new job to learn a whole new skill set. Thus, it was clear Em could probably adapt to this and do quite well at it, too.

"When is it? I'd be happy to help you practice and prepare for your interview!"

The interview was set for a week and a half later, which gave Em plenty of time to review how to answer interview questions, a skill she hadn't needed for a long while, as fishing jobs came about by word of mouth through skippers talking to skippers.

A week and a half later, when Em called after the interview to report back, she sounded down and out. "Mom, I was so anxious, I stumbled and stammered a lot. It didn't flow."

"Oh sweetie, everyone else interviewing was probably as nervous as you were."

"Well, maybe, but still, I'd be surprised if I get it."

"I know you gave it your best shot, Em. And maybe you'll get it. And if for some reason you don't, maybe it wasn't meant to be and a different opportunity will open up later. Plus, it's really good practice for other interviews down the road."

"You're right," Em sighed.

Kathy could tell she was probably rolling her eyes, even though they were on the phone. But two weeks later, after Em had given up hope for the job and moved on to applying to less interesting things, like cleaning for a bed and breakfast or hanging seine nets at the local net loft, Em's cell phone rang—with good news. She had gotten the job and was to start in two weeks. It'd be tedious, lots of computer work, doing all the stuff no one else in the lab wanted to do, but heck, Em was ready and needed something totally different to try.

Her first week on the job went okay. She met the small team she'd be assisting in data and number crunching, and did the prerequisite online trainings and the tons and tons of paperwork required for a state government job. The slow pace was a complete turnaround from the hurry-up-and-find-something-useful-to-do attitude that had been ingrained in her from working with commercial fishermen. But using DBT skills, she accepted the changes with flexibility. It was clear she was starting at the bottom of the ladder, with duties such as keeping the coffee/kitchen area clean and dealing with some secretarial tasks thrown in, but Em also realized she wasn't ready, with her current mental state, to accept a ton of responsibility just now anyway. She was now dipping her toe back into society after months of mainly staying at home in a reclusive state.

And a highlight of the job to her was that she got her own desk and a view out over the water. Having a space that she could make her own was important on a different level, as in all her years of fishing, the only space she'd ever had all to her own was a bunk to sleep in. Her window faced east, out over the water toward Crooked Island, where she could watch the day unfold, the boats go by, and the birds head out and come back in from the sea.

Her coworkers were agreeable, but seemed to keep some distance from her. Ever since the accident, when she'd finally worked up the guts to go out and about in town, she thought she sensed people interacting with her differently. She wasn't sure how much of it was in her head, but it was maybe similar to when someone gets a cancer diagnosis. Everyone knows, but doesn't know what to say, so many just skirt around it, yet inherently treat that person differently. Em now had the label of being one of the two survivors of a tragedy. Thus, people seemed to treat her like a fragile egg, not sure if she was already damaged or about to crack. At her new job, any talk of fishing or her previous profession or the accident was either avoided or never brought up. Sensing these societal changes toward her had made her tend to isolate herself. But now this job was going to slowly force her back out, make her show up to the office at eight a.m. over on the neighboring Near Island (connected to Kodiak by a bridge), and be around people for most of the days of the week. The work itself took just enough concentration, as mundane as it was, that it also kept her thoughts of the tragedy and Todd at bay. Now she only had room for their ghosts to visit after work, on the weekends, or when she woke up with the sweats from a nightmare at two in the morning.

Chapter 35

Job, Stat!

June to October 2013

TODD CARRIED A small plastic bag with the belongings his mom had packed four weeks ago, and when he saw her maroon car pull up, he got up from the waiting room of the reception area at the recovery center, nodded goodbye to the secretary, and walked out.

The whole two-and-a-half-hour ride back, Dianna chatted, her positive energy (because she was a doula and midwife, she had plenty of practice in calming tense situations) permeated the air. As the center had taken away his phone, all the news she and his dad, Rich, had gotten were the initial queries about the accident, and then just a few check-in phone calls from the staff at the center about his progress.

"Todd, did they have you come up with a plan for after?"

"Yes, Mom," he rolled his eyes.

"So, what is it?" she prodded.

"The plan is not to drink again."

"Well, duh, obviously. I mean come on, there must've been more than that!"

"Yes, we of course went over that like the whole last week. They let me come up with my own plan and helped me get to it on my own path."

"So?"

He sighed, and then proceeded to tell her that the plan was to stay away from all situations that involved alcohol for a certain length of time. That meant making it clear to any of his current friends that he couldn't hang out if it involved drinking. He would absolutely need to find a job as soon as possible to help him stay busy and out of trouble, and he was also to continue therapy through online support groups or connect with a local group. In his wallet he had helpline phone numbers laminated on a little card in case any urges to drink came on too strong. He doubted he'd ever call the phone numbers, but he'd promised the center's staff that he'd keep it, at least for a while. Last, he explained to his mom that he'd continue counseling once a week online with the grief therapist, as well.

Dianna nodded her head, seeming pleased and offering to help as much as he would let her. In the meantime, while he looked for a job, she declared that she'd put him to work on her "homestead." As Dianna pulled her car onto the Washington State Ferry, Todd turned on his phone. There were some texts and voicemails, but disappointingly few considering he'd been gone for four weeks. He couldn't help but hope that he'd see one from an Emily Bancroft . . . but his heart sank for the thousandth time when he saw nothing from her. He wondered how she was doing. Was she getting better at all?

There were two messages, though, from his Seattle friend, Jason, just checking in to see how he was doing, and one from Caleb in Port Townsend. While his mom went up to the ferry's upper decks to walk and move a little during the half hour crossing, Todd found a quiet corner of the ferry with a few unoccupied benches and decided to call Jason.

"Hey, man, how you doin'?" he asked as Jason answered.

"Good, brotha', bigger question is how are you? You seemed to have gone AWOL . . . we were a bit worried about you," "we" meaning him and some of the same mutual friends they had. Their friend group consisted of similarly aged fishing buddies that after working hard in Alaska, played hard, spending precious time off gallivanting around Seattle and Washington and sometimes blowing too much of that hard earned cash.

"I did go AWOL. I hit the bottle too hard. Mom checked me in."

"Oh, man, you doin' okay now?"

It didn't surprise Jason too much, as he'd heard word through the grapevine that that's where Todd had maybe disappeared to. They knew more than a few people who had also gone similarly missing for the same purposes, some more successfully than others. So Todd knew Jason could respect the importance of Todd laying off the booze, at least for now, he thought.

"Yeah, yeah, I'm surviving," he muttered.

"Well, where are you heading now?"

"Going back to Port Townsend for now, but hey, you know of any jobs in Seattle? I need one, stat."

"Todd, you know most salmon boats are crewed up already and it's sort of in between the other fishing seasons—"

"No, I don't want another fishing job," he interrupted, feeling ill just thinking about that option. "I guess I was hoping for maybe something in the industry, but not on the boats, like in one of the mechanic shops or net lofts, or some other type of boat work. I just can't do the fishing thing right now." Jason knew what he meant and why, and didn't need to pry further.

"Hey, let me put my feelers out, I'll get back to you."

Soon Todd heard the loudspeaker on the ferry warn everyone to head back to their vehicles, they were approaching the Kingston landing, so he walked back to the car, finding his mom there already waiting.

⚓ ⚓ ⚓

IT WAS EVEN harder than he anticipated to come back to the cabin, no distraction via drinking now. He had also agreed to let his mom hold his wallet and car keys for two weeks minimum while he transitioned, and instead opted to stay busy by picking up a hoe and various other tools for yard work. It did him good to be outside, too. The property was quiet, large trees covering a good two-thirds of her property, with towering cedar, hemlock, and Douglas fir. On the corner near his mom's house was a clearing with a greenhouse and a giant vegetable and herb garden, enough to feed her and share the rest, year round. She also had the chickens and goats that took constant feeding and work, as well. During one of his breaks mucking out the goat stall, he felt his phone vibrate in his Carhartt overalls.

He still had the dang habit of hoping it was Em, and was always let down seeing it was someone else. He wondered if everyone could tell just how disappointed he felt when he realized this and had to pick up and say hello. This time, though, it was Jason.

"Hey, bud!"

"What's up?" Todd asked.

"I was just down in the Terminal and there was this company boom-ing off a sunk boat by the Ballard bridge . . . called Venture Diving & Salvage, not sure if you've heard of them."

"No, don't think so," Todd replied.

"Well, I ran into one of their, uh, I guess they call them envirotechs, and started talking to him. They're based out of the Harbor Island area, you know, down by the Port of Seattle, but they're hiring."

"I'm not a diver," Todd said.

"No, no, this guy said they're looking for more of these envirotechs, or rather "environmental technicians." I guess they go out and boom oil ships when they do fuel transfers in the area, or up at the refineries nearby, and sometimes they help out with small skiff and labor work on these salvage jobs, as the divers are usually crashing the boats around . . . just thought of you. I know you did a lot of skiff driving when you were salmon seining."

"Oh yeah," Todd thought, wheels starting to spin. "Hey, that might work. Maybe I could crash on the *Patricia Ann* for a bit. I know Ethan's not taking it fishing for a time, and he wouldn't mind someone watching it. And it's not too terrible of a drive to make it to Harbor Island from there."

"Yeah, that's what I thought could work, too."

"Did you get anyone's name to talk to?"

"You know I did, man," Jason said with a smile in his voice. "You need to call 'em up and ask to talk to this guy named Andrew."

"Roger that, will do!" Todd hung up with a twinge of excitement in his chest, something he hadn't felt in a very long time. As soon as he finished mucking out the goat stall and topping off the water for the chickens, he rushed back over to the cabin and looked up Venture Diving online. The website portrayed some interesting work, from commercial diving operations, things like dam maintenance and piling repairs, to this environmental booming work, and then also the salvage of sunken or wrecked boats. Seemed intriguing.

When he called up the company, the secretary patched him over to the Andrew guy without asking who was calling. He wondered if that was normal . . . maybe she was new, as usually these kinds of calls got shielded and went to HR instead. But maybe it was his lucky day, as Andrew picked up on the third ring.

"Venture Diving, this is Andrew," he said in a chill manner.

"Hey, I heard you were looking for some envirotechs."

"Uh yeah? Whatchya got?"

Todd felt immediately at home with Andrew's vibe and how this talk was going. It reminded him of talking to the crusty fishing skipper of a boat he might be vying to get on with.

"I got maybe seven years of skiff driving for salmon seining, and even more years of working on various fishing boats, fixing things, doing everything you can think of that's boat related."

With that Andrew hmmmed, then said, "Hey, fill out an application and I'll take a look," and hung up.

Todd rushed through his duties the rest of that day, and then retreated back to the cabin to fill out the tedious online application and scrape together a resume. He didn't even know the last time he'd needed one, so he searched the Internet until he found an online template. One thing he did purposefully omit was any mention of working on a boat called the *Sea Ranger*. He didn't need any extra attention about that. Almost all of the maritime community knew about the accident as it'd been all over the KIRO 7 and KING 5 news for about a week. With one last final review of his resume and application, he hit Submit, and then . . . waited.

Nothing from Venture Diving the next day, or the next. Todd tabled his hopes and continued to work on the homestead and do a halfhearted job search in the evenings, not running across a thing that looked appealing. Then, on the third day, his phone rang with an unknown 206 Seattle area code number. Figuring it was spam, he answered cautiously, but immediately recognized Andrew's voice.

"Hey ya, you said you want to work, just looked over your application. Want to start on Monday?"

Todd's mind raced. That was only three days away. Of course he had to say yes, though.

"Oh, yes, sir! I'll be there, just let me know the time and place."

After getting the details, he hung up and gave a big fist pump to no one but the nearest goat.

His mom, who had been out working by some of the flower beds by the house, looked up with surprise. That night they shared the good news by going out to dinner together.

🪢 🪢 🪢

BY MONDAY AT quarter to seven Todd was in the office's dark parking lot. It was a nondescript building, nestled in amongst the maritime industrial heart of Harbor Island. Behind the main building he noted a large warehouse, then a fenced area filled with all sorts of random gear and equipment, and behind that lay the waters of the Duwamish River and what looked like a dock and some commercial boats tied up to it. Todd knew he'd driven by it many times when going to West Seattle, but had never paid it any attention. The doors were locked and he wondered what to do, but as he sat in his truck with a view of the door, by seven o'clock a woman with a slender frame and blonde, curly hair had come to the front door and unlocked it from the inside. Todd waited another minute or two, then got out, straightened his pants, and grabbed the folder with his hiring documents. He walked up the small stretch of grass to the front door, past a large anchor serving as lawn art, and into the front lobby where the same lady greeted him.

Inside, the building was a hidden gem. It must've been one of the original buildings of the area, dating from the early 1900s as the floors were beautiful dark mahogany and teak hardwood, and there was craftsman quality molding and cabinetry everywhere. Near the front office was a full model of a diver in brass hat and antique equipment. He was liking this place already . . . plus the secretary had a fish tank.

He explained who he was, and Amanda, he learned her name was, motioned for him to go behind her desk and knock on a half open door behind her reception area. He did so with some trepidation, not knowing what kind of boss this Andrew would be in person.

"Come on in," he heard, so Todd gently pushed the door open more and stepped into the spacious office. He first noted a giant shipping spool serving as a decorative table, then a large mahogany desk, surprisingly tidy, and windows with elegant wooden blinds, before turning his attention to Andrew. His new boss was pulling some more formal clothes out of his bike pannier bag, meaning he must have commuted by bike, still sweaty from the ride. Next to his desk was a giant waterproof duffle brimming with travel and work stuff . . . maybe he was on the road a lot, thought Todd. Then he snuck a closer look at this new boss: Andrew was a big guy, tall and stout, red beard and hair, dark rimmed, modern glasses framing a cheery face that seemed to be in a permanent squint and grin.

"You must be Todd," he said.

"Yes sir,"

"Oh come on now, you can call me Andrew. So we got this job going on today over at Manchester near Elliott Bay. Why don't you ride along with the guys . . . they're not leaving for another hour or so. You can go do paperwork, and we'll get you fitted with the right PPE and show you the enviro shack."

Hmmm, a shack. Sounds high end, Todd laughed to himself, but he didn't have high expectations of comfort or glory. This was a job dragging around oil boom at all times of day, in all kinds of weather, at all times of year, just something to keep him out of trouble.

Andrew walked him out, saying hello to various people just getting into the office, past a swanky break room lined with glamorous photos of past jobs that Venture Diving had been involved in, and over to the HR trailer. From there he got handed off in quick succession from HR, doing paperwork and making copies of his IDs, and then to the enviro yard and shack. It wasn't actually a shack, but part of an old warehouse office, thus not very homey, and therefore nicknamed the shack. There he met the supervisor of the Enviro Division, Jeff, who quickly outfitted him with a PFD, safety glasses, gloves, and hard hat, and checked he had steel toe shoes on and raingear with him. Jeff didn't show much overt care or concern toward Todd. Todd got the feeling that maybe he burned through employees, and that was why he put the bare minimum time in to welcome Todd or make him feel prepared. But that was okay, he'd just have to prove Jeff wrong. It sounded like a good challenge to Todd.

Within a few hours, Todd was headed out the door with two guys a few years younger than himself, probably both in their early twenties. They untied a small skiff and headed out past Elliott Bay where an oil tanker was needing a fuel delivery. The weather was crap. They ran into the choppy bay, the skyline of Seattle and the Space Needle painting the backdrop, with just a small wind block for protection, and Todd observed the basics of booming, lending a hand where he could. After all Todd's experience driving skiff, he wasn't impressed with the skills these guys had, but kept that to himself, realizing they were probably city boys, just trying to learn a new job. Compared to skiff driving for salmon seining and towing a huge and heavy fishing net around, this seemed like a cakewalk. There were still tides and currents to contend with, and some fine maneuvering that needed to happen, but all looked simple compared to what he was used to.

With Todd's goal of working as much as possible (to keep him away from the urge to drink and dwell on his sorrow), this new job was perfect, as Jeff set grueling schedules, often demanding Todd work sixty to eighty hours or more a week, with booming happening at all hours of the day and night, and constant last-minute changes and notices. He learned to pack a "go bag" with a week's worth of clothes, as sometimes they'd get dispatched with minimal notice to a different job site to help with some oil booming or salvage work. He realized it would be hard to have a normal social and family life with this job, but that was not what he was looking for just now. So he threw himself into the work, starting out humble but proving himself over time, and soon all the guys were looking up to him, asking him for direction and help when something came up.

THIS WENT ON for a few months. When Ethan needed his boat for shipyard, Todd found another buddy's boat he could stay on. One day as he headed past the main office, he saw Andrew wave him up from his window overlooking the parking lot. Ever since that first day he hadn't seen much of Andrew, who managed all the salvage and enviro work, and whose days were filled with phone calls, business meetings, and visits to job sites. Todd usually saw more of Jeff, his direct supervisor, and worked out of the enviro shack where Jeff had a small office along with Dispatch. There the crew also had a small area to warm up, eat meals, stash their gear, use the bathroom, all attached to a small shop.

"Hey, Todd," Andrew said as Todd knocked on the thick wooden door that was always ajar, and entered.

"Yes?"

"Hey, I've uh, heard good things about your work."

"Why, thanks, just trying to get the job done," he said, striving to sound nonchalant, but very pleased internally—he'd heard Andrew didn't dole out praise lightly.

"So we're doing this ROV job up in Alaska right now, you know, with a remotely operated mini-submarine. The weather has been shit because it's a bit late in the season for this, and now we've also got to send a bunch of folks down to Florida to work on some hurricane cleanup, so I had to pull a person off that job. Well, the deal is we need to refill that spot on the Alaska job. Would you be available?" Andrew asked. "It'd only be for about a week with the travel, just need to get some video, and Loren needs a hand with the ROV stuff."

"Well, I don't know the ROV stuff at all, but if I can be of assistance, I'd be happy to go," Todd replied.

"Sure thing, you'll pick it up. Just basically do what Loren, our ROV guy, wants you to do, and you'll be fine."

"Okay."

"I'll let Amanda know, and she'll get you your plane ticket and fill you in on the details."

"Roger that!" Todd said with some excitement at this unknown and mysterious ROV job in Alaska.

As he turned to walk out the door, he thought of a question, "Hey, what part of Alaska did you say it was in?"

"I didn't," replied Andrew, already pouring his attention into the spreadsheets and profit margins on the screens of his computer. "But you'll be flying into Kodiak and getting on a boat from there."

Todd was grateful he had already turned away, as Andrew didn't get a chance to see Todd's face whiten while his body flooded with apprehension . . . Kodiak . . .

"Okay, sounds good," Todd answered, over his shoulder as he exited, trying to cover a shaky voice, not sure if it would be good at all.

Chapter 36

Close Proximity

Late October 2013

TODD PACKED IN a haze and state of trepidation. His thoughts had gone haywire ever since Andrew had said the word, "Kodiak." It'd only been about six months since the sinking of the *Sea Ranger*.

Amanda emailed him the flight details, set for the next morning at seven twenty a.m., not arriving in Kodiak until late that night due to a layover in Anchorage. Luckily he had his "go bag" packed so had little prep to do, no need to run back to Port Townsend to grab anything. But the jitters kept growing with the hours of waiting. His mind turned to wanting a whiskey to calm his nerves—*No!* he ordered himself, and instead called Jason, asking if he'd go grab a coffee and walk down to the local climbing gym with him, something he did from time to time when he had rare time off, mainly just to keep in shape and meet a few people.

That distraction that night worked well enough to keep him from drinking and let him burn off some of his nervous energy in explosive dynamic climbing moves. But falling asleep was an elusive challenge. Thoughts of Em, what she was doing, wondering if she was there, filled his head. She did not do social media, so he had no clue where she was. He'd thought multiple times of calling Jess to ask, but it just seemed too stalker-ish for him to follow through and hit the "Call" button, even though he'd typed in her number more than once.

Again, in the airport it was hard to pass by the restaurant where he saw people sipping cold tall beers . . . but he walked by, opting to sit as far away from that scene as possible, and tap his leg in nervous energy instead.

He used the time more productively to call Uncle David and Aunt Tammy. They had been checking in about once every few weeks, obviously concerned for him. David was getting through physical therapy and making solid progress.

But on this call Todd quickly dampened their excitement about him coming up to Kodiak, with a "Guys, this is a one-off job. I'm guessing they'll ship me right out to the site and right back in, so I might not have time to see you." Hearing the disappointment in their voices on the other end of the line, he added quickly, "But you know of course I will try to see you if I can!"

He wanted to ask if they'd seen Em, but he hadn't been able to bring her name up yet, not sure if he could handle whatever answers they had.

Flying back to Alaska was also drumming up memories of his time with the guys on the *Sea Ranger*. How many times had he flown into the Anchorage airport and met at least one of them before jumping on another flight to meet the boat at some small Alaskan village? His grief counselor had suggested journaling as a way to cope, so Todd filled some of the time waiting for flights and on the plane jotting down some of his intense feelings, free association style in a little leatherbound notebook he'd brought.

It was dark as he landed in the Kodiak airport, the island blanketed in thick clouds as they approached, and the plane shook in the turbulence as it powered down from the cloud bank into driving fall rain.

As they disembarked from the aircraft, Todd felt himself choking up, fighting back tears with all his will. All he could think of was the second to last time he'd been there, with Em leaping into his arms. *You gotta hold it together, man!*, since within minutes he'd be meeting Loren, Venture Diving's ROV operator who'd come to pick him up and get him to the hotel before their early departure the next morning. Years of practice with bottling up his feelings came into play, and he took a quick break in the airport bathroom to splash some water on his face and pull it together before walking out to meet this guy named Loren.

There were only a few people milling about at the airport at that late hour, and it was clear which one was Loren. He towered over the other people at the gate, sporting a shaved head, dark framed glasses which accentuated very dark and thick eyebrows, and a day or two's worth of salt and pepper stubble on his face. Todd guessed he was in his forties. The obvious sign was that he was garbed in a Venture Diving Carhartt jacket.

"Hey, I'm Todd," he said, as he approached and raised his hand.

"Loren," he said as they shook. "You got a bag to pick up?"

"Yup, just one," he said as they headed to the small baggage carousel. As a few suitcases and several taped-up boxes and Tupperware, probably filled with goods from Anchorage shopping trips, started dropping down the chute, Todd decided to ask, "So where are we headed?"

"It's about a ten-hour boat ride southwest from here."

Todd was pulling up a mental map of the islands and sea off of Kodiak, and the pin was dropping right around the Sitkinak Island area . . . causing his body to tense up.

"Uh, what are we looking for?" he asked, dread in his stomach that he already knew the answer.

"Andrew didn't brief you at all?" Loren asked in annoyance.

"He didn't really have time to, just said he needed a warm body up here to help you out."

"Well, we're going out on a USCG vessel to use the ROV to search for this boat that sank this spring, th—"

"The *Sea Ranger,*" Todd finished for him.

"Yes, that's the one. They're trying to locate it and gather data for the investigation they're conducting on why it sank."

Caught in the shock of this news, Todd didn't see his duffel bag drop down the chute and start to circle away. He knew an investigation was being conducted. It was standard for these sinking events, and he had even gotten a few phone calls from the National Transportation and Safety Board (NTSB). They'd also sent letters informing him that there would be a formal hearing next summer at which he'd be expected to provide testimony. When Andrew said there was ROV work in Alaska, he honestly had never dreamed that it would be for this. Alaska was so huge, with so many applications for ROV work, what were the frickin' chances it would be for the goddamned *Sea Ranger*?! How was he supposed to hold it together? First he had imagined that dealing with knowing Em might be near would be hard enough, but *now*? He really needed to stay poised. He did not want to lose this job. It was good money, and this was a great opportunity to keep advancing with the company, so the thought of dashing right back onto the plane only crossed his mind for a brief second.

"Fuck," he muttered, not realizing until after, that he'd said it out loud.

"Fuck what? Looks like you've seen a ghost," Loren noted, correctly.

Finally seeing his bag come around again, Todd covered with, "Fuck, I missed my bag, it's right here," and went over to grab it and hoist the duffel over his shoulder.

It was late, so Loren drove them straight to the hotel. There was no chance any restaurant was open, so he'd have to try to see Mimi at the Peking restaurant later. Loren handed over a room key and said, "We'll meet out here at oh five hundred." With that he turned and walked off toward his hotel room. *So much for the pleasantries,* thought Todd, as he turned away and put the key into the lock at his door.

It was a sparse room. He dumped his bag on the bed and jumped in the shower, trying to let the water wash some of his nerves away, but it didn't work. The shock of what he'd just gotten himself into was hitting his brain like screaming cars at the Indy 500. As he tackled trying to get at least a few hours of sleep before five a.m. rolled around, the shock settled in further and morphed into a more sickening feeling: *What if I get out there, and they actually find the Sea Ranger? Will I be able to handle seeing it? What if, what if . . . they find bod*—he could not finish the thought.

As four-thirty approached, Todd had only been able to toss and turn. Soon he was up, packing, making a shitty cup of coffee from the room's cheap coffee maker, and checking the weather on his phone. It looked like crap for the next day or two, but then there was a small window forecast in between two big low pressure systems. He was hoping that'd be enough time to get in, get the video, and get out, so he could go back to Seattle, where he'd been doing rather okay lately.

Loren arrived at the truck about the same time Todd did. He wasn't much of a talker at five a.m., either. They drove in silence down to the harbor, where the one-hundred-and-fifty-foot US Coast Guard vessel, one of their large buoy tender ships, was waiting with the engines and generators humming, light on the decks blinding in the early morning darkness. He could just make out the rigging of the *Tammy Sue,* tied up with the fishing fleet on the other side of the harbor.

There were a few US Coast Guard crew on deck prepping for the departure. One already knew Loren, greeted them, and led them inside to give Todd a tour. The ROV and equipment had already been loaded, as they'd made one prior attempt before they'd gotten shut down by weather. Back in August, a boat had been sent out that had used a powerful multi-beam sonar to survey the seafloor in the triangle of the last known position, location of oil slick, and estimation of drift, and had found what they thought was the wreck. The mission of this trip was to investigate that exact spot and confirm if it was indeed the *Sea Ranger,* then search for any clues as to why it had sunk. The site they'd found was at almost two hundred feet deep, so it was a much better application to send in an ROV versus a diver who'd only have short time frames to work in that depth and at greater risk.

The Coastie showed Todd to a stateroom he was going to be sharing with Loren, Todd's bunk on top as Loren had already claimed the bottom bunk. With the size of this vessel, there were a crew of about fifteen, including full-time galley staff. Next the Petty Officer gave Todd a quick tour of where the heads, galley, and mess hall were, and how to get up to the pilothouse and the area on the flying bridge where Loren had set up Venture Diving's ROV control station with computers and monitors.

Tour finished, Todd had gone back to their stateroom and started to unpack a few things when he felt the boat move and engines spur into gear, and heard three prolonged blasts, indicating the propellers were in reverse, while the boat maneuvered back a ways to then move ahead and out of the harbor.

At the oh eight hundred breakfast bell and watch change, Todd eased his way into the mess hall, joined in the short line to get some eggs and toast and standard breakfast fare, then spotted Loren already seated and chowing down. The large vessel rocked in the choppy seas as they entered unprotected waters, forcing Todd to keep a firm grip on his dish.

As they ate breakfast, Loren gave Todd the lowdown on how the ROV deployment would need to go, and what Loren expected him to do. It sounded simple enough. First, he would help the deck crew launch the vessel, then Todd needed to join Loren at the monitors and assist in relaying comms via radio to the deck crew who were tending the ROV's tether and to the captain monitoring the ship's position. It was critical that the boat above and ROV below did not drift too far apart from each other. Todd would also need to help if any technical difficulties came up.

The whole rest of the day, Todd debated if he should tell his big secret to Loren or not. He doubted that even if Venture Diving wanted to yank him off the job, they could, as they were already steaming out across the remote Gulf of Alaska.

By dinner, he couldn't hold it in any longer and decided he needed to say something. He doubted he would be able to hide his emotions if he was watching the ROV live stream and actually saw the carnage of the wreck. But Todd waited until they were both in the stateroom and the door was closed, not sure how Loren would react. It was a good thing he did wait.

"Hey, Loren, I've got to tell you something," he said, eyes cast down, fingers tightly clenching his hands in his lap as he sat at the room's small desk and chair. Loren was on his bunk getting ready to turn in and read, and looked up at Todd warily.

"So, you know how Andrew didn't tell me what job this was before I left?"

"Yes," Loren replied, sensing something was up.

"So, I ah, I used to work on the *Sea Ranger.*"

There was a long pause while it sank in. Then, "What??" he nearly shouted in disbelief, sitting up in the bunk and hitting his head on the low ceiling.

"Yes, I actually had been working on it just a few days before it sank. The only reason I wasn't on it that day was because my uncle, who lives in Kodiak, got in a bad car accident, and Phil, the er, captain, well, he let me stay off for one trip to go help my uncle and family out," he continued, letting it sink in further to Loren.

"Why the fuck didn't you say anything?!" Loren said with utter disbelief.

Why? Todd thought, then answered, "I suppose because I really want to stay working for Venture Diving. It's sort of been my salvation since the accident. It's given me something to do and put my energy into, and I was afraid if I said something Andrew'd pull me off the job and send me back, and I'd lose a good opportunity here." Then he added, "Plus, it was a little bit late. I was already up here when I found out what the job was for." Loren looked over with one eyebrow raised, so Todd continued, "And I guess I thought I could handle it."

"Well, can you?"

"I . . . don't know," he trailed off. Now that they were getting closer to the site with every hour, his doubt was creeping in.

"I guess we'll see," said Loren. "Please just hold it together long enough for us to get some good video . . ." he added, then thought in silence for a moment. "Hey, how about you tap my shoulder three times if you absolutely have to step out. But please," he said, "we really need this video. It may be the last weather window we have in months. There's *a lot* riding on this."

"I know, I totally understand . . . I mean I'll be at the freaking investigation hearing myself."

"Oh, and so will I," Loren said, bewildered at the irony of it all. "Is this even kosher?" he asked. "I mean they may want you to testify for this job as a witness, too?"

"Oh, I bet it's fine, I couldn't help it as I didn't know that this was what the job was for," Todd replied, trying to assure Loren, but he was not actually sure.

Todd saw a flash of melancholy cross Loren's face and then he looked Todd directly in the eye and said, "Hey, Todd. You know sometimes we see some stuff in this work . . . stuff that's not very, ah, pleasant . . ."

Todd was beginning to realize just that. He remembered a job that he'd heard they'd done prior to his time at Venture Diving where a recreational dive boat had caught fire and sank, burning dozens of people alive. He'd heard that the divers had had to recover the bodies, and the ROV was used to obtain video evidence for the years of trial and litigation that ensued. He also remembered when a tender in the Bering Sea had sunk just a few years prior, and that the USCG had similarly sent down an ROV and found in the wheelhouse two survival suits floating like ghosts, with presumed remnants of the crew members in them.

"Yes, I know, I'm trying to prepare myself for that."

With that Loren sighed, shrugged his shoulders, and curled back into his bunk and started to sift through a *Popular Mechanics* magazine.

Todd dressed down to his boxer briefs and crawled up in his bunk, getting out his journal to write, which was about the only remedy that would take a fraction of his nerves off. He was also thankful he was on a dry boat, no alcohol to be found.

✺ ✺ ✺

DAYLIGHT BROUGHT CALM seas. They'd arrived the night before, but it was dark, so they'd jogged behind the island and waited for daylight to begin operations. Todd geared up and headed out on deck to help prep the ROV and jump in wherever he could, not sure of his role yet. He and a USCG deckhand deployed the hydrographic pole, which supported all the electronic components that were required to be submerged below the hull of the ship. Then, after powering up the mini-sub, with the help of the ship's crane they launched the ROV with ease. Once it splashed below the choppy surface of the ocean, Todd radioed up to Loren to start doing his thing. The ROV had a clump weight attached to it that would help it descend. The clump weight, ROV, and a transponder on the bottom of the boat were all pinging their locations, which was what Todd was to help coordinate, making sure all three were in the right places. Todd then headed up to the flying bridge to join Loren, where he'd taken over with his spread of computers, monitors, jog sticks, radios, and a mess of technical equipment and cords.

Loren whispered in his ear as Todd pulled up into the chair at the corner of the ROV spread, "Are you ready for this?"

"As ready as I can be," he said, not sure at all if he was.

"Okay, here we go. And just remember the signal. I'll try to cover this on my own if we have to, but please try to hold it together as long as you can. You can deal with it all after, right?"

Todd nodded, bracing himself as if for battle.

With Todd's mounting anxiety, it seemed to take forever for the ROV to descend approximately two hundred feet to the sea floor. Finally it landed on the sand, random fish flitting here and there, terrified by the sudden onslaught of light. Todd helped communicate with the deck on positioning, as he'd been directed. Loren was hunched over, intent on the screen, his hand manipulating the joystick with expert skill. He was in his element, as it was what he lived for.

There was a strong current to contend with, maybe one to two knots, but eventually the ROV began to make headway toward the ship's presumed location. A halibut scurried away leaving a cloud of sand, and when the turbidity settled, there she was: a wall of steel filled the screen. It was disorienting to figure out what part of the boat they were looking at, but the visual was definitely manmade. Loren panned the camera's view farther left and right, picking up a red bottom paint color. He then manipulated the ROV, backing it up to allow a wide-angle view. It was then clear that the boat was on its side. It had landed portside down, and they were looking at the keel. Loren slowly worked the ROV toward the bow and up above the sand, hoping to confirm the boat's identity, but Todd already knew. He knew because he'd painted that bottom countless times. He knew every through-hull fitting and the shape of the hull like any good deckhand would.

"That's her," he whispered to Loren, voice rigid with shock.

Soon, though, Loren captured a good view of the boat's name in the video. To see the name *Sea Ranger* emerge out of the depths was more jolting than he had expected. It stood out stark and clear, well defined, hundreds of feet under the dark sea now, the finest layer of "marine snow" and silt just beginning to dust it. Todd himself had taken great care in touching up the name in the shipyard that spring. He felt his breathing tighten and tears forming, but he brushed them away with a swift move of his sleeve before any had a chance to escape down his cheeks.

The USCG personnel watching over Todd and Loren's shoulders and on another screen mounted nearby all murmured with satisfaction with the confirmation that this was the ship they were looking for. Loren then continued the ROV's movement toward the wheelhouse windows, but then having a mysterious second thought, turned it away and worked back down the hull, looking for any cracks or holes or signs of cause as to why she had sunk. Then he glided the ROV past the back deck and bait shed, noting all the debris scattered on the seafloor and along the back of the ship. They saw that two doors had been blown out (one imploded and the other exploded), and that the exhaust stack was crumpled, indicating that she'd probably landed on her stern, then rolled over to her side. It took a good long while for Loren to weave through the massive mess of gear in the debris field. If he got tangled in one line, that could spell trouble for the whole mission, so Loren took his time, inspecting certain areas the USCG investigators directed him to, looking for things like the EPIRB. Loren tried to appease the USCG and move with extreme caution, all while fighting the currents and keeping lined up with the clump weight and ship up above. And lastly, the ROV headed up toward the wheelhouse area of the boat.

Loren whispered to Todd, "You might want to look away for this part." Todd then realized why Loren had turned away from the wheelhouse when he'd been close to it earlier. Loren had avoided it as he knew what might be coming and wanted to keep Todd doing his job as long as possible. He'd already gotten over an hour of footage by now.

The video feed from the ROV was astoundingly clear, and in color. It drew closer to the wheelhouse windows facing the bow of the boat.

Some of the windows had been blown out from the impact of landing on the bottom, and some had remained. One of the broken windows allowed Loren to nose the ROV into the wheelhouse. Todd couldn't look away. It was like watching a horror movie. The wheelhouse lay in shambles, manmade objects strewn everywhere, a lone rockfish darted away from the light, and in one part of the chaos there was a bright orange shape, that of a survival suit bag, but clearly the suit was still in it, never having been opened.

Loren turned the camera to the right and kicked Todd under the table, "Look away, now," he said with a forceful whisper. As a good kick can do, it snapped Todd out of his transfixion on the screen, and he looked the other way.

He heard the USCG investigators in their dry investigative jargon recording, "One survival suit bag, one suit deployed, possibly containing a body." After another minute or so, "Possible human remains," and Todd felt the taste of bile in his throat. He tapped Loren's shoulder three times.

"Go down to the deck and help with the tether tender. We should hopefully be hauling it back up soon," Loren directed.

Todd rushed down the stairs toward the head, locked the door, and retched the contents of breakfast into the bowl. He was panicking. How could he hide this? Everything he'd worked through since that tragic day came slamming back at him. All of it. With all his might he forced those emotions down along with the nausea, rinsed out his mouth, again splashed water on his face, gathered all his strength as he unlocked the door, and stumbled out to the deck in a daze. He was worthless as they began to recover the ROV, but at least the work was easy, and he didn't have to talk to anyone. All he had to do was cable coil the tether and direct the crane operator when it came time to hoist the ROV back on deck.

As soon as the deck was all cleaned up and safely stowed and secured again, Todd went straight for his bunk, staring at the ceiling, tears hot on his cheeks, feeling a smorgasbord of rushing emotions and relived memories. Mercifully, it was hours before Loren returned to their room. He'd probably been doing a bunch of stuff Todd should've been helping with, but there was no way in hell Todd could've managed to hold it together. His eyes were dry by now, but red and distressed. He didn't want to be feeling all of this again. He'd worked so hard to get through it. But as he'd learned in therapy, it would continue to come on in waves at times, and well, this was one hell of a rogue wave he was now dealing with.

"You okay?" Loren asked once the door was secure.

"Not really. Sorry I had to bail."

"Hey, you made it through the part I really needed you for."

"I tried," was all Todd could muster.

"You did good enough, we got what we needed, thank god. We're heading back, and Amanda will be getting us the first flight possible out of this blowhole."

"Roger," Todd mumbled. That'd probably be best if they rushed back. Even though he wanted to see David and Tammy, Gunnar, and Oscar, he didn't think he could add the haunting question of whether Em was around on top of all this. The trip back went about as Todd expected. He felt wracked with emotions with nowhere to shove them, either internally or externally, as there was nowhere to run and get his energy out. He counted down the minutes until he could get off the boat.

Unloading gear the next day kept Todd busy, but he felt extremely distracted. He did have enough time to get in a quick call to Aunt Tammy and Uncle David. They came down to the loading dock at lunch, Tammy with Oscar in her arms and David walking now at a slow pace and with a slight limp. They delivered a huge bag of takeout food to share with a ravenous Todd while Gunnar ran around in circles on the dock, getting scolded not to get too far out of reach.

"Wow. Look at you!" exclaimed Todd in delight at seeing his uncle walking again.

"'Wow' is right, Shrimp! It's been a battle, but I'm not giving up," he said as they embraced and he slapped Todd on the back. After digging into the takeout, Todd finally had time to tell them what the job was for, and both David and Tammy looked like they'd been hit by a punch.

"Todd, are you okay?" David asked, deep concern in his voice and worry lines on Tammy's forehead.

"Yes, yes, I'll be fine," he tried to assure them, but not feeling solid in his answer. He felt a bit untethered, just as the ROV was now untethered, packed in amongst a pile of other gear and equipment, buried under five other boxes.

All too soon, Todd was summoned back down to the deck with a whistle from Loren, and he said quick goodbyes to his family. The work trudged along, well past dinner again, as they had to get everything ready to ship on the plane, so they ate a quick bite on the Coast Guard boat.

The next morning couldn't come soon enough. Todd hadn't had a good night of sleep since Andrew first told him about the job. Loren honked the horn and Todd grabbed his bag, heading down to the white rental work truck, dropping his key off at the front desk. The sun was just coming up, and as they drove to the airport, Todd craned his neck and eyes everywhere, searching for some sign of Em, anywhere. He tried to glance into every car, scope out any person walking . . . no sign of her. His heartbreak ached all over again. He desperately wanted to call her, hear her voice, or better yet, *see* her, hold her, enclose her in his arms. But the pain of how they'd left off, and how much torment it might cause her to see him again, held him back from dialing her number that was burning in his pocket.

The flight back to Seattle was long and bumpy, but besides that, uneventful. Todd finally got some sleep through a few small naps on the plane. Loren was sitting a few rows up, so he didn't need to worry about making small talk. As he drifted off to sleep somewhere over the Pacific Ocean and Queen Charlotte Island, Todd resolved to himself that as soon as he got back, he was going to schedule some more therapy appointments. This was going to take some serious unpacking.

Chapter 37

Post Office Talk

January 2014

A NEW YEAR'S Eve had come and gone, and Jess and Em celebrated in a quiet style, staying in to watch the ball drop on TV. Jess had been seeing less of Em since she had a new boyfriend. He lived across town and she spent quite a few nights at his place. At least Em thought this guy, Jay, was decent (the last few she had not been a fan of). The famous saying about Alaskan men was, "The odds are good, but the goods are odd," considering how in most towns men far outnumbered women, but Alaska drew "outsiders' or people looking to get away or escape something, leading to some "odd" prospects for women in the dating scene. So being in a town with the population barely surpassing five thousand, there weren't a lot of good ones to choose from, and the Coast Guard guys turned over in such rapid succession, there was no point if anyone wanted more than just a fling.

Em couldn't stomach the idea of dating again, herself. It was the farthest thing from her mind. What was on her mind, though, was a conversation she'd just had with Tammy, when she'd stopped at the Post Office to pick up her mail. As she turned around from checking her P.O. box, filled with nothing but junk mail and bills as usual, she noticed Tammy standing nearby, deliberating whether to approach or not. But having been spotted, Tammy took a step or two forward and said hello, asked how Emily was, what she'd been up to.

Then, after the basic small talk, she said, "Hey, did you know about the ROV survey they did for the *Sea Ranger?*"

"Yeah, I did hear about that." It had been hard not to hear since it was a small town. That news had set Em back into a week or so of torturous PTSD and depression, but as she processed it, she noticed a small sense of closure from knowing they'd found the boat.

Tammy gave Em a sympathetic look and quick hug, then continued, "Did you know that Todd was on the ROV team that found it?"

"What?" she gasped in surprise. "Why was he here?" She felt stabbed that he'd been here and she'd had no clue. "Why was he involved?" she asked with more confusion, in a building panic.

"Well, he's gotten a job with this Venture Diving & Salvage Company down in Seattle, and he got sent up to help out. They were short a guy."

"Ohhh," stalled Em, trying to process the news.

Sensing Em's distress, Tammy added, "But, he didn't know what the project was for until he got up here. His boss had just said they wanted him to go to Kodiak for an ROV job, and he didn't get any more specifics than that."

"Wow," she said, trying to imagine how that must've felt for Todd.

"Yeah, it was an unpleasant shock for him to find out that's what it was for, but it was sort of too late for him to decline it."

"I can't imagine. Well, thanks for telling me, I had no clue."

"Yeah, he was here only for a day or so, and had zero time off the job. The only way we saw him was by bringing him lunch when they were off-loading."

That made her feel a little less hurt, but heck, she clearly remembered what a struggle their last day had been. Even though he had tried to hide it, she knew how much she had utterly broken his heart. After that, why would she ever expect him to reach out again?

"So, how's your job going?" Tammy asked, trying to change the subject.

"Oh, good, I'm getting the hang of it pretty fast, and it sounds like someone's leaving, so there should be a spot for me to jump into when this temporary job ends, like they could transition me right over." They chatted a little more, then said polite goodbyes.

The whole walk home through the slushy snow (and the next few weeks and months and years), Em thought about how he'd been right there, under her nose. She might have driven by him and not even known it. It was a tormenting thought. And how tormenting it must have been for him to know she was nearby, *and* that he had to go out and see the *Sea Ranger* and keep it together at the same time . . .

Once home, she let herself release and spent the night crying. The hurt that he'd been in town and not looked for her felt like someone had thrown a bowling ball at her stomach. It took another massive effort to climb herself out of that sadness. Once she slowly got back up out of the hole, thanks to her new tools and the steady support from the DBT group, a subconscious seed had been planted . . . she had been toying with the idea of new work some day, and heck, Washington did have a lot more work options than Kodiak had to offer.

Chapter 38

Sink or Swim

Late October 2013

TWO DAYS AFTER his return to Seattle from Kodiak, Todd's phone rang. It was the Enviro boss, Jeff.

"Hey, Todd, can you come in at ten? We have a booming job that just came up."

"Sure, that'll work," he said, pleased it would give him time to first make some breakfast and take a shower.

A few hours later he walked into the shack to see some of the normal crew. Looked like today was going to be an odd cast of characters. There was Lin, hunched over at the table and staring at his phone like he always did, a theme so common to all the younger guys. Then there was Chad Blake. He was pushing the upper fifties, maybe even more, no one really knew, and had worked at Venture Diving longer than anyone could remember. He'd been a diver back in his younger days, when there were far fewer safety regulations. Now that he was older and probably couldn't pass his dive physicals anymore, he'd been adopted into the Enviro Division. Constantly grumpy, he scared many of the younger kids, but Todd, who was used to such gruff characters from fishing in Alaska, got along well with Chad, understanding his humor when most people misunderstood it. Behind the prickly exterior, Todd could see the big soft heart most guys like that had on the inside.

Voices tumbled from Jeff's office, and as he set his daypack down and nodded at Chad (no point in nodding at Lin staring blankly at his phone), he walked to Jeff's office to check in. To his surprise Andrew was there, leaning on a nearby desk, on a cell phone call, as he often was. In the middle of a sentence, Andrew raised his pointer finger to let Todd know not to leave yet.

"Hey, Jeff," Todd said, killing some time.

"Hey, everything's on schedule." Jeff had a screen open on his computer showing the tanker and tug on AIS that they were to boom in, approaching but still far enough out that they probably wouldn't have to leave for another half hour.

Andrew hung up. "Hey Todd, I wanna talk to you for a sec."

"Yeah, no problem, boss," he said, stomach feeling a little unsettled. *What's up? This is unusual.*

Andrew motioned to a chair by Jeff's messy desk and Todd sat.

"Hey, ya, so I talked to Loren about how that job up in Kodiak went."

"Uh huh," was all he could say, bracing himself for impact, for Andrew to let the hammer drop and maybe fire him or reprimand him for failing to provide the support Loren needed.

"What the heck, man, why didn't you tell us anything about that?"

"About what?" he asked, trying to stall for time to figure out if he was in trouble or not.

"I understand I didn't tell you the job it was for, that's on me, but why did you never mention, 'Hey guys, I worked on the *Sea Ranger,* that boat that just sank and three of the five people on it died'?"

"Well, why would that matter? I can still do the job, and I wasn't on it when it sank."

"It matters because . . . well," he stuttered, "dang, I'm just really fuckin' sorry that happened to you." Jeff was typing away on the computer, pretending not to listen, but obviously listening. "Hey, well, thanks for going up there for us like that. I'm sorry I didn't tell you more about the job beforehand. Loren said you did good, considering the circumstances."

"Thanks." He felt like he was blushing, but wasn't sure.

"Well, you interested in doing any other type of work like that? I mean, not like going back to that one, but other salvage or more technical stuff?"

"Yeah, for sure, boss!" Todd replied. "My bag is always packed."

"Right on, we'll see what else we can get you on."

Venture Diving & Salvage was notorious for pushing people off the diving board to see if they'd sink or swim, and while Todd had thought he'd sunk on his first real test, he realized heck, maybe he hadn't yet drowned.

Chapter 39

Searching for Answers

Mid-June 2014

FOURTEEN MONTHS AFTER the *Sea Ranger* sank on April 14th, 2013, the NTSB scheduled a Marine Board of Investigation Hearing to begin on Monday, June 16th. They'd sent notices to all witnesses and experts a few months prior explaining the goal of the hearing, how to testify, and how to communicate if they were going to be able to testify or not.

It was to be held in Seattle, with an online option for anyone who couldn't make it in person. The eyewitnesses summoned included anyone from welders who had worked on the boat in the shipyard, to US Coast Guard personnel that responded to the incident, to sea icing experts, to naval architects, to yup, Todd McClelland as a former crew member, and of course Emily Bancroft and Joel Arneson as survivors. In the end, over forty people were to testify.

Knowing how difficult and emotional it would be, Emily, Todd, and

Joel had all independently thought about skipping out on it, but all had come to the same conclusion: if they didn't assist in the investigation, it might not provide an accurate picture of what had happened. Hence, no lessons for the future would be gained that could help shape policy or help save future mariners from a similar fate. So they all separately decided to do the harder option and testify.

Both Em and Todd had, personally, been in touch with Joel over the last few months, so when the notice arrived in the mail, Todd called Joel up and after a quick hello, asked, "Hey buddy, you coming down to Seattle for the hearing?"

"No man, I won't be able to make the trip, can't get that much time off work. But I'll call in via the remote, online option."

"Roger that. It's nice they have that as a choice. Since I'm down here anyway, I'm going to go in person." Realizing he hadn't talked to Joel in a bit, he then asked, "So, uh, what are you doing for work these days?"

"I got a pretty good gig apprenticing as an electrician. You know I always did okay on that sort of thing with the boat work."

"Right on, that sounds good. Decent money, I've heard."

"Yeah, it's real good. Saving up to buy a fancy sports car."

"Wish I was making that kind of money! My job pays okay, but no fancy cars in the pipeline for me." Todd waited and debated if he should go serious yet. *Why not?* So he asked, "Hey, you doing okay, Joel?" He was guessing this hearing thing might be hard, having to relive the ordeal in such an intense and public setting.

Joel took a deep breath. "I think I'm as prepared as I can be."

"Have you found any ways to deal with it all?"

"Besides just working my ass off, blowing all my cash, and buying my girlfriend nice things? Not really."

After knowing Joel for years, this didn't sound like him at all. Usually he was the solid guy in the group, calm and logical, lecturing them on how to save money, not one to go out and blow cash around.

"Hey, you ever talk to Emily?" Joel asked, surprising Todd.

"No, that fell apart. I think I reminded her too much of what happened. She said she didn't want to hurt me."

"So sorry to hear that. She texts me from time to time to say hi and see how I am. I guess she'll be testifying her part of the story, too, but she'll be attending online, from Kodiak."

"Oh, good to know," he said, trying to hide his disappointment and carry on the conversation for a little while longer. After he hung up, feeling defeated, it was clear that he'd been subconsciously hoping she might be in Seattle for the investigation.

🪢 🪢 🪢

THE DAY OF the Marine Board Investigative Hearing on June 16th came quickly—well, actually the week of it, as it was set to stretch out over multiple days. Most witnesses or experts were interviewed for over an hour, sometimes more. Each day the USCG posted an update on their website, showing the docket that listed who would testify along with estimated times of when. Em, knowing this might be emotional for her, planned to take sick leave all that week. There was no way she could go in and try to concentrate while she knew the event was going on.

She wasn't going to testify the first day, so she stayed in her sweats and when it hit ten a.m., logged in online. A camera was trained on the testimony area where any in-person witnesses would sit, with courthouse-like benches behind them for the public. Then another camera was turned to the front of the room. There was a long table with multiple official-looking people, some dressed in suits or USCG uniforms with all manner of stripes and insignia, and two large screens were mounted above them to display any witnesses who would be testifying remotely so the public could see them.

The investigative hearing was conducted similarly to a trial. The LLC that owned the *Sea Ranger* (it had been a group of three older fishermen, one being Phil, that had gone in together on the business and permits and owned two other boats) had hired a lawyer to represent the boat owners. The hearing began with recapping the facts of what was known, starting with technical details, like how much the boat was worth, when it last went to shipyard, when it last had a stability survey.

The first interviewee was a white-haired old man with spectacles and a weathered face who managed the shipyard at Bronson's in Everett, Washington, where the *Sea Ranger* had last gone for yard work before heading up to Alaska for the longlining season. He was a fellow that still wrote out receipts by hand, so joining a hearing online was a big ask. After some fumbling he managed to get his camera on and audio to work. His background illuminated a messy office with tubs of bolts, nuts, and hardware on the shelves behind him. Once he took an oath and was sworn in, the investigators started out with basic questions, but quickly honed in on the specific shipyard work that the *Sea Ranger* had undergone at Bronson's. Nothing seemed outstanding or of concern. Em followed along while she worked on a knitting project she'd begun. It wasn't too emotionally distressing for her, yet.

The next day, Tuesday, Todd was set to testify. She'd had trouble getting to sleep the night before, knowing she'd be seeing him on the screen for the first time since their Seattle fallout. Currently, she could watch the proceedings with her camera off, but she knew that was soon to change on Wednesday, when she and Joel were set to talk, back-to-back.

Tuesday's hearing began with some boring legal babble, then the Coast Guard Officer introduced an ROV operator from Venture Diving & Salvage, one Loren Schwartz.

Loren was there in person, wearing a nice button-up with a Venture Diving & Salvage logo on a breast pocket. The officer swore Loren in, then asked him the standard fare like how long he'd been working for Venture Diving and with ROV's, his career history, had he ever worked on a project of this nature, etc. Loren presented himself well, exuding an experienced and confident aura. Then the investigators brought in exhibits in the form of a presentation of the ROV findings by Venture Diving.

The first slide showed the sonar findings in a 3D computer-generated image that used a color scale to indicate depth. The shape of a ship's hull popped out of the image in reds and yellows, clearly contrasting with the standard blue and green colors of the seafloor. Then the presentation moved to a map showing the location where the *Sea Ranger's* wreck had been found, overlaid by the location of the last Mayday call, then overlaid with where the oil slick had been, illustrating how the boat had traveled a small distance from the Mayday call and then sunk.

The rote material covered, Loren next jumped into the bulk of it, showing short clips of video and photos from the ROV dive survey. Emily drew in closer to her screen, bracing herself for what she was about to see.

"Hey Jess, they're about to show the videos," she called over her shoulder. Jess didn't have to work until later that day, so had let Em know if there was anything she wanted her to see to let her know, and that she'd be there for her through it all.

The video screen showed the sand settling after a startled halibut flapped away, and there emerged the bottom of the ship, on its side. Loren explained how that was the first time they'd seen it. Then he cut to the image of the name painted on the starboard bow. Em took in a big gulp of air, reality hitting her like a brick in the face. Jess, now sitting next to Em, put her arm around Em's shoulder to let her know she was there. Following that, Loren showed clips of the debris field, back deck, bait shed, and rigging, all in disarray. The presentation ended with some video of the wheelhouse, and that's where Em started to choke up. A flood of memories of the terror of the night rushed back like wind from the outside into a warm room—unwelcome, cold, and shocking.

Jess, arm still around her shoulder, squeezed harder and asked, "Em, are you sure you want to see this?"

She looked a moment longer, enough to see a survival suit bag floating in the wheelhouse. Then, to respect the families of the dead, the video cut out anyway. Loren continued to explain they'd found one suit still in a bag, the one she'd seen in the video, and one had been partially deployed, with possible human remains inside.

Oh my god, oh my god, I should not have watched that, Em scolded herself.

"Em, let's turn that off and take a break," said Jess, sounding a little shaky herself.

"Okay," she said, slapping the laptop shut and grabbing the tissues box, waiting for the old gremlins of PTSD to return. As she suspected, they did return, this time with a flashback to the sound of Manni's last screams, but over time it was as if the volume had been turned down and the screams didn't ring quite so loud. And now she knew how to welcome the disturbing images and memories in and offer them some tea, then sit with them for a few, and then how to show them the door. Still the tears flowed, and Em was thankful that Jess was there with the box of tissues and arm around her shoulder.

Todd wasn't set to talk until two, so once Em had collected herself, Jess and Em took a quick walk in the rare, nice, and sunny day. The town was busy with the usual early summer hustle and bustle, so it was a relief to return to the quiet apartment.

᯽ ᯽ ᯽

"ARE YOU READY to see Todd?"

"I don't think I'll ever be," Em said into the tea mug that Jess had just kindly filled for her.

It was one forty-five, so they turned the hearing back on, and all Em could feel was the pounding of her heart in her ribs. They stuck to the schedule, and at two p.m. the officer called Todd McClelland to come forward. There was a pause and rustle from near the back row of benches. She guessed a lot of the spectators were family members and friends of the crew. Out of the shadows and grainy film of the video recording, Todd came into view. He was dressed in khaki pants with a button-up shirt and sports coat. Words couldn't describe how dashing he looked to Em. Regret filled her at the thought of how she'd left him.

They drilled him with all sorts of mundane questions about the boat, what the safety routine and drills were, did they practice man overboard and flooding drills, did they have a damage control kit, did they have an EPIRB, what was the condition of the life raft? Todd answered them all spot on, reiterating again and again how seriously Phil took safety and kept his boat maintained. But Em had trouble paying attention to what he was actually saying. Instead, she was busy, she realized, regretting what she had let go of.

🐿 🐿 🐿

ON WEDNESDAY, JUNE 18th, Joel was set to testify before the hour-long lunch break, and Em after. She dressed up in a nice blouse, made sure her hair looked good, and figured out where she could sit in the apartment with a solid white background and good lighting. She figured Joel's testimony would be pretty similar to hers, but maybe they'd drill him a little more on the boat itself, as he knew it better than she had. Joel appeared on the screen wearing a nice white shirt and tie, but he looked rough compared to when she had first met him. It was clear he'd been struggling to take care of himself, letting his health slip, gaining a little weight, and sporting bags under his eyes. It was comforting to hear his voice again, though, as they started asking him the basics. The investigators began by directing him to walk through the events leading up to that night, step by slow and painful step.

It was incredibly rare to have the opportunity to interview survivors of a ship sinking as so many factors were stacked against anyone living through such a tragedy. Usually when a boat went down in Alaska in the winter, it took everyone with it, leaving no one to question as to what had actually happened. So with the opportunity ripe, the investigators, hungry for answers, launched question after question at Joel.

When Joel came to explain how he and Em had tried so hard to get the guys out of the wheelhouse he choked up, needing to take a break. The investigators were patient with him. Then he choked up again when he began to describe how he'd swum away from the boat and watched it sink, not sure where Emily was or if she'd made it. Reliving the same story, but through his perspective, she wondered how scared her eyes had looked when he'd first found her again, or how she'd looked from his point of view when they were at the door yelling down to Sam, Manni, and Phil to get out of there. At the end, a bit tired and frazzled by all the questions and emotions, Joel expressed palpable anger at how crappy some of the survival equipment had been and why they didn't all have the small and affordable personal locator beacons on the survival suits. The investigators nodded and took notes.

Em didn't realize until the end of his interview that she'd been clutching the armrests with white and tense knuckles. But she'd made it through listening to him retell it. Surprisingly, the flashbacks were not hitting her like she thought they would, but instead a cathartic feeling was washing over her in his retelling for all to hear, play-by-play. Confused by this unexpected feeling, she investigated it further. Maybe hearing Joel describe in detail as to what had happened was helping her to release everything she'd kept inside for so long. Everyone in town knew she was a survivor, but no one knew what had actually happened, nor did they feel okay asking her to retell it to them. Now the truth was out there for all who wanted to hear it.

🪢 🪢 🪢

TODD SAT IN the third row back, with Jason, Ethan, Caleb, and a few other friends. Carmen and her daughters were in a row in front of them, and some of Manni and Sam's families on either side. Due to his anxiety in knowing he'd soon be seeing Emily on the big screen, he'd barely touched the lunch that they'd run across the street to grab. He realized now that she was about to testify to what he had never actually gotten the painful rundown of, of what had been tormenting and haunting her ever since that terrifying night on April 14th, 2013.

Settling back into the uncomfortable bench seats, he barely heard the introductions, and then the screen turned on and projected Emily Bancroft in the front of the room above the Coast Guard Officers and NTSB investigators.

She was just as beautiful as he'd remembered, maybe a little thinner, more of her cheek bones showing than before. Her dark hair was now just past shoulder length, glistening in the light spilling onto her face from the Kodiak sun, making her green eyes glow even through the video camera. His heart was being wrung by opposing forces, wanting her and knowing he couldn't have her.

She seemed a little awkward and nervous, as had many being questioned, but as the investigators drilled into the meat of the matter, she opened up a little, and began speaking with more fluidity and detail than Joel had been able to manage. She had to draw on a nearby box of tissues a few times, but again, the interviewers let her pause and take her time, even expressing empathy within the formal testimony setting.

After about an hour-and-a-half of gripping testimony, but what felt like ten minutes to Todd, they thanked her and her screen blanked out.

Jason knew how much Todd loved Em, and gave him a quick "bro" hug to show support. That was all Todd could take for the day. At the following recess, people gathered outside the room, talking in hushed chatter. He saw Loren out of the corner of his eye, as he was going to be called back one more time that day for follow-up questions. They made eye contact, and Loren made his way over to Todd to give him a big hug that said, "I'm so sorry."

A couple of the fishermen invited him to grab an early dinner, but

Todd declined, knowing it might lead to them getting a couple of drinks, which would be a temptation for Todd.

Instead he said, "Thanks, guys, but I've gotta head back to the boat." His actual plan was to go work out or maybe stop at the climbing gym to release some of the crazy anxiety and emotion that the day and seeing Em had roiled up.

Back at Fishermen's Terminal, he ditched his original plan, instead lacing up his tennis shoes for a run. Once he started, he ran long and hard, delving right into the pain cave, pushing himself into the zone and not even knowing where he was or how far or hard he'd been running. He welcomed the pain. It was the only healthy remedy he had to deal with the image that kept flashing in his mind of a woman he so badly wanted to be with and the horror she'd lived through . . . all because she'd filled his own spot on the boat that goddamn fateful day.

The investigation wrapped up on Friday afternoon, and they announced that all the material would be reviewed and analyzed. The final conclusions would not be released for many months. However, anyone who had listened to the stories from Em and Joel could fairly certainly ascertain that the sinking was due to uneven ice buildup, then changing course into the Strait, with the new direction of the wind aiding in pushing the heavy ice-laden port side down. He was sure there'd be some major recommendations from the investigation, like having every crew or survival suit being outfitted with a personal locator beacon device, and investigating why the EPIRB released but did not put out a signal, and maybe some issues with the naval architecture and stability surveys. But he'd have to be patient and wait for the official Report of Investigation. Not that it'd bring the guys back.

So life went pretty much back to normal, except for the ever-aching feeling in his heart. Venture Diving put him right back to work and he was busier than ever, too busy to think about much of anything else other than work.

Chapter 40

Goodbyes and
New Beginnings

March 2015

THIRTY YEARS OLD was a big number, and it hit Em like stepping into a hot sauna, making her rethink where she was in life and where she wanted to go. She'd spent the last two years since the accident working for the Department of Fish and Game in the research division in Kodiak, securing a permanent job and jumping up a few rungs on the ladder in the process. Jess had kept her last boyfriend, Jay, and officially moved in across town with him. They still saw each other a lot, but now Jess was busy with him most of the time. Em made enough money in her current job that she didn't need to find a new roommate, nor did she want to, as Jess would've been impossible to replace.

Em had thought about dating, but couldn't quite stomach it, plus she had not yet come across a guy who seemed remotely interesting or attractive to her. Now that her thirtieth birthday was in her face, it set her searching for something else. She began casually scoping out jobs that were out of state, in the Lower 48, as Alaskans called the contiguous United States. Kodiak didn't have sufficient options for promotion, at least in her current role, and she was feeling the isolation and difficulty of living in such a remote place, her parents very far away and getting older by the year.

So she dabbled at searching job postings, especially in Washington as it was the closest Lower 48 state to Alaska and had a significant maritime industry, but for months, nothing interesting came along. She'd begun to lose hope when suddenly she scrolled past a unique job description, unique enough to make her scroll back up. Washington State was hiring a specialist for its Derelict and Abandoned Vessel Program. It was a program funded by watercraft registration taxes that targeted removal of boats that had become abandoned, derelict, sunk, aground, or in danger of sinking, and then worked with state-vetted contractors to remove the vessels from state waters.

She bookmarked the webpage link and planned to look into it more that weekend. At first she'd been thrown off by the sunken boat part of the job description, afraid it would be too triggering for her, but the more she looked at the website about the program, the more intrigued she became. The job was eighty percent land based, but included some time out on the water visiting the sites, and it involved project management, which was something she'd always thought her organizational skills would lend a hand at. So what better was there to do on a Saturday night than apply for a job?

It took about three months from the time she hit Submit for the application. She'd triumphed through two rounds of interviews, then waited and waited to hear back, then finally accepted the job offer with cautious excitement. The next steps were to make arrangements to pack up and drive down to Washington. She hadn't realized how much she missed the excitement of the unknown and trying new things, exploring new places and making new friends, until the reality of finding herself about to move to a place three thousand miles away re-sparked that flame of adventure.

PACKING UP HER little black truck was a bittersweet process. Em culled the possessions she'd take with her and sold or gave away what she didn't want. Jess held a goodbye dinner at Tony's for old-time's sake. The bar was yet again packed with folks that had been in and out of her life in Kodiak over the years. It was a close community, making what "community" was defined as in the Lower 48 pale in comparison. So many hugs and laughs and smiles and a few teary eyes, and Em was overflowing with gratitude.

Getting on the *Tustumena* ferry was harder than she'd expected. It made it final, no turning back, even if she'd wanted to. As the car loading gate closed, Em went up to the top deck and could see good old Jess waving and blowing hugs and kisses at her with Jay at her side from the dock. Em sent back a big smile and wave, her heart full of gratitude mixed with the sadness of a goodbye, knowing true friends like Jess may only come once in a lifetime. She stayed out on the deck until Jess and Jay were just specks on the horizon.

Chapter 41

Coffee Stains

July 2015

NOW THAT TODD had been at Venture Diving a few years, he'd graduated from booming jobs and moved up to the Casualty Response team. And he *loved* it, other than never being home. He'd finally scraped up enough money to buy a place north of Seattle, near Everett, where things were a little cheaper. It was a white, one-story, fixer-upper with two bedrooms and a bath. The key selling point for Todd was that the backyard bordered on some Land Trust property, promising that the woods behind the house would never be developed. From the outside it didn't look like much, but it was something he could call his own and a place to crash and do laundry at when he was back in town. Maybe someday he'd get to the projects he really wanted to, but currently Venture Diving kept him way too busy.

Todd was fresh back in Washington after a month-long job over in Hawaii. It'd been a tricky one and taken longer than first expected. The

Coast Guard had hired Venture Diving to remove a fifty-foot sailboat that had wrecked beneath a two-hundred-foot cliff in a remote corner of the Big Island with very tricky access, if any at all. They'd had to get really creative on this one, which is what Todd thrived on: the challenge, problem solving, thinking up outside-the-box solutions. The normal method of patching the holes and using lift bags to tow it off failed after the first day or two. So instead they'd decided to fill the boat with tons and tons of spray foam, using helicopters to assist, and then using a tug with a really long line to tow it off with this new buoyancy . . . and it had worked (albeit floating upside down due to so much buoyancy so close to the keel). But that was no problem, they towed it right into the Hilo Harbor that way. Just sourcing enough spray foam to fill the hull was a challenge in itself, as it had to be shipped via barge, due to its HAZMAT nature, all the way to Hawaii from California.

Now that he was back, Todd was due down at Venture's headquarters to do some follow-up administrative work of dotting the i's and crossing the t's that followed a big and complex job. Plus it was Monday, when his team had their weekly Casualty meeting. He loved telling people these days that he worked in Casualty. They would often raise their eyebrows in confusion until he'd explain it was a term for salvaging and removing vessel casualties, although, as he very well knew, sometimes human casualties as well.

That week, Kevin and some envirotechs were down on the Columbia River, working on a large fishing vessel deconstruction, so they'd be joining the meeting on the phone, if at all. Andrew was still the man in charge, and he'd be leading the meeting, and then Leif and Scott were probably in the office as well, as they'd stayed local doing an easy thirty-foot sailboat removal down on the Duwamish.

Todd dropped his Pelican case—which had sort of become his man purse, a place to keep all of the essentials for a day's work: work knife, roll of electrical tape, spud wrench, wallet, sandwich—in the office he shared with Scott. The room was filled with random memorabilia from different salvages—old ship's wheels, portholes, brass fittings—along with some windows looking at the drab parking lot, so one could see who was coming and going. Todd headed down the hall to the break room, grabbed a Venture Diving coffee cup, and filled it with the ever-present coffee on the counter, then headed up the stairs to the top level where one of the elegant conference rooms was, its windows facing the main street and train tracks. It never failed that a train would rattle by in a heated part of a conference call, deafening all chances of conversation.

Once Todd sauntered in, Scott and Leif halted their animated conversation about a subcontracting issue. Andrew nodded a hello, and then started the meeting without delay. Leif sat on the end of the U-shaped table, like a giant hulk. He was a big, tall guy with a wild beard. Scott sat a few chairs down, just about the most opposite body type as possible from Leif's, lean and wiry, maritime-related tattoos covering every square inch of his arms, with a clean-shaven baby face. Then there was Andrew taking up the middle of the table, decked in a button-up as usual, but today, it was a plaid shirt that matched some of the red of his hair.

Andrew led the discussion, going over how each current job was going, any issues coming up, then scheduling for the following days, writing up punch lists and what reports needed to get written. Report writing for clients was part of Leif's job, as he was a Senior Salvage Master (such a niche job that fewer than forty people could claim that title in the whole United States), while Todd and Scott were Salvage Specialists, a step below a Salvage Master. Both titles were more of an "earned" title from the actual on-the-job experience. Leif was the brains with more experience, and Scott and Todd were more of the brawn, but they all worked together and collaborated on all aspects of all the projects. In addition to tackling some of the most technical and complicated jobs, Leif also put together bids for clients.

The meeting seemed pretty standard, and Todd was directed by Andrew to join Scott on his job down by Olympia the next day to remove a boat that had caught fire in the marina and had sunk at its slip, when Leif added, "So, looking at the State contracts, I saw a work order come in for a boat removal of the old one hundred-foot wooden passenger vessel that's wrecked high and dry by Jetty Island. We were out there originally to remove the pollution about a month or two ago. You guys remember that?"

"Let's get on that one!" piped in Andrew with excitement. Where they really made their money was on the bigger jobs, *if* they could win the bid against their competitors, and *if* Leif's estimates and project planning were accurate.

"Yeah, for sure," said Leif, then added as a side note, "I noticed a new name listed as project manager."

"Oh yeah, who?" asked Andrew. They almost always worked with just one guy from the State Derelict and Abandoned Vessel team, a fellow named John Bellows.

"It's some lady's name," Leif squinted to look closer at his laptop screen, "It's an Emily, uh, Emily Bancroft."

"What?!?" Todd nearly choked and spit out the coffee he'd just taken a sip of across his project notebook.

Everyone looked up at him in surprise. Then he turned bright red as he tried to sop up the coffee with his sleeve. Eyebrows went up in even further confusion as his face remained heated.

"Do you know this Emily?" Andrew asked suspiciously.

"Uh, yeah, you could say so," he said.

Knowing the true nature of guys, Todd saw the bantering had already begun, with Scott jumping in now with, "Well, *how* well do you know her?"

Seeing where their little innuendos were going if he let them continue, Todd realized the best way to stop it was to tell them the truth, or most of it at least, to sober them up a little. Plus if they knew the truth maybe it'd earn Em a little respect from them. Right now she was just a name to them.

"Scott," Todd said sharply and looking him in the eye, "you remember the *Sea Ranger* sinking up by Kodiak a few years ago?"

"Yes," he nodded.

"Well, I was supposed to be on it the day it sank, except Emily took my place for that trip."

Leif and Scott's jaws dropped. As Andrew already knew at least about the *Sea Ranger* part of it, Andrew sat back and watched Todd handle it, but with some surprise about this new Emily part of it.

"You're for real?" asked Scott.

"I'm not fucking kiddin' you. Why would I joke about something like that?"

That shut them up, and they moved on to the next order of business, although he knew they were still burning with curiosity about what had actually happened.

Chapter 42

Tested

November 2015

EM MIGHT HAVE quit the new job early on if John hadn't been such a supportive and patient supervisor. After months of intense training and countless questions, Em was starting to get the gist of all the complex ins and outs of her job, how to obtain custody of an abandoned or derelict boat, how to put the work out to bid, award it, see the project through, enter data into GIS, deal with constant interactions with the public and other entities, and countless other details. Little did the public know, there were hundreds of derelict vessels across the state with new reports coming in every day. That was the most demoralizing part of the job. Em was witnessing how it sometimes took weeks and months of work to make one derelict boat go away, and in that time there'd be ten new ones reported. Before she'd signed on, she'd had no idea what a massive problem it was.

Her first removal was just a small job, a twenty-five-foot sailboat, but

John led her through it every step of the way in spite of the twists and turns of it breaking free while waiting for custody, then grounding elsewhere. Soon she tackled a few larger vessels.

One thing that she had been naive about upon hiring was who exactly the state hired to do such work. The thought that Venture Diving & Salvage might be one of the contractors had crossed her mind, but she glossed over it, or maybe intentionally tried to block it out, as she had no clue whether Todd still worked there. She did once or twice pull up Venture Diving's webpage and look at the link that showed who's who at the company, although it only listed the Division managers, so she never saw his name included. *Has he moved on to something else? Has he moved away from Washington? Has he gone back to fishing?* Then she had a thought she tried to brush away as quickly as it came to her, *Does he have a girlfriend now?* Maybe she wasn't prepared for the answer, she realized.

Now that she'd been in her new position for almost six months and had a few removals under her belt, she was feeling more confident, but had also been noticing just how often they hired Venture Diving, as they seemed to have a reputation as being one of the most competent outfits around and won a lot of the bids. Besides that surprise, overall she was finding the job engaging enough for her active mind, and she was enjoying the complexities of each new situation with each new boat.

Her next big project was going after a half sunk old seine fishing boat and smaller sunken gillnetter that were causing problems in the sloughs near Marysville. Itching to get out and away from computer screens, Em planned to do a site visit to observe Venture Diving, who'd won the bid. Her boss was always supportive of her getting out in the field, but her week was packed, so she had only allowed herself one day for her site visit.

The spring weather was rainy and about forty degrees, with ninety percent humidity and a dampness that made it feel much colder than it was. Em bundled up as she awaited one of Venture's work skiffs to come pick her up from a public boat launch and take her to the job site.

Getting in skiffs and non-fishing vessel boats had thus far been no problem for her, and the PTSD from the *Sea Ranger* sinking was much better and more manageable now. Thus, she wasn't too nervous about getting aboard the dive-support landing craft, the *Illiamna*. But what she *was* worried about was what she'd do if Todd happened to be there. It was years ago that she'd heard from Tammy in the Post Office that he was working for Venture Diving and almost a year and a half since the investigation hearings. Most likely he was *not* still at the company, or at least that's what she was telling herself in an effort to stay calm. She still hadn't heard his name mentioned, but that was not exactly evidence he did *not* still work there.

Soon she heard the buzz of an outboard and the whitewash of an aluminum work skiff headed down the river, the logo of the dive company plastered across its side. There were two guys in hard hats, PFDs, and rain gear as it pulled up for her. Definitely neither was Todd. She hopped in and helped them push off. They were not a talkative bunch, and Em guessed they were probably wary of her as she was coming from a government agency to "observe" their work, so they rode most of the fifteen-minute journey in awkward silence. They slid under massive highway bridges, past dikes covered in invasive blackberry, a sprawling lumber yard, and then into the heart of the sloughs. There, the original property owners had illegally built docks many years ago, and many disliked any form of government reminding them of this in their largely unregulated, backwater sloughs. The few people out on the docks gave them cold stares as they motored by. Many a neglected, abandoned, or derelict vessel had met its untimely "death" in the sloughs. It was a great place for a boat to go to die.

Around the bend, there sprawled the massive *Illiamna* taking up almost half the channel, several small work skiffs tied to its side. Alongside was a barge with its towering spuds set, anchoring it in place on four corners, with yellow contractor oil boom surrounding it and the wrecks. As they tied up to the side of the *Illiamna,* a gruff-looking giant of a man came over, garbed in a Hi-Vis hoodie that was no longer so Hi-Vis, and introduced himself as Leif. He towered over her, and as he turned to show her the job site said, "Just watch your step," as if she'd never been on a work boat before.

The boat was littered with industrial equipment ranging from big winches and anchors, to diving-related gear, compressors, and apparatus, to a boom crane, and to the Conex that served as a dive shack. The *Il-liamna* had a huge landing craft door on the bow that was currently open with a diver known as a "tender" minding the diving umbilicals stretched out and into the water. At the stern there was a small work room with a head and a ladder going down to the engine room, and then a small wheelhouse was located on the second level above it, where more diving compressors were mounted around the back of the pilothouse. Flying above all the maze of rigging and equipment were crisp American and Venture Diving & Salvage flags flapping in the moderate breeze.

Leif explained there was currently a diver down working on rigging a strap around a piece of the gillnetter to hoist out with the boom crane. After their initial attempts to sling and lift it, they discovered it was rotten and just kept ripping apart like crepe paper as the fiberglass had been underwater for so long. Leif opened the dive shack door, and Bryan, a stout, bearded guy with a round face, who appeared to be in his thirties turned his head, hand on a mic, computer screen showing what the diver's video camera was live streaming. There was a heater blasting, which was very welcome as Em was already chilled from the skiff ride.

"Feel free to hang out here, or up in the wheelhouse, or on deck," Leif said as he turned and walked back out to yell at the tender to unhook the straps from the latest piece of debris that had just landed on deck. Em took a bittersweet sigh. Todd was apparently not here. Instead, it was Leif, Bryan, and three other divers she learned she was going to hang out with for most of the day. Bryan turned his attention back to the computer screen, largely ignoring her and talking to the diver through the mic, then relaying what the diver needed to the tender out on deck, which he had another camera on and a view through the window of.

Em returned to her old habit of trying to stay silent and observe what the scene was on a boat before trying to fill her new role. Her old training from fishing was coming in handy. As she listened, the way the guys talked to one another, joking around half the time and then in an instant getting real serious and yelling at someone for something, then everything going back to normal with no hard feelings, felt strangely comforting. She knew exactly how to navigate this environment, as she'd spent years in it. She guessed commercial divers and commercial fishermen were more similar species than they cared to admit.

Eventually, after Bryan continued to ignore her or just answer her few questions with short yeses or noes or grunts, she caught him looking at his phone on the side, scrolling through diamond ring options. Before she could calculate whether she should ask or not, she blurted out, "You getting married?"

"Well, it's for my girlfriend. We're thinking about it. I was going to take her shopping next weekend." And for some reason that question she'd asked popped open the lock, and Bryan started chatting with her, sharing details about his personal life.

Okay, Em thought, *I can do this*, with relief at breaking through his suspicious reserve toward her.

Some of the other guys would pop in and out, have a heated discussion about how things were going, and leave. Eventually Em left watching "diver TV" and wandered out of the dive shack to go up to the upper level near the wheelhouse where the crane was. Leif was operating it, trying to hoist sections of the boat that the diver below had rigged for lifting. She stayed quiet there, too, for a while standing off to the side and out of the way, but in between lifts, Leif started getting more chatty with her. Em was not normally a fan of garrulous talkers, but the stuff coming out of Leif's mouth about salvage work was fascinating and knowledgeable. Once he got going talking about his work, she guessed he could talk for hours about it. Maybe she could "fish" for information a little, too, she thought.

During another break in activity while the divers swapped out, as one had met his max diving time, Em asked as casually as possible, "So how many of you salvage guys are there at Venture? I know of you, and I've talked with Andrew . . ." she paused to let him fill in the rest.

"There's four of us, then one guy that does more of the command center type stuff."

Damn it, no names, she mused. She decided to go wild and just make up a name to see if he'd correct her, "Is Toby one of them?"

"No, we don't have any Toby's. We've got me, Andrew the Casualty Manager, Kevin, Scott, and Todd." Her eyes widened, and Leif, catching her response, continued with, "I'm guessing you meant Todd."

Leif, who hadn't forgotten Todd's shock at first hearing Em's name in their meeting, adeptly picked up on Em's continuing shift in expression and blushing of her cheeks with the mention of Todd's name. She'd been caught in her now not-so-sly probing attempt. But just at that moment, Leif's phone rang loudly from the dash of the wheelhouse and he excused himself, picked it up, and started explaining to someone else on another job what they should be doing.

After a few minutes to digest the news that Todd did indeed still work at Venture Diving, Leif came back out and continued with, "Yeah, Scott's on a job in Oregon right now, but Todd was here yesterday, you know to sit around and kick the tires."

She could tell he was watching her reaction still with an odd amount of curiosity, and she was having trouble hiding her disbelief. She had missed being in the same space and time as him, after years apart now, by a fucking day!

"Uh huh," she said, not able to come up with anything else. Luckily the new diver had dropped back in the water, and Leif had to turn his attention back to actual work.

She'd already been at her job for over six months and was only now realizing Todd had probably been on some of the jobs they'd won from the State. Were they destined to stay as ships crossing in the night— near, but never actually meeting? Would they ever meet again? If so, how long would it take—a few weeks, a year, or years, . . . or never?

Those were the questions bouncing in her head on the drive home, and *not* how the actual salvage went, like she usually thought about.

Chapter 43

"Mobing" Up

May 2016

TODD WAS AT his desk in the Venture headquarters, and it was getting late in the day. Most of the folks had already left for home. Heavy footfalls echoed down the stairs, and Todd guessed it was Andrew.

He was right. "Hey, Todd," he said. "Burning the midnight oil?"

"Naw, I'm just finishing up here."

"Good. So, slight change to the schedule tomorrow."

This was pretty much a daily occurrence, so Todd said, "Alright, hit me."

"Well, I got a call from Emily from the State. They need to enact the Emergency Contract and hire us for a job up on Dungeness Spit. You know, near Port Angeles and Sequim."

"Oh yeah?" he said, already intrigued, for more than one reason.

"A sailboat wound up on the Dungeness National Wildlife Refuge, and it's a sensitive area, so she's pulling the trigger on it. I took a quick look, and it's way out on the end of the spit. She suggested maybe using an excavator and tracked dump truck, and access should be okay, but at low tide only. That's what I'd recommend, too. Apparently they just removed a sailboat out there, so they already know how to get the permissions from the wildlife refuge and from the neighboring property owner with the only road access to the spit."

"Sure, I can handle that one."

"I told her we'd start "mobing" tomorrow with removal the following day or so. She seemed fine with that."

"I'll get right on it. Send me the info you got," Todd said, already opening Google Earth and zooming in to the spit, but internally his mind racing to . . . Emily.

As Andrew turned to leave, he paused and looked back at Todd with a concerned, almost fatherly look in his eye, his big frame blocking the light from the hallway.

"You okay to do this one?"

"Yes, of course."

"Come on, Todd. I know your track record of accepting emotional jobs."

"Hey, boss, she probably won't even be there, she's not able to make it out to most of the jobs. And even if she is, it'll be fine, I promise."

"Okay, just checking," he said with doubt and left, climbing back up the stairs to his office down the hall.

Todd was already running logistics, what subs he'd need to call, where to get the equipment from, what to load up from the warehouse, how many crew he'd need, where the nearest landfill for disposal was, travel arrangements, and ferry schedules. But one thing he knew he needed an answer on, was Em going to be there or not? Was he by chance (or maybe was it fate?), going to finally see her? Would this be the time their paths *finally* actually intertwined, or would they miss each other, yet again? If not, he figured with a heavy acceptance, maybe the universe meant to keep them apart for good.

AFTER FIGURING OUT the basic plan and making the most essential calls, Todd wrapped up his day, which had already been a long one. At least some of the rush hour traffic was eased up by the time he got back to his empty house. The thought of doing this job for Em dominated his mind, so much so he didn't even think about eating until after nine. The big question of whether she was going to be there kept him up all night, and roused him early due to nervousness he hadn't felt since the days of the Kodiak job and the investigative hearing.

As he rolled back into Venture's headquarters all too early the next morning, his nerves were so high that even though he was sleep deprived, he knew he didn't need the extra shot of espresso in his coffee, but went for it anyway. He had to make a few more phone calls, meet with the two crew he'd have along for the job, grab the equipment they'd need, and start to mobilize for Sequim, a good three to four-hour drive away.

Should I call her or not? He didn't technically need to know if she'd be there. It was standard practice that the client was always welcome to come out to the site and observe, not needing permission beforehand, and often they did not come out. However, he was starting to feel that he needed to know.

"Todd," Mark asked out in the warehouse loading bay, "where do you want this?" He waited a moment, watching Todd staring at a tub of spare hose clamps and fittings, not moving. A little louder this time, "Hey! Todd!" With a quick jump, Todd shook his head and glanced over, where he saw Mark holding a big Sawzall.

"Oh, throw it in the response trailer." His mind had been lost in thoughts of Em, and realizing he was losing focus in a now noticeable way, turned on his heel, shouting over his shoulder to Mark, "I'll be right back." He shoved his work gloves into his back pocket and headed back to his office. He couldn't stand it anymore. He had to get this over with.

Luckily Scott was out on another job, so he had the space to himself and shut the stout wooden door behind him. He knew he had to stay professional. He had so much more to say to her, but he knew this was not the time or place. *Is this really happening? Am I ready for it? Only one way to find out,* he thought as he typed in her number listed on the work order and hit the green Call button, bracing himself as the phone began to ring.

Chapter 44

No Other Choice

May 2016

"HEY, YOU COMING out for this one?"

The caller ID had a 206 area code number she didn't recognize, but the voice she *did* know. It felt like she had just walked into a glass door. This was no doubt Todd McClelland calling her about the Dungeness Spit job. A blur of possibilities and factors raced through her mind. Then her reply came before she could think further, "Oh, ah, let me check the ferry schedule."

"Sounds good. With the tides we got, we're going to start up around oh nine hundred tomorrow."

"Okay, I'll see what I can do."

And after a quick, "Sounds good, see you there," he hung up. She stared at the phone in disbelief. It had been years now of thinking of him every day, but now—to see him in person?! Was she ready for this? She couldn't read from his tone during their strictly-business, thirty-second phone conversation whether he wanted her there or not. Was there a hidden invitation in it? She didn't want to get her hopes up, so she tried to push that thought aside.

As she opened up the webpage for the ferry reservations, she realized her heart had been beating like a hummingbird trying to get out of her chest, and her palms had grown sweaty. Late spring was a tough time to get an open spot on the ferry. She plugged in the dates, only one day away, and prepared herself for disappointment. The page loaded, and dang, she was in luck as there was still space available. As for timing, she realized she would have to stay overnight, so she then prepared herself to be disappointed about the return options which would need to be the next day, and, and, and, she waited for the page to load—boom! To Em's great surprise, space was also available late that second day for the return trip, not at the best time that day, but still there was a spot open. And she decided to take it.

"Hey, John." She tried to sound cool as she talked to her boss. "It looks like that *Mystic Sea* job on the Spit is going to happen tomorrow. I checked the ferries, and it looks like I could make it over there. I think it might be good to observe this one, you know, connect with the wildlife refuge folks, and all."

"Yeah, no problem. That sounds fine to me. Get yourself a hotel."

So yeah, to stay overnight, that was a reservation she hadn't quite thought of where to make it at yet. Way out on the Olympic Peninsula, there weren't many options. She did a little more Internet searching and came up with the standard motel that looked the cleanest and most economical, trying not to think about where the Venture salvage crew were going to be staying.

THE NEXT MORNING, as she pulled up to the wildlife refuge's parking lot, yet again Em felt her heartbeat begin to pick up. She couldn't believe this was finally happening. After a quick check in with the park ranger, she headed back out to the parking lot, daypack in hand. She discreetly glanced at her reflection in a car window to make sure she looked half decent, and headed toward the trail. The ocean pounded in the distance, and the salt was heavy in the air. Her footsteps were muted on the golden pine needles and spongy Pacific Northwest earth, and she glided as if in a dream. As she neared the bluff, the vastness of the ocean spread out over the horizon, and the calls of seagulls started to build along with the nostalgic odor of low tide, the smell of where land meets the sea.

There, at the beginning of the five-mile-long spit of sand, the longest natural sand spit in the nation, she saw a white truck with an excavator on a trailer, a Morooka (tracked dump truck), and three guys in hard hats gathered round in a circle. They'd already taken all the equipment down the private road, accessed from a different neighborhood from the refuge.

She took a look at the crew, looking small from her high spot on the overlook. They must be doing their morning tailgate safety meeting, she thought. Todd was easy to spot. His strong build and generous height stood out against the lanky guy next to him and the other with the beer belly. *Here I go*, she told herself with a gulp, in an effort to boost confidence and quell the anxious nausea brewing in her stomach. It took a few moments to climb down the trail from the bluff, and as she approached the guys it looked like they were getting ready to head out. "Beer Belly" was climbing into the Morooka. Todd was opening the door to the truck, and as he looked back over his shoulder saw Em approaching. He paused and looked right at her. She swore she saw him take a quick inhale, as if he was bracing himself for a storm.

"Hey, good timing," he said with a smile, a smile that was betraying so much history between them.

"Yeah, I got lucky. I was the last car on the ferry this morning."

"Good thing you made it, then. We were just about to head out. Hop on in," and he nodded to the passenger side.

❧ ❧ ❧

EM PLANNED ON getting in the back, but Todd's nod signaled to the other guy to relinquish the front seat, so Em sheepishly walked around, giving the lanky guy a smile and "Sorry" look at the same time for taking his front seat. Once inside and after stashing her bag at her feet, Em took a deep breath and took another sidelong look at Todd. It had been three years since she'd been this close to him. He looked as ruggedly handsome as ever, a little more worn and older, but so was she. Words wanted to flow, but she didn't know where to start. She wanted to blurt out, "Todd, I'm so sorry. I know I deeply hurt you. I still love you . . . I always did, but I was just too much of a mess." Instead she checked all that at the door, especially with an onlooker sitting behind them.

She did manage, "So, looks like it'll be a good weather window for this one." It was dumb, of course it was. It was obvious it was going to be a bluebird spring day and not a breath of wind forecast for the next few days.

"Yeah, you should've seen the sunrise this morning."

"Well, I did, sort of, from my drive."

"Oh yeah? Where'd you come over from?"

"Bellingham."

Todd's eyebrow rose. "Oh really? I've got a place in Everett now." Bellingham was only about an hour or so away from him when there was no traffic.

Changing subjects he asked, "Hey, do you know Jeremy?" nodding toward the guy in the back.

With introductions made and a slow bumpy ride out to the site, they made small talk, catching up on recent jobs he'd done and where in the country he'd been. She was completely enthralled with his every word. She wondered if he'd noticed just how much her hands were shaking. None of their small talk really mattered, except, actually it all really did matter.

🪢 🪢 🪢

ALL TOO SOON, they were at the site, the forlorn boat beached high up at the high tide line, debris strewn up and down like the scene from a plane crash. The trip out had flown by, Em's eyes and mind barely looking at anything else but Todd, forgetting Jeremy was even in the truck with them. All of the PTSD she'd once associated with Todd and her fear of hurting him had long since melted away. It was mostly thanks to the endless therapy work, the strangely cathartic reliving of the event during the hearings, and her support network of Jess, her family, and a few friends from the DBT group. She wondered if he had forgiven her for leaving him so coldly in Seattle years ago and never reaching out again. How could he have? He certainly didn't look her up when he'd had a chance to in Kodiak.

Now, at the site, came the awkward part. She was used to working her ass off as a commercial fisherman, always finding something to do, some way to be helpful. Now in her state agency role, she couldn't lend a hand as she was formerly trained to do. Instead of jumping in and getting dirty, her role was to "observe," so she awkwardly took a post nearby on some driftwood and made herself as comfortable as she could. Next she fished out her binoculars and notepad to look busy and give herself a distraction. *Maybe there'll be some interesting birds to watch*, she told herself, but realized she'd probably be watching something else . . .

Once the guys got going, it was impossible not to notice the command, authority, and confidence Todd carried in what he was doing. It dawned on her that she'd never actually had a chance to watch him do his thing, as it was *his* shoes she'd been filling on the *Sea Ranger* when it sank. It was impressive to watch him work, directing the other guys, hopping in and out of the excavator, finessing the machinery, grabbing a Sawzall, taking a work phone call amidst it all. And dang, as the sun started to rise toward noon and the beach slowly warmed up, it was impossible for her not to stare when Todd stepped over to the truck and took off his hoodie. He was wearing a worn blue T-shirt, and through it she could see the musculature of his back, and by god, the sight of his sculpted arms instantly made her flush. Em quickly looked away and fumbled with her water bottle. *He shouldn't be allowed to do that—work in just a T-shirt!* She scolded herself for gawking. A few people trekking out to the lighthouse stopped by, curious about the action, providing a good distraction and excuse to feel somewhat useful instead of gazing at Todd.

🪢 🪢 🪢

THE SUN SHIFTED, the tide went out and came back in, and it was time to head back before they were trapped by high water. One more day, and the job would be done. The ride back flew by too fast. This time she could smell the sweat and grime off of him, and it was intoxicating. Just from being in proximity, she felt a jolt or two of electricity run up and down her body. *How has he changed in the last few years?* she wondered.

Back at the mobilization spot, as Em got out of the truck and turned, she found Todd standing in her path, blocking her exit. Jeremy had gone off to unload some things from the back of the truck. Em was cornered, as the truck was behind her and Todd directly in front. He took another step into her space, but she wasn't running anywhere, nor did she want to.

He looked her right in the eyes, and said, "Hey, we're going to grab some dinner, want to join us? On us . . ."

She couldn't believe this was actually happening, and stammered, "Uh, sure, where were you going? But hey, you know with this job, you know I can't take gifts. I can cover my own dinner."

He said, "Just look the other way when I pay the bill, you'll be fine. How about McNeal's, maybe in an hour or so?"

She gulped and nodded.

"Call me if you get lost," he said over his shoulder as he turned to help the guys unload. Her heart was already racing as she started the steep hike back up to the top of the bluff, which only increased it further. *What the heck?!* she said to herself as she glided the rest of the way through the forest trail to her truck, as if there were wings on her feet. *What am I getting myself into? This is going to be trouble . . . !* But she knew there was no turning back, no saying no, no regretting. She needed to find out where this path of fate would lead. So much had happened between them, but she was a different person now. She was healed, and all that time spent wondering about him, knowing he might be near but unattainable, was about to draw to a close. She'd find out who he was now. Strong feelings started to unleash inside of her as the reality of the situation set in.

After checking in at the motel, Em took a quick look in the mirror. Her hair was windblown and her face etched from a long day out in the elements, but Em had time to take a shower and change into some more appropriate "town clothes." It would have to do. She didn't have any other options so couldn't try on multiple outfits. She'd packed light.

The guys were already at the restaurant when she timidly opened the door and did a quick scan of the dimly lit interior with its bar and a few pool tables in the back. There was some 80s music playing in the background and a lot of old-timers at the bar, none even looking up when the blast of cool air entered with her.

"Hey ya," he said as Em approached. They were at a round table, and the seat next to him was open. "You clean up pretty nice," Todd said just loud enough for only her to hear.

Totally inappropriate! But of course she loved it. It reminded her of their first playful days . . . before the ship sank. There hadn't been enough of that.

"You, too," she returned, looking him up and down. He had showered too, had nice(er) work pants on and a clean plaid shirt, top button or two undone enough so she could see some of his tantalizing chest.

She was getting all kinds of signs from him that he was glad she was there. The walking on clouds and disbelief at what was happening were starting to build like a thunderhead, a feeling she hadn't felt since before the accident.

The conversation returned to the other crew and how the day went, but under the table, as they all started to flip through the menus, Em felt Todd's leg next to hers, and goddamn, another jolt of electricity ran through her, so much so that all she could do was try to stare at the entree section, unable to read it. The building thundercloud had released its lightning and she did not remove her leg from next to his. She took a sip of water, trying not to look at him. *So, it's confirmed. After all these years, he still has feelings for me.* There was no denying it now with his body language. She started to feel hot and wet. Her face flushed. Another sip of water, and then the waiter was there. Em ordered the first thing her eyes went to, not even caring what it was.

Jeremy left and went to the bar to order everyone a drink and came back with beers and a few shots. Feeling so flustered, Em wanted to take a shot, too. She still drank some, but only occasionally now and moderately at that, but this time she resisted. She wanted to keep her wits about her. She pushed it back toward Jeremy with a thanks, but no thanks look, and he shrugged, then downed it with ease. She glanced at what Todd was drinking, and noted it was an Athletic, a nonalcoholic beer. She wondered if he'd gotten sober.

The conversation at the table was full of wild salvage stories, reminding her of her fishing days and hours spent around galley tables listening to sea stories from the fishermen of Alaska. They're similar types of lifestyles in a way: gone from home for long periods, doing crazy work no one else would understand unless they've been there themselves. She wondered if Todd would appreciate that about Em now, that she could understand two types of lifestyles he'd been in, that she could get the things he was passionate about. *Most girls he's probably dated had no clue what he really did,* Em thought. Nor could he connect to them about it. That made her wonder what she'd reluctantly thought about so often: *Does he have a girlfriend now?* She snuck a glance at his roughened hand, dirt under the nails, a scar or two, but no ring. *At least maybe he's not married. Has he stayed single this whole time?* she wondered. She doubted it as he was so attractive. *How could he not have constant girlfriends? But, well, that's fine if he did. He's allowed that,* she concluded, pushing down ugly envy at the thought.

🪢 🪢 🪢

THE WAITER TOOK their plates. Em had hardly touched hers. Jeremy and the other crew guy, Mark, decided to play a game of pool. Of course that left just Todd and Em, together. This was the first time since their dramatic departure that they'd been so close and alone. He pushed his chair out and motioned to the bar.

"Let's get one more." As she stood up, he boldly grabbed her hand and led her over. It was clear he didn't care if the other crew saw. She was hoping she wouldn't get fired. He was a contractor hired by the State. But they were in the middle of nowhere on the Washington coast, and consequences seemed very far away and hard to comprehend at that moment. Her head was starting to spin from what was happening, and not from any alcohol. Tom Petty's "Free Falling" was playing in the background. The bar stools were tall and spaced closely together. Todd asked what she wanted, and she returned, "Whatever you're having." He motioned for two more, and the bartender had them opened and in front of them promptly.

He glanced over sidelong, his brown eyes staring into her green eyes, and said in his low, smooth voice without a blink of an eye, "Well, Em, do you know how long I've been thinking about you? I see you in my dreams so often, I can't get away from you, even if I wanted to."

Here was the answer she'd been wondering about for years, and hearing it now was such a relief, it felt as if a thousand doves were gently pulling her up into the air. She could have said the exact same thing to him. Instead, after a breath, she replied, "Are you kidding?" He had a quick look of disappointment, but she quickly followed with, "And do you know how much I've thought of you? You haunt me in my dreams, too. When I started this new job and then heard you were still working for Venture Diving, I about went crazy knowing you were near. Ever since I left you in Seattle," she paused to look up and give him a huge heartfelt "Sorry" look with her eyes and continued, "and ever since I started to heal, which took years, I have *so* regretted how I ran from you and hurt you like I did. Seeing you at the hearings just tore me up, Todd." He leaned in closer to her, encouraging her to whisper into his ear as she continued, "Do you know how crazy I felt when I found out you might be working on some of our program's projects, or that once I missed seeing you on a job . . . by one day?" He nodded in complete understanding of her feelings and let her continue, "You know there's not a day goes by where I don't think of you . . . what we could have been, if I hadn't been such an emotional wreck and messed it all up."

With these confessions, the trickle of relief continued to lighten her spirit. Just as one can go months without seeing the sun in an Alaskan winter and not realize just how much it is missed until that rare day when it peeks out from behind the clouds, she was now feeling just how much this had been weighing on her.

In spite of the heavy topics, a big slow grin had broken out on Todd's face, and his eyes sparkled with his old sense of mischief and relief. "Well, you don't say. So why'd it take so long?" accepting her apology and letting her know he returned the feelings, all in one question. Then he laughed and gave her a devilish wink. He motioned Em to lean over closer again. As she did, she got a scent of him, and it turned her insides out.

"Where you staying tonight?"

"I got a room at the Double Inn."

"Well, I'll be damned, that's where we're at, too."

"Oh, shit."

"Oh, shit?"

"Yes, oh, shit, how am I going to stay away from you?"

"You're not. No one needs to know. I'm not sharing a room, and it's not near the other guys." He let that sink in for a moment, then continued with "Hmmmm, Emily, why is it I feel this way with you?"

"How does it feel?"

"It's just this uncontrollable feeling." He took a sip of his drink, then continued, "Do you know how badly I've wanted to kiss you again, and for how long?"

"Well, I hope I don't disappoint," she said as she completed the lean and felt the gentle touch of his lips. The world around her stopped. All time stopped. No one else existed, it was just her and Todd.

"Don't worry, you don't disappoint," he said as they drew apart.

"Hey, what the fuck, Todd! You shouldn't be making out with the client!" Mark was standing tall over them at the bar, in the process of ordering another drink, but eyes wide with shock, frozen as if he'd been playing freeze tag. Todd had obviously not shared any information on their prior relationship.

"Leave us alone, we've got some history to sort out," was his reply.

"I'd say so," Mark said as he unfroze and rolled his eyes with a smirk and jab in Todd's ribs as he walked back to the pool table with a new beer in hand.

"Let's go," Todd said, slapping some cash on the table. "We're close enough to walk." He grabbed Em's hand and led her out the door, slinging his worn jacket on his other shoulder as the night air grabbed them.

The stars were out and the temperature had plummeted, so Em gratefully sidled up next to him. They walked and talked the few blocks back to the hotel, both of them confessing how they'd driven each other wild all these years and how they'd been recovering, and laughing at the ridiculousness of it all. Their journeys sounded similar—years of slow healing, grief and trauma work, setbacks, counselors, even both finding meditation in more recent years, on different yet parallel paths.

"Your room, or mine?" he asked, another glimmer in his eye.

"Yours."

He again led her, this time up the stairs, Em following fate. She could feel the rough calluses on his hands. He fumbled in his pockets, finding the key card. It flashed green, and he put his arms around her as they entered. They barely had the door shut, and he had Em up against the wall. She was already at the buttons on his shirt. Em could feel his strong abs and chest underneath as she fumbled at his belt buckle. She couldn't believe it; it was finally really happening. Was this real? So many years of thinking about him, so unattainable, not even knowing if he had an ounce of interest in her anymore, so hurt after finding out he'd been in Kodiak and had not tried to find her. And here he was directly in front of her, hands all over her, then lifting her up in his strong arms and flinging her onto the bed. It felt like the first time, but so much more passionate, all their years of sorrow and grief pouring into their lovemaking. It was urgent, and wild, and strong. After, as they both lay gasping, trying to catch their breath, tears of release ran down Em's face. She smiled at Todd, and he smiled back, knowing, understanding, and with a finger gently wiping her tears away, he reached in close again to give her a gentle kiss. Things had come full circle, in that weird way of life, and she knew she was home again.

Chapter 45

Full Circle

May 2016

TODD DREAMED THAT night, and it was one where Em appeared. Most often she'd be in his dreams, but distant, and he'd try to get to her but she'd remain elusive, unattainable to actually start a conversation with in the dream, no way to get closure, even in his subconscious. There'd only been one or two dreams where he'd made it close enough to talk to her and look her in the eyes, but he usually woke up shortly after.

This time when he woke up, though, she was there, directly in his arms, and real. He wanted to pinch himself to check it wasn't still a dream, the way Em had needed to go check if the wolf tracks were still in the snow in that story she'd shared years ago, but with such a glowing feeling, he knew it was real. He moved in as close as he could to the curves of her body, smelling her delicious scent, savoring the reality that she was actually there. With his movements, she stirred, her eyes fluttered, and she grabbed his arm tighter around her.

He whispered in her ear, "I love you, Em."

She was still half asleep, but she murmured, "I love you, too, Todd."

Soon they both fell back into a deep sleep.

The hotel alarm clock blared loudly at six fifteen, jolting them both awake and out of their love-filled reverie. Todd sat up, it finally dawning on him there was another very long day of work ahead, and he had Em in the bed next to him. He leaned over and gave her a kiss on the cheek, as she was still orienting herself, realizing the day ahead, too. Todd was quick at getting ready in the morning. All he usually needed was a half hour or less, while Em usually needed a bit more time, so with a glance at the red digital numbers on the clock, she groaned and started searching for her clothes. He could tell she looked worried and guessed what it was about. She'd just slept with a contractor, and she probably wasn't sure how ethical that was.

He didn't give a shit if it was "ethical" or not, but to assuage her fears he said, "I'll make sure on the drive over to tell the guys not a word is to peep out about last night. What happens in Sequim stays in Sequim. They'll keep their mouths shut, I'll make it clear to them, k?"

"Okay, thanks." She was now zipping up her jeans. "I don't know how I'd exactly explain that to John."

"And if word ever somehow gets out, don't worry, I'll fall on that sword, say it was all my fault. They won't fire me. They need me too much." As she continued to dress and search for her socks now, he added, "Heck, someone once took a company work truck out on a bender and no one knew where he was for over a week, and he didn't get fired."

Now fully dressed in the clothes she'd been wearing the previous night, Todd, only in his briefs with toothbrush in hand, stopped her before she got to the door by stepping in front of it. "Em, you are the love of my life. You always have been since I first laid eyes on you in Sand Point. Promise me I'll see you again after this job?"

"Todd, I want that more than you know. Here, I'll give you my personal number," and he followed her to the desk where she found a pen and paper and scribbled her number and personal email, figuring he probably still had it saved in his phone, but she didn't want to take any chances in case he didn't.

Todd embraced her again as she reached the door, lifting her off her feet, savoring her scent, her petite body in his arms. As he set her back down, he playfully slapped her butt, and turned her around toward the door.

"Todd!" she cried in righteous indignation. "You ass!"

"No, that's your ass," he said, cracking himself up. "I'll see you in a few, boss," laughing even more.

She burst out laughing, too, at the ridiculousness of it all. "Promise me you'll behave?"

"I promise," he swore, as she opened the door and when she turned back to give him one last smile, he returned it with a devilish wink.

Oh boy, she thought to herself with a childish giddiness, *this is going to be an interesting day.*

Epilogue

April 14, 2028

FIFTEEN YEARS HAD come and gone, fates entwined, and, in the end, inseparable, like a good master Turk's head knot should be, where one cannot find the beginning or the end of the line.

After a year of dating and trying to keep their relationship on the down-low from their co-workers, although she often wondered just how well they hid it, Todd proposed to Em and she accepted. Now they owned their own salvage company, much smaller than Venture Diving, but doing well picking up the small jobs, and it allowed them much more time together. Todd was no longer gone to all parts of the country for months at a time, just to different parts of the state and usually only for a week or two, a much better balance for both of them, but still enough adventure to keep it fun. They had soon discovered that they worked incredibly well together, each balancing out the other's strengths.

As was their tradition since they'd reunited, on every anniversary of the *Sea Ranger's* sinking on April 14th, Todd and Emily would take a day off from work and drive down to Fishermen's Terminal. Once there, they'd usually get a coffee at Caffe Appassionato or a meal at Chinook's, then they'd walk slowly and steadily, arm in arm, to the marble and bronze statue. They'd always leave fresh flowers, and now also added an extra bouquet for Joel. His name wasn't on the memorial as he hadn't died at sea, but just four short years after the sinking, he'd passed away on scene in a car crash in Anchorage at an intersection, of all things. He deserved flowers too, nonetheless.

This year being a big marker of fifteen years since the tragic date, Todd whispered into Em's ear that he had a surprise this year.

As they approached the memorial they found it empty, with only a fat herring gull perched on the rail surrounding the square. They ran their fingers along the bronze names. Part of the tradition was that Todd would recall a funny story about each of the guys. Then Em would pull out a battered book of Mary Oliver poetry and read a fitting poem or two.

This year it was a beautiful Seattle spring day. The cherry blossoms again lined the parking lot, opening to the return of the sun. A breeze stirred a few wisps of hair from Em's knit hat. Todd leaned in and put an arm around his girl, the girl he thought he'd lost forever. More than once.

Then he released his arm from around Em, reached into his pocket and pulled out a pair of her old blue panties, crouched down, and draped them neatly at the base of the memorial for all to see their sexy lace edges next to the bouquet of flowers they'd just laid down.

"See, I got you again," he teased.

"You little devil!" she cried. "How long have you been holding on to those?" And then, "Oh my god, I never got you back like I said I would!"

"I may have swiped them from your apartment in Kodiak, just under fifteen years ago."

"And you didn't tell me this whole time?"

"Nope. And you've got to leave them there, Em, it's for the guys. Plus, I know where I can get more."

She laughed, looking into his face. The playfulness and joy, the glint in his eye that she remembered from when she'd first met him, played into her soul.

"Alright," she conceded in defeat, knowing there was no way to win this one, just as Todd himself had realized years ago when he'd lost her purple panties on the fo'c'sle floor.

"At least the statue doesn't have a flagpole, or you know where they'd be," he teased.

And they both laughed—a laughter with true merit and wisdom to it. Todd picked her up, swung her around, and they walked arm in arm back to the truck.

 THE END

Glossary

AIS - Automatic Identification System, a way to broadcast a ship's position to other ships, tracking systems, and coastal authorities.

Brailer - A device made for unloading fish, consisting of a metal frame and small-mesh webbing attached to the frame that the fish get loaded into from the fishhold and which then gets hauled up to the cannery with a crane.

Bulkheads - Vertical walls inside a vessel that partition different spaces off, and can aid in adding stiffness to the hull to prevent different compartments from flooding.

Bulwarks - The extension of the vessel's sides, above the weather deck up to the gunwales, that acts as a railing to prevent crew and gear from being washed over.

Bunt - The end of a seine net that forms a pocket into which all the fish are forced and which is then hauled up over the side of the boat. It consists of heavy-duty webbing to withstand the weight of the catch.

Corks - The floats that help keep a net on the surface of the water.

Fo'c'sle - The forward part of ship, usually the living quarters, short for forecastle.

Gen-set - Short for generator in the ship's engine room.

Head - Maritime term for the bathroom on a boat.

Helm - Another word for the ship's wheel used to steer the boat.

Helm alert - A device used on fishing boats meant to keep people awake at the helm. The person on watch can set a time from one to fifteen minutes, which will show as a countdown. When the time reaches zero, it alarms unless the watchperson hits the Reset button, and then it begins counting down again.

Jog stick - A small device that can be controlled with one hand, used to steer the vessel in lieu of a ship's wheel.

Lead - A weighted line at the bottom of a seine net to help keep the net down.

EPIRB - An Emergency Position Indicating Radio Beacon device that, when activated or submersed in water, will broadcast its location to a satellite system for Search and Rescue.

Lazarette or **laz** - A compartment in the aft end of the boat used to store goods or supplies.

Longlining - A method of deep-sea fishing which uses a long line with hooks spaced out at intervals and an anchor on each end with marker buoys to keep it in place on the seafloor to catch groundfish.

Loudhailer - An intercom device to allow the captain to speak to the crew out on the deck or other parts of the ship.

"Mobing" up - Slang for preparing and mobilizing for a salvage or dive job.

Pancake - Nickname for a flat, metal, spring-loaded device used to attach a skiff to a seine vessel, but which could be released and opened with the pull cord attached to the spring.

Port - The left side of a vessel when facing the bow.

Purseline - The line used to draw a seine net closed that runs through a series of metal rings along the bottom of the net and lead-lines.

Purse seining - A form of fishing that uses a net consisting of a cork line, leadline, purseline, auxiliary lines and rings, that can encircle large groups of fish and then prevent their escape from the bottom by drawing it closed, like a purse.

RPMs - Rotations per minute.

Satphone - A satellite phone that vessels use to communicate with each other over long distances.

Scupper - Opening in the bulwarks that allows the sea to drain from the weather deck.

Set - Can mean one revolution of hauling out the net and closing it and hauling it back in for seine fishing; may also refer to one series of skates of longline with baited hooks, with an anchor on each end.

Skate - A long line with hooks attached at regular intervals that can be attached to other skates to make up a set, used for longline fishing.

Starboard - The right side of a vessel when facing the bow.

Sole - Maritime term for the interior floor of the boat.

Spud - A large pole or pipe that a barge can raise up and down and use to set the vessel in place, similar to anchoring, sometimes in pairs of two or four on different corners of the barge.

Track phone - Slang for a type of satellite phone system used on fishing boats to communicate with each other over long distances.

Web locker - A storage shed that fishermen use to store their nets, spare web, parts, and fishing gear.

About the Author

GROWING UP IN the Midwest surrounded by a loving family, the author read a few too many Jack London and Robert Service books and dreamt of more: more wildness, more mountains, more adventure. And so she moved to Alaska at the age of twenty-two. She spent over nine years in the Great North, and it has never left her heart, nor will it ever. Of those years, seven were spent working on various types of boats, but the most beloved of those were commercial fishing boats. She spent those years adventuring and working, plying all the waters from Sand Point to Southeast, and even down to southern California and back up to Alaska again.

Then, after turning thirty, she moved to the Pacific Northwest, a little closer to home but still close to the sea. There she found the love of her life, and lives with him and his three children on a beautiful, wooded property with a big garden, where she has remained with a foot in the maritime and derelict vessel/salvage industry.

The author has updated the Interior section of *Fodor's Alaska* 2009,

2010, and 2011 guidebooks. She has also published articles in *Social Education* and *Alaska* magazines, along with articles in the *Seward Phoenix LOG* newspaper, and *Cipher* and *Contour* magazines.

The author longlining on the F/V Trask,
back when she used to commercial fish.